Welcome to Silver Town, where shifters are hot and the romance sizzles

"Terry Spear weaves paranormal, suspense, and romance together in one nonstop roller coaster of passion and adventure."

— *Love Romance Passion* for *Destiny of the Wolf*

"Riveting and entertaining…makes one want to devour all of the rest of Terry Spear's books."

— *Fresh Fiction* for *Wolf Fever*

"Another great story sure to amaze and intrigue readers…sensual, passionate and very well written… Terry Spear's writing is pure entertainment."

— *The Long and Short of It Reviews* for *Wolf Fever*

"Fascinating characters and exciting, action-packed crime drama plot. A great fantasy twist and yet another way to interpret the legend of weres."

— *RT Book Reviews* for
Dreaming of the Wolf, 4 Stars

"Intense and swoon-inducing… The chemistry is steamy and hot."

— *USA Today Happy Ever After* for
Dreaming of the Wolf

"The outstanding and gripping plot will appeal to paranormal fans, and romance junkies will take delight in the red-hot love story."

— *RT Book Reviews* for *Silence of the Wolf*, 4 Stars

Also by Terry Spear

Heart of the Wolf

Heart of the Wolf
To Tempt the Wolf
Legend of the White Wolf
Seduced by the Wolf

Silver Town Wolf

Destiny of the Wolf
Wolf Fever
Dreaming of the Wolf
Silence of the Wolf
A Silver Wolf Christmas
Alpha Wolf Need Not Apply

Highland Wolf

Heart of the Highland Wolf
A Howl for a Highlander
A Highland Werewolf
Wedding
Hero of a Highland Wolf
A Highland Wolf Christmas

SEAL Wolf

A SEAL in Wolf's
Clothing
A SEAL Wolf Christmas
SEAL Wolf Hunting
SEAL Wolf In Too Deep

Heart of the Jaguar

Savage Hunger
Jaguar Fever
Jaguar Hunt
Jaguar Pride
A Very Jaguar Christmas

Billionaire Wolf

Billionaire in Wolf's
Clothing

BETWEEN A WOLF AND A HARD PLACE

TERRY SPEAR

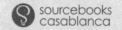

sourcebooks
casablanca

Published by Sourcebooks Casablanca, an imprint of Sourcebooks, Inc.
P.O. Box 4410, Naperville, Illinois 60567-4410
(630) 961-3900
Fax: (630) 961-2168
www.sourcebooks.com

Printed and bound in Canada.
MBP 10 9 8 7 6 5 4 3 2 1

To Jan Buker, a friend and fan with an orange-striped tabby named Merlin who loves my books as much as Jan does and honors me with the cutest pictures. In Savage Hunger, *I mentioned Merritt Island where I attended high school, and Jan contacted me to learn why I had mentioned that location. We discovered our lives had paralleled each other's—our families having moved from California to Merritt Island, our fathers working on the Apollo space program. It truly is a small world, and though I didn't know Jan back then, I'm thrilled to know her now.*

Chapter 1

"I THINK THERE'S SOMETHING WRONG WITH ME," ELLIE MacTire told her triplet Laurel as she vacuumed the lobby of their Victorian inn one last time before Brett Silver and his brothers moved their great-aunt's baby grand piano to the sisters' inn as a gesture of friendship.

The ghost maid, Chrissy, stayed in the old, recently renovated inn in Silver Town, but Ellie wasn't having any luck with her. The ghostly woman often turned the attic room's light on and off, and sometimes the sisters saw her peering out the window. Ellie hadn't been able to connect with her. And not being able to connect with a ghost didn't happen very often for her. She was eager to help the maid find closure so she could go on her way, and in order to do so, the sisters needed to learn what was keeping Chrissy there. Maybe fear of the unknown? The inn had been her home forever.

Their triplet Meghan raced through the closed hotel and dashed into the nearby bathroom in her reddish-gray wolf coat, leaving a trail of red, black, and gray hairs on the floor in her wake.

Ellie let out her breath in exasperation. "Meghan."

From the bathroom, Meghan called out, "The wolf door in the basement is working properly now."

Leaving the bathroom dressed in jeans, boots, and a soft blue sweater that complemented her straight flaming-red bob, Meghan grabbed the mop. "Sorry for the wolf hairs. I had to make sure that wolf door was working right and didn't squeak when anyone used it." She paused. "So...what could be wrong with you?" Meghan didn't sound serious in the least as she mopped the floor right behind Ellie.

"Great on the wolf door. Who needs a handyman when we've got you?" Laurel asked.

Meghan gave her a thumbs-up.

"I can't reach Chrissy, the ghost." As if they didn't know who Ellie was talking about. "I've tried and tried to make a connection, but she isn't responding to me."

Laurel was the oldest and had always been the one in charge. She usually gave Ellie sound advice when her ability took a powder. They didn't tell just anyone about their abilities, though Laurel's weren't as clear-cut with respect to ghost sightings. Meghan had a heightened ability to locate spirits like Ellie did. Even though witch-hunting was a thing of the past, a lot of people didn't believe in ghosts and frowned on anyone who did. Silver Town was wolf run, and nearly everybody living there was a *lupus garou*. Ellie always figured they should be open-minded about other supernatural beings since, as wolves, they were clearly part of the equation. But it didn't work that way.

"You're trying too hard." Laurel tucked her hair behind her ears. Both she and Meghan had the most beautiful, clear-green eyes. Ellie's were blue like their Aunt Charity's, though she often wished hers were also green. "You know you get blocked when you're really trying too hard to reach a spirit instead of letting the spirit move you. Chrissy seems content enough. So she's not really a problem."

"Yeah. Except we're booked for the next several months, which means the attic room will be occupied. I'd rather that she didn't mess with the light while someone is in the room." Ellie always wanted to help spirits find their way to their resting place, but in this case, she was feeling pressured to make it happen sooner rather than later for the sake of their guests. And she felt guilty about it too. Ghosts couldn't help being trapped between worlds, and Ellie never knew for sure if releasing one was the best thing for it. They never came back and let her know she'd screwed up or anything.

Meghan agreed. "I'm having the same problem. None of the incense I've used has helped either."

"The same goes for you, Meghan," Laurel said in her usual reasonable way. "You're trying to force it to happen. You know it only works if you're not trying to beat a deadline."

Checking on reservations, Laurel shook her head, her short, curly, red hair bobbing while she worked at the computer. "We are booked solid for the weeks before, during, and after the Victorian Days celebration. For the four months after that, most of our guests are booking rooms so they can go skiing. So we still have a week's break before the place is filled to capacity and more time to decorate for the holidays. Good thing we renovated the basement so we'd have a few extra rooms."

"What about the Alaskan retreat guest room? Who's renting it?" Ellie had suggested decorating one room in a winter wolf theme. She wasn't sure if Arctic wolves would prefer a room like that, or if gray or red wolves would because it was so unusual for them. Or just plain humans even. Maybe the white wolves would want something different from what they were used to.

Ellie and her sisters were excited because their first Arctic wolves were coming to stay at the beginning of the year. In fact, the whole town was excited. Most of their pack had never seen white wolves, shifter or otherwise.

"Most popular room in the bunch," Laurel said. "It was booked right away. The Arctic wolves want it when they come for New Year's. Gray wolves have it the rest of the time. The tropical room we did up for jaguar shifters—can't wait to see if any come to stay—and then the forest room are the next two most popular choices. The mural of the northern lights against a midnight-blue sky with a pack of wolves howling at the moon in the Alaskan retreat room is pure genius."

"I agree. It's beautiful. What are we going to do about Halloween decorations?" Meghan asked.

"We go all out like we usually do," Ellie said cheerfully.

"The inn is haunted! Do we want to make it *look* haunted too?" Meghan asked. "I say we don't put up spiderwebs or creepy spiders. Or skeletons. Make it appear...sweeter."

Ellie had already hung black and orange lights around the porch and set their collection of ceramic jack-o'-lanterns on the check-in counter and bookcases in the common room. They'd even bought a carved jack-o'-lantern featuring a wolf's head, visible especially when a battery-operated candle was set inside.

"No tombstones in front of the inn or by the fountain out back?" Ellie said. "You're no fun. We have to put our stout, white candles out with the black candleholders, and really, we should have the fake spiderwebs. I'm okay with not having spiders dangling from them. I keep thinking they're real and need to be killed."

"Okay," Laurel said. "We'll do everything but the spiders. We'll put out more light strings so the inn is awash in lights—orange for the lower half and along the walkway, and pink lights for the top—to give it that sweeter appeal. I agree with Ellie. We have to have spiderwebs. And the 'cemetery plot' can be set up out back. We can play Victorian music, which can be scary sounding enough, especially pieces with heavy organ sounds. Like *Phantom of the Opera*—hauntingly beautiful. We'll have a ton of candles for light but also to give that Victorian look."

Ellie was thrilled. She loved Halloween. So did Meghan and Laurel, but Meghan was afraid of scaring off potential customers now that the sisters had decided to stay in Silver Town. They hadn't participated in Halloween last year because they were so busy finishing the renovations. Ellie couldn't wait to see how the child and adult trick-or-treaters were dressed this year.

She was going to wear a blue Victorian ball gown embroidered with gold and green designs and a low-cut bodice. She hoped Brett would drop by, because that's who she really wanted to wear it for. The sisters had each bought several Victorian gowns to wear when guests stayed at the inn, so Ellie wasn't sure which her sisters would choose for Halloween. She had others to select from for Victorian Days. Picking out all the different gowns and dressing up had been a lot of fun this year.

Laurel studied her and said, "Okay, is something else bothering you?"

Yeah, not that Ellie wanted to discuss it. The only reason she had considered speaking with Laurel was that two of Laurel's mate's cousins had found their future mates by first having steamy dreams about them. Maybe fantasizing about the wolf she was dating was normal.

She'd seen Brett naked, of course. Wolves shifted, and they had to get naked to shift. And yes, she'd fantasized about boyfriends before. What would it be like to go all the way? They couldn't do it unless they were mating, since wolves mated for life. What if this was just like her previous dreams, and Brett Silver wasn't meant to be her forever mate?

Meghan was watching her now, and that made Ellie's cheeks warm.

Both her sisters were waiting to hear what had made her blush.

"Well, spill," Meghan said, putting up the mop.

"Meghan says you haven't been sleeping well. She hears you getting up in the middle of the night. And you're off to bed earlier than normal. Maybe because you're tired from getting up in the middle of the night. Is something worrying you other than Chrissy and the trouble she might cause with our guests?"

"I'm having sex with Brett!"

Her sisters' eyes widened, and their mouths hung agape.

Ellie hadn't meant to say it quite like that and give her sisters heart attacks. "I mean, I keep fantasizing about it."

Both her sisters audibly sighed in relief.

"As long as you're not actually doing it with him,

then we're good. Before you get involved with him in an intimate way, you have to tell him about your ghost-whisperer abilities," Laurel said. "What if he can't live with the notion that you can see and speak to ghosts?"

"I dream about guys I've been dating. I know you have too, Ellie." Meghan shrugged. "No big deal."

What if it *was* a big deal? What if it was like what Jake and Darien Silver had experienced? Both of them had dreamed vividly about their future mates. Darien had even had the dreams *before* he met his prospective mate.

What if the dreams were different for her? What if Brett had been having dream sex about *her*? Or what if he was fantasizing about her like she was about him and it had no darker, psychic meaning?

She couldn't really ask him. Yet how else would she know for certain? If he wasn't dreaming about her, then she was fantasizing about him in a normal way. She frowned at the notion. If he wasn't dreaming about her when she was about him, that wasn't good either.

Trying to get a handle on this, Ellie could see herself asking him over lunch, "Hey, by the way, have you been having dream sex with me? Oh, can you pass the ketchup, please?"

He'd smile and she'd blush.

Meghan might have sounded like she was brushing off the idea, but she and Laurel were still waiting with bated breath to hear more.

"You're thinking of Jake and Darien," Laurel finally said, as if relieved that's all the matter was.

"Dreaming up steamy sex scenes with a hot wolf who could be your forever mate... Wow." Meghan put her hands over her heart and looked heavenward. "That's not happening to me either."

"Peter's family isn't the one who has the dream-mating talent. Only the Silvers," Ellie said, since Meghan had been dating Sheriff Jorgenson fairly regularly. "I've dreamed about hot guys whether I'm dating or not. I just wondered if..." Ellie couldn't say it. What if Brett *was* having the same kind of dreams about her? Then again, he probably was. But probably not like his cousins had. "Why were Jake's dreams connected with mating? I could understand if he had never seen Alicia and then had these sexy dreams. But he had seen her, so why couldn't he simply have been fantasizing about her?"

"I don't know. Really. All I know is that he was dream mating with her, and I just assumed it was the same kind of thing. It just never came up in any conversation. Do you want me to ask CJ about Jake's experience?" Laurel asked.

Since CJ was Brett's cousin and Laurel's mate, that might work. "Wouldn't CJ think you had a reason for asking?"

Laurel raised a brow. "What you really want to know is if Brett is dreaming of you."

"Heavens, no."

Laurel gave her a big-sister annoyed look. "*Yeah*, you do. Do you want me to ask if any other family members had that ability? Just ask in a curious way, not like I'm trying to learn anything about any particular Silver brother."

"Don't you think CJ will figure it out?" Ellie asked. "Brett's the only one seeing anyone. And CJ's closest to him."

"I'll bring it up in such a way that CJ won't guess I have ulterior motives."

Ellie sure hoped that wouldn't backfire. What if CJ believed Laurel's query was about Brett? And he asked Brett if he was having dream sex with anyone? If he thought Ellie was having dreams like that, CJ would probably look at her differently. Worse, Brett would too.

Ellie felt her whole body warm in an instant, and she knew she had to be blushing all over.

The more she saw of Brett, the more she knew she had to tell him about her gift. It wasn't a situation where it didn't matter whether he could accept what she could do or not. Having different opinions wouldn't usually be a problem in a long-term relationship. All relationships had to have some give-and-take. But this was too important to her to dismiss.

She could envision talking to a ghost, trying to discover why he or she was stuck here, and her mate thinking she'd flipped out. Or teasing. Or even being embarrassed by her behavior. Without full acceptance and understanding, she could see the relationship between them crumbling. She didn't tell most people about her abilities, but her mate would have to know and accept what she could do.

Laurel sighed, patted Ellie on the back, and headed for the front door. "If he truly cares for you, he'll be fine with your gift. If he isn't, then he's not the right one for you. Dream sex or no."

Ellie frowned at Laurel, hoping that the dream sex wouldn't be the topic of conversation between the sisters from now until she mated the right wolf.

Ellie wanted Brett to be the right one for her. He was

fun, protective, funny, and endearing. It didn't matter what he was working on as the local newspaper reporter. No matter how gritty or gruesome the day's business was, he was always ready to let it go and concentrate solely on them when they got together. She kept telling herself she needed to tell him about her ability, but she couldn't talk about it easily with someone who might not be receptive.

How would he react if he learned she could commune with the dead?

———∿∿∿———

Brett Silver hoped that the old piano wouldn't break down once it was situated in the MacTire sisters' inn. He was thrilled to be able to give his great-aunt's treasured grand piano a home where visitors would enjoy it. His younger quadruplet brother, CJ, a deputy sheriff of Silver Town, had helped him polish it one last time before they moved it.

"I think this is a great gesture and the perfect place for the piano," CJ said, working on the instrument's clawed feet. "Even if it stops working again, it fits in with their Victorian decor, and it's a grand old piece."

"It's been properly tuned, and Remer Cochran, the pianist and piano teacher, has tested it and made sure it's working beautifully. Though, according to Ellie, neither she nor her sisters play any instruments. But if anyone wants to drop by and perform on it, he or she is welcome to do so." Brett would love to hear someone play like Great-Aunt Matilda had when she was performing for the family.

"I hear Eric, Sarandon, and the piano movers pulling up now." CJ headed for Brett's front door.

The piano had been sitting in a corner of Brett's living room where no one but a few friends and relatives saw it. Now it would be seen by all kinds of visitors to the inn. Brett felt really good about that, though he suspected he'd miss seeing the piano in his home. It was more than just a piece of furniture. The piano was a reflection of older times when the family would gather and sing songs at weddings, birthdays, and especially Christmas.

Brett set aside the polish and cloth and greeted his brothers and the movers.

Eric slapped CJ on the back. "I'm surprised you didn't think of giving the piano to the sisters first, as much as you were trying to make an impression on Laurel."

"No need," CJ said. "Laurel was already head over heels for me."

The brothers laughed.

"At least Brett didn't make the mistake of mispronouncing the MacTire sisters' last name," Eric said.

"I learned to spell phonetically," CJ said. "*Tire* should be pronounced 'tire.' Not like 'tier.' Besides, if you'd said hello to them first, you would have made the mistake instead."

Brett was glad he hadn't.

"As for the piano, it was Brett's to give away. Frankly, since he's always at my house and I don't drop by his often, I never even gave it a thought," CJ said.

Brett watched as the movers covered the maple piano with blankets to protect it and carried it out to their truck. Snowflakes were beginning to fall, making the day feel magical. The Colorado autumn air was cold and crisp. In that instant, Brett had the greatest urge to pick up Ellie and go running with her as wolves. The movers came back for the piano bench. Once it was loaded, the brothers took two vehicles to lead the way.

Brett drove, and CJ rode with him on the way to the inn. "Hey, are you having any more trouble with that artist?"

"Which one?" Brett asked. Modeling nude for art students had been good money when he was in college, but since then, three women had periodically sent him prints of paintings they had done of him in the nude, asking if he was still as buff and could model again for them.

He'd declined, but the women had been persistent.

CJ chuckled. "You didn't realize you'd become a modeling sensation for female art students. Did you go out with any of them?"

"No. It was strictly a modeling job, though I had all kinds of offers."

CJ shook his head. "How are you making out with Ellie? You've been pretty quiet about it."

"I don't kiss and tell." Though the truth was that Brett and Ellie hadn't had that first kiss. Not for lack of wanting. Brett thought Ellie was hiding something from him, but no matter where he took the conversation, he hadn't been able to learn what the problem was. He was afraid that was why they hadn't had their first kiss.

Not that he wasn't imagining a whole lot more with her. He'd even talked to CJ about it. Not about her specifically, but about their cousins finding their mates through dream mating, and he'd asked if any of his brothers thought finding a mate that way would be possible for them.

Brett really cared for Ellie, so he didn't want to

suddenly have a fantasy about another woman. All he wanted was to make some headway with her. He loved her Irish lilt and even heard it in his mind when he wasn't with her. He couldn't imagine being with anyone else.

CJ had been quiet until they reached the inn. "Have you told Ellie about your modeling experience? How the women are still hassling you to model for them?"

"No. I won't unless it looks like something will really come out of our relationship. Hell, everyone in the pack knows about the modeling. I'm sure she and her sisters heard about it sometime during the year they've been here."

"I wouldn't rely on that. Best to mention it to Ellie before she learns about it on her own, if it looks like something more permanent might come out of the relationship."

Brett wondered how she would react. Would she be amused? Or annoyed?

He really wasn't ready to discuss it with her. How would it sound? Like he wanted her to know other women lusted after his body for the purpose of art, which they regularly sold? He wouldn't have done anything differently. He had needed the money, and it was an easy way to earn it without neglecting his studies. He wasn't an exhibitionist, but he loved art and hadn't seen anything wrong with modeling. Wolves got naked in front of each other all the time, so it came naturally. It would have stayed in the past if the three artists—best friends who'd attended the same art class—hadn't kept trying to get him to model further for them.

When Brett and CJ arrived at the inn, they got out to help guide the piano movers. Laurel met CJ outside, giving him a big hug and kiss. Brett sighed. He'd love it if he and Ellie got to that point in their relationship—and soon. They'd both been busy lately, she with the inn and he with reporting about Victorian Day festivities. So he hadn't seen her as much as he would have liked.

As soon as they went inside, he saw Ellie showing the movers where she thought the piano should go, while Meghan insisted it should be more to the right of the stairs.

Then Ellie caught his eye and smiled, and he felt his whole outlook brighten. She was the darkest-haired redhead of the bunch, her long, curly hair auburn in color, and to him, sexier and more mysterious. He wanted to ask her out tonight. He could cook, though he'd do better grilling outside.

She turned her attention to the piano again, frowning. And Meghan was frowning too.

Poor movers. Brett thought the two ladies would have the men relocate the piano all over the lobby before settling on the perfect place for it. Instead, Ellie suddenly looked pale and said it was fine where it was. Meghan quickly nodded, looking just as ashen.

CJ and Eric readjusted the burgundy, brocade-covered bench in front of the piano, which made Brett remember he needed to box up all the sheet music and books and bring them over. He'd taken them out of the bench when he'd had its seat cushion reupholstered last year, and they were still sitting in a box in the spare bedroom.

Brett paid the movers and they cleared out.

"Got to get back to work," Eric said, giving Brett a knowing look. "Late shift working as a park ranger tonight."

"Yeah, I've got to get back to the business of

sheriffing." CJ smiled at Ellie. "Can you drop me off at the station, Eric?"

"Sure thing," their eldest brother said.

Sarandon was admiring the piano, arms folded across his chest, when he realized his brothers were leaving and snapped out of his thoughts. "Yeah, I've got to get back to work too."

Brett knew Sarandon didn't have a guide job in the park tonight, so he was glad Sarandon was vacating the premises pronto, taking his brothers' cues. Now if only Ellie's sisters would leave the two of them alone.

Laurel took Meghan's arm and hauled her toward the back door. "Let's go fix supper, why don't we?"

"For two, three, or four of us?" Meghan asked with a smile in her voice as they disappeared outside.

Brett didn't hesitate before he moved toward Ellie, placed his hands on her shoulders, and leaned her gently against the piano, blocking her from escape if she thought to put on the brakes again. "Would you be up for dinner for two? You don't have any guests for the next week, unless something has changed." He rubbed his thumbs against her shoulders, loving the feel of her, the sweet, fresh fragrance of her. She looked beautiful in her soft teal sweater, rust-and-teal-plaid skirt, and high-heeled boots, her dark-red hair in silky curls around her shoulders.

She was soft in his arms and appeared receptive when he leaned down to kiss her. It seemed like the perfect time. No one was around. The piano had been the perfect gift. Now it was time to kiss her like he'd wanted to since they'd first started dating. As soon as their mouths touched, she responded by wrapping her arms around his back, but then Eric felt her jump a little and pulled his mouth away, wondering if he was going too fast. If he'd done something wrong.

She quickly moved against him, pushing him away from the piano, her heartbeat racing, her breathing unsteady, the color that had infused her cheeks instantly draining from her skin.

"What's wrong?" he asked as Ellie moved him even farther from the piano. He thought maybe she had gotten static-electric shock from touching it.

"Let's go have dinner," she said, her Irish accent more pronounced, as it was whenever she was overly worried. The sisters had been born in the United States, but their parents had been born in Ireland, and they'd picked up their parents' accent. He loved it. "Any place is fine."

Yet she was visibly upset, and he wasn't sure what the difficulty was.

"Thanks for the piano. It's beautiful." Ellie glanced back at it, but not in an admiring way. She was looking off to the right of it, a frown marring her forehead, which he thought was odd.

"Why don't I take you to the Silver Town Tavern? They have great cuts of steak, and we can catch up on what's been going on."

"I hear you're working on some interesting stories."

"Yeah. My favorite? The last time the Silver Town Inn was part of the Victorian Days celebration. The idea seemed appropriate since this will be the first time the inn is open for business during the festivities since then."

"I can't wait to read it." Ellie glanced back at the vicinity of the piano one last time before she shut and locked the front door to the inn.

"We can help you move the piano again if you don't think it's in the right place," Brett offered, getting the car door for her.

"Uh, no, I think it's fine." But she didn't sound like she thought so.

He was afraid he'd pushed her too fast on the kiss, yet she'd seemed so willing. He didn't know what he had done wrong, but he had every intention of proving how much being with her meant to him, no matter what the difficulty might be.

———

Ellie couldn't believe that not only had Chrissy shown up, looking interested in the piano, but so had some other woman. She was older, with white hair and dark eyes, and had appeared when Brett leaned Ellie against the piano and gave her the beginning of a spine-tingling kiss. It was so reminiscent of the start of the dreams she was having about him that Ellie could have screamed. Seeing the ghost shook her up and ruined the in-the-flesh fantasy with Brett.

Ellie couldn't help being shocked at seeing the other woman, who shook her head and tsked at her as if Ellie shouldn't have been kissing Brett like that. He was so kissable too, his dark-brown sweater complementing his dark-brown hair and eyes, and his soft, blue-denim shirt and blue jeans covering hard muscles, the best combination a girl could ask for.

But the woman's tsking had ruined Ellie's concentration, even if the woman was a ghost! And then there was Chrissy again, hands together held against her chest as if she wished she had been on the receiving or *giving* end of the kiss.

Ellie hated that she'd ended the kiss after being startled, but she couldn't concentrate on Brett while the older woman gave her the evil eye, punctuated by sounds of annoyance. Or with Chrissy eating the whole thing up.

So who *was* the other woman? Ellie guessed she was the one woman who had loved that piano more than anyone else. Brett's great-aunt Matilda.

Chapter 2

AT THE TAVERN, ELLIE COULDN'T STOP THINKING about the woman who had appeared near the piano. She listened to Brett talk about some of the stories he'd researched and written recently for the newspaper. She usually found these behind-the-scenes reports fascinating, but this time she was having a devil of a time concentrating.

The tavern was filled with wolves having a meal in the wolf-members-only establishment. No one had to have a membership card to join; they just had to be a *lupus garou*.

"Do you have a photo of your great-aunt Matilda?" Ellie suddenly asked, and Brett set his glass of wine down on the table. Her question had come totally out of the blue, and she wished she'd done a better job of leading into it. "I was thinking it would be nice to dedicate the piano to her and have a little memorial plaque with her picture on it on the wall behind the piano."

How was that for thinking quickly on her feet? Though she knew it was also the best way to commemorate the gift. She would have thought of doing it eventually.

"I'm sure I can find a family photo of her. I'll check. That would be nice."

Brett seemed to buy her story and appeared pleased. She sighed. Had their kissing brought the ghost to life? Disturbed her? Ever since Ellie had seen the woman, she'd wanted to call her sisters and warn them of the new ghostly trouble they might have. Unless the new ghost didn't bother making any more appearances. How likely was that? From Ellie's past experiences with ghosts attached to people or an object, not very likely.

"How did you say she died?" Ellie realized she'd completely changed the subject again. Brett had said something about the weather and snow, and she had barely heard his comments until he frowned at her.

He sat back a little in his chair this time and studied her. She really had to concentrate better on what he was saying. Brett would think she wasn't interested in being with him. Which wasn't the case at all. She just couldn't stop thinking about the new ghost.

"Sorry." She took an oversize swig from her glass and nearly choked on the wine.

"What's wrong?" He reached across the table, taking hold of her hand and stroking it, which only fed into the way she would view him in tonight's dream fantasy.

Nothing was wrong, except that the piano had stirred up two ghosts in the inn. Ellie hoped the women didn't get into a fight over territory. She'd never seen it happen before, but anything was possible when paranormal stuff was involved.

"I was just thinking that we could mention a few details…for the memorial. The date of death and so on."

Brett released her hand and took another sip of his wine. "She was seventy-five in human years, and the doc we had at the time said she died of pneumonia. It simulates drowning; her lungs were filled with fluid."

What if Matilda had *really* drowned? What if she was staying around because she had been murdered?

Then again, ghosts of people who had died of natural causes could still attach themselves to prized possessions or people. Any number of things could be ghost magnets, depending on the individual spirit. In one case in the nineteenth century, a man had built a home for his beloved wife, but when she died of sickness and his daughter died a couple of years later, he continued to live there. Upon his death, he remained there as if tied to his wife and daughter and that home. Forever. The historical home was a museum in Texas now, and many visitors had seen the man in his ghostly form.

Ellie took a deep breath. Okay, no more thinking about ghosts. "So about the weather…" What had Brett said? "You said it's going to snow?" She usually checked the weather every once in a while, but she'd been busy and hadn't for a few days, though she had smelled snow in the air.

He smiled and reached across the table, taking hold of her hand and squeezing. "I can't tell you how much I enjoy being with you, Ellie. You're just fun to be around. I've been really wrapped up in work lately, but I wanted you to know it's not always like this. I know you've been really busy lately too. I hope you enjoy being with me as much as I enjoy being with you."

She smiled. If he only knew what she had been thinking about him in the privacy of her bedroom at night! "I love going out with you. I just…" The last time she'd told a guy she was dating that she was a ghost whisperer, he had stranded her at a hotel restaurant. He'd told her he had to go to the men's room but skipped out on her instead, leaving the bill for her to pay! What an ass. Then she'd had to call a taxi to get home.

Of course karma can be a bitch. When she remembered he was staying that night at the hotel where the restaurant was—figuring he'd get lucky, she suspected—she'd given his room number to the waiter, paid him a really generous tip, bought a round of drinks for everyone at the bar, and gotten the most expensive bottle of champagne she could to share with her sisters and celebrate. She smiled at the satisfaction she'd gotten from that.

Considering how much she cared for Brett, she really wanted to deal with her current situation in the best way possible, not wanting to upset what she and he had for now.

"Brett, do you believe in ghosts?"

He didn't say anything for a moment. She knew he wouldn't pull what the other guy had. Not with his brother married to her sister and Brett too decent to do that anyway. But that didn't mean he would accept what she could do.

He was still studying her, like a wolf trying to anticipate how to handle this best, and she wondered what he was really thinking. "I think anything's possible," he said slowly, as if he didn't want to say the wrong thing.

Which she really, really appreciated.

"I've never experienced any ghostly phenomena, so it's hard for me to really believe in them. But anything is possible."

Well, that response was better than she had expected. "What about your brothers?" It really didn't matter if they believed in ghosts or not, unless they'd put Brett down if he did. He was close to his brothers, like she was with her sisters, and she liked to think they would be receptive too.

"Believe in ghosts? Eric and Sarandon? No. CJ, not sure. He says no, but I think he's seen some stuff he can't explain away. He and our cousin Tom both."

Good thing she and Meghan weren't dating either of the brothers who didn't believe in ghosts. Though she wasn't sure about Peter Jorgenson, the sheriff.

"What about the light going on and off in the attic at the inn?" She knew Brett had witnessed that when he was taking pictures of the inn to do a feature on it for Christmas.

"Faulty electrical wiring, I've heard."

So he didn't believe. "The electrician checked it out and said it's fine."

Brett pondered that for a moment. "Okay, so you're saying…?"

"Nothing. I just wondered if you were totally against the idea that ghosts exist."

"Not totally against it. No." He finished his wine and sat back in his chair again. "Do you believe in ghosts?"

His dark-brown eyes mesmerized her. When she went to bed at night, that's what she saw. Oh sure, the wolf's hot body too, but his eyes were what drew her in—like now, concentrating on hers and showing his interest in what she had to say. He was a lot more attentive to her than she'd been with him while she was pondering the ghost scenario. Normally, she would have been all eyes and ears, soaking in every bit of him.

"Yes," she said. "I do believe in them." She wanted to be clear on this point.

"Have you had any experiences?"

"Uh, yeah."

"So tell me about your experience. I'd love to do a feature on it for Halloween, if you don't mind." He leaned forward in interest, his arms resting on the table. Maybe as a reporter, he would be more open-minded. Maybe this was the opening she'd been waiting for.

"As long as you don't include my name." Ellie didn't want the whole pack knowing she saw ghosts.

Brett smiled. He had the most beautiful smile, warm and inviting, and his lips were perfectly kissable. Or at least in her dreams when a ghost, or two, weren't interrupting them.

"So you would be an unnamed source. I can do that. No problem."

"Okay, here goes." If he could believe her story, that would be a point in his favor.

"The first time I saw a ghost, I was five." Meghan had seen it too, but Ellie didn't want to tell her sister's secret. That was for her to share. "The little girl was about my age and playing near a creek. I thought she was real. I talked with her, and we skipped around the woods near the creek. But she kept wanting me to go into the water with her. I knew better. Mama had told us girls never to go into the creek unless she was with us. She told us how easy it was to drown. One of her cousins had drowned that way when she was seven, so Mama had really impressed upon us the danger of the water's swiftly moving currents.

"When I went home, I told Mama about the little girl near the water. Mama came with me the next afternoon to see if she could witness the phenomenon too. When she saw the ghost, Mama choked up and told me the girl was her cousin who had drowned. She hadn't seen her for years. She supposed Sybil wanted to play with me, and that's why she had shown herself to me."

"So your mother could also see the ghostly girl?" Brett acted interested, not like he didn't believe her.

Ellie felt a modicum of relief. "Yes. After that, I didn't see her again, or any more spirits for years."

"But you have since then," Brett said.

She didn't think he was ready to hear about *all* the encounters she'd had, or how she could actually communicate with the ghosts. "I've seen the woman in the inn. Chrissy. She was a maid working there and died of a fever. It was due to natural causes, but the inn had been her home since she was born."

"That's the one you were asking me about earlier. Her mother had the little girl out of wedlock, and the owner of the inn made accommodations so she didn't have to send her child away. She raised Chrissy there and then taught her how to clean the inn so she'd become a maid too. But you didn't tell me she was a ghost now staying at the inn."

"Well, she is. She's harmless, but we've all seen her. CJ denies he believes in ghosts, but we think he's seen her too."

"Well, I haven't seen her, but I did see the lights go on and off in the attic. So I guess that means I've had my first ghost experience." He offered her another of his warm and sexy smiles.

Was he teasing her? Her gaze locked onto his mouth, and his lips curved up even more. Ellie knew what she would be thinking about when she closed her eyes tonight after going to bed. *Him*. His darkly intriguing eyes, his warm and willing mouth, and his hot, naked body pressed against hers. Yet it wasn't the real thing, and she wanted more. Wanted to feel him writhing against her, making her hot and bothered and…

Grabbing her glass of ice water, she gulped down a quarter of it. She didn't have to wait until tonight to feel the heat between them, even if it was just a fantasy. She mentally shook her head at herself.

Sighing, she appreciated that Brett didn't appear to think she was crazy. Though he didn't act like he truly believed in the supernatural, he wasn't making fun of her either.

Brett's dark brows pinched together in a frown. "Was she there when the piano was delivered?"

"Yeah." But not *just* Chrissy!

He pondered that for a minute. "You looked kind of spooked."

"I was a little taken aback. No matter how many times I see a ghost, it's always a little startling." Especially when a new and totally unexpected ghost showed up, one that was most likely Brett's relation.

"I understand." He fingered his napkin, his gaze steady on hers. "*And* when we were kissing?"

"Yeah, sorry." Her face felt flushed. Omigod, he was such a hot kisser. She remembered their breaths mingling, her skin tingling, her tongue longing to stroke his when ghost number two popped into the picture and completely ruined the moment.

Brett let out his breath, then smiled. He had dimples when he smiled. Cute little dimples. And his dark, smiling eyes were framed by beautiful black lashes. "So it wasn't me."

She couldn't believe he'd thought he was the one who had turned her off. But what else would he think? He couldn't see the ghosts. Poor wolf.

Ellie smiled. "No, it definitely wasn't you."

His smile broadened. She melted. She couldn't help it. His smiles said he really, really liked her, and he hadn't indicated once that he was ready to ditch her and leave her with the bill.

She felt lighthearted and hopeful that when he learned what she could do, he would be able to accept her gift. She couldn't tell him who was haunting the piano until she knew for sure who it was. She might not need to tell him at all. She'd try to exorcise the ghost and never let on that it was his great-aunt. It was one thing to come to terms with knowing ghosts existed. Quite another to realize that the ghost was the spirit of a deceased loved one. What Brett didn't know wouldn't hurt him. Especially if he didn't believe in it anyway.

"So, next time, we'll have to spend time together somewhere a little less crowded," Brett said.

Ellie smiled again. She really liked him.

Then she wondered, did his great-aunt not like that Ellie had been kissing her grandnephew? Matilda probably believed in the old ways, that an unmarried maid should be chaperoned when visiting with a gentleman suitor, and all that business. Definitely no kissing allowed with or without a chaperone.

"Do you or your brothers ever play the piano?" Ellie asked, trying to get off the subject of ghosts *again*.

"I can play by ear like my uncle could."

"Oh, that's cool."

"Yeah, it is. Matilda wanted to offer my uncle lessons, but my grandfather didn't think his sons should play. Not manly enough. I was the one of us four brothers who had the talent, but we lost my mother when I was young and my father wasn't the least bit interested in me learning to play. After that, I never really considered it."

"You can still play by ear?"

"Yeah. It takes me a few minutes to figure out the keys, and I can play some songs. Not a whole lot. Certainly not like a trained pianist. It's an inherited trait for some of us. First time we learned of it was in the days of bootlegging and Prohibition. One of my German great-uncles made bathtub beer. Folks didn't have a lot of money during the Great Depression, but some were desperate for alcohol. One time, a man gave him a piano in payment. Johann would play songs by ear for the rest of the neighbors. Life was hard, but they made the most of it."

"Yeah, same with my family. We have some funny Prohibition stories too. My great-grandfather was a doctor who also owned a pharmacy. He sold bottles of extracts and other cooking items. During a celebration, some guys bought out his banana extract since it was one hundred and sixty proof, but after the celebration, they told him they would never eat another banana."

Brett laughed. "So the Wernicke ghost-buster cousins of yours… Can they help with the woman's spirit?"

Ellie snorted.

Brett smiled. "Fakes, huh?"

"I'm sure they put on a good show. I don't know if they're for real or not. I haven't watched any of their shows yet, but no way do we want them using our inn to pump up their ratings. I can see it now: 'See our cousins' sensational haunted Silver Town Inn.' Maybe my cousins can do something with spirits, but I'd rather not get them involved."

Since both she and Meghan had enhanced sensitivity

to ghosts, it was possible her cousins did too. Maybe that's why they had created the ghost-buster show. But she could take care of the ghost just as easily, and she didn't want her cousins trying to make a profit off Chrissy.

Only now she was faced with two ghosts.

"Want to take a wolf run tonight?" Brett asked.

"Yeah, I'd like that. Know anywhere that's forbidden?"

He laughed. "I would have taken you for a more law-abiding wolf."

Everyone always saw her that way. Sweet, innocent Ellie.

"Most of the time." Except when she was trying to make peace with a ghost. She'd broken a few laws at times to do that. She felt she owed it to them to give them some peace of mind, and as long as she didn't hurt anyone in the process, everything was good.

"A few silver mines in the area are off-limits, but no way am I taking you down into one of those. I would never put you at risk, and Darien would have my head if he learned about it. Not to mention your sisters and my brothers would too. Some trails are off-limits because of the threat of rockslides."

Ellie sighed dramatically, loving how he wasn't about to put her in harm's way, even if she said she wanted some adventure. "Okay, take me to the place you loved to go as a kid."

Brett laughed. "As kids, that was forbidden. As adults, no problem."

Before long, he drove her out to the woods and a river that ran through the pack's territory. A waterfall cascaded from cliffs in the distance, the foamy blue-green water splashing into the river. From there, the river rushed downhill over boulders and well-worn stones. It was a beautiful place and would be a lot of fun to revisit in the summer.

Right now, the temperature was just at freezing, the snowflakes fluttering about them as if practicing for an upcoming snowstorm later.

Ellie ran with her sisters and a large group of pack members on a regular basis, but hadn't done so with Brett alone on a wolf date. Wolf courtship was just as important for *lupus garous* as human dating activities. They had to learn how to play and protect and enjoy each other's company as wolves too.

"So what made this area off-limits? I guess your parents worried you'd drown."

"Eric. He was in charge of us, and he didn't want to be responsible for us getting injured or drowning here."

"So your brother made it off-limits."

Brett smiled and pulled her into his arms, his warm body wrapping around hers as he looked down at her, the cool breeze tossing her hair to the side. This was heaven.

"Only if Eric didn't come with us. When he came, we were allowed to tackle the rapids. Mom probably would not have allowed it, had she been alive. After she died in the hunting accident, Dad didn't care how we occupied ourselves as long as we got our chores and lessons done. Eric was only a few minutes older than us, so though he was alpha enough to take charge of us, he was still a kid at heart."

"I'm so sorry about your mom." She'd heard that the boys and their mom were out hiking, planning to shift, but hadn't yet when the hunter saw movement and thought their mother was a deer.

Ellie soaked up Brett's warmth, trying to concentrate on the conversation and not what his touch was doing to her, making her all hot and mushy. "Did any of you get hurt out here?"

"Are you kidding? Four boys roughhousing out here over the years? Lots of scrapes and bruises, one broken arm, and one near-drowning. All in all, it wasn't a really safe place to play."

She laughed.

He smiled and leaned down to kiss her. No ghosts out here to interrupt them. Just a chilly fall day when green-needled pines rubbed elbows with quaking golden aspen, their leaves dancing gaily in the cool breeze.

Brett's gentle kiss turned hot and needy. No way was she pushing him away this time, ghost or no. This was what she'd needed. A kiss from a wolf who didn't automatically dismiss her ghostly abilities. A man who was warm and gentle, but also passionate and oh so desirable.

This time Ellie did what she'd wanted to before, slipping her tongue into his mouth and stroking his. He crushed her against his body, revealing how passionately needy he was. She'd never seen a male shift who was aroused like that, and she had every intention of adding the image to her bedroom fantasy tonight. His lips continued to brush against hers, slowing the pace as if he were trying to get his rampant urges under control.

As hard as he was, he wasn't succeeding.

He finally brushed his mouth against her hair with a long, lingering kiss. "Ready to run?"

His voice was heavy with lust, and she was having a difficult time backing off and letting the poor wolf get his erection under control. Instead, she wanted to rub against him, like wolves did, to show she was just as interested in him as he was in her.

Their pheromones had already spiked, boosting the burning need to consume and claim each other as mated wolves. Consummating a relationship only ended one way for wolves: mated for life.

Brett's angular face softened as he pulled away, still holding her arms as if he wasn't quite ready to let go.

"One of the things I wanted to show you is my great-aunt's home," he said as Ellie rested her hands on his hips, barely hearing what he was saying as she remembered how his erection had felt against her abdomen.

"It was my uncle's after that, but it's in ruins now. Lightning hit a pine tree, which caught fire. It started a fire in the woods, and my great-aunt's home was consumed. The stone floor and the two chimneys are still standing. The forest has regrown up around it. It's a lovely place to visit, near the river."

That got her attention. "Did anybody die there?" She really didn't want to meet any ghosts on this wolf run.

"No. My great-aunt had already died, and my uncle made it out just fine. Are you ready to run?"

"I am." Though she'd really enjoyed all the kissing that led up to the run. She was relieved she wouldn't be plagued by ghosts. At least she hoped she wouldn't be. That didn't mean someone else might not be haunting the area.

They finally released each other and began to yank off their clothes.

Because of the cold, Ellie hurried to strip as fast as he did. She had fully intended to avert her eyes and not check out his arousal, but she couldn't resist peeking. As soon as she did, she got an eyeful—the cold didn't seem to affect him one bit. When she glanced up to see if he had seen her look, Brett pulled off his shirt and smiled at her.

Her whole body warmed, and she swore waves of heat were radiating off her.

Naked now, she quickly called on the warming quality of the shift, her body transforming in the blur of the change, the cold on her skin dissipating. She dropped to her four paws, her winter coat warming her as the snowflakes settled on the outer guard hairs and keeping the snow from melting against her skin. Brett had already shifted and was waiting for her. She nudged his face in greeting before he licked hers and raced off downstream away from the falls.

She watched him loping through the woods, the strength of his muscles, his beautiful furry, black-tipped tail held stately behind him, and his head held high, smelling the air, watchful, alert. Even though no hunting was allowed on these lands, someone could be out poaching. No matter what, wolves like Brett and Ellie always had to be watchful while they were in wolf form.

When they reached the shell of his family's old home, Ellie thought how beautiful it must have been there in the woods, with the view of the river nearby and the stone fireplaces giving the home warmth in its glory days. Stone pillars still welcomed guests onto the cement slab. Someone had cleaned all the debris away, and the stonework was covered in pale-green moss.

Ellie thought a couple of picnic tables set there—maybe a little pavilion, and a memorial to the family—would be nice. A perfect spot to sit awhile and enjoy the view. Then she saw a wrought iron trellis, and nearby, a gazebo, its small, octagon-shaped cement slab and stone pillars still standing. Around the base of the slab, she saw rose canes and red climbing roses. Oh, wouldn't it be beautiful to rebuild the gazebo and train the roses around it like Matilda most likely had done?

After exploring for a time, smelling the animals that had been through the area, most of whom she recognized, she and Brett ran back toward the falls. She was happily exhausted. Ellie felt the freshwater spray on her face, the breeze carrying a light mist toward them. It would be so nice to come here with him in the summer, to splash around in the water with him and cool off. Now, she was ready to do anything and everything.

They trotted back to where Brett had parked his vehicle. He looked happy to have run with her, to have shown her his special place to visit when he was a kid. She'd lived all over, but if she'd been here growing up, this would have been her special spot too.

Once they had shifted, dressed, and were on their way back to her place, she said, "I loved your special place. It really was beautiful. I was thinking that a couple of picnic tables would be really nice there. Maybe a pavilion for inclement weather and a memorial to show who owned the home."

"I love the idea. I'll tell my brothers and see what they think. I bet they'll love it too."

Ellie was glad she had suggested it.

Now she had to get back to the business at hand of

telling Laurel they had a new ghost to deal with. Could she convince Laurel not to tell her mate? Knowing Laurel, she wouldn't want to keep that from CJ. But if he didn't really believe in ghosts, what would it hurt to keep the secret from him?

—∿∿—

Brett couldn't have been happier to have finally kissed Ellie and know she felt similarly about him. He'd really been shocked when she'd pushed him away by the piano, thinking he'd misread all the wolf cues she was giving off.

He wasn't sure what to think about the ghost issue, but he was willing to keep an open mind. He'd seen the lights on in the attic. If a ghost had anything to do with turning them on and off, he'd witnessed it too.

More than anything, Brett was so glad he'd been able to kiss Ellie, to show her he was ready to take this further, to reveal how she made him feel. The issue with ghosts—that she believed in them when he might not— must have been what was holding her back before. It was understandable. He thought he was a progressive kind of guy, willing to see things in a new way. That's why he loved being a reporter so much. Sometimes a news story would really open his eyes.

They talked about the inn and how excited Ellie was that they'd renovated the basement and that the hotel would be full for the winter season and beyond. He was glad the women had decided to stay and were doing so well.

When he reached her house, Brett parked and saw the living room lights were on. He suspected Meghan was still up, waiting for Ellie to return. Laurel's car was gone, so she probably had returned home to CJ. Brett escorted Ellie to her front door. The snowflakes collected in their hair as he moved her under the cover of the front porch. She seemed to have loved the wolf run as much as he had. And he really appreciated that she had thought enough of his family's old homestead to suggest a way to make it an even more special place for visitors.

"I had a lovely time with you, Ellie."

"I did too. I'd invite you in for a drink, but Meghan's still up."

"No problem. I'm working on a couple of short deadlines, but if I get through early, do you want to have dinner with me again tomorrow night?"

"Yeah, sure." She pulled him in closer for a kiss, melting against him, all softness and warmth.

She felt damn good in his arms. He had to smile at the way she had been checking him out when he'd dropped his pants to shift. He couldn't get his raging erection under control no matter how much he'd tried to think of something other than her. She was a contradiction in terms. He'd always thought of her as so sweet and innocent. But not when he'd caught her wicked little smile.

As soon as he began to kiss her, she stiffened, her eyes widening as she looked up at the inn. Brett glanced in that direction to see what she was staring at. The light was on in the attic room. "Is Chrissy up there?" He couldn't see anyone, and he still wondered if it was a faulty wire. Once he'd had a car with that problem, but when he took it to the mechanic, the man couldn't find anything wrong with it.

"I don't see her. Just the light going on."

They watched for a moment, and then the light turned off.

Brett rubbed Ellie's arms and kissed her nose. "I take it seeing ghosts is something you don't share with the world."

"You're right."

"Does CJ know?"

"We told him Chrissy haunts the attic room mostly, but I'm not sure he believed us."

"Okay. Well, your secret is safe with me."

"Thanks. Some don't like the idea that I am sensitive to things like that. We can't help it. We're just born like that."

He looked around the lighted area. "Are there any more hanging around?"

She smiled. "No, you're safe."

He laughed. "Dinner tomorrow night?"

"My place. Meghan is supposed to be eating out with someone."

"Good call. Tomorrow night then. And I'll bring you the photo of my great-aunt." He wanted to make this a regular occurrence. He thought Ellie looked like she did too. He had to find a ghost-free zone so she wouldn't be so distracted again.

―⁓―

As soon as Ellie closed the front door and locked it, she saw a smiling Meghan curled up on the couch, turning off the TV. "Well, how did it go? Did he finally kiss you?"

"Yes, but we have a problem."

"With Brett? Nooo. He's perfect for you. Well, as long as he believes in your ability to deal with ghosts."

"No, not with him. With the ghost—"

"Chrissy? I know. We have to work harder at sending her on her way, despite what Laurel said. We can't just wait for it to happen."

"No, not Chrissy. Though I agree she needs help to move on." Ellie went into the kitchen to get a glass of water.

Meghan's eyes widened. "Another ghost? Who?"

"It might be Great-Aunt Matilda." She sipped from the water.

"Who? The Silver brothers' deceased great-aunt? The one who owned the piano? No. Really?"

"Well, maybe. Brett is going to bring over a picture of her tomorrow so I can see if she's the one I saw."

"You told Brett that?"

"Of course not. I just said I thought it would be nice to make a memorial plaque for her on the wall behind the piano."

"Oh, good save. Did you tell Laurel?"

"I didn't have time this evening. And I'm sure CJ's home by now. But whoever the ghost is, she wasn't happy that I was kissing Brett or that he was kissing me."

Meghan's jaw dropped. Then she said, "No."

"Yes. She tsked at me in a disagreeable way."

Meghan smiled.

"It's not funny. The last thing we need is a Victorian chaperone haunting the place. See how you feel if you're kissing some guy and you have a disapproving ghost looking on and making annoyed sounds of disapproval. See if you can concentrate any better than I could. I wonder if she would disapprove of CJ and Laurel kissing, since they're mated wolves."

"Seriously, that calls for an intervention," Meghan said.

"Right."

"We have to tell Laurel."

"We will when she comes over here in the morning. I don't think it's a good idea for CJ to learn about it."

Meghan's lips parted, and then she frowned. "You don't think the woman died due to something other than natural circumstances, do you?"

"Probably not. She loved that piano. So she stayed with it."

"But what if...?"

"It's possible, of course. Brett said she died of pneumonia. So that's probably all there is to it. I don't think it would benefit the brothers to tell them of her presence, even if she died like they thought she had. Brett said neither Eric nor Sarandon believe in ghosts, and Brett's never witnessed ghostly happenings, except the light turning on and off in the attic. So I think it's better if we just quietly take care of the matter and never mention it to them."

"Agreed. Though I suspect Laurel won't go along with that." Meghan got up from the couch and walked over to the front window and looked out at the inn.

"It's late. Ready to go to bed?"

"I want to see her. Besides, we could put up some"— Meghan let out her breath as if it really killed her to mention it—"put up some spiderwebs. We need to finish decorating before Halloween's here."

Ellie was exhausted and really wanted to go to bed. She wasn't that interested in seeing the ghost again, but she knew if Meghan had seen it first, she would have felt the same way about getting to see it too. If Meghan was offering to hang spiderwebs, she was all for it. She grabbed her jacket. "All right. Hurry up. I'm tired and want to hit the sack as soon as we finish decorating a little more."

Meghan threw on her jacket and opened the door. Then she was out of it and headed down the path to the inn. "Maybe we can talk her into leaving tonight."

Like that would happen. When ghosts were really attached to something, they often had a hard time letting go.

"I wonder if she'll become angry if anyone comes to play her piano. Maybe we should rope it off until we know more about this. We could just say it's an antique and can't be played," Meghan said.

"We've already told everyone they can play it if they know how to."

Meghan sighed. "Yeah, but if she gets violent, we'll have to say something."

"'It's not working,' I guess. But I'm afraid that if Brett or any of his brothers hear of it, they'll send a repairman over to fix it right away."

As soon as they reached the back door to the inn, they heard music playing in the lobby.

Meghan looked at Ellie and whispered, "Beethoven's Piano Sonata no. 14, *Moonlight*." Meghan loved classical music, as did Ellie, but Ellie rarely knew which song she was listening to. "And now that's *The Marriage of Figaro*, by Wolfgang Amadeus Mozart."

Ellie took a deep breath and let it out. This was so not good.

Chapter 3

As soon as Ellie and Meghan opened the back door to the inn, the music stopped. Neither of them were surprised by that. Ghosts could be unpredictable. Ellie was afraid the woman wouldn't show herself to Meghan now. Would Ellie have to kiss Brett near the piano again to force the woman to appear so her sister could see her?

They would really have trouble if the ghost decided to play the piano in the middle of the night when guests were staying at the inn. Ellie could envision dissatisfied guests leaving early or writing bad reviews on the inn's website, complaining about the bizarre happenings there. And what could Ellie and her sisters do? They could move the piano out of the inn, but that meant upsetting the Silver brothers, who would want to know why. Everyone in town knew the piano was on display in the lobby, and it was going to be a big part of the show-and-tell for the town's Victorian Days celebration. Each of the older establishments were showcasing something special from that time.

When they reached the lobby, Ellie saw no sign of the ghostly woman. She glanced at Meghan, but her sister shook her head, indicating she didn't see the ghost either.

"Okay, we want to show off your treasured piano, to dedicate it to you," Ellie said for the new ghost's benefit.

"In fact, Brett's bringing a photo of you tomorrow, and we'll add a memorial on the wall behind the piano." Ellie acted as though she knew just who the ghost woman was and that she was standing there right before them. Even if it wasn't Brett's great-aunt, the woman had to have played the piano. The music they'd heard was beautiful, as if she'd played with one of the prestigious orchestras. "If it bothers you that we have it on display here and you'd rather it remain with Brett in the quiet of his home, we can move it back there. We really want to do what you wish us to."

Both Meghan and Ellie waited for a response, but no one appeared or uttered a sound.

Meghan folded her arms and looked cross. "Listen, if you want some changes, you'll have to let us know. You undoubtedly are able to communicate with us, and we're happy to make it right, however you want to do this. But we can't read minds."

Ellie knew she only half meant it. Yes, they wanted to accommodate the ghost. If she wanted her piano returned to Brett's home because he was family and it was more private, then they'd have to honor that request and deal with the repercussions. If she wanted to keep her piano here and play it when she wanted to, that was another story.

"Come on, Meghan. Let's at least hang up the spiderwebs. It's late. I'm tired. We'll deal with this tomorrow. We'll see what Laurel has to say too."

"I was hoping we could avoid having to tell her." Meghan grimaced as she pulled out a handful of fake spiderwebs.

They spent an hour hanging the webs all over the

furniture and the check-in counter. Then they hung them around the mirrors. After that, they met in the lobby and looked at the piano. Ellie draped some spiderwebs off the piano, hoping Matilda—if that's who the ghost was—would be all right with that.

Finished with the webs, they headed outside and locked the inn door.

"I can't believe we've got a second ghost haunting the inn now," Ellie said, exasperated.

"I know, right? What if the two women don't get along?"

"Or they might become best buds and team up to cause more trouble for our guests."

Meghan eyed the inn. "Laurel's not going to like hearing about this. She won't want to keep secrets from CJ. And if he learns his great-aunt is the one haunting the piano, he'll want to tell his brothers about it. Who would have thought such a sweet gesture on the Silver brothers' part would create all kinds of angst?"

Ellie unlocked the house, and after they went inside, Meghan locked the door behind her.

"I know." Ellie really wanted to tell Laurel tonight. They always told each other about things right away. Especially something like this that could affect their livelihood.

"I know you, and you're dying to tell Laurel. Don't. She can't do anything about it tonight, and neither can we. We'll see her tomorrow after CJ goes to work and let her know then." Meghan headed up the stairs.

Ellie let out a breath and followed her sister. "She's not going to like that we didn't tell her right away. This could be a real disaster." She'd thought she would be dreaming about Brett again tonight, when instead she could be dreaming up ways to talk a ghost—or two— into leaving.

Laurel climbed into bed with CJ, but while there was time for conversation before they began cuddling, she said, "Tell me about Darien's and Jake's dream-mating experiences. I've only heard a little about them." She was hoping she could learn more about the subject without tipping CJ off.

CJ smiled a little and pulled her on top of him. She rested her chin on her hand and said, "Well?"

"Brett and I were talking about this earlier today, but is there any reason this is coming up right now?"

Laurel couldn't help being surprised any more than she could fib her way out of this.

"You were?"

"Yeah." He rubbed her back. "According to our cousins who were dream mated, they were obsessed with locating the she-wolf that was to be their mate. There was a mix-up in Darien's situation, and Jake's was rather unusual, which goes to prove every case can be different."

"Right. I thought it was something like that."

"Why do you ask?"

She shrugged.

He smiled. "Is Ellie dreaming about Brett?"

Laurel smiled and then sighed. "I'm not supposed to say. I swore I'd keep it secret."

"I know you too well. I won't say anything to anyone about it."

"Is Brett dreaming about Ellie?"

"I'm certain of it—when he's asleep and when he's not."

Laurel chuckled. "Okay, I'll tell her that to be dream mated, she has to be completely obsessed with him, and no other wolf would do."

"At least in Jake and Darien's cases. Who knows how it will happen for someone else?"

"It could be just dreams then. Fantasies about the other person."

"Did you fantasize about me?" CJ asked, kissing her on the cheek, the forehead, and the other cheek.

Laurel just smiled and leaned down to kiss his most kissable mouth—and that was the end of the conversation.

―⁓―

Ellie closed her eyes, hoping to dream about Brett, but she couldn't. She tossed and turned in bed, trying to put her mind at rest. Unable to sleep, she kept thinking of how they were going to have to deal with two ghosts in the inn now. Did she and her sisters have enough sage for cleansing? Incense? If they had to try a séance, they would have to perform it before the guests arrived.

She rolled onto her back and stared up at the dark ceiling. She hadn't been able to do anything about Chrissy. Had she lost her touch? Or was Chrissy just happy where she was? Maybe she wouldn't haunt the guests when they began arriving. The only one who had stayed in the attic room was Deputy Sheriff Trevor Osgood, and he said nothing had happened. So maybe Chrissy had left the light switch alone while he was there at night. What if she got upset when they had someone staying in both her bedroom and the attic?

Ellie didn't think she would ever get to sleep, so she tried to envision hunky Brett standing in front of her, pulling off his shirt while the rest of him was naked, his erection jutting out proud and ready. She hadn't seen him naked when he was aroused like that before. Except in her dreams, when she'd seen a hazier version of him. What a gorgeous hunk of wolf man! Then she recalled the amused gleam in his eyes, the way his oh-so-appealing mouth had turned up because he was tickled that she was gawking at his beauty.

Then somehow, between the images burned into her memory, the lateness of the hour, and the tiredness she was feeling, that image of Brett turned into something more—hotter, sexier, a fantastical dream.

Approaching her in the bed, he moved like a wolf on the hunt, slowly, focused, his dark gaze on hers, a predatory gleam in his eyes, the soft moonlight giving them a greenish tinge. Her heartbeat sped up in anticipation. She pulled her long, brown T-shirt over her head and tossed it to the floor. He climbed over her in one smooth move, pressing all that hard muscle against her body, telling her he wanted her, now, tonight, right this moment.

He was kissing her, his mouth so perfect for hers, warm and sweet and passionate. His tongue stroked hers, and she writhed against him, wanting more than just his tongue in her mouth. Tendrils of pleasure coiled around inside her, making her eager to feel his cock penetrating her. In the dreamlike fog, she felt his fingers stroking her, pleasuring her, tantalizing her. How could this be so real? He seemed to know just what she needed to make her come.

He moved his mouth down to her breast and suckled a nipple, and that was all it took. She cried out, clutching his shoulders, reveling in the way he made her rocket to the moon.

He slid inside her then, thrusting, and he felt good there—huge, but good. She stroked his back as he began to kiss her again, and she fell completely under his spell. He truly was the wolf of her dreams. "Brett," she whispered, stroking his waist and loving the feel of his soft skin stretched over hard muscles.

*"Ellie," Brett whispered in her ear, and she came again, her heart pounding, her breath short as she woke…*to find she was alone.

She groaned.

—⁂—

"Ellie," Brett whispered, feeling her beneath him and around him, hugging his cock deep inside her, stroking him as he stroked her. He felt the end coming, the stage of near-completion, so real, and then he growled and released.

He opened his eyes, expecting to be with Ellie. To wrap his arms around her and hold her tight the rest of the night until they made love again. But she wasn't there, and he growled in his frustration.

He rolled over on the bed and ran his hand through his hair. He'd been having these dreams more frequently the more often he saw Ellie. It wasn't dream mating. At least not the same as it had been for Jake and Darien. Maybe that was because everyone was so different. The experience had been so incredibly real, not dreamlike at all. Brett felt like he'd really had sex with her. Which meant she was his, in the way a wolf claims his mate.

He'd never had such strong dreams before where he couldn't separate fantasy from reality.

He groaned and stared at his phone sitting on the bedside table. Then he grabbed it and called Ellie. "Are you still awake?"

She answered on the first ring. "If I weren't, could you tell?"

He smiled, got out of bed, and began changing the sheets. "I couldn't sleep."

"No wild and sexy dreams?"

Her voice was drowsy and sexy, and he envisioned her in bed wearing the moose T-shirt she'd had on before she tossed it and was completely naked.

"Yeah, actually, I was having this really hot dream about this incredibly hot and sexy she-wolf."

Silence.

He was afraid he'd shocked her. "Are you still there?"

"With me?" she asked, sounding startled.

Who else would he be dreaming of? He laughed though. "Yeah. I didn't embarrass you, did I?" He finished changing the sheets on his bed, then climbed back into it.

"Hmm, what if I said I was dreaming about you?"

He paused. "Really."

"Yeah, but you know everyone fantasizes about people they're dating, right?"

"Yeah, sure." He pulled the covers over his waist. "So what was I wearing?"

"No shirt, no boxer briefs, just your jeans. What was I wearing?"

"A brown T-shirt with a moose on the front of it."

"*No*."

"Yeah. It's weird what you'll envision in a dream, right? So what were you really wearing?" Brett asked.

"That's what I was really wearing."

Both were silent for a few seconds, then Brett said, "Okay, so tell me exactly what happened in your dream."

After she gave him an abbreviated version, he whistled. "I know you can see ghosts, but are you…psychic?"

"No."

"Hell, Ellie. You know what this means?"

"We are *not* dream mated."

"Okay, so if you went out with someone else, you'd see that you wouldn't dream about him in the same way we dream about each other—and you'll know we're meant to be together." He couldn't imagine a better way to prove it, not that he really meant for her to do so, nor would he suggest it in a million years. But he assumed that's what would happen.

"Are you serious? What if I start dating a wolf, and he thinks I'm really interested in him? What if I am? Okay, fine. I'll ask Sarandon on a date."

"No, wait. I didn't mean for you to do that. It was just a hypothetical comment." No way did he want Ellie asking Sarandon out. What if his brother was interested in her? Besides, the news would spread through the pack like wildfire.

"No, I think it's a good idea. A great social experiment. If we're meant to be together, then we will be. Listen, it's really late and I've got to get up early tomorrow. I'll talk to you later. Night, Brett." Ellie hung up on him.

"Wait!" Ah hell, he'd just been talking off the top of his head. If they were dream mated, it was a done deal and they needed to make the fantasy come true. He was certainly ready. He called her back, but she didn't answer.

Brett let out his breath in a growl. He didn't want her to date anyone else. What if she was angry with him over suggesting that and she called it off between them completely?

Then he smiled. She couldn't. Not if they were dream mated. She would want him back no matter what. Then again, what if they weren't? No way. Though there were a couple of minor discrepancies in what she had seen and what he had witnessed during their heated dreams, any two people experiencing the same dream would surely each see things a little differently. He had to try to convince her once and for all that they were meant for each other.

Ellie couldn't sleep after she hung up on Brett. She wasn't an unreasonable person, but she didn't plan to date just anyone as an experiment to see if she felt the same with him as with Brett. He had a good point, but what if she didn't have any feelings for whatever other guy she dated? Just because she went out with someone didn't mean she'd automatically begin fantasizing about him. That only happened when she really got to know the person. Like Fred Pippin, the wolf who had stuck her with the bill at the restaurant—though not for long.

That had happened only a couple of months before she and her sisters sold their last renovated Victorian inn and found this one. Which meant she hadn't seen Fred for more than a year. She hadn't dated anyone else when she arrived in Silver Town because she and her sisters were renovating the inn. Once that was done, they'd begun to join in pack activities, and Brett had made his interest in her abundantly clear. And she'd loved him for it.

She had other things to deal with right now though.

———

Up super early the next morning, Ellie paced across the living room floor, waiting for Laurel to arrive so she could tell her about the other ghost. She suspected CJ was working a later shift today, or Laurel would have already been there. When Meghan woke, she headed straight for the kitchen and the coffeepot, glancing in Ellie's direction with a look that said, *Really? How long have you been up?*

"CJ must be working later." Ellie couldn't help being annoyed. Not that she wasn't glad that Laurel and CJ could spend some extra time together, but she really wanted Laurel at the inn so they could deal with this ghostly business.

"So how long have you been up?" Meghan took a sip of her favorite mocha.

"Three hours." But that was because Ellie was always an early riser. Meghan could sleep until noon with no trouble at all.

"Any more piano playing?"

"No. Maybe she got the message last night that if she doesn't behave, she'll be out of our place and back at Brett's." Ellie fixed herself another mug of lavender green tea.

"I hear Laurel pulling up now," Meghan said, but she'd let Ellie be the one to tell Laurel what was going on.

Ellie put her mug on the marble kitchen counter and hurried out the door. "Laurel, we have a real problem."

Her older sister frowned when she learned what the trouble was. "Why didn't you call me last night and tell me?"

"We didn't want to upset CJ about this if we could take care of it ourselves." Ellie walked back into the house with Laurel. "What if it isn't even their great-aunt?"

Laurel gave her a get-real look.

"I don't believe it could be anyone else," Ellie said. "Still, I need that photo from Brett to verify that's who the ghost is."

"I can't keep this from CJ if it is his great-aunt."

"Well, if she died of natural causes and the brothers don't see the ghost, what difference does it make? We could send her on her way without the guys ever being aware of her."

"And if the piano starts playing when one of them is here and we have to explain we already knew about it?" Laurel walked with Ellie into the kitchen and made herself a peppermint mocha.

Meghan nodded sagely.

"Can we *just* hold off until I see the photo of their great-aunt?" Ellie asked. "If it's not her—"

"All right. If it is, I'm talking to CJ about it."

"Fine." Ellie understood where her sister was coming from, but she really wished she could send the ghost on her merry way and not involve any of the brothers.

Laurel shared the information CJ had given her about Jake's dream-mating experience.

"So he was obsessed with his mate before he saw her again."

"Yeah, he couldn't eat or sleep and dropped out of pack activities. He was a mess. He kept searching for her, desperate to find her. They were really worried about him," Laurel said.

Ellie wasn't feeling like that, but then again, she was dating Brett, not absent from his life. It made her wonder if what Brett suggested would really work. She wasn't sure what was going on between the two of them. Maybe he'd just guessed what she was wearing last night. Tonight, she'd wear something different. Wouldn't that tell her something was really up between them if they discussed their dreams and he got her outfit right again? Wouldn't that indicate something more than just normal dreaming about each other?

She swept her hair back into a tail and tied it off.

After finishing their drinks, she and her sisters headed to the inn to add decorative touches to the basement rooms and then finish with the Halloween lights. Ellie knew Laurel and Meghan were just as wary as she was, listening and watching for any sign of ghosts.

Ellie let out her breath in an exasperated way, unable to keep her secret from her sisters. Especially since she decided to go through with the plan. "Brett suggested that the way to figure out if we're dream mated for sure is for me to date others. And that's just what I'm going to do."

----~~~----

Brett had tried to get ahold of Ellie this morning, but she wouldn't answer her phone or return his calls. He had to turn in a news story on Silver Town Ski Resort's new trails and new ski lodge, both opening with the first good snowfall. Otherwise, he would have run over to the house or inn to see her in person. Because his brother Eric's new pack and a couple of other wolf packs liked to come to the ski resort in winter and run on the closed trails at night, Silver Town had needed more accommodations. Brett had worried that the added rooms at the lodge would impact the MacTire sisters' Victorian inn and the Hastings' bed-and-breakfast, but all the places were booked for the coming season and for Victorian Days. So it looked like that was no problem.

After Ellie had hung up on him last night, Brett had left the bed and stayed up way too late searching through old photos, looking for one of his great-aunt Matilda. He finally found one he really liked where she was seated at the piano with him and his brothers gathered around her. He liked it best because it showed her at her piano, displaying the importance that her playing had to the family. He hadn't stopped there but had made up a little blurb about her and put it in a glass-covered picture frame— one that matched the Victorian style of the inn. He hoped the sisters appreciated it, but he would be sure to tell them they could display it differently if they wanted to.

He couldn't wait to see Ellie tonight. Hopefully, she wasn't serious about seeing anyone else, though the fact that she didn't answer the phone didn't bode well. Maybe she was really busy. He sighed. If she went out with a couple of different wolves, she would realize Brett was the one for her. Then they could get on with what was meant to be—the mating between the two of them. He thought her dating could still be a sound idea. If he could just let go of the notion she was dating anyone else but him.

For now, he was having lunch with CJ at the Silver Town Tavern, hoping to learn more about the ghost named Chrissy.

Like most of the town's business establishments, the tavern was all decorated for Halloween. Everyone had fun with that. Silva, Sam's mate, had probably done all the decoration both here at the tavern and at her tea shop, but Brett hadn't visited the tea shop yet, so he couldn't say for sure. Here, everything was skeletons and special bottles of liquor: Spider Cider, Bewitching Brew, and Haunted Ale, which suited the tavern. Sam was making special Halloween drinks for the adult crowd, while Silva planned to give away treats at the tavern door Halloween night since her tea shop was closed in the evenings.

When Brett saw CJ enter the tavern, he waved and his brother smiled and headed his way. "Did you order us Sam's famous roast-beef sandwiches?"

"Sure did," Brett said.

Sam brought them bottles of water. Towering over them, he narrowed his eyes, looking like an unhappy grizzly. "Hope Darien's not going to approve of much more building in the area. I like the quaint feel of the town."

Sam always seemed like a rugged mountain man, but he was really a big teddy bear—unless anyone messed with Silva. He'd also been concerned about the town drawing too much of a human crowd. His tavern was open only to wolves so they could visit without worrying about what they might say.

"Nope," Brett said. "We all voted on the new trails and the ski lodge. No other plans in the works."

"Well, maybe a movie theater and an ice cream

shop." CJ twisted off the cap of his chilled bottled water. "That's what all the teens have been pushing for."

"The kids want a drive-in. Darien and Lelandi aren't going for it," Brett said.

"Ice cream and a theater, no problem. Just don't need any other taverns or anyone to compete against my mate's tea room," Sam growled.

"No problem. Everyone wants to have variety. So if anything else moves in, it has to be something that doesn't compete with existing businesses. And it has to be wolf run." Brett loved the way Darien and Lelandi ran the town. They were good about ensuring that everyone's vote counted. Even the teens'. They also let the younger kids participate as a learning experience for when they had a real say in pack politics.

Sam nodded and returned to the counter to finish making their sandwiches.

"So, CJ, have you ever spied the ghost named Chrissy at the inn?"

"Nope."

"Ellie told me about her. She said she and her sisters thought you'd seen her."

Sam delivered their sandwiches, fries, and pickles, then returned to the bar.

"Have *you*?" CJ asked.

"Nope. And I have to admit I have a hard time believing in a ghost. I've seen lights going on and off in the attic room. I still feel that has something to do with the old wiring."

"Could be."

"What about that letter *C* that kept appearing on the wall in the lobby?" Brett figured that could be easily explained away too. Some oil-based paint that had bled into the wall and couldn't be covered up.

"Not sure about it. It comes and goes. So the ladies covered it up with one of Jake's floral photos of the mountains and purple daisies in spring."

Brett had never actually seen the letter, but he felt there had to be a viable explanation for it. "So you've really never seen a ghost at the inn."

CJ leaned back against his chair. "I've seen... something. Or thought I'd seen something. Don't tell Sarandon or Eric, all right? Just a shadow, and then it's gone. I'm sure it's just car headlights casting shadows through the front windows or something."

"Your secret's safe with me. I know Eric and Sarandon don't believe in any of this stuff."

"What's this all about? The sisters believing in ghosts? They do, you know." CJ took a bite of his sandwich.

"Well, Ellie told me she does."

"Okay, so what's the problem? You're not sure you can live with the idea?"

"No, it's not that." Though Brett realized that Ellie might feel it could be an obstacle to their relationship if she truly believed and he truly didn't. He would either have to shrug her comments off, which he didn't want to do, or pretend he believed, which he didn't want to do either.

"What then?"

"Did you see how pale Meghan and Ellie were when the piano was set in its final spot at the inn? Ellie said she'd seen Chrissy, and the ghost had startled her." Brett ate more of his sandwich.

"Laurel didn't seem perturbed over anything. I was

watching her, waiting to see if she wanted the piano moved further."

"Maybe she didn't see Chrissy."

"Laurel says she believes in ghosts and told me for certain the inn, especially the attic room, is haunted. Well, and the basement."

"Yes, but maybe they don't always see the same thing at once. I was wondering if their cousins might know of a way to exorcise Chrissy. Ellie didn't seem to care for the idea of getting her cousins involved. Maybe you could ask Laurel."

"If the ghost doesn't bother her—"

"It bothers me." Brett took a bite of his pickle, really not wanting to tell CJ the details, but if he was going to convince him why it was important, he knew he'd have to.

"You said you don't believe in them."

"Ellie does."

CJ frowned, and Brett knew his brother wasn't getting the whole picture, though as close as they were, they rarely needed to overexplain things to each other.

Brett leaned forward. "I was kissing Ellie when the ghost upset her."

CJ smiled. Brett knew CJ had been dying to know when Brett was taking it to the next level with his mate's sister.

"I'm serious. *This* is serious."

CJ chuckled. "Okay, I know it is, or you wouldn't have told me about your first kiss. I'll ask Laurel if she saw Chrissy when we were moving the piano around, and I'll see what she has to say about the Wernicke brothers and if they have any idea how to get rid of a ghost. Are you sure that's the real reason for Ellie pulling back?"

"Yes. She said it wasn't because of me but because of the ghost."

"All right. I'll see what I can do. I'm not promising anything though. The sisters don't want their cousins involved in the inn in any way, shape, or form."

"I understand." Brett didn't have a lot of hope that the ladies would change their minds about their cousins, but he had to do something.

"Hey, and congratulations, Brother. Ellie's worth it."

"Yeah, well, I agree, but I kind of messed things up between us last night."

CJ arched a brow.

"I was just talking off the top of my head. Hey, if Jake or Darien had seen other women, they wouldn't have felt the compulsion to be with them like they did with their dream mates, right?"

"Yeah." CJ leaned back in his chair. "And…?"

"Well, I had the notion that if Ellie dated another wolf, she would realize that no one else would be right for her but me."

CJ groaned. "Are you crazy?"

"I didn't mean for her to go off and actually do that. I was just making a comment, thinking out loud. You know how it is. I still think it's a good idea to prove we're meant for each other. But I wasn't suggesting she really do it."

"Well, make it up to her, Brother, because I don't want to have to deal with the fallout from Laurel when she learns about this." CJ shook his head. "Now if only we could get Sarandon hooked up with Meghan…"

"Yeah, except that your boss is wooing her big time."

"True. Peter's quiet about it, but I know he's really interested in her. I'll talk to Laurel tonight. Oh, and if you have a spare moment, the ladies want to put up lights on the inn for Halloween. They put up some out front, but the roof of the inn..."

"I'll be sure to drop by to help."

"Okay. Good. Maybe you can tell Ellie what a dumb idea you had and get back on her good side."

"I hope so." Brett hoped she had no intention of going out with anyone else. What if she thought he'd only said that because *he* wanted to see other wolves? Great.

Brett and CJ paid for their meals, said good-bye to Sam and several pack members eating lunch there, and then headed out.

Brett saw the Wernicke brothers' blue van drive by and wondered what they were doing here this time.

"They're doing a story on the Silver Mine ghosts," CJ told him. "Wait until I ask Laurel about the situation."

"I will." Brett wished he could talk to the brothers, but he didn't want to annoy the MacTire sisters by doing that. He was used to taking care of things and all too willing to do the same for Ellie—if he could wrap his mind around the idea that ghosts exist and that there was a way to make them leave.

CJ got a call and said to Brett, "Hold up."

Brett knew some kind of trouble was brewing.

"All right, Peter. I'll let everyone know." CJ turned to Brett. "Eric called in an alert that a young boy is missing in the park. He wants all of us who can to go out there to search for him, knowing that our kind can find someone faster than humans can. I'm running over to the inn to tell the ladies."

"Thanks," Brett said. "Who do you want me to call?"

"Sarandon was in the park taking a group on a hike. See if you can get ahold of him."

"I sure will. I think the MacTire sisters should stay with one of us since they're fairly new to the area." Brett wanted to be the one who stayed with them, though he wasn't sure they'd want him to if Ellie had told her sisters about him suggesting she date others.

"Sounds like a good idea. I've got to help organize the search. If you want to watch over the sisters, that works for me. I'll let them know first." CJ hurried off to his vehicle.

Brett called Sarandon and gave him the news. "Call Eric to see where he wants you to begin a search."

"I'm sure the hikers on my tour will be eager to help," Sarandon said.

"Good. I just saw the Wernicke brothers. I'm going to try to contact them and then bring the MacTire sisters out to join the search."

"Okay, good luck."

"You too." Brett got in his vehicle and drove off after the blue van and pulled up beside it at the light. "Hey, if you want to help out, we're all searching for a missing kid," he called out to Stanton. He gave the coordinates of the search area.

"We'll head out there," Stanton said. He was the eldest of the three brothers and the one who was always in charge.

"Thanks. See you out there." Then Brett headed home to grab some cold-weather gear and first aid supplies.

—〰—

Ellie saw CJ pull up at the inn, then climb out of his vehicle, looking concerned. He met with Laurel outside to talk to her in private.

Ellie couldn't help but watch them as surreptitiously as she could through one of the windows.

Slipping in beside her, Meghan tsked. "They're just having a newlywed moment."

"Laurel looks guilty, like she has a secret. CJ's going to pick up on that. Besides, he doesn't usually drop by during his shift unless something's wrong."

"You are so paranoid. And if he sees us both standing here watching out the window, he's going to really believe something is up."

Laurel gave CJ a hug and kiss and then headed for the inn while CJ went to his vehicle.

"Okay," she said once she'd walked inside. "Eric called and said they're organizing search parties for a four-year-old boy who wandered off from his tent at the park early this morning. Because of our wolf senses, he's asked Darien for our pack's help. He spread the word to the sheriff's department to tell everyone we need to find the child pronto. It's going to get too cold for him to be out on his own tonight."

"Omigod, that's terrible." A ghost problem didn't mean anything compared to a missing child. Ellie was reminded of the case of the Arctic wolf child that Lelandi had received a call about. The Arctic wolf boy had wandered off and ended up with a jaguar shifter family in Texas. Ellie still couldn't believe it. If jaguar shifters were as elusive as wolves, did other kinds of shifters exist that were just as secretive?

As bad as that situation with the boy had been, Lelandi

had given the whole Silver wolf pack a talk about what to do if any of the kids—or adults even—got lost or injured. Ellie remembered everyone looking CJ's way and him turning a little red, because he had fallen into a killing pit and no one had known what had become of him. So really, anyone could be at risk at any time, and it never hurt to go over emergency procedures again.

"I'm going to run and put on some really warm clothes. It's getting colder by the hour," Ellie told her sisters.

"Pack blankets, coats, and first aid supplies in case we have to stay out through the night." Laurel locked up the house and hurried after Ellie and Meghan. "He's a cute little kid. Blond curls, blue eyes, wearing neon-green-and-blue sleeper pajamas. They won't be warm enough for him the way the temperature is dropping." She showed her sisters a photo of the boy. "CJ said Brett's coming with us. We'll meet him at the newspaper office."

"CJ's afraid we're going to get lost?" Meghan asked.

"Yep. He's in an overprotective mode, so I figure we'll humor him," Laurel said.

Meghan smiled at Ellie. "Are you still mad at Brett?"

"I'm not mad at him. I think it's a good idea." If Ellie hadn't been worried about finding a little boy...? She figured the question of dating others wasn't important right now.

"Wait, you don't think Brett wants you to go out with others because he wants to, do you?" Laurel asked.

"No." At least Ellie didn't think so. But what if that's what this was about? He'd just throw it out there to see if she wanted to do it. Then once she said yes, he would be free to date others too. How would she feel about that? Ellie told herself he would be trying to learn the truth about their interest in each other the same as she was. Would they still be dreaming about each other? And why was she feeling super growly about the whole notion?

The sisters had just pulled up to the newspaper office when Brett parked beside them.

"Do you want us to follow you?" Laurel asked. "We've got a lot of stuff packed in the car."

"Yeah. Same here. Do you want to ride with me?" he asked Ellie.

"Sure." Ellie joined him, figuring she'd tell him she was planning to date others, so she wouldn't be able to see him all the time.

"There are the photo and the memorial plaque I made, if they work for you," Brett said, pointing to the backseat as he led the way to the park. "I had them ready and sitting in the car for when I came over tonight. Guess we might have to postpone our dinner date."

Her heartbeat quickened as she eyed the framed picture. "We will. We might have to skip it all together. I sure hope we can find the boy in time." She pulled the framed photo and plaque out of the bubble wrap and felt a chill sweep up her spine. Yes, it was Great-Aunt Matilda, with four little boys she swore were Brett and his brothers. The woman looked stern, like people in most photos of that time. One of the boys was smiling. She thought it was Brett. "This is you and your brothers, right?"

"Yeah. I found a couple photos of my great-aunt, but this was the only one where she was sitting at the piano. I thought it had a nice, warm, family feel."

"I love it." Would Matilda love it too? Would she leave them alone if they mounted the memorial behind the piano? "It's beautiful."

"I was afraid you might have had some other idea in mind."

"No, the frame is the same color as the piano. Nice and Victorian. I love the way you used antiqued paper, and the sentiments are perfect."

"I hoped you'd like it. It won't hurt my feelings if you change anything."

"It's perfect." But any hope that the ghost was someone else was instantly dashed.

"I have a box of sheet music and song books in the car too. I'd forgotten I'd removed them and stored them in the box while we had the piano bench refinished."

"Oh, that's great." Before, she would have loved for someone to use the song sheets to bring the music to life. Now, she wanted to hide them away so no one could play the piano and possibly upset Matilda. "That's you smiling, isn't it?"

Brett chuckled. "Yeah. Eric had just made a crack about how I always smiled in pictures. I was trying really hard not to, but his comment made me laugh. He teased me about that for years."

She laughed. She was sure she would have loved Brett when he was a little boy.

They finally reached the park and met up with some search parties just getting started. Ellie and Brett and her sisters quickly smelled the child's sweatshirt that the parents had given to Eric. He was sharing it with all the wolves so they could recognize the boy's scent. Ellie figured the humans gathered there were wondering what that was all about. Then she and Brett and her sisters took off to try to locate the boy's scent anywhere they could.

Working as a park ranger, Eric was normally really good at locating missing people of any age. He'd found several people over the year he'd been working there. One had been an older man with early-onset Alzheimer's. Eric had also located a couple of kids and even some dogs. Faced with the cold weather and its danger for a child so young, he'd called his pack and Darien's to get more wolf help.

Through the trees, Ellie saw her cousins searching for the boy. She was surprised they were here. Who told them about the missing boy? And why were they in the area again?

People kept thinking they'd spotted the little boy and reported the sighting, but the reports always turned out to be false alarms. Dusk was falling, though the wolves could see well in the darkening night and would continue to search until they found the boy. The humans were beginning to panic, worried that they wouldn't find him before it got too dark. The light had nearly faded when CJ reported that he'd located a fresh trail. Ellie and her party hurried that way.

Ellie and Brett spied an old wolf den dug out between some boulders, the rocks' thick understory hiding the entrance. If they hadn't smelled the boy's scent, they wouldn't have noticed it. Wolves didn't hibernate in dens. The females used them to have their pups, so at this time of the year, the den should be empty. Ellie and Brett crouched in front of the small opening and listened for any sign of the boy.

"Billy?" Brett called out. "Are you in there? We've come to take you back to your mom and dad."

"Billy, can you crawl out of there?" Ellie asked.

There wasn't any response. Either he wasn't there but had been at one time, or he was sleeping or hypothermic and they'd need to go in and get him. Crawling into a den as adult humans would be challenging, if not impossible. The opening was only about fifteen inches high and maybe twenty inches wide. Best to do it as a wolf. Unless humans caught them in the middle of the rescue. They'd truly be between a rock and a hard place then. Or…a wolf and a hard place.

"I'll go," Ellie said, already yanking off her jacket and hat.

"Okay. If you have any trouble, let me know and I'll come and help."

"We'll wait to hear if you've found the boy," Laurel said.

"Right. We don't want everyone to converge on the wolf den if he's not there," Meghan agreed.

Meghan and Laurel served as lookouts while Ellie finished stripping, shifted, and ducked her head to slip into the den. As shifters, most of them never went into dens, so this was a first time for her. She wasn't sure what she would find. She moved through about fifteen feet of tunnel until it dead-ended, forming the top of the capital *T* and continuing to the right and left. She smelled the earth and recognized that the boy had taken the left tunnel. She moved down it another fifteen feet until she reached the birthing chamber, about three feet wide and two feet high, where Billy was curled up in the soft dirt sleeping, his brightly colored pj's barely visible in the darkness. Ellie was glad he wouldn't be able to see her in case he was scared by the big "dog" that had suddenly found him. She moved closer and felt him shivering. Though the den would offer some protection from the wind and cold, he needed pack mates to keep him warm like the wolf pups had when they were born here.

She shifted and called out that she'd found Billy. She wished he was a wolf shifter because they could easily get him out of there then.

"Brett's already on his way with a backpack," Laurel called into the den.

"Good, thanks!"

He hadn't even waited for her to reach the boy, maybe worried she had run into trouble herself.

She was so glad to have found Billy, but he wasn't out of danger yet. And she was thankful Brett had already come for them. She shifted again and shared her wolf's body heat with Billy like a big family dog might do, trying to warm him. He was shivering badly, which was good. No shivering was even worse. But his eyes were closed, and he was curled up into himself as much as he could to keep warm. Laurel would have to call Eric and let him know what the situation was so that only wolves would come to take care of the boy. They didn't want any humans to see wolves rescuing him from the den.

As a wolf, Brett joined her, dropping the pack in front of her and then checking them both over. She quickly shifted, yanked out a blanket, and wrapped Billy in it. They would have to rig up a carrier that they could pull him on. The backpack appeared to be big enough that they could actually put him in it. Then maybe the two of them could pull it with their teeth as they walked backward until they reached a point where only one had room to move it. The entrance was too small for them both to pull at the same time.

As she tried to move the lethargic boy into the bag, Ellie realized he was too big, so she set him on top of it and tied him to it while Brett waited. He was too big and wouldn't have been able to maneuver inside the den with another human in the small space. Then she shifted and moved to where Brett was. He nuzzled her face, and she greeted him back. Then each grasped a strap between their teeth and backed up, sliding the backpack and the boy over the soft earth.

Pulling him took so long that she didn't think they'd ever reach the main tunnel that led back to the entrance to the den. They could still move the backpack side-by-side, but when they drew within about eight feet from the entrance, the tunnel narrowed too much. Brett nuzzled her in a way that said she should let him do it. He was stronger and could pull the boy by himself. She was afraid Billy might still slide off the backpack, so she maneuvered around him and followed at the boy's feet, just in case.

"You're almost here," Eric said, peering into the den with a flashlight trained on them. "Just a few more feet, and I can grab him and bring him out."

But Brett hauled the boy the rest of the way out. Eric and the wolf paramedics quickly took care of the boy while Brett and Ellie shifted farther away in the woods. Meghan had already brought their clothes over and returned to see if she could help with Billy.

Thrilled to have located the boy but apprehensive about his condition, Ellie and Brett dressed and then checked on Billy. He had hypothermia and was slurring his words, but as dark as it had been in the den, and as out of it as he was now, he'd never remember that a couple of wolves had rescued him. Once the EMT crew stabilized him, they carried him out of the woods to a waiting ambulance. Brett wrapped his arm around Ellie and gave her a kiss on the cheek, warming her to the marrow of her bones on the chilly night, while Meghan and Laurel tried to pretend they weren't there.

"Good job, you two," Laurel said, her back to them as they hiked to the parked cars.

"Yeah. The boy's going to be all right because of you," Meghan said.

"We all had a hand in finding him." Ellie smiled up at Brett as he kept her snuggled under his arm. She was rethinking her mission of dating anyone else.

Chapter 4

"WE'RE STILL HAVING DINNER, RIGHT?" BRETT ASKED. He hoped Ellie wasn't too exhausted from their ordeal of locating the missing boy or too upset about it and wanting to call off the date.

He was relieved they had found the little boy before it was too late and that he was going to be okay. Brett loved how the packs would come together and search for missing persons. They were perfectly suited for the job. And he was glad he was able to search with Ellie and her sisters. He realized that the more he was with her, the more he wanted to do pack-related activities as her partner.

On the drive there, she'd been somewhat reserved, and he wasn't sure how she'd be on the way back.

"Yeah, I'd really like that—a way to unwind after all that's happened. I don't have anyone else lined up for a date tonight." She smiled at him.

"I wasn't really serious about that."

"I still think it's worth seeing what happens, don't you? I mean, you could even go out with another she-wolf."

"Hell no." Surefire way to really screw things up between them.

"I saw my cousins searching through the woods at one point. I was surprised to see them there," Ellie said as Brett drove her back to her home to have dinner.

"Yeah. I saw them driving through town and asked if

they wanted to help. I believe they're eager to get on the pack's good side."

"Good. As long as they leave our...inn alone, I'm happy to be friends with them."

Brett heard the hesitation in her words and wondered if she and her sisters were still aggravated about how the brothers had harassed them about the inn. "I meant to ask if I could bring anything for dinner. Do you want me to stop and grab anything?"

"No thanks. You paid for dinner last night. I have all the fixings we need."

"Okay, good. When the weather warms up this spring and summer, I'd love to grill steaks, chicken, ribs, or anything that you'd like to eat outdoors. I'm not quite as handy in the kitchen."

"I've heard you often eat over at CJ's."

"Yeah. I bring the food; he cooks." Brett wondered how she'd feel about him not being much of an indoor cook. It was nice to give a mate a break from the daily chore of cooking. He'd be happy to grill all summer long. "Maybe I can hang some of the lights on the inn tonight for you too. And I'll help hang the picture of Matilda next to the piano when we finish dinner." When Ellie didn't say anything, he wondered if she needed to get Laurel's permission to hang it there. "If you want to."

"Uh, yeah. That would be nice." She sounded a little apprehensive.

"Are you thinking of the little boy? I still feel my blood pumping faster from the worry that we wouldn't find him and then, when we did, that we wouldn't get him out of the den in time before he died from exposure."

"Yeah. Me too. I'm so glad it was happily resolved, but I may be having nightmares about it tonight."

"Agreed. It's always a worry when something like that happens. It reminded me of when CJ and I got lost in the woods once. We'd both had bad colds, it was summer, and we were searching for magical stones."

"Magical stones?"

"Yeah. You know. The ones with the quartz crystal in them." He realized once he'd mentioned it that she might think what they'd been doing was dumb. He and CJ loved collecting colorful rocks. "We were maybe five miles from home, couldn't smell anything worth a darn because our noses were so stuffed up, and boy, did Eric give us hell when he caught up to us." Brett still remembered how red-faced Eric had been. Sarandon had stayed out of it.

"When Eric had realized what we'd been doing, he swore. Though he also appeared damned relieved and said he'd help us search for the rocks. Sarandon told CJ and me later that Eric had worried we'd run away because we didn't like that he was in charge of us, and he'd really felt hurt about it. No way would he tell us that. So that's why he offered to help us hunt for the special rocks. He looked like a huge weight had been lifted from his shoulders."

"Aww, your brothers are so sweet. Your dad wasn't upset with the two of you for being lost like that?"

"No. Eric never told him. He wasn't sure how Dad would have reacted. As far as Eric was concerned, he had lectured us enough all the way back home. He and Sarandon had spent hours trying to catch up to us. Thankfully, they weren't sick so they had no problem following our scent trail."

"That's good. Did you ever find your magical rocks?"

He smiled. He had magical rocks all right.

"Your quartz crystals," she said, her cheeks coloring crimson.

Brett cleared his throat. "Eric found some and said we could have located them easily ourselves if we had been able to smell them."

"When you got better, *could* you smell them?"

"No." Brett chuckled. "We never went off on our own like that again when we didn't have all of our senses. And we always let Eric know where we were going. Some members of the pack had trouble with bears, so it was important that we didn't go off without alerting anyone. Well, Eric. As to our sense of smell, we don't realize how much we rely on our senses until we don't have our heightened abilities."

"Yeah, I agree. Do you still have the quartz stones you picked up that day?"

"You bet. Eric said we'd better never get rid of them after the ordeal of finding us. We really loved them, and they meant something special to us. Especially since Eric was the one who located them for us." Mainly because of what Sarandon had told them about Eric's concern. Brett would never have guessed his brother would worry that he and CJ planned to run away from home—just because of Eric telling them what to do.

Ellie loved how the brothers were with each other. Without a mother, and with a father who was mostly absent in their lives, they'd had to fend for themselves.

No matter what, they had been there for each other. "So, did the magical quartz bring you luck?"

"Absolutely. You and your sisters came into our lives."

She laughed. "You sure had to wait a lot of years for anything magical to come of it."

"Completely worth waiting for. Believe me."

Maybe he could deal with her ghost issue and not be bothered by it. She wanted to tell Laurel what she'd learned first: that the ghost was the brothers' great-aunt.

Which made her think of her aunt. Ellie was still trying to figure out how to run into a guy she could go on a date with. Maybe she could visit her aunt Charity's candy shop in Green Valley to buy something, say hi, and see if she could casually run into someone in her pack. She hadn't dated anyone in so long that she wasn't sure how to go about it.

When they arrived at her house, Ellie fixed steak medallions in mushroom-and-wine sauce, asparagus, mashed potatoes, and brown gravy. Glasses of Chablis and chocolate cheesecake made the dinner perfect.

"Loved dinner." Brett helped her clean off the table. He handed her the last rinsed-off plate to add to the dishwasher. "Let's head on over to the inn, and I'll hang those lights for you. Do you want to find a spot to hang Matilda's picture too?"

Ellie hesitated, afraid that Matilda would pop up out of nowhere again. "Sure. Let me grab a picture-hanging hook and a hammer."

He walked her down the path to the dark inn. No attic light on this time. She was glad for that.

"I'm kind of surprised the inn was empty for so long. It's been booked solid since you opened it before Christmas last year," he said.

"We left a monthlong break in reservations. We wanted to do the basement addition without disturbing any guests. Often guests are out sightseeing, exploring, hiking, whatever they want to do, but sometimes they return to the inn to have lunch and take a nap." Ellie flushed a little after she mentioned it, thinking that napping guests were honeymooners and not exactly napping. "Anyway, we didn't want to have construction going on while we had guests. The dust, the noise, the mess."

"Did you have any trouble with Chrissy while you were doing all the remodeling downstairs? I understand she lived in one of the rooms down there."

"We've had some strange occurrences. A roller brush went missing. Rolls of wallpaper were moved from one room to another. We did each of the rooms in different color schemes: lavender, blue, a Alaskan retreat, a jungle retreat, a forest-decorated room, and the black, red, and white rose room. I think lavender must have been Chrissy's favorite color because she moved the lavender paper rolls into the blue room and the blue wallpaper rolls into the hall. Just dumped them on the wooden floor. The lavender rolls were neatly stacked on the marble-topped table." She glanced at Brett to see his reaction.

"So she liked the furniture." He looked like he was still having a hard time believing someone real hadn't done it.

"Must have. The room has a window, and she took down the blue curtains. So we had to redo them in lavender. Luckily, the new blue room's window was the same size as the new lavender room."

"And then she left the lavender curtains alone."

"Yep."

"Couldn't it have been someone else messing with the stuff?"

"Anything is possible because a lot of wolves have lockpicks for emergencies if they have to shift and hide somewhere. But we didn't smell anyone in the room."

"Could have used hunter's spray."

"Right. And the only ones I know who might have pulled something like that would be our cousins. But they're trying really hard to please everyone in the pack, so I don't think they would have had anything to do with it."

They entered the lobby, and Ellie turned on the light. Brett smiled to see all the Halloween decorations inside. He held up the framed photo against the wall behind the piano, putting it in various positions, but Ellie was staring off to his right. "What is it?" he whispered, as if the ghost couldn't hear him. Who else would be garnering her attention?

Instead of answering, she said, "Okay, there. I think that's the perfect spot."

He wondered if Chrissy was telling her where to hang the picture. He couldn't believe he was starting to think ghosts existed.

Then he hung the picture and plaque where Ellie thought they would be seen the best. He set the hammer on a nearby table and went to fetch the ladder out of the basement storage room.

Soon, they were hanging the lights out front and Ellie was smiling. "This is going to be beautiful. Thanks for helping, Brett. We had planned to all get out and do it, so it was nice of you to help."

"My pleasure. It will be the showiest Halloween spot in town. I'll have to take pictures of it for the special section in the newspaper we'll have on Halloween activities."

When they finished, he put up the ladder, then carried the box of sheet music from his car to the inn and set it near the piano. He took a seat on the bench.

She looked shocked, maybe because she didn't think he could play very well. "What are you... What are you doing?"

He smiled. "I'm going to play a little for you. If it's too bad, I'll quit and we'll go for a wolf run, if you'd like." He knew he could do a fairly decent job of it, or he wouldn't have offered. And he wanted to play for her.

She looked torn between letting him play and getting out of there as fast as she could.

"Really, I'm not half bad. But you can be the judge of that." Brett started to play "Silent Night," and he didn't do all that poorly, he thought. Then he played a little of "Greensleeves." He didn't know all of it, but he loved the song and wanted to learn how to play the whole piece.

Glancing at the door, Ellie still looked like she was ready to leave any second.

Brett sighed. If she was worried about how he'd view her ability to see ghosts, he would have to act as though it didn't bother him. Then maybe she wouldn't feel so troubled about what she could see when he was there.

"I know mostly Christmas songs because I loved listening to my great-aunt play them when we were kids. You don't know how much I miss her." Then he played

"Jingle Bells" and "Away in the Manger," smiled, and rose from the seat, taking Ellie's hand and pulling her in for a hug. "Well, what do you think?"

"I'd love to go for a run."

"Don't think much of my potential as a pianist, I take it." But he didn't think that was the trouble.

Then, to his delight, she smiled and wrapped her arms around his neck. This was what he'd hoped for. Not a standing ovation, but a hug and a kiss. "I think you play beautifully. I'm sure with a lot of lessons, you could be as great as your aunt. Although, I thought it was lovely just the way you played."

He leaned down to kiss her. She kissed him back, then pulled away quickly and took his hand. "Let's go for a wolf run."

She didn't look back at the piano, but he did. He felt that she sensed Chrissy's presence, and it was making her feel uncomfortable being intimate with him, as if a real person were there, watching their every move.

He hoped that if she came to his house, she wouldn't see ghosts there. She'd never mentioned it, so he suspected there weren't any. He realized then that Ellie didn't exactly say Chrissy was watching them. Yet something seemed to have caught her attention.

"Maybe we could both take up piano lessons. Then we could play duets." He would love playing with her like that. Maybe practicing with him would take her mind off whatever was bothering her in the lobby.

—⁓—

Ellie smiled at Brett's suggestion. "I'm afraid I'm not very good at sticking with things like that. I've tried to create all kinds of crafts, but rather than learning how to do anything well, I'm off to the next project."

He was trying so hard to please her, probably after the dating-others issue, when all she could think about was his great-aunt scowling at her for being in the same room. Maybe Matilda didn't like him playing her piano when he hadn't learned how to do it properly. Or she just didn't like that Brett was kissing Ellie again.

"Maybe taking piano lessons would be a different experience for you. You never know until you try. And if we did it together, it could be fun," he said.

After she exorcised his great-aunt, maybe. "Later. We would have to do it when we weren't disturbing anyone." Which could be never.

"You're on."

She could see Brett had his heart set on doing something with her that would mean something to the two of them. What if she couldn't manage it at all? And wouldn't she have to play for years before she would be halfway decent, if she had any talent at all? Then again, she was good at trying things out for a short while.

"I've always wanted to take lessons." Brett walked her back to her house where they could shift and run.

"Why?"

"I don't know. Maybe because my great-aunt was the most huggable, loving woman in my life. My mother had died. My dad was not affectionate in the least. He didn't want me taking lessons. He felt we had to do chores and school lessons that meant something. Playing the piano was a waste of time. So, when I could, I'd sneak over and see her, and she had me sing instead. I was awful at singing."

"Let me hear you sing."

"Don't say I didn't warn you." He sang a little bit of "Silent Night."

She grimaced.

"I told you I couldn't sing. Neither could my great-aunt. For fun, she and I both sang off-key while she played the piano. For me, it was a fun time spent with my great-aunt. My brothers all thought I was crazy."

"You bonded with her."

"I did."

"And now?"

"I wasn't sure if I could ever perform well, but the idea that we could learn together? That makes all the difference in the world to me."

Ellie smiled.

After all the hiking they'd done while searching for the lost boy, she was really tired. But she knew Brett didn't want to end the night with her this quickly, and she knew once she began running as a wolf, she'd have fun and her energy would be renewed. Yet, how was she going to get out of taking piano lessons with Brett? Maybe if she kept putting him off until they could get rid of the ghost, then she could try the lessons and that would be the end of it.

She could just hear her sisters laughing about her taking lessons. She never took training for anything. She was a do-it-yourself kind of girl.

They both shed their clothes and shifted, then bolted out through the wolf door.

She ran with Brett, really enjoying the time spent with him. The snow started to fall again, and they were covered in flakes, making them look like white wolves as the snow began to accumulate. Their second coat kept them warm, but none of the snow melted on top of their coat. It was the perfect coat for winter weather.

When she stopped to look at him, he had snow accumulating on his snout and sprinkles of snowflakes around his cheeks. He stopped, panting for a moment, then licked her cheek and the bridge of her nose. She did the same to him, laughing inside. Then, to her surprise, he raced around her, leaned down, and told her he wanted to play in their wolf way. She tackled him without hesitation.

She'd never played like this with him before, and she wasn't sure how much strength she needed to use against a bigger male wolf. With her sisters, she knew how much power to use in her lunges. She used more with Laurel than with Meghan, because Laurel was the true alpha and nearly always ready to give it her all. Meghan was more delicate in her response than either Ellie or Laurel, which meant they always took her down first. Then Ellie and Laurel went after each other. Well, almost always. Sometimes Ellie and Meghan ganged up on Laurel, just on principle. But only in a fun-loving way.

Ellie tackled Brett, but he was like a solid wall and she bounced off. She laughed at her inability to budge him. She tried again while he waited to give her another chance, and this time, he moved to her left, and she ran right past him. She woofed.

He barked joyfully back. He was teasing her, and she loved him for it.

She went after him again, only this time he tackled her, pushing her into a pile of snow and holding her down with his huge body. She smiled up at him, loving the way he played with her. She should have been studying how he played with his brothers. Instead, he'd been watching her with her sisters so he knew all her moves. Smart wolf.

———~~~———

That night, while Ellie was having dinner with Brett, Laurel fixed CJ halibut fillets, fried potatoes, and broccoli—one of his favorite meals—before she talked to him about the latest ghostly issue at their inn.

CJ talked about taking one of the teens in their pack on police patrol for the day and how he thought the boy might like to be a deputy sheriff someday.

"He's a good boy." Normally, she would be interested in his conversation, but all she wanted to do was clear the air about his great-aunt.

"I told my brother to straighten things out with Ellie."

Laurel hadn't expected CJ to bring that up. She hadn't planned to speak of it. It was between Ellie and Brett now. "No problem. I doubt she's going to go looking for any other guy."

CJ frowned. "Wolf?"

Laurel shook her head. "She's not really outgoing. If someone pursued her, she'd go out with him, but trying to track one down on her own? That's a different story."

CJ snorted. "I ought to tell a few of the bachelor males that Ellie's looking to date some other wolves. Teach Brett to say she should go out with other guys. Even if it's to prove a point."

"Don't you dare," Laurel said. "It could be a big mess, and Ellie would be right in the middle of it. Your brother would strangle you over it. Besides, from what I understand, she said he was just throwing the notion out there, but she thought the idea had merit."

"Well, he shouldn't have told Ellie to date other guys, no matter what the reason was." CJ finished eating his fish. "Man, that was good."

"I know how much you enjoy halibut for a change."

"Yeah, it's great, honey. Thanks. So how was Chrissy today? Was she giving you any more trouble?"

"Not Chrissy."

He set his fork down on his plate and took a sip of his decaf coffee. "Not Chrissy. Don't tell me your renovations in the basement stirred up more ghosts."

"Not the renovations."

CJ sat up a little taller, his expression more serious. "What happened?"

She sighed, realizing that telling him about his great-aunt was going to be more difficult than she'd thought. She started clearing away the dishes, needing to do something.

Frowning, he helped her with the leftovers while she started the dishwasher.

"It all started with moving the piano into the inn."

"The piano."

"Well, not just the piano, but when Brett kissed Ellie next to it."

"Chrissy's not happy with the piano being in the lobby? You said she didn't like the color you chose for her room. But now she's not a music lover either?"

"Not Chrissy."

CJ frowned again.

Laurel pulled him into her arms and looked up at

him. "Your great-aunt Matilda." She immediately felt
CJ stiffen in her arms.

CJ pulled away from her. "What?"

"I know you aren't one hundred percent certain about
my sisters' ability to see ghosts, but—"

"How do they know it's her? It could be anyone.
Even Chrissy."

"No. Brett gave Ellie a photo of your great-aunt, and
she verified that's who she saw near the piano."

"When Brett was kissing Ellie."

"Yes." Laurel folded her arms. "You don't believe
me. Have you just been humoring me whenever I've
talked about Chrissy? Don't tell me you don't think we
really see, hear, or feel what we do."

"I don't believe my great-aunt is haunting the piano.
We've never had any indication that she's been hanging
around since her death."

"You don't see anything, or maybe you do, but you
are in such denial that you don't want to believe it."

"Laurel—" CJ sounded totally exasperated with her.

"Isn't that so?" Now she was furious with CJ. How
could he not believe her and her sisters when he had
acted all along like he had? She was beginning to think
Ellie was right. She shouldn't have bothered telling
her mate. A whole lot of good it did. She and her sisters could have worked to exorcise that ghost from the
inn and their lives without sharing any of it with the
Silver brothers.

"Brett said he thought Ellie and Meghan were shaken
up when we were moving the piano. He assumed it was
because of Chrissy. But now you're saying that wasn't
her all along? It was my great-aunt?"

"No. Only Ellie saw her. And she seems to disapprove of Brett and Ellie's kissing."

"I don't believe this."

"Fine." Laurel stormed up the stairs to their bedroom, grabbed a bag, and packed a few things. Then she headed down the stairs, while CJ was coming up and saw the bag slung over her shoulder.

"Where are you going?"

"I'm staying with my sisters. We have a lot of work to do. I'll be home when we're done."

"Laurel—"

She passed him on the stairs and headed for the door. Without a backward glance, she shut the door on her way out. She was so annoyed with CJ that she couldn't think straight.

Chapter 5

THAT NIGHT, ELLIE WAS JUST GETTING OUT OF THE shower when she heard the phone ringing and hoped there wasn't more trouble. With a towel wrapped around her torso, she snapped up her cell.

"Hey, Laurel. Did you tell CJ about his great-aunt?" Ellie was afraid of what Laurel would say about that. CJ probably hadn't been happy to learn his great-aunt was haunting the inn, which was probably why Laurel was calling at this late hour.

"He doesn't believe us. Well, you… Since you're the only one who has seen her."

"I told you we shouldn't have let him know. But Meghan heard her playing the piano too."

"If it was her. Maybe Chrissy was playing it."

"Unless she had lessons, I doubt it."

"Normally, I'd say you were wrong about me not sharing with my mate. This time, I agree. I'm on my way over now."

"Wait. What? Don't tell me you two had a fight." They were so happily mated that Ellie hated for anything to come between them. With her and Brett, it was different. They were still getting to know each other.

"Yeah, well, I'm staying with the two of you until we resolve this. Matilda has to go, or the piano has to."

"Maybe she was annoyed with me for kissing Brett. Maybe if we don't do that in the inn anymore, everything will be fine. I even wondered how she'd react if you and CJ kissed, since you're mated wolves."

"Too late to try that now."

"Wolves mate for life," Ellie reminded her sister. Laurel and CJ would have to resolve this issue between them.

"Right. I'm not leaving him forever. Just long enough to take care of his great-aunt."

Ellie threw on her tiger-striped pajamas as she heard a car pull up in the parking lot. Peeking out the window, she saw it was Laurel. "Okay, see you. Do you want me to make us mugs of hot chocolate?"

"Sure, thanks. Be right in. Who put up all the lights on the inn?"

"Brett did. He did a great job."

"It's just beautiful."

A few minutes later, Ellie and Laurel were sitting in the living room with hot mugs of cocoa on the chilly fall night, the wind whirling and moaning about the house. "So what do you want to do first?" Ellie asked. She knew CJ would talk to his closest brother Brett first. Then Brett would probably be annoyed with her for not telling him she had seen his great-aunt at the piano, even if he didn't believe in ghosts. Which was the perfect reason *not* to tell him.

"Meghan's still out on a date, I take it," Laurel said.

"With Peter. Yes."

"He'd better believe in ghosts, or she's going to have to quit seeing him for her sanity's sake."

Ellie considered her relationship with Brett and knew the same thing went for him. If CJ didn't believe in them, then what would Brett think? It just wouldn't work out. She was thinking she needed to post a letter in the Lonely Hearts column in the *Silver Town Gazette*: "She-wolf seeking male wolf who believes in ghosts. No others need apply."

―――――

Brett was watching a cop show when CJ called. He was usually wrapped up in his mate when he was off work, so Brett worried something was wrong. When his younger brother told him what the problem was, Brett couldn't believe it.

"That's why Ellie wanted the picture of Matilda?" Brett couldn't help sounding annoyed.

"She didn't tell you?"

"No. She said she wanted to have it for a memorial." To some extent, Brett understood why Ellie felt she couldn't tell him. He was noncommittal about believing in ghosts. Also, he assumed she thought he'd be upset. Who wouldn't be when they learned a dead relative was still hanging around because of some unsettled business? "So they think our great-aunt was murdered? No way was that the case."

"No. The other ghost, Chrissy, died of a fever, so everyone says. Apparently people can hang around after death even if they died of natural causes—if any of this can be believed."

"Now you're saying you don't believe in it?" Brett was really surprised.

"Let's just say I have a hard time believing in ghosts sometimes."

"How does Laurel feel about that?"

"She left me."

Brett was stunned into silence.

"She'll be back as soon as they've finished work over there."

"What? In another two weeks? You're just going to let her leave without chasing her down and begging her to come back? Apologizing or whatever you need to do to make this right?"

"What would you do in my place? You don't believe in ghosts any more than I do."

"I'd chase her down and beg for forgiveness."

"Is that what you're going to do with Ellie?"

"We went for a wolf run and had dinner. Everything seems to be okay. Concerning Matilda, they say that ghosts can remain behind for all kinds of reasons. Not just because of foul play."

"Right. So?"

"I remember Dad saying something about how Aunt Matilda had been sick. She had a cough and had been running a fever on and off."

"Which contributed to her having pneumonia."

"She was still running around when everyone had told her to take it easy. Then she took a bath or shower and went to bed with damp hair that night."

"Which Dad said she always did. She didn't have a hair dryer. She just toweled it dry and went to bed. He thinks she got even more chilled because of it. What, Brett? I know you and your investigative mind. What makes you think it could be anything more than what it appeared to be?"

"She'd been dead for several hours when they discovered she wasn't just sleeping in her bed. If she'd towel dried her hair, wouldn't it have been dry by the time they discovered her body in the morning?"

"Maybe she washed up really late, and her hair didn't dry all the way."

"Her nightgown was on backward."

"Which can happen to anyone. If she was delirious, that could have been the reason for it."

Brett pondered the situation further, though his brother was right. But he was trying to remember something else that might lead to the conclusion that she hadn't died naturally. "What about the rowboat?"

"What about it?"

"A few days after she died, they found it snagged on some rocks several miles downriver."

"Because someone hadn't tied it up properly the last time they used it. The boat had been carried away. One of our pack members found it while running as a wolf."

"I remember Dad remarking about the old gal having a little fun with someone in the rowboat and being amused. You know that was unusual in and of itself for Dad."

"I don't recall anything about it. What did he say?"

"They'd found her sunbonnet in the bottom of the boat with an empty wine bottle and a man's glove."

"I must not have been around to hear that. When did that happen?"

"Dad assumed that before she got sick, she must have gone out with some guy. They had to have both been a little tipsy when they returned, or they wouldn't have left any evidence behind."

"But you think this happened when she was sick? That she accidentally drowned or was drowned— and someone redressed her and put her to bed?" CJ sounded skeptical.

Brett didn't blame his brother for thinking that was a far-out notion. He would never have given the matter another thought if his great-aunt hadn't suddenly returned as a ghost. Why would she? Maybe her arrival had nothing to do with her death. But he had always wondered how the boat got away if it was tied to the dock. And the business about her partying with some guy before her death and not being more discreet about it?

"I'm sure she died the way the doctor said she did. But why not double-check? I just want to go over the information that's available through Doc Oliver's medical records and the coroner's report and see if I can learn the truth. Either she died of natural causes, or there's the slim possibility that she didn't. I wish Doc Oliver were still alive so we could ask him." Brett paused. "All the sisters have seen our great-aunt's ghost, I take it."

"I don't know. My conversation with Laurel ended rather abruptly. Truthfully, I was in such shock that I didn't know what to say."

"Exactly. So Laurel has got to be worried about what will happen when the new guests begin to arrive. I think we need to get in touch with the MacTires' ghost-buster cousins to see if they know how to exorcise a ghost. What would it hurt? If one is really there, even if it's our great-aunt, and the brothers can help the spirits go to their final resting places, maybe they can do it. The problem would be solved."

"I can see *that* backfiring since the sisters don't want the cousins involved."

"Okay, so how can we help? Laurel told you about it for a reason. You know she had to worry about telling you any of this. Disbelief on your part. Maybe even defensiveness. We have to do something. She's obviously concerned about the situation. Ellie told me Chrissy moved rolls of wallpaper from one place to another. If she could do that, was our great-aunt doing something completely disruptive too?"

"I don't know. Like I said, we didn't get to talk much before Laurel stormed off."

"What if Matilda starts creating havoc like Chrissy has been doing? What if a ghost is doing something, and the sisters have guests at the same time?"

"Hell," CJ said.

"Yeah, see? They're probably stressing about what could happen, based on whatever already has."

"Okay, gotcha."

"So what are you going to do? Call Laurel and apologize?"

"What are *you* going to do concerning Ellie?"

"I told you. We're doing fine. I'll do some research about Matilda. After that, we can talk about it and go from there. But if I were you, I'd clear things up with Laurel now."

"Did you tell CJ we heard the piano playing?" Ellie asked Laurel as they finished their cocoa.

Laurel shook her head and took her empty mug into the kitchen. "I didn't have time to explain much at all. I was too angry. Of all the brothers, I really believed CJ thought our claims were real. And to think he's just been humoring me all along!"

"I really don't think he has been. I believe he's just

shook up that we think we can see his great-aunt. You've got to agree that it could be unsettling if you don't see ghosts yourself and never had any indication your great-aunt was still hanging around Brett's house."

"Okay, you may be right."

"So are you going to tell CJ you love him anyway?"

Laurel laughed. "Just don't get yourself into an ordeal with Brett over this."

A key turned in the lock to the front door, then opened. Meghan was smiling like she'd had the time of her life as she came in and locked the door. Then she frowned. "What are *you* doing over here? Is CJ working late again?"

"If Peter doesn't believe in ghosts, dump him." Laurel headed for the stairs.

Meghan stared after her. "Aww. She told CJ about his great-aunt, and he doesn't believe us."

"Or doesn't want to believe us. What did you expect?" Ellie asked.

"True. I don't blame him, really. Is she going to stay here for the night?"

"Yes," Laurel said from upstairs.

Ellie and Meghan laughed.

"You can't stay mad at him forever," Meghan called out.

"He'll come around or else," Laurel hollered back. Then she shut her bedroom door, and they heard the master bath's shower turn on.

"Well, I'm ready for bed." Ellie headed for the stairs.

"I haven't talked to Peter about any of this. I guess I need to before we go much further with any kind of relationship."

Ellie turned to look at her. "You haven't talked to him about this ghost business?"

"Nah. Never came up. And I guess I've been avoiding it."

"I don't blame you. It can really be a dead end to a relationship."

"So what did the two of you do?" Meghan asked.

"Dinner, Brett hung the photo of his great-aunt on the wall next to the piano, helped hang lights, and then played some Christmas songs by ear."

"On the piano?" Meghan closed her gaping mouth. "Did he kiss you there again?"

"Yeah, but nothing happened this time. Maybe your little talk convinced Great-Aunt Matilda to leave well enough alone."

"Or she's waiting until the place fills up with guests to show us who's got the upper hand."

Ellie groaned. "Okay, tomorrow you and I are going to try everything we know to get her attention, speak with her, and try to convince her she doesn't belong here."

"Sounds good to me. If that doesn't work?"

"I'll research what I can about her. With the guise that if we get questions about the piano, we'll know more about the previous owner."

"Sounds good. What about Laurel?"

"I'll be helping with the whole project," Laurel said behind her closed door.

"Good," Meghan said. "Did you leave me any hot water?" She headed into the spare bathroom to take a shower.

Ellie figured she wouldn't get any sleep tonight, not with worrying about how Brett was taking the news. She was certain CJ would have talked to him about it, as close as they were.

She had just climbed into bed and pulled up the blanket and comforter when her cell rang. She looked at the caller. *Brett*. She took a deep breath, unsure how she was going to approach this. "Hello?"

"Life is too short," Brett said, and she was afraid he planned to propose a mating. Maybe he'd decided he might lose her if she started dating someone else.

No way could she go along with a mating until they settled the ghost issue.

"I've always wanted to take piano lessons but couldn't when I was younger and never made time later. You know Remer Cochran? The piano teacher? He came here in the beginning of the year, and he said he'd be willing to teach us how to play."

Ellie started to object. She really didn't think she could sit at a piano for hours and practice all the time. Besides, what if doing that set Matilda off?

"Remer has a piano at his home in a private room where he teaches students of all ages. He said he'd accommodate our schedules and is eager to teach some older pupils. I think it's more that my cousin is the pack leader, and my brother is one too. It never hurts to get good publicity for your business. And he's having a bit of a time encouraging the local wolves to sign their kids up to play the piano. This way, we'll will help him, something we always try to do to encourage new wolf businesses to stay in the area, and we'll have fun at the same time."

Ellie didn't think practicing to play a piano sounded like fun.

"So starting tomorrow, he'll take us. Please, please say yes. I don't want to do this on my own, but I want to see if I have at least half the talent my great-aunt did."

Ellie couldn't say no when Brett was begging her like that. He really was a sweetheart. "Okay—"

"Yes!"

"Wait. Hear me out. If I can't do it, I'll drop out and you can continue playing because that's your dream. I'm not good at sticking with things. Especially something like programmed lessons."

"I completely understand. Thank you for saying yes. We can celebrate after each lesson, just for having given it a shot."

She was waiting for him to mention having spoken to CJ. Maybe because of the disagreement CJ and Laurel had had, CJ hadn't talked to Brett about their ghostly great-aunt visiting the inn. Ellie didn't want to open that can of worms tonight. "What time are we doing this?"

"Would ten work for you? Then we can have lunch afterward and go back to our respective jobs."

"All right."

"Ellie, no matter what, I want this to be fun for us. Not a chore. We're not trying to be concert pianists. If it stops being fun, we can quit and try something else."

That made her feel better. And she loved that he was interested in doing something else with her if this didn't work out. "We could take up macramé."

"Yeah, like that."

She couldn't believe he'd agree. "Do you know what it is?" She couldn't really believe he'd be interested in anything like that, but she'd always thought it would be fun to try.

"Braiding wool and knotting it, or something like that. But let's try the piano lessons first. You might find you have a real talent for it."

She secretly hoped she would.

"And we can do the macramé too, if we find we have more free time on our hands."

"You know what? I'd really like to try my hand at wood carving. My dad made my sisters and me all kinds of small carvings—fish, beaver, bear. He always made them in threes, one for each of us."

"I'd love to. I've whittled some, but not made anything more than a primitive bear."

"All right then. Tomorrow, we'll start the piano lessons," Ellie said, getting excited about the prospect. She was always enthusiastic when she began a new project.

"I'll pick you up and drive you over there."

"Sounds good. Night, Brett."

"Good night, Ellie."

After they ended the call, Meghan headed down the hall to her bedroom. "Got another hot date with Brett?"

"Piano lessons."

"Piano lessons?" Meghan sounded like she thought Ellie was kidding.

"Not on Matilda's piano," Ellie said.

"Okay, so you know that after you take the lessons, you're supposed to practice. Every. Day. On. A. Piano."

Ellie opened her bedroom door and frowned at Meghan.

"And the only one we have ready access to is in our lobby, being guarded by a persnickety ghost."

Ellie hadn't considered that part of the equation. Once Brett said they would be using Remer's piano, she'd thought that was all there was to it. "Well, we still have two weeks before our guests arrive."

"Right. Where is Brett going to practice? With you? With his great-aunt supervising?"

"You know, maybe that would be a good thing. If he hears her or senses her, we can get this out in the open."

"And if he can't? But only you can, and it's so bad that you can't practice?"

"We'll just have to give it a try and see what happens."

Laurel opened the door to her bedroom. "You are taking piano lessons? With Brett?"

"Yeah." Ellie smiled at the shocked expressions both her sisters were wearing. "What? You don't think I can learn how to play?"

Meghan sighed.

Laurel shook her head. "It's not so much whether you can or can't play, but that you are going to aggravate Matilda."

"What if that's the key to her happiness? One of her grandnephews learning to play?"

"You playing the wrong notes or at the wrong tempo could really annoy her." Laurel let out her breath. "It's not that you can't learn to play well, but in the beginning, any of us would make a lot of mistakes."

"Yeah, but it's like I told Meghan. What if Brett senses Matilda's presence? That could be a good thing."

"Be sure he's not just saying what you want to hear and doesn't really believe in your abilities."

"Amen to that," Meghan said. She walked off to her bedroom. "Night, Laurel, Ellie."

Ellie wanted to prove to her sisters and to herself that she could play the piano. Not that she would be a concert pianist, but enough to play a simple song or two. Putting on special programs for their guests at the inn could be really fun. But with her history of not sticking with anything long enough to perfect it, she was afraid her sisters were right.

"We're doing a séance early tomorrow morning," Laurel said and went to bed.

They rarely did séances. When they did, one of them— usually Laurel—would act as the medium and guide the session. Sometimes a spirit would talk through Ellie, sometimes through Meghan, but never through Laurel.

Once, a friend's departed mother had sought to speak with her daughter and begged the sisters to have the séance. To make things right. It wasn't normally done that way. Usually, when a grieving family learned the sisters had the gift, the family wanted help in saying good-bye to their family member. The mother wanted to beg her daughter for forgiveness for not liking her choice of mate and for disowning her. She wanted to make amends. Since the sisters knew both parties—and the mother was causing them grief with her constant appearances—they had agreed. But the daughter didn't believe. The mother finally thanked the sisters, gave up on trying to convince her daughter she loved her with all her heart, and found the light.

The sisters believed the mother had been happy when she gave up her quest to make amends with her daughter, believing she had done all she could. But the séance hadn't gone as planned at all. Anything could happen at one. Unwelcome spirits could appear. Here at the inn, they already had two to deal with. They didn't want any more.

Ellie sighed. Tomorrow, first thing, they'd have the séance. But she was going to contact Matilda on her own before that because Matilda had only appeared to her.

When Laurel went to bed, Ellie put on her coat, dug out one of the sage smudge sticks they had in the pantry for emergencies, and headed over to the inn. Everything was quiet and dark there, as would be expected. Ellie turned on the lights and lit the sage, then went from room to room waving the smudge stick, hoping to cleanse the inn. She and her sisters didn't mind living around ghosts, but the same didn't hold true for guests staying at their inn. Afterward, Ellie sat down at the piano and looked up at Matilda's memorial. If the sage hadn't worked and Matilda was still here, Ellie hoped she liked the picture and sentiments.

Ellie sighed and spoke from her heart in case Matilda was around. "We know you loved to play the piano for family gatherings when you were alive, and your family loved you for it."

Ellie spied the box of sheet music and stood, then opened piano bench and began to neatly place the music books and sheet music in the storage compartment. "Brett has always wanted to play the piano because of your talent. And he's asked me to take lessons with him." She thought it was important to let Matilda know. Maybe she would be more understanding if Ellie shared their intent. If not, so be it, but she felt she owed it to Matilda to tell her first. If she hadn't moved on.

"He really cares for me, and I really care for him. So I think he wants me to do it as something we could enjoy doing together. But I don't know the first thing about playing a piano and… Well, the thing of it is, we'll have to practice on yours, but I don't want to disturb you by doing so. I might be horrible at this."

She'd finished placing the music in the bench when the keys depressed from one end of the keyboard to the other in a neat, orderly way. Chills swept up Ellie's spine. She didn't see the older woman, but the room had grown decidedly colder. The keys depressed in the same way again. Was Matilda telling her to follow her lead?

It had to be her. The sage hadn't worked. Though she wondered if it had worked on Chrissy.

"Brett doesn't believe in ghosts. I haven't told him I've seen you, but my sister Laurel told her mate, CJ, that we did. He's not happy about it." Ellie pressed the keys down the way Matilda had. "I want to tell Brett that I can sometimes commune with spirits, but I'm afraid he won't believe me and that will be the end of any kind of relationship we could have."

The keys slowly depressed in a pattern this time, playing a tune Ellie didn't know. After Matilda finished, Ellie did the same and smiled. She couldn't believe Matilda was showing her what to do, encouraging her even. Which made her feel a little guilty that she'd tried to exorcise her.

"I really care for Brett. He's the most kind-hearted, interesting wolf I've ever met, but you see the dilemma we have? It's not like I haven't had trouble with this before. A guy I was seeing didn't like that I could sense or commune with spirits and ditched me. So I've been reluctant to tell Brett the extent to which I can get in touch with ghosts."

Matilda played more keys, and Ellie copied her. This wasn't so bad at all. She actually enjoyed it.

Then Ellie said, "I wish you could be with us today. My father died of pneumonia. He was getting better but relapsed, and we lost him. I haven't told Brett that yet. But we missed my dad so much. He just kept telling us he'd get better. And we knew he would, because he said so. Was that what happened to you? I guess it would be hard for you to know."

A bunch of keys were pressed in a discordant way. Then Matilda banged on the keys for several seconds before she stopped and the lobby was filled with quiet.

Ellie closed her gaping mouth, blinked, and stared at the keys as if they would magically move again. She whispered, "You didn't die of pneumonia?"

The piano remained silent. The room seemed much colder, and feeling chilled, Ellie turned off the light, locked the inn, and hurried home. She had the dreadful sense that Matilda wasn't staying here because she loved the piano so much, but because she had died of something other than natural causes and needed to see justice done.

Before Ellie reached the door to the house, Laurel opened it and Meghan greeted her, ushering her inside.

"What in the world was that all about?" Laurel asked, sounding half shocked and half annoyed. "I thought we'd try to exorcise her spirit tomorrow morning. Were you trying to get a head start so you could take piano lessons with Brett without having any ghostly interactions with Matilda?"

"We were practicing just fine together. Matilda was playing and then waiting for me to copy her. But then I mentioned Dad dying of pneumonia, and I think...I think maybe she didn't die the way everyone thought she did." Ellie sincerely hoped that wasn't the case. The sisters headed upstairs to retire for the night.

"Great," Laurel said. "So we don't tell the brothers? Or we tell them? If you're right, what a nightmare."

"I agree." Ellie had decided she wasn't going to

dream about Brett. She refused to. She didn't want to. She had to make room for dating other guys and see what happened then.

Which was why when she curled up in bed, drifted off…*and saw Brett standing in her bedroom peeling off his clothes in front of her, she ignored him.* Not. *She quickly tugged off her tiger pajamas, eager to feel his hands on her, as eager as she was to lay her hands on him. But right in the middle of making love with him, she heard a wolf howl—and it snapped her right out of her dream.*

Ellie lay quietly in her bed, listening for the wolf's howl again. She'd never heard that howl before, so it wasn't anyone in her pack. Had she dreamed it?

She got out of bed and peeked out the window, swearing that the howl had come from the inn. She threw on a robe and slipper boots and headed over there. What if Matilda began appearing in the lobby as a wolf? She'd give their human guests seizures.

When Ellie entered the hotel, everything was quiet and she saw no sign of Matilda. Sighing, Ellie figured she'd imagined hearing an unknown wolf howl while she was having a sexy time with one hot Silver wolf.

Chapter 6

EARLY THE NEXT MORNING, ELLIE AND HER SISTERS were ready to head over to the inn for the séance when CJ called Laurel. Even though Ellie had heard her sister talking to him last night in her bedroom, Laurel wouldn't go home to be with him. But this morning, Laurel had agreed he could drop by at nine with freshly baked cinnamon rolls from Silva's tea shop.

"Did you hear a wolf howling last night?" Ellie asked Meghan.

"No one's supposed to be howling within the town limits, if the wolf was howling that close," Meghan said.

"Right. But the howl sure sounded like it was coming from the inn."

Meghan groaned. "Great. It's one thing to have a piano playing on and off, but if Matilda begins howling…" Meghan frowned. "Was it Matilda or Chrissy?"

"Chrissy never howled before. You know the owners had to be strict about anyone who worked in the hotel howling or showing themselves in wolf form. They would have been fired. So it must be ingrained. I figured it had to be Matilda, if I hadn't just dreamed it."

Meghan sighed. "Well, that would be just great. First she's playing the piano, and now one of them is howling. If you didn't just dream it."

"What if they start making an appearance as wolves?

Or they begin to howl in chorus?" She and her sisters had to resolve this before it got any worse.

"Then we really do have to take care of this sooner rather than later."

Ellie waited for Laurel to finish speaking to CJ, wondering if she would tell her mate why he had to postpone their meeting. It was six now, and the sisters were going to begin their séance as soon as they had everything set up. Ellie thought Laurel might even ask him to join them, but she didn't. They said all the loving things that newly mated couples say to each other, but Laurel must not have trusted CJ to join them with an open mind.

When they arrived at the inn, Ellie told Laurel about what she'd heard last night, but again saying it might have been a dream.

Laurel didn't say anything right away as they all began to set up candles in the center of the table, then turned up the heat so they'd be comfortable if the spirits chilled the air a lot and turned off their cell phones to avoid interruptions.

"Maybe you dreamed it," Laurel finally said.

"I sure hope so."

Meghan echoed their sentiments.

Conducting a séance could take a long time, so they always got as comfortable as they could. No holding hands. That wasn't necessary, and it could be distracting. No music. They had to keep their minds open and their senses on the highest alert. Ellie hoped they wouldn't call on a slew of ghosts at the same time and create more problems. That's why they didn't do séances very often.

"Ready?" Laurel asked.

"Go ahead," Meghan said.

Ellie nodded.

Laurel took a deep breath and exhaled. "Dear Matilda, we would love to speak with you. These are my sisters, Ellie and Meghan. I'm mated to your grand-nephew, CJ. Ellie told us you were upset when she mentioned that our father died of pneumonia. Can you tell us what happened?"

The four candles flickered, the room grew colder, but no entities revealed themselves.

"Ellie wants to thank you for teaching her a lesson on the piano. It was her very first, which made it really special for her. She loved it."

Even though Laurel was always the medium in a séance, Ellie wanted to be the one speaking to Matilda, not having Laurel speak for her. She bit her tongue, mindful that the sisters had to be unified if this was to work. Otherwise, they could risk causing negative energy and negative forces to appear.

She had to give Laurel a chance to connect with the ghost. But she wasn't feeling anything, except that the dining room was colder. They probably should have done this in the lobby, near the piano.

Then Ellie saw Chrissy pacing back and forth behind Meghan, her arms folded across her waist. "She's annoying. Make her go away." Chrissy was looking directly at Ellie, her blond hair coiled on top of her head, a long black dress sweeping past her ankles, her white pinafore nearly as long, and her buttoned leather boots polished. She was swinging her white cap around by the ties, but when she saw Ellie frowning, she quickly tied it back on.

Ellie glanced at Laurel to see if she would agree to have her speak with Chrissy. But Laurel wasn't looking at her, just across the table in another direction. Ellie raised her brows at Laurel, trying to get her attention, but she only caught Meghan's eye. She raised both her brows and mouthed the word *what*?

Laurel must have caught their interaction, because she cleared her throat and said, "Do you wish to speak with Ellie?"

Her brow furrowed, Chrissy looked annoyed.

Before Chrissy left in a huff, Ellie said, "Chrissy"—to make everyone aware that she wasn't seeing Matilda— "make who go away?"

"This is my home. She doesn't belong here. Make her go away." Then Chrissy vanished.

"Chrissy…?" Ellie felt the ghost's exasperation. She knew how she'd feel if someone was suddenly in her space when she'd had the run of the place for years. Ellie could imagine that Matilda, being older, would think Chrissy would have to live by her rules.

When Chrissy refused to return, Ellie said, "Matilda, will you talk to us? To me? Thank you for showing me how much fun it could be to play the piano. I might not ever be really great at it, but I'm eager to continue taking lessons."

Laurel frowned at Ellie.

Oops. That's why Laurel was the medium. Ellie hoped she hadn't given Matilda the idea she wanted her to continue giving her lessons. Not that she didn't love it, but that wouldn't help their guests when they all arrived.

They sat for a long time in silence, maybe a half hour.

Ghosts didn't have time schedules, but Ellie knew that eventually CJ would come by to bring the cinnamon rolls and get a kiss and hug from Laurel.

Ellie turned to Laurel. "Maybe we should move this to the lobby, closer to the piano."

"Did you see Chrissy?" Laurel asked Meghan.

"Nope. I got nothing."

"Okay, so she's unhappy that Matilda is here now, invading her space," Laurel said. "And that's completely understandable. She's tolerating us, maybe because we've made the inn beautiful again. So what's going on with Matilda?"

Ellie shook her head. "Chrissy just said Matilda doesn't belong here, and she wants her to go away."

"Why is she speaking to you? And only you? As if you're the only one to help her?" Laurel asked curiously. Matilda hadn't appeared before any of the sisters other than Ellie, and now Chrissy was interacting only with Ellie.

"Maybe she thinks I'm the one who brought Matilda here."

"You didn't. The movers brought the piano. CJ and his brothers were involved because it had been their family's piano."

"But Matilda didn't appear to me until I was kissing Brett. So maybe Chrissy thinks my actions had something to do with Matilda making her presence known."

"Okay, that makes sense." Laurel glanced at the clock. "If you are all willing to try it again, let's do what Ellie suggests and move this closer to the piano."

They took their places there, Ellie sitting on the bench before the piano, with Laurel and Meghan a few feet away on high wingback chairs in the lobby.

"Do you want to start this here?" Laurel asked.

"Sure. Maybe I can reach her." Since Ellie had never served as a medium before, she copied what Laurel had said. Nobody responded. Not Matilda. Not Chrissy. Ellie let out her breath. "You seemed upset when I mentioned our father having pneumonia. Do you feel someone neglected you when you were so ill?"

Dead silence.

Ellie wanted to ask Matilda if she had been howling, but then she'd want to tell the ghost she couldn't keep doing that—and she figured Matilda wouldn't appreciate it.

They stayed there until it was getting close to time for CJ to arrive. Then Laurel said, "Come on. Let's go."

"I'm going to sit here a while longer," Ellie said.

"Good luck," Meghan said.

Laurel nodded. "We'll keep a cinnamon roll warm for you."

And then they left.

Ellie tried again. "Do you believe you didn't die of pneumonia?"

The music sheet sitting on the stand flew off the piano and landed on the floor.

〜〜〜

Trying to get his mind off the way Ellie had looked in her wild tiger pajamas last night when he made love to her in his dreams, Brett hurried to finish another story for the newspaper so he could have lunch with CJ. They'd hired a woman to start a lonely hearts column, which, since they had more bachelor males than females in Silver Town, was filled with lonely heart letters from guys. She'd also started a recipe column. Brett hoped to try some of the recipes so he could cook something really great for Ellie that he didn't have to cook outside on the grill. A couple of teens were writing a column about the fun things to do in Silver Town and the surrounding communities for kids of all ages. One of the suggestions had been to run as wolves on the new ski trails before the owners had enough snowfall to open the ski resort. He'd like to do that with Ellie.

For now, he could hardly concentrate on anything but what he was going to be doing with Ellie tonight. He sure hoped she loved playing the piano, and that they could find other pastimes to share. He'd already picked up carving tools and blocks of wood to use in creating their first projects and a book on macramé, in case they wanted to try it too.

Brett glanced out at the gray sky, which showed the threat of a winter storm coming in. Tomorrow was Halloween, and he hoped the snow wouldn't stop everyone from enjoying the parties and trick-or-treating. Even he had decorated his office with a jack-o'-lantern candy dish filled with treats, and a black cat and raven oversaw the office.

He pulled out the file he'd created concerning Great-Aunt Matilda. He'd gotten a copy of the coroner's report and the medical records Doc Oliver had for his great-aunt. She'd died so long ago that they didn't have forensic tests like today. She'd been sick, gotten pneumonia, and died. No bruising or other trauma that would indicate she'd had a struggle with anyone. That was all the medical report said.

Next, Brett called Stanton Wernicke to ask if he knew

how to exorcise a ghost. Brett wasn't about to say it had anything to do with Stanton's MacTire cousins. If Brett learned that the brothers couldn't really get rid of ghosts, that would be the end of that notion. But maybe Stanton could tell Brett how to do it. He felt it was his responsibility because Matilda was his great-aunt and he'd offered the piano to the sisters in the first place.

"Hey, Stanton, this is Brett Silver." Though he was sure the ghost-buster TV personality would have caller ID. "I'm Darien Silver's cousin."

"Yeah," Stanton said. "And your brother CJ married my cousin Laurel."

"Correct."

"Great. So...what can I do for you?" Stanton sounded a little distrustful, probably because of the trouble the Wernickes had had with Darien and the pack. When they first came to town, the brothers shouldn't have tried to claim the MacTire sisters' inn was theirs.

Even though the brothers had mended their ways, the pack was still a bit wary of their intentions. But if the Wernickes could help the ladies, Brett wanted to solicit their aid.

"Can you really help ghosts find the way to their final resting place?"

"Yeah, but if we do, we want to include the story on TV. That's what pays the bills."

"How do you send them away?" Brett knew the ladies wouldn't go along with a televised show in their inn, and he didn't want his family included in a ghost show either. He was certain his brothers would agree. He still thought this was a lot of hocus-pocus, sleight of hand, television magic. Not anything that was real.

"Let's first discuss where this malevolent being is located."

"I can't say. I want to know for certain if you can send a ghost on its way if it's causing people trouble. If not, I'll have to look elsewhere."

A long pause followed. Stanton was probably trying to figure out where the ghost was so he could still use it for his show.

"This…doesn't have to do with my cousins, does it?" Stanton sounded serious, yet there was a hint of excitement in his voice.

"No." As far as Brett was concerned, it didn't. He was the one looking into soliciting the Wernicke brothers' help. He wanted the best for his great-aunt, for her to find peace in this world—and the next, if she truly was stuck in this world. In no way did he want to upset Ellie and her sisters.

"We always have to conduct our research first. So we can't do gigs where we don't know the situation better than that. If the ghost is happy where it is, we really don't want to force it to leave. People need to realize that some spirits have found their home and don't want to be anywhere else. People need to learn to coexist."

"Okay, I agree." If Brett could wrap his mind around the idea that ghosts even exist. "Can you do it as quietly as possible? Just have one of you show up to do the job?"

"We all know each other's jobs in case one is sick or otherwise incapacitated and can't make it, but we usually work as a team to achieve better and quicker results. If this needs to be done in secret, I suppose I could handle it."

That's more like what Brett was thinking of. "I guess you don't just do a job for free." He would pay them a set amount if they could do it. But no TV show. He still had to find a way to get them into the inn without creating a big deal over it.

"For a couple of hours, five thousand dollars. Our work is fully guaranteed. If it doesn't work, we keep coming back until it's finished. No extra charge."

"For just one of you? That's way over my budget." Though if Brett solicited his brothers, they could each pay something for the Wernicke brothers' services. But he wasn't certain Eric or Sarandon would go along with the idea. Maybe not even CJ.

"Okay, well, if you change your mind, get ahold of me. You have my number. Have a great ghost-free day." Stanton hung up on him.

Brett shoved his phone in his pocket and got ready to pick up Ellie. If he was going to pay anyone that kind of money, he wanted to know for certain that Stanton truly could do what he said he could. The only way Brett could guarantee that was if he had someone else verify the ghost was really gone. That meant one of the sisters would have to do it, since he didn't know anyone else who could see them. Unless CJ could and he was in denial.

Brett didn't entirely trust the Wernicke brothers. He could see that working with Stanton could be a disaster. He called CJ on the way to Ellie's house. "Hey, are you speaking to Laurel yet?"

"Of course. I took her home, spent some quality time with her, had cinnamon rolls and coffee, and returned her to the inn to work."

"So she's no longer mad at you?"

"We still need to talk. But no. So what did you learn about Matilda?"

"Records say she died of pneumonia. Fluid in the lungs. No really great forensics back then though. But when I looked into other possible causes for fluid in the lungs, I found drowning and severe pulmonary edema. Even today, not one pathognomonic autopsy finding can definitively prove drowning in a victim. Since she'd had a cold beforehand, was elderly, and found dead in bed with no signs of any trauma to the body, the doctor concluded she'd died of pneumonia in her sleep. In other news, I talked to Stanton Wernicke about the ghost situation."

"Do you want to stir up a hornet's nest with Ellie and her sisters?"

"I didn't tell him the ghost was at the inn. I wanted to know if they could really exorcise a ghost."

"And he said they can, right? But where's the proof?"

"That would be the problem—verifying they were successful without asking the sisters. He charges five thousand for a job if he's not able to use it on their TV show."

"That's highway robbery!"

"Right. I was thinking if all of us pitched in—you, me, Eric, and Sarandon—it wouldn't be quite so much."

"I can tell you right now that our brothers won't go for it."

"Okay, so the other problem is that we'd want to know if they'd handled the job successfully. Unless you can see ghosts or sense them or something, we'd have to ask Ellie or one of her sisters. Whoever can see them."

"Which gets us back to them learning we're doing this with their cousins in the first place. And I say no."

"We've got to do something."

"You exorcise the ghost then."

How could Brett do that when he couldn't even see or sense spirits? "Okay, I'll research it and see what I can learn." He would do anything he could to try to help out.

CJ laughed. "Good luck with that." He didn't sound the least bit serious.

"Okay, so if I try to do this on my own, can you tell if a ghost is still there?"

"You'd have to ask Ellie, and I don't think you want to go there. By the way, how are things with you and Ellie? Is she dating anyone else yet?"

"Nah, she hasn't had time and I don't think she's interested."

"Lucky for you, Brett. Talk to you later. Got to go on patrol."

"All right." Brett loved to research things. Even if he didn't exactly believe in all this, he could look into it. What if he found an easy solution? Attempting to exorcise the ghost would be less of a trial than sneaking Stanton into the inn. More than likely, an exorcism wouldn't cost him much, if anything. Hell, maybe he could just talk to his great-aunt and see if that worked. The problem was that he didn't really believe she was still here. If she were, why hadn't she let him know all these years?

When Brett arrived at the MacTire sisters' home, Laurel and Meghan were heading to the inn. They told him to have fun at the piano lesson and continued on their way. Ellie met him outside, looking like she was getting ready to take an exam and hadn't studied the night before. He took her cold hand in his and led her out to the car.

"Now remember, no worries. If we have fun at this, fine. If not, we can quit."

"I didn't even ask how much it was going to cost," she said.

"It's free."

"No, we have to pay the teacher what he normally charges."

"It's a promotional tool for him. I'll pay him. The first two lessons are free to see if we even want to do this."

"Are you sure? I can—"

"No. My suggestion, my treat."

As soon as she got into the car, she saw the macramé book and smiled. "You were serious."

"Weren't you?"

She laughed. "Yes." Then she saw the book on wood carving beneath it. She began flipping through the pages of the macramé book first. "Oh, oh, I want to try this one. It would be perfect to hang off the back porch holding a pot of flowers in the spring. Or maybe a wall hanging. Oh, I don't know now." She checked out the book on wood carving and smiled at the picture of a wolf carving. "This one." She knew that was the one she wanted to do.

"I haven't seen the macramé project I want to do yet, but I'll look later. We can pick up the supplies we need once we're ready to try it out. I did get what we needed for wood carving. The wolf was my choice too." He was glad he'd pleased her. He wanted her to know he was serious, and that he wanted to share in things she wanted to do too.

"Hey, if we get really good at it, or at least if one of us does, we can offer carvings and wall hangings for sale in the lobby," she said.

"Gifts for family. The possibilities are limitless." As long as they turned out well!

Laurel really liked the piano teacher. He was in his mid-to-late fifties, and like Brett had said, he was really eager to teach them how to play.

He started teaching them the notes and gave them some online lessons to work on so they could practice.

Remer had dark-red hair like Ellie, which made her wonder if he had Irish roots too. Or maybe Scottish. While Brett was practicing, she asked.

"To be sure," Remer said. "My maternal and paternal grandparents were from Ireland. They came over about the time the Silver family was starting the town."

"I thought you were new here. That you've only been here a year or so."

Brett was still practicing the piece the teacher wanted him to play.

"Yes. We moved away for a time. I was performing in an orchestra in New York, but I got tired of not being around our kind. So I returned here."

"No family now?"

"Nope. I was an only child." Remer gave Brett some more notes to practice. "Both of you are doing great for your first time. I'm surprised you didn't learn some from your great-aunt or your grandmother," he said to Brett.

Brett was frowning as he pressed down the keys. "My grandmother didn't play the piano as far as I knew."

"Oh, she played. She didn't play as well as Matilda though. Your great-aunt taught me piano lessons for a number of years. She taught a lot of kids. Matilda even asked your grandmother to take over lessons one day after she suddenly got an emergency call. Your grandmother didn't play or teach half as well as your great-aunt. Maybe it was because she didn't play that often. But she didn't seem to have a natural affinity for it either. I think there was some jealousy between the two of them over it."

"I never knew that," Brett said. "I know they lived together at the end, but I never saw Grandmother play."

Ellie hadn't lived here back then, but she was surprised Brett's grandmother had kept her training a secret from him. Even if Ellie never learned to play well, she wouldn't hide the fact that she'd tried to learn. She was always trying new stuff. No big deal if she didn't master it and make a big success of it. If one of her sisters was better at something than she was, she would be happy for her.

"Your great-aunt made a good income off her lessons. She performed a lot too, before she settled down and began teaching local kids."

They heard someone enter through the front door.

Remer smiled. "Another student just arrived. So what do you think? Are you willing to continue lessons for a few more sessions?"

Brett looked up at Ellie, and she swore he was holding his breath, waiting for her answer. She smiled. "Of course. You can tell me when—I mean, if—you think I'm a hopeless student at any time. You won't hurt my feelings."

"Truthfully, I've never seen a student play so well for the first time."

She was going to say he must have had some really bad students, but since he hadn't said the same about Brett, she smiled again. She thought about Matilda really giving her the first lesson, but she wasn't about to mention that. "Thanks."

When she and Brett left Remer's house, Brett wrapped his arm around Ellie's shoulders and gave her a squeeze in the crisp fall air. "That wasn't too awfully bad, was it?"

"No. I really had fun."

"Good. Me too. You did very well. I thought we'd go to Silva's tea shop for lunch if you like."

"Oh, I'd love to. She'll love it." She was glad Brett had suggested the tea shop and not the pub for lunch since they had dinner there recently. Both were first-class establishments as far as meals and service went, but Silva's tea shop was only open for lunch.

Ellie was glad she had tried the piano lessons. At least so far it had been fun. "That was a surprise about your grandmother playing piano, wasn't it?"

"Yeah. She didn't want my Uncle Ned to take lessons. She always said it wasn't a masculine enough activity for him. Maybe she didn't like the idea of her sister teaching him because she could play better than my grandmother."

"Brett, do you know for sure that Matilda died of natural causes?"

―◦◦◦―

Brett glanced in Ellie's direction, shocked she'd ask about his great-aunt's cause of death. What did she suspect? Or know?

"You saw her, didn't you? Not Chrissy, but Matilda," he asked.

Ellie nodded. "I know you don't exactly believe in ghosts, so I didn't want to mention it. She didn't like that you and I were kissing. I figured it was her Victorian upbringing. Unmated girls had to be chaperoned."

He couldn't believe it. Yet that did sound suspiciously like his great-aunt. "And?"

Ellie let out her breath on a heavy sigh. "Meghan and I heard her playing the piano in the inn the other night."

Brett pulled into the parking lot of Silva's tea shop and cut the engine. He stared at Ellie in disbelief. "What are you going to do about it? With your guests coming?"

"Do you believe me?"

She looked so hopeful that his heart went out to her.

"Well, like I said, it's kind of hard to believe in something I can't see or hear. I can rationalize that others can experience ghosts when I can't, I guess, but still, it's hard to imagine."

"Well then, we'll just have to kiss by the piano."

He smiled, certainly ready for that.

"Then again, you probably wouldn't be able to see her if she suddenly appeared. I'd be the only one who was unsettled. Maybe I can talk her into playing the piano for you. She showed me some keys to play last night."

He shut his gaping mouth and processed that. "I thought you went to bed."

"I-I just had to talk with her. So I went to the inn and told her we were taking piano lessons together. I didn't see her this time. I don't always see the physical ghost. She began to show me keys to play, and I copied her. I think that pleased her."

"Why did you think she might not have died of pneumonia?"

"I mentioned my dad dying of pneumonia to her."

"I didn't know. I'm sorry."

"Thank you. We were devastated. It seemed to bother her when I asked if she'd had a relapse like my dad had. She made a horrible noise on the piano, banging on the keys. She seemed really angry. I can't imagine that anyone who loves the piano as much as she did would mistreat it. Maybe she was angry that she had died from pneumonia. Or she believed that someone hadn't taken care of her like he or she should have, even if they had. My mother was devoted to my father. So were my sisters and I. He still died. His body didn't have time to fight the infection before he lapsed into a coma and died."

"Do you think she might be telling you someone neglected her and that's why she died?"

"No. Like I said, it could be she's angry about it, despite receiving the best of care. It doesn't mean anyone did anything wrong."

"Okay, I wondered." Brett took a deep breath and let it out. "She had a cold beforehand. Maybe she had walking pneumonia, unaware that she was that sick. But what if something else happened? What if she actually drowned?"

Ellie stared at him in disbelief. "What makes you consider that?"

"It's all supposition. Probably just a crazy, far-out notion. I keep thinking that if she showed herself to you, she needs some kind of closure to move on. It's possible that something else, nothing sinister, is at stake. But what if that's not the case? Especially if she's upset you think she died of pneumonia. What else would she have died of that could simulate pneumonia? Pulmonary edema can cause a buildup of fluid in the lungs. But drowning can too. I ran the idea past CJ, but he doesn't believe the cause was anything other than what the coroner's report stated."

"She died in bed though, right?"

"That's what everyone thinks."

"So what makes you think that she could have died elsewhere?"

He explained about the missing boat and what they'd found in the bottom of it—the man's glove, the empty wine bottle, and his great-aunt's sunbonnet.

"Scandalous," Ellie said very seriously. "I mean, if she had issues with us kissing when we're not mated, and she was partying with some guy in a boat on the river behind her house, her sunbonnet off... Well, it sounds rather scandalous."

"And out of character? Of course, the old gal might have had a secretly wild side. We don't really know."

"Any idea who the gentleman suitor might have been?"

"A couple of men were hanging around. One loved to play the piano. The other was Remer's grandfather, Theodore. I don't know the name of the first man."

"Two gentleman suitors?" Ellie tsked. "And she was giving me the evil eye because we were kissing? Okay, so when were the items found in the boat?"

"Well, Theodore was actually seeing Grandmom. After Matilda's death, they discovered the boat had gotten loose from its moorings, and the river had carried it downstream a couple of miles. Someone in the pack found it stuck on some rocks."

"Did anyone notice it was missing before she died?"

"No."

Ellie frowned. "So, if she had drowned, someone would have had to carry her to the house, change her clothes, and put her to bed."

"Her hair was damp the next morning, though everyone assumed she'd had a bath and taken more of a chill. A couple of damp towels were hanging on the rack. Grandmom said Matilda must have been really delirious because she'd used both Grandmom's towel and her own, and her nightgown was on backward."

"Or she could have been drunk on the wine. Then again, she could have drowned, and the man who brought her back dried her the best he could, making the mistake of using both towels, then dressed her in her nightclothes and made it look like she just didn't wake up the next morning. That means he would have left water all over though, if he'd had to pull her out of the river and carry her back to the house." Ellie shook her head.

"Or he went back to the house and used the two towels to mop up the floor."

"Did anyone notice a bunch of wet towels?"

"No. Just the two."

"And her wet clothes?"

"He might have disposed of them."

"So she was living with your grandmother?" Ellie asked.

"Yes, her twin sister, my grandmother, but she wasn't home at the time. Grandmom was out with a couple of lady friends and was completely distraught that she had been gone when my great-aunt got so sick and died. She'd believed Matilda was home, not wanting to go out with the ladies because of her cold, and instead playing her piano as usual. But what if she went out with some guy, and it had a tragic end?"

"Accidentally? Or on purpose?" Ellie lifted a brow.

"Or not the case at all. I'm sorry you've had to deal with this. It's hard for me to believe she's been hanging around the piano all these years when none of us had a clue."

"I understand. I have to admit we were sure shocked."

"I saw the way you were upset when I was kissing you. I'm glad it wasn't because of me."

She smiled. "It wasn't because of you. So what are we going to do about the possibility that your great-aunt didn't die of natural causes?"

"I'd say we might need to team up and do research. What do you think?"

Ellie nodded. "Yeah. I'm all for it. I'm starving. Do you think you can eat anything?"

"I sure do." Despite being hungry and wanting to spend as much time as possible with Ellie, Brett was distracted. He had been thinking way ahead about this situation. He needed to learn who the other man was. Had anyone seen them go out in the boat? Or know anything that would prove she had gone out that night and not stayed at home like his grandmother had believed.

Brett and Ellie entered the tea shop. Round tables covered in lace, antique teapots and teacups, botanical prints, and vases of roses adorned the quaint Victorian shop. Silva also had decorated pumpkins filled with flowers on each of the tables. Ghost and Frankenstein petit fours were sitting on a platter underneath glass, and a pot of witches' brew—orange spice tea—was scenting the shop for that sweetly Victorian Halloween flair.

Silva greeted them with a cheery smile and then showed them to their seats at a table next to one of the windows overlooking a covered street-side patio with café chairs and tables. Brett had a triple-stacked Reuben sandwich and swore Silva had made it more man-sized just for him, so he'd encourage more of the guys to stop in at the tea shop. Ellie had chicken and dumplings, and the women in the tea shop twittered as if seeing a man in the lunch room had gotten them all excited. Most were mated, so he was amused.

"You're getting all kinds of attention," Ellie said to Brett, taking another spoonful of her chicken and dumplings. She smiled at him.

He chuckled. "They'd react that way if any guy turned up here."

She laughed. "Enjoy it while you can."

A red car pulled up outside the window and parked. The license plate immediately caught his eye. "Art4Hire." Ah hell. Not only was the driver Ginger, one of the former students who had painted him when he was modeling nude, but Thera and Renea, both water-color artists, climbed out of her car. They lived in or around Breckenridge, and all had been in one class or another that he had modeled for. There wasn't any way that they would know he had come here for lunch. And though they'd mailed him free prints that he didn't keep, he'd never given any of the ladies his phone number or email address.

No one knew he was going to be here today except Ellie. No way had he wanted to mention this to her here and now, but he could see the trouble he might be in with her when the women entered the shop and saw him—if they didn't already know he was here.

He reached across the table and took her hand and squeezed. "Trouble is on its way."

"Oh?"

"Yeah. You see those three ladies?"

She glanced out the window and raised her brows as one of them saw Brett and began waving and blew a kiss to him. The others started waving frantically too. *Damn*.

"Former lover?" Ellie sounded like she was trying to keep her tone of voice even, but he heard a hint of annoyance.

"No. I used to model for art classes at a college in Breckenridge so I could pay for my journalism degree."

Her gaze switched to Brett, and her jaw dropped. "A *nude* model?"

He was afraid she was going to dump him right then and there.

"Not always. Sometimes I had something draped across my lap."

Her lips were parted in surprise, but then her attention shifted to the door as the bell jingled and the three women walked in. They were all lookers: Ginger, the redhead; Thera, the brunette; and Renea, the blond. They were great artists, displaying their works in galleries all over. But Brett's modeling days were done. Not that he couldn't still model and do a good job of it, but he was a news reporter now, and that's all he cared about doing.

Ellie leaned back in her chair as if distancing herself from him and the women, who happily surrounded him, all smiles and hugs. What could he do but smile back and return the hugs? Platonically, of course. He didn't want Ellie to think this was how he was with everyone and that he had a bunch of women interested in his body, just because he'd posed for some art classes a couple of years back.

"We came here to see if we could find you," Ginger said. "We thought if the three of us got together, we could convince you to model for another session. We'd pay for it, of course."

"Truthfully?" Renea said. "Ginger made such a mint off her last oil painting of you that we all wanted to have another chance. We're in competition to see who can make the biggest sale this time. We all have our own technique so our paintings turn out differently for each of us."

"We even have one of those fake bear rugs you can pose on," Thera said.

Brett noticed that everyone in the shop was watching them now. Ah, hell. The word would get around the pack pronto.

"My answer is still no. Sorry, ladies. My modeling days are over."

Ginger turned to Ellie. "Have you seen our work?" She pulled an envelope from her large bag and handed it to Brett as if he were going to open it up and show off his nude poses. Yes, it was art, but somehow it didn't seem as much like it when he was trying to court a she-wolf who didn't know anything about his modeling days.

Everyone waited expectantly. Ellie's cheeks turned crimson.

Silva dropped off a slice of chocolate cheesecake for Ellie and raspberry-topped cheesecake for Brett, both garnished with candy pumpkins. "I know you have to get back to work, so I wanted to drop this off before you have to leave." Silva turned to the ladies. "Three for lunch?"

They were still eyeing Brett like *he* was on the menu. "Nice to see you again, ladies." And then he turned his attention to Ellie, not waiting for the ladies to say good-bye. He was there with Ellie and wanted only to be with her.

Ellie was poking at her cheesecake, ignoring him and the ladies. The women moved off to the table farthest from them near the kitchen. Brett would have to thank Silva for the rescue later.

"She must have guessed we'd want a slice of her award-winning cheesecake," Ellie said, sounding like nothing had just happened.

"My brothers are always ordering pies or cheesecake from her. They're the best."

"They are." Ellie poked at her cheesecake some more.

"About the modeling," Brett said. Ellie eyed the manila envelope on the table. "I've said no to modeling ever since I finished my degree."

She shrugged as if the modeling didn't matter and poked her fork into her cheesecake again.

If she didn't want to discuss it, he was fine with that, but he was afraid they needed to get this out in the open. "I didn't date them, and I didn't do any private modeling for anyone. It was strictly through the college."

"How did they know you live here?"

"They wanted to send me prints of how their paintings of me turned out. I said sure, not really thinking about what I'd do with them. They've done really well with them, but that has a lot to do with how well they paint."

Ellie sat back in her chair again. "So…paintings of you, and prints, are all over the place? In your home even?"

"Uh, well, I guess. I don't know. I mean, really, who would want a painting of a nude guy hanging on the living room wall? I really don't see how they could sell all that well. And no, I don't have any hanging up in my home." He lowered his voice. "I didn't keep the ones they sent to me. I mean, it seems kind of narcissistic."

"What are you going to do with those?"

"The same thing I did with the others. I certainly don't intend to share them, frame them, or keep them tucked away."

She eyed them again, and he wondered if she was curious to see them. He certainly wasn't going to offer to show her and risk her being further annoyed with him.

"Listen, Ellie, if you're upset about this, I understand, and I'm more than willing to talk further to you about it. But I need to get on the road to Green Valley to interview your aunt Charity about her candy store's anniversary. I'll be getting back by six. I thought we might have some dinner and then practice our piano lessons a little, if you'd like."

She hesitated, and he hated that she might be rethinking their relationship.

Then she finally nodded. "I'd like that. What if we have some trouble with your great-aunt's piano?" Ellie sounded worried that they might and he'd be upset about it. Maybe that was all that bothered her.

Brett reached across the table to take her hand, and he swore every eye in the room was on the two of them. "No problem. We can deal with anything." He stroked the top of her hand with his thumb.

Ellie blushed.

He knew then that she didn't mind his attentions. Not even with the other women looking on. The problem was his disapproving great-aunt. He couldn't wait to see Ellie tonight. But he had to get to Green Valley and return home before the weather turned bad.

He paid for the meal and gave Silva a generous tip. She gave him a big smile back. "If I hadn't already taken Sam for a mate, I might have considered choosing you."

He laughed. As if she had ever wanted anyone but Sam.

Silva winked at Ellie, and she blushed again.

"Okay, I'll call as soon as I get back, and we'll have dinner," he said, escorting Ellie out of the tea shop.

"Thanks for lunch, Brett. I look forward to tonight." She glanced again at the envelope tucked under his arm.

He was certain she was curious about what she would see. Truth be told, so was he. Which was another reason he didn't want to show them to her. He slipped the envelope into his leather briefcase before he climbed into the car and then drove her home.

When they arrived at Ellie's house, he kissed her in a way that said he wanted more than just a casual relationship. He didn't care if her sisters caught them kissing if they happened to glance out the inn windows. He only cared about this moment with Ellie. She wrapped her arms around his neck and was kissing him right back, as if she wanted the same. She was warm and soft, bright and cheerful. No matter what was going on, she always had something nice to say, a positive outlook on life, real kindhearted. She would make the perfect mate.

She was teasing his tongue with hers, their breaths

frosty in the chilled air, their bodies pressed tight against each other's. Despite the bulk of her wool coat and his ski jacket, he still felt her heat pressed against him. He smelled her pheromones telling him she was enjoying this intimacy between them as much as he was, and he loved it.

She finally pulled away from him, looking serious. "You'd better get going, or you won't have time to get back from Green Valley before the snowstorm hits."

"Nothing will stop me from getting home in time to have dinner with you. But you're right. I need to get on the road. About…Halloween. Do you mind if I come over and help you and your sisters hand out drinks or candy?"

"We'd love it."

He pulled her into his arms for one last serious hug, kissed her mouth and forehead, and then said he'd see her soon.

She smiled, waved at him, then walked on the path to the inn to work. He wondered if she'd tell her sisters about his modeling stints, or if either of them already knew. As close as they were, he suspected that if they had known, they would have told her.

He was over the moon and sure he and Ellie were headed for a mating. As soon as he could, he'd research how to exorcise a ghost, and once he had done it to his satisfaction, he would have a serious talk with Ellie about the direction their relationship was going.

Even though Ellie was dying to see the paintings of Brett in the nude, there was no way she would ever ask to see them.

This afternoon, she had important business to take care of. She called the newspaper and put in her letter for the Lonely Hearts column. She figured if she was going to date someone, he should be a wolf, if she was going to prove their theory that she and Brett were dream mating. As far as she knew, dream mating never happened between a wolf and a human. No way was she going to leave town to try to hook up with a human. And she'd make it known that she was just dating for fun, nothing serious. Still, she felt awkward about doing this. She wondered if anyone even read the column.

She thought about Brett posing nude for all those art students and sighed, reminding herself it was just art, and he was right. Who would want to have his nude body plastered all over their homes? Sure, she wanted to take a peek, but no way would she want to put him on display for everyone else to see.

Then she recalled what the redhead had said—they'd brought a bear rug for him to lie on while they painted him? Now all Ellie could think of was him stretched out nude on a polar bear rug, looking sexy as the devil.

Her sisters had probably been watching her and Brett. They would have heard his car pull up and would have checked to see if he was bringing her home or whether they had some other visitors. So it wasn't like they would be spying on her. Though she suspected they'd watch to see how far they were taking the relationship. The problem was the whole communing-with-ghosts issue.

She had no intention of telling her sisters that she was going to post a letter in the Lonely Hearts column. They'd probably tell her it was a bad idea. She'd hear about it soon enough.

When she walked into the inn, she half expected her sisters to approach her and want to know more of what was going on between her and Brett. Laurel and Meghan were in the basement, one of them running the noisy vacuum. Maybe they hadn't heard or seen her come in.

She headed down the stairs, and Meghan spied her first, smiling and turning off the vacuum. "So, anything you want to tell us?"

Laurel came out of one of the bedrooms, a white splotch of paint on her cheek, the paintbrush in hand, with the lid to the paint can held beneath it to catch drips, her brows raised in question.

"About…?" If they hadn't been watching Ellie with Brett, maybe this was about the ghosts.

Laurel smiled but shook her head. "About Brett, of course. Where is this going between the two of you?"

"You were watching."

Meghan snorted. "We just checked to see if it was you, and it was. We didn't expect the steamy scene to play out before us."

"And you kept watching."

Meghan smiled. "The show was great."

"We still want to know if Brett is on board with your abilities, or you're still keeping it secret from him. You can't, you know. We were honest with CJ, or at least about the fact we knew Chrissy was haunting the inn. It's up to you to tell Brett it's a little more than that with you and Meghan," Laurel warned.

"I will." Ellie just had to wait until the time was right. Maybe tonight she could convince Matilda to play the piano, and hopefully Brett could hear her too. If he did, and he believed that ghosts existed, she could tell him how she could commune with them.

"So what's next on the agenda?" Laurel asked.

Ellie smiled. "I'm going to start decorating for fall. That way, the day after Halloween, we can take the decorations down, and we'll be all set with the autumn decorations for Victorian Days and Thanksgiving."

Both her sisters looked exasperated with her. "With Brett," Laurel said.

Ellie sighed and headed up the stairs to decorate. "Dinner, of course. Piano lessons."

"On the haunted piano?" Laurel asked.

"Yes." Ellie turned to look at her sisters. "And if Matilda plays, which I'm going to try to convince her to do, then he'll know ghosts exist and I can tell him the rest."

"Good luck with that," Meghan said, but in a sarcastic way.

"If you need our help with it, let us know," Laurel said in a way that said she meant it.

"Thanks, Laurel." Ellie gave Meghan a peeved look and ascended the remaining stairs. She decided she would try to talk to Matilda now, just to prepare her for tonight.

Chapter 7

WITH EVERY INTENTION OF DOING A WELL-THOUGHT-out interview, but still making it back in time before the snowstorm really hit, Brett made the drive to Green Valley and stopped in on the MacTire sisters' aunt, Charity Wernicke, who owned the Candy Shop. He'd nearly walked into the shop with his briefcase when he remembered the darn manila envelope with prints of his nude poses in it, pulled it out, and tossed it in the trash can outside the shop.

The candy store was bright, colorful, and welcoming. The fragrance of chocolate, maple, and other delicious scents wafted in the air. Halloween-decorated candy, jack-o'-lanterns, witches, and black cats decorated the storefront windows.

This would be the perfect place to pick up a fancy autumn-decorated box of chocolates for Ellie for Halloween tomorrow night.

Charity looked like her confections, wearing a pink wool dress, her white hair in a bun, and a big smile on her face as she greeted him, her hand outstretched. He was glad to do this to help her business, especially since he cared about Ellie and her family.

While he interviewed Charity, they sat at a little glass table next to the big windows, where they could see the snow falling fast and furiously. The store was already closed for business so he could interview her in peace, but because of the weather, he imagined the shop would have been devoid of customers anyway.

"You may have to stay the night with me," Charity offered as they had cups of hot chocolate and pieces of Frankenstein fudge. "My nieces would be mighty upset with me if I let you drive home in this weather and you had any trouble."

"I have a date with Ellie tonight and don't want to miss it for anything. Thanks so much."

"All right. Don't say I didn't offer. And don't let me keep you then. The road isn't going to get any better. And, Brett, thanks so much for interviewing me for an article on the Candy Shop. When Ellie told me you wanted to do that, I was ecstatic."

"Anything to help out another wolf," he said quite seriously.

"And help become part of the family?" Charity asked.

He smiled, then bought Ellie one of the fanciest boxes of assorted chocolates that Charity was selling, sure Ellie would want to share some of the candy with her sisters. Maybe even him.

Charity sighed. "Ellie thinks the world of you, by the way. But the girls are rather special."

"They see ghosts. I know."

"It's not just a hobby for them. It's a way of life. The only way some male wolf is going to do right by her is if he believes in her abilities one hundred percent." She came around the counter. "Enough of us talking." Charity hurried him out the door. "You've got to get home safely before Ellie worries too much about you."

"Do you have their ability?"

"Heavens no. I sense things like they do, but I don't actually see ghosts."

He nodded and gave Charity a hug. She seemed pleased that he did. "You take it easy, and I'll let you know when this comes out in the paper. Probably by the weekend."

"Thanks again, Brett."

"You're most welcome." Then he headed out into the blowing snow. He realized it was worse than he'd thought when he actually got on the road. But he was certain he'd get home all right. He might have to take it a little slower than usual. Anything to make sure he got home safely.

Two hours later, he'd finally reach a point about ten miles from home when he saw headlights approaching in the blinding snowstorm, headed straight for him. He swore he was on his side of the road, but the piled-up snow made it impossible to see the center line or where the shoulders of the road began and ended. He pulled over a little farther and slowed down even more, but the vehicle, a big 1930s classic Plymouth, continued its deadly approach as if his car wasn't even there, sideswiping him.

A loud bang sounded as they hit, and metal scraped metal for a few seconds. His heart thundering, Brett twisted the steering wheel, trying to get out of the car's path but still stay on the road. The tires lost traction on the icy, snowy pavement, and despite him trying to stop it, the vehicle slid off the road.

The car landed in the deep ditch next to the shoulder. Though Brett tried to drive out of the ditch, his vehicle wouldn't budge. He hated to think about how much damage could have been done to his car.

"Damn it!" Brett climbed out of the car, which was tilting toward the gentle slope downhill, though it wasn't going anywhere. He moved around the ground, stumbling over rocks. He glanced back in the direction the car had gone after hitting his vehicle, thinking it might have stopped or slid off the road too. The red taillights continued on their way, never slowing down, the driver never pausing to see if he was all right. *Damn hit-and-run driver.*

Because of the blowing snow, Brett couldn't even catch the license plate number, or he would have called it in. Luckily, with his enhanced wolf's night vision, he would be able to give the description of the car though. Dark steel-gray, old. He wasn't sure what exact year, but it was from the 1930s, a vintage collectible. Who would be crazy enough to drive a classic car like that in these conditions? Though the heavy old car sure had knocked his lightweight Ford Taurus off the road.

He growled and pulled out his cell phone. And got no reception. *Hell.* With as bad as the weather was, he was certain the emergency crews would be out trying to rescue people. He didn't need to add to the mess. He climbed into his backseat, removed his clothes, opened the door, and hurried to get out. He quickly locked the car with the keypad, then shifted.

Warming at once in his thick wolf fur coat as his wolf took over, Brett tore off for Silver Town, hoping he wouldn't be so late that Ellie would call Darien and send out search parties. In case they did, he stuck close to the road—not on it, but close enough to see if anyone he recognized was out looking for him. He hoped not. He didn't want anyone searching for him in this weather

when others might be in need. He was already an hour
and half late returning home by car. Trotting as a wolf
would take another two hours in this weather. When he
got closer, he'd howl to let anyone who could hear him
know that it was him and he was fine.

He just hoped he didn't find anyone else who had run
off the road.

—⁓—

Ellie quit pacing long enough to call her aunt Charity
while Meghan and Laurel looked on, both frowning, as
anxious as she was. "Hi, Aunt Charity?"

"Ellie? Hasn't Brett arrived home yet?"

"No, he's a couple of hours overdue for dinner, which
can be expected because of the weather. I didn't know
when he'd left your shop exactly."

"He left two hours ago," her aunt said.

"Okay."

"The weather has been so bad that he could still be
driving in it and on his way."

"Right." Ellie still worried since she hadn't been able
to get ahold of him.

"You tried calling him on his cell, I take it."

"Yes. I can't get through."

"Did you call Darien?"

"Not yet. I wanted to first learn exactly when Brett
left your shop."

"He could still be on his way. Visibility is nearly nil.
I slipped twice just walking to my home. It's a real mix
of ice and snow on the roads."

"Okay, thanks. I'll let Darien know, just in case. He's
put out word that no one is to be out in this weather

except for emergency vehicles." Ellie looked at her sisters and raised two fingers.

Laurel got on her cell phone right away. "Darien, there may be no reason for alarm, but Brett was interviewing my aunt Charity in Green Valley and left her shop two hours ago. He hasn't made it home yet. Ellie isn't able to get ahold of him on his cell either."

Ellie said to her aunt, "We'll let you know when we hear from him."

"All right, dear. You stay home. I don't want you or your sisters out in this weather looking for him… Uh, Ellie?"

The way her aunt said her name sounded like she was concerned about something else. "Yes?"

There was a long pause.

Ellie said, "Are you still there?"

"Uh, yeah." Aunt Charity let out her breath on a heavy sigh. "I don't know what to say about this, but I care about you and your sisters. You're my nieces after all. I'd like to think you don't mind if I act like a mother hen every once in a while."

"No, of course not." Now Ellie really wondered what was going on.

"Brett threw a manila envelope in the trash container in front of the store before we had the interview."

Ellie barely breathed. Omigod, her aunt couldn't have looked at naked Brett in the prints.

"Um, well, I had just emptied it before he came along because the shop was closed and trash day is tomorrow morning if the trucks can get through. So I was going to toss his trash in my city trash can, but I got curious because it wasn't junk mail. It was a brand-new envelope with his name written on it in a woman's handwriting. I just thought it was odd, and you know how we wolves are. Curious."

"He was a model for art classes when he was in college," Ellie said before her aunt could continue.

She saw both Meghan and Laurel's eyes widen.

Her aunt didn't say anything for a moment. Then she said, "Oh, okay, so you've seen them."

"No, I haven't seen them." Ellie explained about lunch and the artists.

Her sisters' mouths were gaping, and then Meghan smiled.

"Oh, did you want me to save them for you?"

Yes! But not to keep. Well, maybe to keep under her pillow at night. "Um, thanks, I'm sure they're beautiful, but no. Okay, I'll let you go. Laurel's telling Darien that Brett's still on the road. I'll call you when we know anything." Once she ended the call with her aunt, Ellie waited to see what Laurel had to say.

"All the emergency crews are out. CJ's on one of them, looking for a missing teen driving to the grocery store. Eric's stuck at the park, and Sarandon's with him, having had to cancel a hike with a group because of the weather."

"Then the three of us will go and find Brett," Ellie said. "As wolves."

Laurel lost her frown and smiled. "I'll tell Darien."

Meghan began stripping. "So what's this about with Brett being a male model? Nude and bear rugs?"

Ellie knew this would be the next hot topic of conversation.

"And women are chasing him down in Silver Town?"

Meghan laughed. "I can't believe Aunt Charity saw the pictures when we haven't. Why didn't you tell her to overnight them?"

"I don't want them."

Meghan shook her head. "Yeah, you do. You're fantasizing about him when you go to bed at night. What better way to help you with imagining that hunk of burning love?" Meghan shifted.

Ellie finished stripping, not commenting, and shifted, as Laurel ended the call with Darien. "He doesn't want us to stray from the road Brett will be taking. He says that Brett will stick close to the road in case anyone is out looking for him."

Unless he was injured, Ellie thought morosely. Then she woofed, telling Laurel to hurry up and shift already.

Once Laurel had shifted, the three of them were out the wolf door in a heartbeat and took off down the road, hoping that if any human was traveling through the area, they wouldn't notice any of the wolves in the whiteout.

They had run, trotting sometimes and sniffing the air, but the wind direction was wrong. Every once in a while, Laurel or Meghan would bump into Ellie because they were trying so hard to pick up any sign of Brett's scent trail.

Then Ellie thought to howl. She stopped, lifted her chin, and let out a long, *where-are-you* howl.

Immediately, a male wolf howled back, and her heart raced across the snow-filled sky. It was Brett. She howled again, eagerly, exuberant.

Her sisters howled too, as if to let him know they had all worried about him.

He howled back, letting them know he was all right and on his way. Maybe he was only about a quarter of an hour away, she thought. She was so glad to hear from him, and he sounded fine.

They alternated between trotting and sprinting to reach him, and when they didn't find him quickly, she realized he'd been farther away from them than she'd envisioned. She kept thinking she saw a glimpse of a wolf headed their way, but she was just imagining seeing him in the curtain of snow.

And then she observed his hunky wolf body, his ears held erect, his eyes squinting in the blowing snow but looking straight at her. He sprinted for her, and before long, they were nuzzling and licking each other. Her sisters joined in, nipping and licking him, telling him they were glad he was safe. Then they headed home, Laurel and Meghan in the lead, while Ellie nuzzled Brett, keeping her body next to his, wanting the closeness until they arrived home.

When they reached the house, Laurel had already shifted, dressed, and was on the phone with Darien, updating him. Meghan was upstairs getting dressed.

Ellie realized they didn't have any men's clothes at their house for Brett.

She raced up to her bedroom, shifted, dressed, and hollered down, "Brett will need some clothes if someone can drop some by."

"All we need is a bear rug," Meghan said.

Ellie could have socked her.

"Calling CJ next," Laurel hollered back.

Meghan called out, "I'm calling Aunt Charity to let her know Brett's safely back home."

"Thanks!" Ellie said. When she went back downstairs, she found Brett peering out the front window in his wolf coat. "Attic light on?" she asked.

He shook his head.

"Well, Meghan's date canceled on her because the sheriff is helping to coordinate rescue activities, and the same thing with CJ. If you don't mind, we can all have dinner together."

He woofed, indicating that was fine with him. It would be nice for them all to be here together during the brunt of the storm.

"I'll bake some chicken and potatoes," Ellie said.

"I'll make a spinach salad," Meghan added.

Laurel was still on the phone with CJ. "All right. Love you too. I'll let him know." Laurel ended her call. "Well, CJ said it would be a couple of hours before he can drop by your place and then get here. He's really tied up helping stranded motorists. He said maybe you could wear something of ours?" She looked at Ellie to emphasize that he should wear something of hers.

"Pajama loungers? They're flannel, might be a little short on you, but that way you can shift." Ellie waited for Brett to agree.

He woofed his assent.

She placed the baking pan with the seasoned chicken and potatoes in the oven and set the timer. "I'll be right back."

Jogging up the stairs, she tried to remember which pajamas she'd washed. Pink hearts, snowmen on a blue background…oh, her Irish plaid ones. She hoped they would fit okay. She crossed the floor to her dresser and pulled open the drawer. She'd forgotten a fragrant lavender sachet scented her clothes. Hoping he didn't mind, she guessed he'd rather eat dinner as a human wearing sweet-smelling clothes than have his meal as a wolf.

"I've got some," she called out to Brett. He might as well change in her bedroom instead of in the smaller bathroom downstairs. She smiled when she heard him loping up the stairs.

"Hope these aren't too short in the legs. You can wear my fluffy robe if you want instead of the shirt. You're probably too broad shouldered for it. Or we can turn up the heat for you."

He shifted and she smiled at him, trying not to look at his nakedness. "They smell a little flowery, but—"

"Like you," he said, pulling her into a hug and beginning to kiss her. "I was so afraid I'd miss our date. Well, we have a few more for dinner than we'd planned, but I wouldn't miss this for the world."

Her whole body was on fire, pressed against the hot, naked wolf-man, yet knowing she should let him get dressed, she wrapped her arms around him. Her sisters would be sure to speculate about her not leaving the room when he must be shifting. She was always so good. Never doing anything she shouldn't. With Brett, she wanted to have fun, misbehave, be a wolf.

His burgeoning arousal pressed hotly against her, and she felt utterly wicked in his arms. "Hmm," she murmured against his mouth, really loving the way he made her feel sexy and desirable. "I'd better help my sisters with dinner before they send a rescue party."

He smiled and pressed a warm kiss against her forehead. "For me? Or for you?"

She chuckled. "For me, probably, but they would be mistaken."

He grinned. "Why, Miss Ellie MacTire, I believe I haven't even begun to know all there is to know about you."

If he only knew how much more there was to her. "I could say the same thing about you! I had to hear from my aunt Charity that she was concerned about you because you threw out that manila envelope in her trash can in front of the store, and she had to look inside to see what it was."

Brett's eyes rounded.

"Yeah."

"What did she say?"

"I told her what it was all about. I think she was worried you were posing for a male escort service."

He laughed.

"Why did you throw it out there?"

"It seemed like a good idea at the time. Far from here. I didn't know she was watching me or that she would go Dumpster diving. So what did you tell her?"

"To toss them." She smiled and pulled away, glancing at his beautiful, fit body. Then taking her eyes off him for a moment, she pointed to the plaid pajamas lying on her blue bedspread that she'd left out for him. "If those don't suit, I have others in the drawer."

"Is that your MacTire plaid?"

"Aye."

He smiled again. "I will be proud to wear your plaid, lassie."

She laughed. "See you downstairs then." She didn't make a move to leave him alone.

"And piano lessons after dinner, right?" He began to pull on the pajama bottoms.

She swore he was more interested in the lessons than anything else. He must really want to learn how to play the piano, and she admired him for it. "Sure. Of course. Then I can drive you home."

"I can run home as a wolf. No sense in you going out in this weather in your car. Besides, what would the neighbors think if they saw me returning home in just a pair of pajama pants?" Since the pajamas puddled around her ankles when she wore them, they weren't a bad fit on him.

She smiled at him. "Don't like living dangerously, eh? Afraid of idle gossip?"

"In a pack, the news would spread like wildfire." He pulled her close again. "And then you would have to agree to mate me so my reputation wouldn't be tarnished."

She laughed again. "You're so funny."

"I don't think the shirt will fit. I don't want to rip it."

"I've got a fluffy white robe you can wear so you don't get chilled. Or we can turn up the heat," she reminded him.

"Unless your sisters don't want to see me shirtless at dinner…"

"We're wolves." Not that she really knew how her sisters would feel about that.

He smiled and snagged her hand. So much for her leaving Brett alone to dress. She was just comfortable around him, when she wasn't usually that bold with a guy.

They headed downstairs where her sisters were sitting on the couch watching *The Three Musketeers*, the sound so low it was nearly muted. Both Laurel and Meghan looked in their direction.

"Well, the pajama bottoms look like they fit really well," Laurel said.

Meghan considered Brett's torso. "Shirt wouldn't fit, would it?"

"Afraid not. As long as you ladies don't object to me eating dinner with you shirtless…"

"We're wolves," Meghan said, casting Ellie an amused look as if she'd heard her say the same thing in private to Brett minutes ago. Considering the way they had the TV turned down so low, they probably had heard.

Ellie was grateful her sisters didn't mention the nude modeling. She made hot eggnog with brandy and served the Tom and Jerrys to everyone in the living room. Meghan brought out a bag of chips to snack on before dinner was served.

Laurel asked, "Are you hot enough?"

Ellie smiled. She couldn't help herself. As soon as Brett glanced at her, looking like he was waiting for her to answer that question, she felt her face heat again. She swore she never blushed as much as she did when she was around him.

He finally said, "I'm hot enough."

"I'll say," Meghan said, laughing and stretching out on the couch, while Laurel sat on one of the chairs.

That left another chair and a love seat.

When Ellie didn't automatically sit on the love seat, Brett took her hand and led her there. "Live dangerously," he whispered in her ear.

Both Laurel and Meghan were smiling. Ellie knew

this was all well and good, but only if Brett believed in her abilities.

When the timer went off, alerting them that the food was done, they all headed into the kitchen to serve up dinner and then settled in the dining room to eat.

"So, Brett," Laurel started. "We know you really care for Ellie—"

"This is between Brett and me, Laurel," Ellie said so vehemently that Laurel looked a little taken aback. Ellie didn't need her sisters setting down rules about her dating life.

"We just worry about you, Ellie," Laurel said, frowning at her.

"Because of the ghost issues." Brett sat down at the table.

"Right," Laurel said.

"Laurel," Ellie warned. She would handle this in her own way. It was her gift, and she'd decide when the time was right to approach him about it. She didn't want to ruin things between them.

Laurel raised her hand and made a dismissive gesture. "We think you're wonderful, Brett. Don't get me wrong. We're just looking out for Ellie's best interests."

"I don't need anyone to look out for my best interests. I do just fine on my own." Ellie took a bite of her chicken.

"Uh," Brett said. "I would never hurt Ellie."

"Not intentionally," Laurel said.

"Table. The. Discussion. Now." Ellie gave Laurel a look that said she meant it. Or hell, she was going to shift and run as a wolf to Brett's house and have wild and crazy almost-sex with him. Because she couldn't consummate the relationship or she'd be mated to him forever.

Meghan was watching to see how Laurel reacted. She was the alpha among the sisters, always in charge. Though they always had a say in things, Laurel made the final decision. It looked like it was killing her not to have the final say this time. She wasn't mean; she was just the eldest triplet and she always felt responsible for Ellie and Meghan. It was part of their wolf upbringing.

"I just don't want you to get hurt," Laurel said, her eyes brimming with tears.

Ellie had never expected her sister to get upset like this. Ellie left her seat and gave Laurel a hug. "I know. And I love you for it. Really. I can deal with this myself." She sighed. "Really."

Laurel nodded, but she didn't look like she believed Ellie. Which was probably because of the last time when the guy had left her at the restaurant and Ellie had been devastated. Even though she'd repeatedly told herself he hadn't been worth the energy and upset, she'd really thought he was the one for her. Yet she should have suspected Fred Pippin wouldn't believe in what she could do, considering how many times she'd tried to broach the subject and he'd abruptly changed the topic of conversation.

Ellie swore she wouldn't fall apart if it didn't work out with Brett. She returned to her seat, the mood quiet. Meghan took up the slack and started talking about Victorian Days and their first ball to celebrate the occasion, since they hadn't participated last year with all the renovations going on at the inn. She engaged Brett in conversation, while Ellie and Laurel ate their dinner in silence. It was really awkward between all of them.

They were almost finished eating when the doorbell rang, and Laurel hurried to get it.

"Oh, CJ, thanks so much. Come in and have supper with us. We're nearly done eating, but the rest is still in the warmer and ready for you."

"Is everyone all right? Brett?"

"Yeah, we're great." Laurel led CJ into the dining room.

CJ grinned at his brother. "You look great in the MacTire plaid. I've got to run back out, but I wanted to leave off some clothes for you and grab a bite to eat."

"Thanks, CJ." Brett finished the last forkful of his baked potato. "Be right back." He grabbed the bag of clothes from CJ and headed for the downstairs guest bathroom.

Ellie was almost disappointed that Brett was going to be wearing his own clothes. He looked cute in her plaid.

When Brett returned, CJ asked, "So what happened?"

"I got sideswiped by a tank. You know, one of those vintage Plymouths that's built to last. Not like the flimsy cars we own today."

"Color?"

"Dark steel-gray. Reminded me of a gangster car of the thirties."

"Oversized white sidewalls?" CJ asked, taking notes.

"Couldn't see them for the snow."

"Approximate year?"

"Well, when I did the article on the vintage car show last year, I saw some that looked similar and were built anywhere from about 1932 to 1939."

"Do you remember one that looked like that—same color—at the show?"

"Maybe. I'd have to look at the photos and my notes. I wrote down who owned them and why they bought those particular models, though with being wolves and living so long, most were the original owners."

"Maybe you can pick it out of a lineup of photos then. No clue on the license plate?"

"No. It blended in with the snow. And it was headed out of town. Might not have been one of ours. Plus, humans were at the car show too."

"Okay, well, you check out the photos, see if any look similar, even if they're a different color, and I'll run the owners down."

Ellie was glad Brett had a deputy sheriff for a brother.

———

Brett didn't think he'd done anything to make Laurel feel he had any intention of hurting Ellie, so he wasn't sure why she was so concerned. Maybe Laurel felt Ellie was being a little bold with him? But he loved it. It seemed so out of character for her, which made him feel that she really cared for him. That's what was important, because he sure the hell cared for her.

"Did you want me to drop you off at home before I run out again?" CJ asked when Brett returned to the dining room.

"Ellie and I have piano lessons once she's ready to go over to the inn. Unless you need me to help you."

"No, go have your lessons. I know how much you always wanted to do that when you were younger."

"Are you sure you don't need my help?" Brett asked.

"No. I don't have any more rescues to make. I'm just patrolling in case someone is stranded and doesn't have a way to contact us. Like you, unable to call us on your cell phone."

"Okay, if you're sure. If you need me, just come by the inn and pick me up."

"Need a ride home?"

"I'll run home as a wolf. That way you don't have to drop by here if you don't need to."

"CJ needs to drop by here later," Laurel said. "He has to take me home, but I'm staying until he's done tonight."

"Okay, well, we'll see about the time then," Brett said to Ellie. "Are you ready?"

"I sure am."

He wasn't sure if she wanted to practice, or she just wanted to get away from her sister's meddling. In any case, he was glad to be alone with Ellie for a while.

Chapter 8

ELLIE SO HOPED SHE COULD COAX BRETT'S GREAT-aunt to play the piano while he was there to see if he could see the ghost too.

"Is she here?" Brett asked.

"Nope. At least not that I can see."

"Okay." He pulled out a sheet of piano music of "Mary Had a Little Lamb." "I noticed this was marked as beginning sheet music, so I thought we could try it. And we can pull up the practice lessons on the Internet too. Did you want to go first?"

"No, go ahead. I'll watch you play, then I'll try." Though she was going to have a hard time watching him while keeping an eye out for his great-aunt.

But no ghosts showed up that she could see.

He smiled up at her, and she told him how beautifully he'd performed.

When she sat down at the piano, she practiced like his great-aunt had taught her, and she felt good doing it. Even though Matilda didn't make a physical appearance, Ellie felt like the elderly woman was there, encouraging her. For the first time ever, Ellie thought she could do this.

She played the simple piece Matilda had showed her before, and afterward she played the sheet music Brett was using.

"Bravo! You're doing great." Brett pulled her from the seat. "Isn't it fun?"

"Yeah, I really like this."

"Well, one of these days, maybe a few months from now, we could perform really complicated duets."

She laughed. "Maybe years."

"Not the way you're playing." Brett pulled her close. "About what Laurel said—"

"Don't think anything about it. She was being her usual big-sister self who needs to let me live my life."

"I get the impression this goes deeper. That you've had a prior bad experience that upset you."

She really didn't want to tell Brett how foolish she'd been. "Let's go sit in the common room." They sat on one of the comfortable love seats in there. "I didn't want to talk about this. It's not that important to our relationship."

"I think Laurel seems to believe it is."

"All right. It really isn't, but I was dating a wolf a couple of years ago. We were living in Florida at the time. I…thought he was the one. It turned out he didn't like the notion that I could see ghosts and…well, speak with them sometimes. I was really broken up when he left me, though I realized how fortunate I was that it had ended the way it did. Laurel felt bad she hadn't intervened before I totally lost my heart to him."

Brett frowned. "Were you mated?"

"No, but it was leading up to that—until I told him about myself. First, he just laughed at me, like I was telling a joke. Then he got mad and said ghosts didn't exist. How could I be such a fool? Anyway, Laurel blamed herself for my folly, but, of course, it wasn't her fault at all. I blamed myself for allowing him to change the subject every time I tried to tell him about it earlier on.

"When you and I started dating, I knew I had to speak to you about my ability, but I couldn't right away. I suspected you knew something about it from CJ, but I had to explain to you myself. It's not enough that you know, but that you believe that what I can do is real. Just as your job is real, and my working at the inn is real. I can't come home to tell you your great-aunt spoke to me, and you either don't believe and pretend you do, or you dismiss me, thinking the same as the man who left me. That I'm foolish for believing anything like that."

"I don't think you're foolish at all, Ellie. I think that you and your sisters are more sensitive to seeing things that the rest of us can't."

"Does that mean you believe me when I say your great-aunt was here?"

"Of course I do. And I would never treat you like that guy did. It does bother me that Matilda hasn't moved on. I just never considered that she would be hanging around since I'm unable to see ghosts or sense them in any other way. I'm sure when Laurel told CJ about it, he was in shock as much as I was."

"That's what I told her. Anyway, the music I was playing, that's what she showed me to play."

"So she still loves to teach piano lessons. Maybe she'll teach me." He sighed. He glanced at the clock and realized they'd been lost in conversation and it was nearly one in the morning. "It's getting late, and I need to run on home and let you get your sleep."

"Will you come over early tomorrow night? We could make mummy dogs or something for dinner, and then we'll hand out treats."

"Sure thing."

"Are you sure you don't want me to drive you home?"

"No. The roads are too bad. My paws do better, considering the icy conditions."

They locked up the inn and headed back to the house. Meghan had retired to bed. Laurel had already left with CJ, and she figured his brother hadn't wanted to interrupt Ellie and Brett's "date."

"If you don't have your car tomorrow, I can come and get you," Ellie said. "Or CJ can bring you over. He said he was going to help with the treats too."

"Either way." Brett gave her a hug and kiss. Then he went into the bathroom to strip and shift.

Ellie took his clothes and folded them up. "Night, Brett. See you tomorrow."

He woofed and headed out the wolf door. As she was climbing the stairs, Meghan called out, "How'd lessons go?"

"Great."

"Any ghostly appearances?"

"No, but I told Brett anyway."

Meghan's bedroom door opened, and she frowned at Ellie. "You told him you can send ghosts away?"

"No. That I can see and talk with them. If he can accept that, the rest is all the same."

"He accepted what you can do?"

"Yes. So, no worries."

Meghan smiled. "Good."

"Did you tell Peter?"

"No."

"Meghan…"

"When the time is right. Going to bed. Night."

Ellie sighed, went into her bedroom, and closed the

door. She supposed Meghan wasn't that serious about Peter, or she would have told him about herself already. Not once had Ellie heard he believed in ghosts, so that wasn't good. Tomorrow, she would tell Laurel the good news, so she wouldn't feel she had to protect Ellie from Brett any more.

Meghan called out from her bedroom, "She's playing the piano again!"

Ellie opened her window and listened to the haunting sound. "Beautiful," she said, her breath frosty in the night air. "Why didn't you perform when Brett was there?" She closed the window and got ready for bed, looking forward to trick-or-treaters if the roads were clear enough and the kids and adults could brave the snow.

Maybe Matilda would even play something nice and spooky for Halloween, and then Brett would know for certain that ghosts existed.

Ellie closed her eyes, ready for Brett to come to her in her dreams, when she remembered the Lonely Hearts column was coming out first thing in the morning. Maybe nobody would read it. Even if no one but a couple of bachelor wolves saw it and she went out with them, the word was sure to get out. She folded her arms across her chest, frowned, and closed her eyes.

Brett had suggested she do this, so it was all on him.

Chapter 9

THE NEXT MORNING, WHILE BRETT WAS SITTING AT HIS desk in the newspaper office, he looked through all the vintage car photos he'd taken at the car show last summer and found three cars that looked somewhat similar to the one that had hit his vehicle on the road. Then again, the snow had been blowing so hard that he could be mistaken. None of them appeared to match the dark steel-gray color. One was pale silver, another was glossy black, and the last one was light blue. Though like CJ had said, between now and last year, the owner could have repainted the car.

Brett called CJ and told him the names of the three car owners. They were all members of the pack, so he really didn't think that any of them would have been so careless or callous. Unless the driver had been inebriated.

"I'll check them out, but like you, I doubt any of our people would have done that. I'll let you know what I learn."

"Thanks, CJ."

He had shared Ellie's ghost story anonymously in the newspaper as she had requested and had been fielding calls on that all day. "Excellent story!" "Was it true?" "Which wolf had the experience?" A number of wolves had shared their own stories, maybe to be included in the paper next Halloween.

Anxious to exorcise the ghosts at the inn, Brett began

searching the Internet to see how he could do that himself instead of involving the sisters' cousins.

He found an article on performing a cleansing for ghosts. Simple. Just bundle some sage together and burn it, scenting the air throughout the inn with it. But he couldn't do that surreptitiously.

He found sage-and-citrus candles, for adding fragrance to a room, and figured that would work. It was supposed to be relaxing. He thought of giving them to the sisters to use, but what if they accepted the candles and then didn't burn them?

Then Brett had another thought and looked up sage in recipes. There was a recipe for a spice ball of sage, rosemary, thyme, tarragon, and marjoram, which would be added to soup, sauce, or stew. Or he could make sage sausage, or coat chicken with orange-sage marinade and bake it. Or he could make sage dip. The soup or stew would bubble away and add the scent of sage, along with the other herbs, to the air. Soup or stew? He liked chunks of beef, potatoes, and celery. So that's what he'd make. He hoped it turned out great.

Glad to have come up with a plan that cost under a hundred dollars instead of paying Stanton's exorbitant fee of five thousand, Brett was eager to help his great-aunt and the sisters find peace.

—◦◦◦—

When Ellie went to the grocery store, she saw little kids dressed up as everything from fairy princesses to Batman and other comic heroes. She planned to drop by the craft store to pick up materials to make her first macramé project from the book Brett had picked out. A plant holder? A bracelet? A wall hanging? There were lots of good choices.

"Hey," Sarandon said, joining her at the checkout counter, his dark-brown eyes even darker now. He didn't look like he planned to purchase anything, but just wanted to speak to her—and from the scowl on his face, he didn't look happy. "I saw your letter in the Lonely Hearts column in the paper." He pulled the torn-out column from his pocket. "'Woman interested in dating guys who love wolves, love to run, believe in ghosts, and love to howl at the moon'?"

Her jaw dropped. She'd almost forgotten about the ad because of all the excitement over Halloween. Mindy, the clerk, smiled at her. "You go, girl. Tell me if it works."

Ellie smiled back at her. She didn't say anything to Sarandon as she finished her transaction, but before she could carry her groceries out to the car, he grabbed the bags. He didn't look the least bit like a wolf who had seen her letter and was interested in dating her. He looked annoyed with her. Not that she was interested in dating him either. It was one thing to date other wolves, but not one of Brett's brothers.

"What?" she asked, unlocking the hatchback.

"What does Brett think about you dating other guys?"

"*He's* the one who suggested it!" She waited for Sarandon to deposit her bags in the car, but he was staring at her like he couldn't believe it. "Ask him!"

Sarandon didn't budge. She began to take one of the sacks out of his hand, which seemed to bring him back to the here and now, and he placed them in the trunk. "Don't date anyone until I have a talk with Brett about this. He thinks the world of you, Ellie."

"Go talk to him then, but I'm not changing my mind. This was all Brett's idea, not mine." She didn't feel she owed Sarandon an explanation of why Brett had come up with the idea either.

His stern gaze still on her, Sarandon immediately whipped out his phone and called Brett while she closed her hatchback. She was certain Brett wouldn't like to hear that she had posted the item in the *Silver Town Gazette*. She was surprised he hadn't called about it before now. He must not have read it.

"Hey, Brett. Sarandon, here. Did you tell Ellie to date other wolves?"

Sarandon was eyeing Ellie as she slid into her driver's seat. If she was going to date other people, she'd choose who.

"Ah hell, Brother. Well, you might want to check out the Lonely Hearts column this morning."

Ellie smiled, closed her door, and waved good-bye to Sarandon before she took off.

Sarandon pocketed his phone, and hers instantly rang. *Darien*. She sighed and answered his call. He was the pack leader and Brett's cousin, after all. Maybe it wasn't about the letter, but she suspected it was.

"Hey, Darien."

Beeping on the car panel alerted her that she had another incoming call to pick up. She smiled when she saw it was one of the two brothers who worked ski patrol.

"I'm calling as your friend and Brett's cousin to ask you not to date other wolves in the pack," Darien said. "Lelandi's in a session with a patient, but when she's through, she wants to talk with you too."

Ellie wasn't talking to Lelandi about this. She didn't need counseling. "I've got another call coming in." She hung up on Darien, knowing he wouldn't be happy about it, but tough. Yeah, he and Lelandi were in charge of the pack, but courting a wolf was her business, not pack business. She guessed her sisters hadn't read the paper yet, or she would be fielding calls from them too.

She answered the next call, this one from her first gentleman suitor. Everyone called Cantrell and his brother, Robert, Viking gods. They were both blond haired, both handsome, and both had a great sense of humor.

Before she could say anything, someone else was trying to call her. *Brett*. She ignored his call because she was busy with Cantrell. She would talk to Brett *afterward*.

"Hey, Ellie, I hear you're looking for some action. I'd take you out in a heartbeat, but I wanted to make sure you're really available. I don't want all the Silver wolves to take action against me if I pursue you," Cantrell said.

"Hey," Robert said in the background. "I'm asking first though, as long as it's okay with the pack."

Hmm, maybe it wasn't going to be easy to date a wolf in the pack, as closely knit as they were.

"Brett wanted me to start dating others as a social experiment," she said, being perfectly honest.

"Count me in," Cantrell said. "When would you like to go out to dinner?"

"But me first," Robert said.

She laughed. Now *they* would be perfect to go on dates with because if she was dating both of them, they couldn't take her too seriously.

"One of you can take me out to lunch tomorrow, and the other for dinner. You decide."

—⁓—

Hell and damnation! Brett couldn't get ahold of Ellie, and all of his brothers had already called to find out what the hell had happened between them. Then Darien called with a warning that Lelandi wanted to discuss this matter with him personally. That meant she intended to use her psychology training on him.

Damn it to hell. No way had he said he wanted Ellie to go dating wolves. Talk about a feeding frenzy!

Each of his brothers had told him to tell her he had made the dumbest mistake in the world—even though he had explained he hadn't meant her to seriously consider it—and let him know in no uncertain terms if he even thought of dating anyone else himself, they were disowning him. His Silver cousins read him the same riot act.

All Brett had thought was that it was a way to prove to her that she would dream only of him—and no one else—no matter who she went out with. Most of his Silver kin said that was the most harebrained notion they'd ever heard.

Lelandi called next while he was driving to Ellie's house. He was trying to catch up to Ellie as she headed home from the grocery store since she wouldn't answer his calls. Brett thought Darien had said Lelandi was in a session with a patient. She must have thought this was a real emergency. It was just a typical bachelor male's wolf crisis—worry about losing his girl to a bunch of hungry wolves.

"Okay, I know what you were trying to do with Ellie, and I understand. I don't think this is the way to go about it. I truly believe the two of you are perfect for each other, both from your actions and conversations I've overheard at gatherings. Would you like me to have a counseling session with the two of you?"

"No. We're fine. Really."

"Okay, but I'll warn you right now that this could lead to real trouble between the two of you."

"We'll be fine," Brett said, hoping the hell they would be. They ended the call, and he arrived at the sisters' house to see Ellie's car parked out back. He had all kinds of plans for tonight, which included exorcising a ghost and being with Ellie. What if Ellie canceled their plans so she could date someone else? He knew she'd get a blitz of calls. That may have even been why she couldn't answer *his* call.

He parked beside her car and stalked toward the house, not sure if she'd be there or at the inn. He couldn't wait until tonight to talk to her. And what was he going to say? He couldn't tell her she couldn't see any other wolves in the pack. Not without coming off as an overbearing lout.

As soon as he approached the house, he heard Laurel scolding Ellie and paused at the door.

"You are going to cause so much trouble, Ellie!" Laurel said.

"This was what Brett suggested, so I'm doing it. I'm not going to say it again."

This was *not* what he wanted.

He knocked on the door.

Everyone got quiet inside.

Then someone headed for the door. He was practically holding his breath when Meghan opened it, shook her head at him, and held the door open.

"Aren't you early for dinner?" Ellie asked.

"Can we talk?"

"Tonight. I've got stuff to do." Ellie's phone rang, and she answered it. "Hi, Radcliff? I'll have to look at my calendar. I think I'm free for dinner the day after tomorrow."

Brett opened his mouth to speak, but Laurel grabbed his arm, stepped out, and shut the door behind her so they were alone on the front porch. She released him, scowling up at him. "Fix this! CJ's mad at Ellie, and he's mad at me, as if *I* had anything to do with it!"

"I'm trying, but you see the way she is. She won't even speak to me."

"Be the big, bad wolf and make her listen to you. Or else." Laurel opened the door, walked inside, and slammed it shut.

Hell.

Ellie pocketed her phone and looked at her sisters: Laurel, who was scowling, and Meghan, who was smiling at her. She was about to say something, but then her phone rang again, and the front doorbell rang simultaneously. With phone in hand, Ellie answered the door and the phone at the same time.

Radcliff's brother, Kemp, wanted to take her out. Both of them were also on ski patrol. And the delivery man had a Red Hot Rush package for her. She couldn't remember ordering anything and hoped one of her brand-new suitors wasn't giving her a gift already. She'd told everyone this was just for fun, nothing serious. She suspected everyone was hoping they had a chance with the single she-wolf since they had a shortage of females in the pack and Meghan was seeing Peter.

She wondered if they all truly believed in ghosts or were just willing to say so to get a date with her.

When she opened the bubble-paper mailer, she found pictures of Brett in the raw. Artistic painted versions. He was beautiful. She turned around to see if either of her sisters was watching her, but Meghan was coming down the stairs, two gowns in hand, and Laurel was in the kitchen.

"Hey, was that something for me?" Meghan asked.

"No." Ellie quickly stuffed the pictures in the envelope and fought hiding them behind her back.

Meghan held up the two gowns. "Which should I wear tonight?"

"You have a mask that matches that one," Ellie said, pointing. "Why don't you wear it?"

"Okay." Meghan headed back up the stairs.

Ellie followed her, then slipped into her bedroom and tucked the envelope underneath her pillow so she could really look at all the pictures later without either of her sisters catching her at it!

Chapter 10

LATER THAT DAY, WITH *PHANTOM OF THE OPERA* MUSIC playing in the background, Ellie handed out treats to early trick-or-treaters. Her favorite was a darling Little Red Riding Hood and her daddy, the wolf. After the wave of trick-or-treaters left, Ellie saw a dashing masked Zorro arrive at the inn dressed all in black—cape, hat, pants, shirt, and boots. She knew he was Brett. It helped that she could smell him. Well, that and a ton of sage, which she thought was odd. She'd know that sexy, wolf-ish smile anywhere, mask or no. He could sweep her off her feet any day. And she was glad he didn't look pissed at her for planning to date other wolves. In fact, she thought he looked eager to prove he was the only one for her. So that was a good thing, really.

She wasn't sorry about scheduling all the dates she had for the next couple of days. If Brett was right, she would still dream about him. If he wasn't, then the dream mating just wasn't happening between them. She was certain the dates would only make their relationship stronger. She'd decided from the get-go that she would only go out with each wolf one time. Unless he happened to sweep her off her feet more than even Brett did. And she didn't think that would ever happen.

She greeted Zorro wearing her blue ball gown, her favorite, just for him. His gaze immediately shifted to the swell of her breasts. He was such a rogue. He took her hand and kissed it, just like the romantic Zorro would have done, but he moved his mouth to her neck and trailed kisses along the skin, heating her up on the chilly night. She quickly ushered him inside the lobby and shut the door before anyone saw them. She was glad her sisters were still getting ready and CJ hadn't arrived yet. Though she imagined he'd go to the house first to see Laurel there.

Zorro pulled her into his arms and crushed her against his body, kissing her soundly on the mouth.

"My, what a big sword you have, sir," she said, sweeping her hand over his sheathed sword.

"I'm fully armed," he said, "with that and more."

"A pistol?" She looked up at him, surprised.

"And fully loaded."

She reached down to feel where he had the pistol holstered, not believing he owned one unless he had borrowed one of CJ's. Brett laughed. "You won't find it there."

She pulled her hand away, and her face heated. He was such a tease. "You, sir, are a rogue."

"And you love me for it. Where is everyone?"

"Oh, still getting ready."

"I have something for you. Just wait here and I'll get it."

He was so enthusiastic that she wondered what he'd brought. She suspected it was a peace offering of some kind. He went to his car and pulled out two huge canvas bags. After she led him into the inn, he set the bags on the check-in counter and started digging things out. "These are candles that are supposed to promote relaxation. I read that some yoga instructors use them in classes. And I had to bring you flowers."

He handed her the lovely bouquet of white roses, purple mums, sage, and mint. And then he fished out a large box of chocolates.

"From my aunt Charity's shop!" She was thrilled.

"Yeah, I picked it up yesterday, but until I could get my car towed, I couldn't give them to you. Hope they're okay after sitting in a freezing car overnight."

"They'll be great. How was your car?"

"It was in good shape, surprisingly. The snow helped to protect the undercarriage when it landed on the rocks. The scrape on the side will need to be repaired, but I'll have it done later. The auto body shop is swamped right now with repairs after all the minor accidents." He lifted a huge pot out of a second bag that smelled like beef stew.

"Wow, Brett, this smells delicious. I didn't expect this."

"I know you said you were making mummy dogs, but I thought we could have this too."

"We didn't make them yet. They cook up so fast that we were waiting for you, CJ, and Peter to arrive. Should we take this to the house and—"

"No, let's have it here in case someone comes for candy. I've got bowls and utensils in here."

"Okay, let's take it into the kitchen, and we can sit at the breakfast table." They moved into the kitchen, where she placed the flowers in the center of the table. Ellie set the pot on the stove and turned it on low. "I'll let my sisters know the food is on and not to make the mummy dogs."

"I'll be right back," Brett said.

"What are you going to do?" She wondered if he'd

gotten more stuff for tonight. She couldn't believe all he'd done already. Was he trying to prove that he was the perfect boyfriend?

"I'll set out the candles."

She smiled. "Okay, I'll serve some stew for us in the meantime." She took a taste and chuckled. No wonder he smelled of sage. The stew was still hot.

She quickly called Laurel. "Hey, Brett brought dinner. Don't bother with the mummy dogs."

"What are we eating?"

"Beef stew. And it's delicious. See you in a minute."

Brett returned in a flash, still wearing his mask, and asked if he could get anything for them. He was already setting out the silverware and napkins.

"You have enough here for my sisters, CJ, Peter, and guests that drop in. This is great."

"I hope everyone loves it. I thought it tasted good."

"It does. Sure smells good too."

He poured glasses of ice water for them. Then they took their seats, and she spooned out some of the stew and ate a bite. "Really delicious."

Still wearing the mask and looking perfectly mysterious and roguish, he studied her. "You're not just saying that to be nice, are you?"

"When I fill my bowl with a second helping, I'd say no, I'm not just saying so to be nice." It was delicious.

He sighed audibly.

She smiled. "See, you *can* cook." She realized he must have really worried about it and hoped she had set his mind at ease.

"Sometimes it works, and sometimes it doesn't. Since I'm sharing it with you, I'm glad that it turned out okay." Then he studied her for a moment, and she knew what was coming next. "About the dating business…"

"No worries about that."

He frowned.

"I'm just going to date each guy once."

"In the pack."

"Yep."

He grunted.

"This is what you suggested."

"Which was a complete mistake."

"Hey," Meghan called out from the back door. "Is that stew I'm smelling? Much better than having hot dogs wrapped in crescent rolls."

"We're in the breakfast nook having Brett's delightful beef stew."

"Brett can cook?" CJ asked, sounding like he was trying to give his brother a hard time.

Everyone laughed.

CJ, Laurel, and Meghan joined them and sat down to eat. Her sisters were wearing low-cut Elizabethan gowns, Laurel's in pale blue and Meghan's in rich burgundy. CJ was sporting a sexy Robin Hood costume, which was funny because he was a deputy sheriff. Before long, Peter, the sheriff, showed up as Han Solo, another rogue, and Meghan got him a bowl of stew.

"Oh, this is great." Peter smiled at the ladies. "So did you all make it?"

"My brother did," CJ said, sounding proud of him. "Now I know he was lying all those years when he said he couldn't cook so I'd make the meals."

"It worked, didn't it?" Brett said, grinning.

Ellie was glad everyone loved his stew. "Peter, Remer said you took piano lessons from Matilda."

"Not for very long. My mom made me take them. She said it would give me focus and that maybe I'd even have some real talent. But I hated it. When the other boys were down by the river having fun, I was stuck at home playing the piano. I was so moody and difficult to live with that my mom finally said I could stop taking the lessons. I had no talent for music at all. Remer and a few of Matilda's other students were really good at it. Mervin was one of the best."

"Mervin? He never plays the piano. Lots of other instruments though," Ellie said.

"He couldn't afford to have a piano back then. And at our celebrations, he always has instruments that are more easily transported." Peter finished his beer. "Bertha Hastings also took lessons and plays beautifully, but she met John when they were young and mated. So if she'd had any thought of playing professionally, that ended that. Instead, her mate opened the hardware store, and she opened their house as a bed-and-breakfast."

"And Remer took lessons from Matilda," Brett said.

"Yeah." Peter helped himself to more stew. "He and Mary Nicholson were the only two who took lessons from Matilda and ended up playing professionally."

"Mary Nicholson? I don't remember her." CJ served himself more of the stew too.

Peter shook his head. "Don't doubt it. She was one of Matilda's first students. She was so proud of Mary. She told all of her students about the child prodigy. Mary was five when she started lessons with Matilda. She was only ten when she started playing for audiences all over. Matilda had always hoped she'd find another genius among her students. I certainly wasn't one." Peter chuckled.

"What about Remer?" Brett asked.

"He was really good at it. Enough to make a living. He worked hard to get somewhere with piano. Just like Bertha and Matilda's other students who stuck with it. Mary had a rare gift. Matilda followed Mary's career in the papers for years. She shared with us all about Mary's fame. Your great-aunt was just like her, you know. She had a real gift. She started playing when she was four and never stopped. She was so proud of Mary, but I think it hurt her feelings that the girl never kept in touch with her."

"Because she'd been her first teacher from a small town?" Ellie asked. "Well, and a wolf from her pack?"

"That was the real kicker. Mary wasn't a wolf. Her family lived in a nearby town, and her mother drove her here for lessons. They couldn't afford a piano, so she brought Mary to Silver Town several times a week to practice on Matilda's piano. Matilda even offered for Mary to come live with her so she could teach her everything she knew—even though she wasn't a wolf and that could have been a hardship for Matilda and everyone around here. The parents felt their daughter needed a *real* teacher to hone her talent so they moved to New York City. They thought of Matilda as the only local piano teacher around here."

"I bet Matilda was upset." Ellie could imagine how much Brett's great-aunt had wanted to help the girl find real success.

"She was. She never had such a brilliant pianist to

teach. Most of her students were like me, hating to go, hating the lessons, while Matilda loved to play. And she loved teaching. She'd played solo and in concerts all over. She didn't talk about it much to others. Just to her students. Still, she was a wolf, and she finally gave it all up to come home to her family and find a mate. And teach ungrateful students like me." Peter smiled.

"Was she disappointed that you quit?" Ellie thought Matilda would have felt like a failure if she couldn't show every student the joy of playing the piano.

"No, she knew my heart wasn't in it. That it was my mother's notion, not mine. Matilda was really good at understanding her students. Really patient with all of us. She wasn't a taskmaster. She wanted me to have fun while we practiced. One time, I was in a particularly sour mood. Teen hormones, you know."

Meghan chuckled.

Peter smiled at her. "I really liked this girl who was going out with a bunch of kids to run to the waterfall as wolves. They wouldn't budge on the time, and my lesson was for that same period. Matilda told me to go, run, be with my friends. She'd cover for me and secretly give me a lesson some other time when it was more convenient. She knew what it was like to be a teen. Her mother had made her take singing lessons, and she hated them. So she understood."

Ellie nodded. "I always wanted to try things out, so when I saw the *Nutcracker* ballet, I aspired to be a ballerina."

Brett reached over and squeezed her hand. "Now that I'd love to see."

She smiled at him. "I took a few lessons and discovered it was grueling work. The teacher kept making us do things over and over again, but I just wanted to wear the pretty costume and dance around onstage to the beautiful music. Mom had paid for lessons for the year, and it was the worst time of my life."

"Yeah, but you got to dance in the *Nutcracker*, and Meghan and I were so envious," Laurel said. "You were beautiful."

"You were jealous? I thought you were mad because Mom had to spend so much time taking me to lessons and rehearsals and such."

"We were," Meghan said. "Then you got flowers from a secret admirer at the theater, and we were so jealous."

Brett smiled at Ellie. "A secret admirer, eh?"

"I think it was Dad. But today, I got flowers from a masked man—even more intriguing."

Laurel suddenly took an interest in the flowers on the table. "Lovely bouquet of flowers." She cast a glance CJ's way as if he should have thought to bring *her* a bouquet. It was never too late to keep up the courtship rituals of a wolf, even if they were already mated.

Meghan then looked at Peter, who appeared just as sheepish.

"He brought candles too." Ellie was proud of him for making this Halloween so special.

"I smelled the citrus and sage when we came in the back door," Laurel said, giving her a look that said she thought more was going on than met the eye.

Ellie agreed. She thought Brett must have read that sage would chase spirits away. She couldn't fault him for trying to help, though she wished he'd talked to her about it. She had already tried sage, and it hadn't worked.

Then they heard knocks at the front door and kids calling out, "Trick or treat!"

Laurel jumped out of her seat. "I've got this one."

"I'm going too," Meghan said.

CJ, a.k.a. Robin Hood, hurried after them, a quiver of arrows slung across his back, bow in hand, and green velvet hat on his head. In his tights and belted velvet tunic, he looked pretty dapper.

"Do you know how to use that thing?" Laurel asked him as they hurried toward the front door.

"The greatest shot there is."

Meghan laughed.

Peter finished his stew and saluted them as if he were Han Solo. "See you around." And he headed out into the lobby.

Ellie heard them greeting someone and saying, "Come on in for some of Brett's stew."

After that, Ellie and Brett were busy serving stew and cleaning dishes. She overheard CJ ordering a couple dozen roses for Laurel, to be delivered to the inn pronto.

More of their friends dropped by from town, and Ellie went back to serving stew.

Everything was perfect, Brett thought as he helped to serve more stew to their visitors. "Maybe I need to get more of the stew for hungry visitors."

"You have more?"

"I made two batches—the big pot and a smaller one—but I wasn't sure you'd like it."

"Love it, but you don't have to get it. We have chips and dip. We hadn't planned on having anything else for guests," Ellie said.

"Omigod, CJ, you shouldn't have," Laurel said near the front door, but clearly she was thrilled.

"Two dozen roses," Ellie said to Brett, "to make up for not bringing her flowers like you brought me."

Brett smiled and began washing more of the dishes.

The piano began playing "Ride of the Valkyries." Brett hesitated, a scrubber in one hand, a bowl in another, his skin chilling as he glanced in the direction of the lobby.

"You hear the music playing?" Ellie asked, her voice nearly a whisper as if she were afraid the ghost would hear her and vanish.

She also sounded so hopeful that he was hearing what she was hearing that she grabbed his wrist before he could respond. He quickly put the scrubber and bowl down, and she led him into the lobby.

Mervin, the barber, was playing the song with exuberance. "Playing for my meal," he said smiling.

He often played various instruments for wolf gatherings, and Brett could understand how he might want to play the old baby grand. Brett was relieved that the music didn't mean the sage hadn't worked. He wished he could have heard Matilda play just once so he could say he'd had a ghostly experience too. Maybe then Ellie would believe him when he said he believed in her abilities.

Ellie smiled at Mervin. "You play Wagner's song beautifully. That's who wrote it, right?"

"Yeah," Meghan said. "Just beautiful. You have real talent, Mervin."

They took Mervin back to the breakfast nook to feed him, glad they still had some stew left.

"I haven't played that piece in years. I swear Matilda was moving my fingers on the keyboard, keeping me from making any mistakes."

Brett looked at Ellie, but she shook her head, most likely indicating she hadn't seen any sign of his great-aunt. That was good.

Then the trouble began. Four of the guys who served on ski patrol at the ski resort—Kemp, Radcliff, Robert, and Cantrell—all showed up. None of them wore costumes, but all bore gifts. *For Ellie*.

CJ and Laurel had followed them back to watch the proceedings, possibly worried there'd be a fight. Peter soon joined them, while Meghan was handing out candy and shouting, "Don't do anything until I'm done here."

Brett knew that for Ellie's and his sake, he should just stand by and watch, acting as though the attention from other wolves wasn't any big deal. But he couldn't. He slipped his arm around Ellie's shoulders and held her loosely at his side, saying in a wolf way *mine*.

She might be going out with other guys, but he wanted the bachelor males to know this could get serious if they thought they had any chance with her. He wasn't confining her, so if she really wanted to leave his side, it was her choice. He wasn't going to play the big, bad wolf like Laurel had suggested unless any of the wolf pack members got out of hand with Ellie. He just wanted to tell them in a subtle way that she wasn't *really* available.

They were all good-natured guys, all with a fun sense of humor, and they didn't seem to mind. He almost took them showing up with boxes of candy and vases of flowers for Ellie as a way to rib him because of her letter in the Lonely Hearts column.

He wasn't going to interfere, even though Laurel had already emailed him Ellie's calendar of dates. He was surprised they were all going to be at the Silver Town Tavern, maybe so Sam would be a witness and her pseudo-suitors wouldn't get into trouble with Darien. Or Brett. Or his brothers or cousins. That was a lot of male muscle.

Brett and his brothers and cousins often had lunch there—all except Eric, because it was too far for him to drive when he was working at the park. But Brett would try to avoid the place for the next couple of days while Ellie dated in peace.

"Well," Cantrell said, "since Zorro's looking perfectly lethal, I guess we'll see you later. Night, Ellie." He winked at her.

All the others did the same, Robert patting Brett good-naturedly on the shoulder, and then they left.

When the men were gone, Meghan joined them. "Darn, what did I miss?"

"Nothing," Ellie said.

"Ha! As crimson as your cheeks are, I know that's not true." Meghan eyed all the boxes of candy and vases of flowers, giving Peter a look that asked where her candy and flowers were. "Hmm, maybe I ought to put a letter in the Lonely Hearts column."

Peter scowled at Brett. Brett hoped Peter wouldn't drum up a traffic ticket for him on principle the next time he was out driving around.

Meghan started hauling some of the loot out to the house, and Laurel and Ellie joined her.

The guys hung back.

"What are you going to do about this?" CJ asked Brett.

"Nothing. It's her choice. She'll realize I'm the one for her, and that will be the end of it."

Peter shook his head. "This was the dumbest idea you've ever had. If Meghan places a letter in the column…" He shook his head again and stalked off.

"He's the sheriff," CJ reminded Brett. "And you've never really seen him riled." He motioned with his head for Brett to join him. "I saw the not-so-subtle way you were holding on to Ellie when the guys showed up."

"I thought I *was* being subtle."

CJ smiled darkly at him. "And the brooding look on your face—like a wolf who was ready to put a pack of wolves in their place. Not just one, but the whole lot of them at once."

"Do you think it worked?"

CJ laughed.

Mervin agreed to hand out candy for them a little while longer, and CJ and Brett walked to the house where they all shared the box of chocolates *he* had given Ellie and drank cocoa and watched *Sleepy Hollow*, the TV series about the headless horseman.

Halfway through the second episode, they heard the piano playing "The Ride of the Valkyries" again at the inn and then several other tunes.

"Mervin plays beautifully." Ellie cuddled against Brett, and he loved that she didn't seem to mind his behavior with her suitors. It was almost as though she was glad she had him in her life, and all this other was just for fun.

He also noticed everyone else watching them when

they took their seats together, seeing if their relationship was truly in trouble.

"Mervin does." Brett had his arm wrapped around Ellie, enjoying this too much to check out the inn to ensure Mervin was really playing the piano. It had to be him. But what if it wasn't?

What bothered Brett most was that he couldn't stop thinking about all the dates Ellie would be going on this week. Lunches and dinners? She wouldn't have any time for him at all.

When he went to sleep at night, all he would think of was Ellie.

———

Later that night, alone in her bedroom, Ellie pulled the pictures of Brett from underneath her pillow, set the envelope aside, and began going through them. She sighed, enjoying the way the ladies had captured him in paint. At least he wasn't aroused in the pictures, like he'd been when he was with her. He was a perfect, wolfish kind of Rodin's *Thinker* as he sat with his chin resting on his hand, his elbow on his knee, pondering life in one of the pictures. In another, he was a Greek god lying on his side, a piece of cloth draped over his private parts. So the pictures weren't all explicit. He was gorgeous, but she was glad he wasn't showing off his beautiful wares to anyone else anymore.

She knew what she would be dreaming of tonight: joining him on the couch, removing the sandal he was tying on, or giving him something to really ponder—like making red-hot love to her.

Chapter 11

BRIGHT AND EARLY THE NEXT MORNING, WITH THE snow melting off everything, Brett arrived at work feeling good about the ghost situation. He was certain he'd taken care of his great-aunt and Chrissy and that they'd found peace. He wasn't happy about Ellie dating other wolves though. From what Laurel told him, Ellie was having lunch with Cantrell and dinner with Robert. And tomorrow, she was having lunch with Kemp and dinner with Radcliff. She didn't eat big breakfasts and Brett had to be at the paper so early, so he really couldn't have breakfast with her.

He reminded himself he should be glad about the ghost situation. The MacTire sisters wouldn't have to worry about their inn guests, whose arrival was fast approaching. He just hoped he could square things between Ellie and him.

As soon as he began to type up his next story, CJ called.

"Hey, Brett, you're busted."

"What?" Brett didn't have a clue what his brother was talking about, but CJ didn't sound like he was in *real* trouble.

"Just so you know, Laurel said she suspected you had brought all that stuff packed with sage into the inn in an attempt to get rid of their ghosts."

Brett barely breathed. What could he say? It was all true.

"They were amused," CJ said. "I think."

Brett was relieved. "Did it work?"

"Since we all heard Matilda playing the piano while we were watching *Sleepy Hollow*, I'd say no."

"What? I thought Mervin was playing." Brett couldn't have been more surprised.

"Apparently not. Laurel was curious whether your sage gifts worked, because neither she nor her sisters had seen Matilda or Chrissy during the Halloween festivities. She called Mervin and asked him about the music, but he said he hadn't played the piano any more after we left. He'd only handed out candy to a couple more families. The street was empty, and he wanted to go home and watch some TV, so he locked up the front door and left through the back."

"You're sure the sisters were amused?"

"I think so. Amused that you'd do it on the sly, with the hope you could help them and Matilda at the same time. I think Laurel was a little disappointed it didn't work."

"So, it does work sometimes?"

"She says yes. Every entity is different, just like in life. Apparently, the sage or Halloween or something moved Matilda to play after everyone left."

"If Matilda plays only when everyone is gone, I guess that won't cause trouble for anyone." Though Brett reminded himself that Matilda had appeared when he was kissing Ellie, so she didn't always stay away when people were around.

"Unless she's annoyed that people are there when she wants to play," CJ said.

While listening to CJ, Brett hurried to look up other ways to expel ghosts from a place, glad that what he had done helped sometimes, even if not this time. Though he might have helped to send Chrissy away. But then he considered that the only way this might work was if he and Ellie could learn what had really happened to Matilda.

"How much did it cost you for everything?" CJ asked.

"Under a hundred."

"You sure impressed the ladies."

Brett chuckled. "It sounded like Laurel loved her roses."

"Yeah, about that... If you're going to do something like that for Ellie when Laurel and I will be there, let me know beforehand, will you?"

Brett laughed. "Peter didn't seem to be bothered that he hadn't gotten anything for Meghan."

"Laurel said Peter sent her *three dozen* roses this morning. Must have cost him a fortune."

Amused, Brett shook his head.

"Anyway, I just wanted to tell you that your scheme didn't work, the ladies are onto you, and they'll take care of the ghost issue themselves."

"I didn't think they could. Why else would the ghosts be hanging around?"

"True. They haven't had any luck so far."

"What about Stanton?"

"No. Not only is the price he's asking ludicrous, but the sisters wouldn't have any part of it."

Brett began reading how mirrors in every room could help get rid of ghosts. But the sisters had mirrors in all the inn's rooms, including in the attic. Yet, he didn't think they had one in the lobby. Still, he couldn't just hang a mirror there without first asking if the ladies wanted one.

Priest-blessed water was another option. But the one he liked the best was talking to the ghost.

"Can you help the ladies take down the Halloween lights and put up the crystal lights for the holidays? They'll be good through New Year's after that," CJ said.

"Sure thing."

"Thanks. That's a sure way to ingratiate yourself with the ladies, if you hadn't already. I'll be by a little later to help."

Brett had helped CJ set up Christmas lights all over the inn last year, so it seemed natural to do it again this holiday season. He was happy to help.

"And by the way, the first of our ski patrollers is having lunch with Ellie at Silver Town Tavern at noon. Just in case you forgot."

As if Brett would forget. He had every date listed on his calendar. He was trying hard to convince himself not to drop over there.

"Do you want to have lunch with me there? I can cancel on Laurel. She'll understand. Probably welcome it."

"No, that's okay. I've got work to do."

"All right. See you later."

How would it look if Brett did drop by to eat lunch at the tavern? Like he was checking up on Ellie. That's how.

Ellie really liked all the wolves she had scheduled dates with, but she wasn't interested in dating any of them. She figured she'd just have a meal and some conversation with them, and then she'd go out with the next guy. She was wearing jeans and a nice shirt, boots and a ski jacket like she usually would when she went out to eat.

What she hadn't expected was to see Darien and
Jake Silver sitting at a table near the one where Sam had
seated her.

"Hey, Ellie," the brothers both said in greeting. They
were smiling and didn't appear to be upset with her for
dating wolves other than their cousin. She knew that the
Silver brothers often ate here, so she should have remembered that when she had agreed to the dates. Maybe she
should have chosen to go to Silva's for lunch instead.

Then Brett's brothers sauntered in, Eric and Sarandon,
who both nodded in greeting, then joined Darien and
Jake. Tom and CJ showed up and sat at a table on the
other side of hers. Talk about feeling like she was on
view at the zoo! She'd gotten here early to get a good
table and realized Darien usually sat at a different table
back in the corner from which he watched all the com-
ings and goings as the pack leader. He wasn't usually
this close to the front door and big windows.

Tom and CJ were best friends, both the youngest by
a few minutes. Brett was best friends with them too,
and she was surprised he wasn't here having lunch with
them. She gave him credit for staying away, because
she was certain if the others knew she was eating here
today, so did Brett. She thought CJ had a lunch date with
Laurel. Ellie hoped she didn't end up here too.

Her date, Robert, arrived all smiles, wearing jeans
and a pretty blue wool sweater, and he was carrying
yet another box of chocolates and a bouquet of flowers.
Rose from Green Valley sold the flowers to everyone
in Silver Town because she was a wolf and they didn't
have their own florist shop. She actually had a nursery
too and was probably thrilled at all the recent sales.

Ellie noticed that, like the other boxes of chocolates, this one was from her aunt Charity's shop. She hoped Aunt Charity didn't learn the boxes were all for her because she was dating a bunch of different guys.

"You're early." Robert greeted the men with a tilt of his head. He didn't seem to mind that the Silvers were there watching them. Ellie knew they were without even looking in their direction because instead of conversing, they were deadly quiet.

"You're early too." She was glad he had made the effort to come early.

"I thought I'd grab a table first. I couldn't miss this for the world."

She thought he might be referring to the chance to rib Brett rather than their actual date. And she loved what a good sport he was. She wondered if CJ would tell Brett the details of the date since he wasn't here.

Then the door jingled. She tried not to look, tried to concentrate on what Robert was saying, but as soon as she heard the door close and smelled Brett's sexy scent, her pheromones began pinging all over the place.

A fine sheen of perspiration appeared, and she felt self-conscious. All because Brett was the one she wanted to be with. No one else. Still, she held her chin up, smiled at Brett in greeting, and then tried once again to concentrate on Robert's conversation. He was talking about taking her up on the slopes for more advanced ski lessons. He was on ski patrol, but he also took turns giving lessons.

Private, one-on-one lessons.

She knew all the Silver men were excellent skiers, and all but Darien gave lessons from time to time. So she suspected Brett wouldn't like it if she signed up for private lessons with any of the guys she was dating. She also suspected that all of them would make the offer.

She hadn't realized how much of a strain going out with other guys could be though. She'd become familiar with Brett, and she liked the easiness they had between them. Of course, some of the uneasiness she was feeling was because Brett was now watching her. Maybe he wasn't. Maybe he was just visiting with his brother and cousin. They were awfully quiet over there. Like they were listening in on the conversation.

"So, do you believe in ghosts? Have you seen any?" she asked Robert, because that was one of her stipulations for dating anyone else.

"Nah, never saw one, but I like to keep an open mind."

Well, not that she really wanted to take this dating business with Robert anywhere, but she realized that some of the guys might have wanted to go out with her whether they were into ghosts or not. At least she was a little further along with Brett with regard to the ghost issue.

She glanced in Brett's direction, unable to keep from looking. He smiled at her and winked, the cad.

"Do you have time to take a walk after lunch?" she asked Robert, her mind made up to remind Brett that this was what *he* had suggested.

Robert glanced at all the Silver men as if deciding if he could do it without having a pack of wolves at his throat.

"That's okay. I've got to run." She was really glad he hadn't wanted to. She thanked him for a lovely lunch, and he quickly paid the bill and hurried after her as she carried her flowers and box of candy outside. "Were they intimidating you?" she asked Robert as he joined her and opened her car door.

"Nah, not really. I knew if I asked you out and had lunch here, the pack of them would show up. Everyone's looking out for everyone's welfare. So I knew what to expect and it didn't bother me."

"You didn't ask me to go anywhere else for a date."

Robert smiled. "I want to live a few more years."

She laughed. "I had fun. And thanks so much for the roses and candy."

"I have to warn you... So many of us dropped by your aunt Charity's candy shop for boxes of candy that she asked who the lucky girls were. When we all said you, she pursed her lips and didn't look real pleased. You might be getting a call later."

"All of you went in at the same time?" Ellie couldn't believe it.

"Yeah, to make sure we all got something different. Once Charity realized all the boxes of candy were for you, she told us which you preferred."

"Anything chocolate."

"That's what she said."

Ellie wondered if she was going to get a call from her aunt with more motherly advice. Tonight she had dinner with Cantrell, but afterward she had to get back home to help put up lights so she'd still see Brett. It should have bothered her that he was going to do all that work for them when she was seeing other guys, but he had offered.

Before she could climb into her car, Eric headed out of the tavern, glanced at them and nodded, then hurried to his vehicle. She was kind of surprised to see him here because he had such a long drive to make from the park as a ranger. Darien and Jake left after that. Then Sarandon. It was a steady stream of Silver wolves checking out the situation.

Robert looked like he was waiting for everyone to take off so he could give her a kiss, but she smiled and said good-bye and headed out, not wanting him to kiss her and think she might be interested in more.

"He's not going to kiss her," Brett said to CJ and Tom.

"Hell, we're talking about Robert here," CJ said. "If he could get away with it, he'd kiss her."

Tom raised his bottle of water in a salute. "I'm sure my brothers and your brother thwarted him."

Brett was certain of it too, as quickly as Eric left the tavern after Robert and Ellie. He knew Eric had really left so soon because he had to get back to the park. Brett couldn't believe Eric had made the time to even come here for this. Appreciating his older brother's concern, Brett knew Eric was still annoyed with him for even suggesting that Ellie should date anyone else. All the Silver men were still in agreement over that, no matter how much Brett tried to explain his perfectly plausible supposition and mistake in sharing it with her.

When CJ had texted Brett that he and the rest of the gang were at the tavern and missing him, Brett had smiled and texted him back, saying he was on his way. It reminded him of the old days when they'd looked out for each other when a wolf encroached on their territory.

"I thought you had a date with Laurel." Brett finished his sandwich.

"She canceled on me and said if I didn't get my ass over here and watch over Ellie, I was in the doghouse. And you know that's pretty bad. Hell, I've got to come back here for dinner too."

Tom and Brett laughed.

"So how long are you going to let this go on?" Tom took another swig of his water.

"She's got dates with four guys. That should be enough."

"To realize you're the one for her?" CJ asked.

At least Brett hoped so.

CJ finished his sandwich. "Are you still hanging lights tonight?"

"Yeah, whether she'll be there or not." A promise was a promise.

"Have any dinner plans?" CJ asked.

Brett smiled. He sure as hell did.

Chapter 12

BRETT WASN'T SURE WHAT KIND OF RECEPTION HE would receive when he arrived at the inn, but he saw the sisters already had the ladders set up and the lights were spread out, ready to hang. He swore Meghan and Laurel were smiling at him more today. Clearly, they were amused by his antics with the sage last night. Luckily, they didn't seem annoyed over the dating business with Ellie.

Ellie was just as friendly as she had been, not aloof or anything, so he assumed he was still all right with her.

They had already finished taking down all the Halloween lights along the walkways. Laurel and Meghan were concentrating on decorating the white picket fence out front with bows and garlands, while Ellie helped him remove the Halloween lights off the roof.

Out of earshot of her sisters, Brett said, "I hope you're not upset with me for the sage gifts."

"Yoga? The candles?" Ellie asked, brow raised. She was wearing formfitting jeans, suede boots, and a short-waisted ski jacket as she took the lights from him. She looked sexy and huggable.

"For relaxation. Sure. You can find the explanation on the Internet."

"For ghosts? Or to cover up what you were up to?"

He sighed in an exaggerated way. "Forgive me?" He handed the last of the orange lights down to her. Then he climbed off the ladder, took the lights from her to set on the porch railing, and gathered her into his arms. "I was only trying to help."

He couldn't last at this courting business. CJ's had been such a whirlwind affair with Laurel, but Brett really wanted to woo Ellie like a wolf should. He wanted more. Everything. The intimacy only two mated wolves could share. She felt so warm and soft and loving in his arms. He wanted them to be together every night, not just have dates and have to say good-bye over and over again. He didn't want to dream of her after she left; he wanted to have her in his arms.

Even so, she had her hands against his chest in a way that said they still needed to talk about last night before she could forgive him. "And the bouquet?"

"I was planning to get a flower bouquet for you, just something pretty. I didn't even know anyone added herbs to them. I checked out Rose's online catalog of floral arrangements, and I saw the one with sage and mint and asked for it."

"For the ghosts."

"It couldn't hurt. I just thought the sage would help 'clear the air' and you wouldn't have to worry about my great-aunt disturbing your guests. Not to mention I thought she needed to find her way to the light and join my great-uncle, if that's what happens. Anyway, I looked on the Internet to see what would work, and lots of ghost sites said sage did the trick. I guess not with Matilda though."

Smiling, Ellie ran her hands up his chest and circled her arms around his neck, pressing her breasts against his body. "So what else did you learn?"

"I read that mirrors could work. You have a mirror in the attic room where Chrissy messes with the lights. And a mirror in the lavender room in the basement where she used to stay. None in the lobby. It doesn't really seem to work on one ghost, so I'm not sure it would on another. I'm sorry I wasn't successful."

Ellie sighed. "We've tried different things. The sage, of course, but not to the extent you did. Matilda obviously wasn't bothered by it. But you did hear her playing."

"And so did CJ and Peter. Unless Mervin really was playing, and he didn't want to say so."

"I doubt he would have fabricated his story."

"Then you know what that means?" Brett asked.

"You have to believe in ghosts."

"Absolutely. Will Laurel now believe I'm fine knowing about your abilities?"

Ellie pulled away and handed him the clear lights to hang on the inn. "She was really amused by your sage display last night. She was impressed you had researched it when you didn't really believe, and that you were trying to help us so we wouldn't have any further trouble. So I'd say you earned some big brownie points." She smiled up at him, and he wanted to howl at his success. Even if he hadn't succeeded with the ghosts.

"I was surprised to see you having dinner at the tavern tonight with CJ while I ate with Cantrell. And yet I should have figured you or some of the other Silver relations would be there."

"CJ asked me. He mentioned something about Laurel ordering him to or he was in the doghouse."

Ellie laughed. "At first, I didn't think you were

coming to the tavern for lunch when I was there with Robert. Did you get hung up on a job?"

"Truly? I had planned to give you your space. Then CJ called and said everyone was there. I couldn't be the *only* one who didn't show up for a Silver gathering for lunch."

She shook her head. "Luckily, Robert isn't easily intimidated."

"Which is why we were all there!"

———✳———

Ellie couldn't help but love the way Brett was trying to aid them with the ghost issue. She sure appreciated him helping with the lights too. With his and CJ's help, it had taken them half the time. Speaking of which, CJ pulled up in their parking area and hurried to hang the remaining lights. Ellie was glad Brett was concerned about her dates too and couldn't fault the alpha male for making sure nothing got out of hand.

"I would love more of that stew you fixed for us," Laurel said to Brett as they finished the decorating and went to the house. "I guess we'll have to make do with corned beef, cabbage, and red potatoes tonight, even though I know a couple of you had a light dinner earlier."

"Works for me," CJ said. "I just had peanuts and a beer at the tavern."

Brett agreed. "Salty peanuts and a soda."

Ellie had eaten a salad because Laurel had told her in no uncertain terms that she was eating dinner with Brett and CJ tonight because they were putting up the lights for them, so she'd gone light on lunch and was hungry again. She had told her sister she didn't even think salads were on the menu at the tavern, but Silva had made one especially for her. Ellie suspected Laurel had called Silva beforehand.

Ellie wondered about Peter and Meghan's relationship, but she thought something was a little off. Brett had taken it slower with her, but that had a lot to do with her concern about the issue of ghosts. And Laurel had hooked up with CJ so fast. Though they were good for each other and she was thrilled for them, Ellie had preferred a slower pace to get to know Brett. She'd been rethinking that idea when he'd begun to ask her out every night. She enjoyed being with him. They seemed to suit each other perfectly. And now that he was finally initiated into the world of ghosts, she really thought they had a chance.

Tomorrow, Ellie had the notion of going for an early-morning wolf run with Brett at the ski resort since she was tied up for lunch and dinner again. The resort wouldn't open for another couple of days. Though pack members often ran along the ski trails when the ski resort closed for skiing at night, she wanted to see the new ski trails before anyone got to ski on them.

As soon as she mentioned the plan, both Laurel and Meghan wanted to go too. Which would be fine, but Ellie had really wanted a wolf date with Brett. Still, when they all sat down to eat, CJ said, "Sounds like a good plan. I'll ask if anyone else wants to run with us."

Ellie wanted to groan out loud. CJ was probably concerned about ensuring everyone remained safe. She smiled at Brett when he winked at her, and she figured he knew she'd only wanted to run with him.

"Piano lessons after dinner?" Brett asked.

She'd almost forgotten about them. Which was why she wasn't very good at sticking with something like that. "Sure. I'd like to." Once she had it in mind to do it, she was fine with the notion.

"This is delicious, ladies," Brett said. "I never thought of having the meal for any day other than St. Patrick's."

"We love to have it any time of year," Meghan said. "And thanks so much for all the help with the lights. We really appreciate it. We were thinking of paying someone to hang them next year."

"I don't mind doing it," Brett said.

"Me either. With all of us hanging them, it's done in no time," CJ agreed.

"Okay, well, we really didn't want you to feel like we're imposing." Meghan took a sip of the Irish beer.

"You're not imposing," Brett said. "Believe me, if we couldn't do it, we'd say so."

"Oh, and I checked with the owners of the vintage Plymouths. I went by and had a look at their cars. They were the same color as when you took the photos for the newspaper. None of them had any scrapes on them. And all the owners said some variation on *Are you crazy?* No way would they have taken their pride and joys out in that kind of weather," CJ said. "They were all stored for the winter."

"Okay, good. Hope no one was too put out about it. I'm glad the driver wasn't one of our people," Brett said.

Ellie figured he would never get to the bottom of who hit him having not seen a license plate, unless he miraculously saw the car come into town at some later date. Which really irritated her. She wanted the person responsible to pay.

After dinner, Ellie and Brett began practicing their lessons. They were having so much fun with it—even though they alternated between doing a great job and messing up big time—that they tried playing a duet listed on the Internet for beginning students: "Garry Owen," a good old Irish drinking song.

"My dad used to play this on a fiddle. I wonder what he'd think of me attempting to play it as a duet on the piano."

"He'd be proud of you."

The music was beautiful, but their version had them laughing out loud. They had to place their thumbs side by side, not together, but it was hard for them when moving fast. If they practiced their scales and exercises to increase finger coordination, they'd master it. She was certain.

"We have to keep practicing that piece," Ellie said, "and play it during Victorian Days."

"I agree. It'll be great. Want to try again?"

They practiced for another hour, and Ellie even forgot to watch for Matilda like she had earlier because she was having such a great time. They really were getting better at this.

For the first time in her life, Ellie thought she might be able to stick to lessons and enjoy them. Only because Matilda had started teaching her and Brett was taking them with her.

She didn't know what to think of his great-aunt's distress over the comment she'd made about her dad dying of pneumonia. Had her death really been foul play? Ellie wasn't sure they could learn anything about his great-aunt's death any other way other than what she could find out from Matilda. Brett was an investigative reporter though. Maybe they could learn the truth by digging into the past.

Brett took Ellie's hand and helped her from the bench, pulled her close, and started to kiss her slow and easy, building up to something hot and sexy and sizzling. Her blood was on fire as he held her face tenderly in his hands and pressed her back against the piano. A small voice warned her that Matilda could show up at any time, tsking away, but Ellie didn't want to lose the moment. She wrapped her arms around his neck and kissed him right back. She needed this after a day of dating other guys who didn't make her blood heat and her senses spin out of control.

She needed Brett, needed the closeness, the heat of his body, the warmth of his touch, the way he was caring, protective, and always so helpful. Would she dream about Robert or Cantrell tonight? She doubted it. She and Brett had chemistry that neither of the other men had with her. She wanted to cancel the other two dates. She'd already turned down a handful of men, and then the calls had halted. She was amazed at how quickly the word spread around a pack.

Ellie assumed the word also had gone out that the Silver men had shown up at the tavern in protective pack mode, and anyone who wanted to go out with her while Brett and she still had a chance to be mates didn't have a prayer.

Brett was pressing his wickedly aroused body against hers now, and she knew he could smell how aroused she was too. She wanted to tell him she was ready to cancel her next two dates, but she couldn't.

He finally ended the kiss, pressing his forehead against hers, and sighed in a frustrated way. "I'll walk you back to the house."

"No need," she said, but he was all protective wolf, so he did anyway. With one last kiss, she said good night and watched him go, heading inside to find Meghan watching her. CJ and Laurel had already left.

Meghan smiled, holding up a chocolate bonbon from one of the many boxes of candy. "Aunt Charity called. She said business was so brisk because of you that she wanted to know when I was going to do the same thing."

"If you do the same thing and we eat all the candy, we won't fit into our wolf coats. So Aunt Charity wasn't upset that I was seeing all these different wolves?"

"No. She was more amused than anything because they all came together to pick out the boxes of candy, making sure no one bought a fancier box than the others. Not only that, but she assumed Brett and his Silver kin were watching the situation closely. Laurel said the guys all chaperoned you." Meghan laughed. "I love the Silver Town wolf pack."

So did Ellie. She couldn't imagine living anywhere else. "Night, Meghan. Tomorrow will be here before we know it, and we've got a wolf run first thing."

"Night, Ellie. We'll need to run ten times daily after eating all these sweets."

Ellie took a hot shower, thought about how wonderful it would be if she were taking one with Brett, and finally climbed into bed. And felt the Red Hot Rush package with the prints of him under her pillow. She quickly pulled them out, settled back against her mattress, and smiled at the sexy hunk in her hands again.

No wonder when she closed her eyes that night, all she could think of was him stripping out of his clothes, aroused and looking devilishly sexy, like a wolf hunting for a she-wolf mate.

———

"Damn it, Ellie," Brett said, frustrated when he woke to find she wasn't on top of him as he had dreamed. No way was this anything but dream mating, as far as he was concerned. He slipped into the shower and took a cold one. He didn't care if she was dating anyone else. He was going to ask her to mate him. He was just trying to decide the perfect occasion to ask her. After all, he would only do this once and he had to do it just right.

Chapter 13

EAGER TO RUN WITH BRETT EARLY THE NEXT morning, Ellie was a little disappointed they wouldn't be running alone.

She gathered with the rest of the wolves, who had left their clothes in the lockers at the ski hut and run out into the snow in their wolf coats. At least twenty-five wolves had shown up to dedicate the trails before the ski resort opened for the season. She smiled at Brett as he headed straight for her and nuzzled her. Those around them watched. It wasn't nosiness on the other wolves' part, but a way of keeping up on which bachelor wolves were off-limits to others, how pack dynamics might be changing, and what it meant for the rest of the pack. Especially when Ellie had dated two other wolves so far. With the way she and Brett reacted to each other, he was showing just how much he loved being with her. She saw Robert and Cantrell, both of whom wagged their tails at her, but neither dared approach when Brett was there.

Ellie and her sisters were well-liked and she knew the other wolves were glad she and Meghan were courting wolves in the pack. It gave the pack stability, camaraderie, and a sense of place within the pack.

Wolves split off into smaller groups, some going on the trails, others cutting through the fresh snow and making their own trails. Even though the point was to check out the new ski trails, Brett led Ellie up an old trail, all the way to the top of one of the ridges, away from the others. He wanted her all to himself, just as she had planned to run with him alone. She was having fun watching the other wolves playing and running along the trails below, and disappearing from sight behind the pine trees, while she was on the top of the world.

Then Brett nuzzled her, standing next to her, his body heat warming her. Up here with him like this, she felt like she was his mate, like they were pack leaders of the mountain. It felt just right.

He led her down the back side of the mountain where no trails existed, and they ran and ran until they stopped at a flowing creek and sipped water, smiling at each other. They were alone in the woods, enjoying nature like wolves would, except that they didn't have to worry about where to find their next meal.

She sat down and watched the river flowing by, and he nuzzled her face. She smiled at him and nuzzled him back. He nipped at her muzzle and rolled onto his back in a playful, loving, submissive way. She rested her foreleg over his chest and licked at his chin, enjoying the moment. She wanted to return here with him another day.

They heard rustling in the underbrush nearby, and both instantly stood, peering into the woods and searching for the source of the noise. And saw a cougar. The golden cougar soon spied them, its green eyes watchful, wary, its body ready to attack if the wolves approached him. The big cat knew it didn't have any recourse but to move out of the territory. Even so, Brett lifted his chin and howled. And Ellie quickly followed suit.

Several howls came in response.

The cat slunk off into the pines, and Brett and Ellie headed up the mountain again, their hearts pounding. She knew two wolves could fight off a cougar, but the cat's wicked claws and teeth could be dangerous.

As soon as they came down off the mountain, Brett and Ellie went into the ski hut to shift and dress, then met outside. Others had already left to go to work. Some were still enjoying the run.

"I hope no one else ran into the cougar," Ellie said.

"With all of us howling, no way. And the others will amass and chase it off if it lingers in the area."

She loved how the pack worked together.

Brett and Ellie were headed for the parking area when they saw her ghost-buster cousins.

"They sure are spending a lot of time in our pack's territory," Ellie said.

Brett loved when she talked about the pack like that, acknowledging that she was a full member now. "They're producing a new ghost show here. The inn isn't the only place that is haunted. They're doing one about the ghosts in the silver mines."

"As long as they don't come looking for one at the inn."

They saw Stanton in his black wolf form leading his brothers toward the ski hut, but as soon as they observed Brett and Ellie, the Wernickes hesitated.

"Come on. Let's go." Ellie quickly climbed into Brett's car and waved at her cousins, and then Brett backed out of the parking lot and drove toward one of the exits.

"You don't think they just want to be friendly?"

"No. I don't believe so."

"You might be right." Before Brett left the parking area, a vintage, dark-steel-gray Plymouth that looked suspiciously like the one that had hit his car caught his eye. He pulled in beside it, parked, and got out of his vehicle.

"Don't tell me that's the car that hit yours." Ellie hurried to join him.

"It sure looks like it." Brett walked over to the driver's side of the car and examined the paint to see if he could find any scrapes or other damage. He didn't see any. But the likelihood of two cars that looked so much alike being in the same vicinity at the same time was miniscule. And since the ski resort wasn't open yet, the vehicle had to be wolf-owned.

Brett took in several deep breaths next to the door handle. "Stanton Wernicke." He couldn't believe Stanton could be the hit-and-run driver when he'd acted as though he wanted to be on decent terms with the pack.

"I was thinking the same thing. But, Brett? This car is…inhabited."

Brett shifted his attention from the car to Ellie. "A ghost?"

"I feel it. A strong sense of it. I can't see anything. I don't always see a ghost."

"So you're saying Stanton's driving a haunted vintage Plymouth? Maybe he's driving it to see if the car is haunted, and they're using it for one of their TV shows."

"Could be. Do you see any damage on the car?" Ellie was leaning over to get a closer look.

"No. But I smell new paint."

"Yeah, me too."

"I can't believe there's another car that looks so much like the one that hit mine."

"I agree, and I believe the fresh paint smell confirms it. I guess you'll want to wait for them and talk to Stanton," Ellie said.

"Yeah. If you don't mind."

"No. You need to learn if he did hit you and make him pay for the damages."

Brett pulled Ellie in for a hug. "You know we're going to have to do something about this…thing between us."

"I feel that 'thing' between us growing."

He laughed and kissed Ellie's cold nose. "That too." He saw Vernon Wernicke headed for the brothers' blue van. Stanton and Yolan continued on their way to the vintage car, the brothers' brows raised in question to see Ellie and Brett standing beside the vehicle.

"Can we help you with something?" Stanton was being congenial but wary.

"The blizzard was really something the other day, wasn't it?" Brett asked.

"Yeah. I'm surprised the ski resort isn't open already."

Brett leaned against the Plymouth. "It's opening tomorrow. Did you see anything unusual when you were driving to Green Valley from Silver Town during the blizzard?"

Yolan cleared his throat as if he wanted to say something, but since Stanton was the one in charge of his brothers, Yolan didn't venture a comment. Vernon pulled the van up on the other side of the Plymouth and got out.

"Got something to say, Yolan?" Brett asked.

CJ and Peter headed their way across the snowy parking lot, their boots crunching in the partially frozen top layer of snow.

"What are you suggesting?" Stanton folded his arms across his chest.

"You sideswiped Brett's car the night of the blizzard, forcing him off the road." Ellie sounded highly irritated, her face red with annoyance.

Before Stanton could say anything, Peter motioned to the vintage Plymouth and asked Brett, "Is that the one that hit you?"

"Well, Stanton? You want to make amends with the pack. You want to be accepted whenever you come through our territory. So what happened the other night?" Brett asked.

"Hell, none of you would believe me." Stanton glanced at Ellie as if thinking she might be the exception.

"Okay, so what happened? You hit Brett's car and were afraid you'd lose control and continued on your way? Your actions still constitute a hit-and-run, you know," Peter said.

"And you caused Brett's car to land in the ditch, leaving him stranded. What if he had been injured?" CJ asked, his voice terse.

Yolan finally found his tongue. "It was the ghost."

"What ghost?" CJ still sounded highly irritated, a pair of cuffs now dangling from his hand.

"The one we're doing a new show about." Stanton frowned at Ellie. "You sense it, don't you?"

"Yeah, but the ghost wasn't driving the car. You were," Ellie said.

"The entity took control of the car. Yolan and Vernon can verify that it did. One minute I was driving, and the next, I wasn't. I was trying to move the car over to my side of the road. Visibility was low, but I saw the car's headlights approaching. I couldn't turn the wheel, no matter how much I tried. I managed to slow down, but I couldn't stop it. I had no control over the brakes. I told my brothers at the time that I couldn't avoid the oncoming car."

"He did. He's telling the truth," Yolan said. "We were hollering at him to pull over, in case he didn't see the car. He yelled back at us that he was trying, but that the ghost was pulling the steering wheel the other way. I think we would have had a head-on collision if Stanton hadn't been trying so hard to turn the wheel in the other direction. As to the brakes, we had the car checked out when we took it to the shop—"

"For a new paint job?" Brett asked.

"Uh, well, yeah. We have to return it to the owner in pristine condition, but we're still driving it to verify what's going on for the show," Yolan said. "The only time the ghost—Shorty Bill Smith, the owner of the vehicle originally—takes over is when the road is covered with snow, or when it's snowing. We had to see if we could document his presence during the blizzard. Stanton had driven the car several times on clear roads, no hint of snow before this, and nothing happened. The current owner, Shorty's grandson, insists the car is haunted during the winter months, and he wants us to do something about it besides use it in our show. He wants us to get rid of the entity."

"During a blizzard," Brett said incredulously. "You could have destroyed the car and killed yourselves or me in the process."

"We didn't," Stanton said, sounding defensive. "Shorty wouldn't let me stop to see if you were okay, though I didn't know who you were. We tried to call the sheriff's department to let Peter know that someone was in the ditch, but we couldn't get any reception. If you tried to call on your cell phone, you probably learned the same thing and know that we're telling the truth."

"About the cell reception, yes. I couldn't reach anyone out there. About the ghost?" Brett raised his brows.

"Yeah. Yolan tried to exorcise it because we were afraid Shorty was going to try to kill us for driving his car," Stanton said. "Hey, you write for a newspaper. You could do an article about this since you were a firsthand witness."

"Oh, I'm sure your producer would love to hear you caused a hit-and-run accident, leaving a man stranded out in the blizzard, someone who could have died if three sisters hadn't come to his rescue." Ellie smiled evilly. "Yeah, maybe Brett should write that story."

Brett smiled at her.

"On second thought, maybe not," Stanton said.

"Why would anyone take a classic car out in the winter though? Most car owners in snowy climates like ours put their cars in storage," CJ said.

"The problem is the engine revs up and the horn blasts with one of those *ahh-woo-gah* sounds, disturbing the grandson and his family in the middle of the night, but only once it begins to snow. It's like clockwork. The owner removes the battery to winterize the car," Stanton said. "So even if someone were trying to play a prank on the grandson, the prankster would have to bring his own battery with him."

Brett nodded, conceding that it sounded plausible, if any of this could be.

"You're under arrest for a hit-and-run, Stanton Wernicke," Peter said, and CJ placed the handcuffs on him.

"Wait. I'm telling you the truth. Why would I be driving the old Plymouth if we hadn't suspected it was haunted? Call the producer. He'll tell you we're investigating this." Stanton rattled his bracelets. "You don't need these anyway. I'm going with you. Just call them."

"You were at the wheel. You didn't report a hit-and-run accident any time after the accident, not even when you were closer to town and could get reception. We could have searched for the driver of the other vehicle and made sure he or she was okay." Peter pulled Stanton toward the sheriff's car.

"Call my lawyer," Stanton told his brothers. "Right now."

Vernon got on his cell phone while Peter escorted Stanton the rest of the way to his car. "I thought you were working on a story about the silver mine ghosts."

"We were, until we got sidetracked with this project. The guy was begging us to take his case," Stanton said.

Yolan motioned to Stanton. "He was telling the truth."

"It doesn't excuse him from not reporting the accident as soon after as he could have." CJ glanced at the damage done to Brett's car.

Ellie shook her head. "If the car isn't safe to drive, you shouldn't be taking it on the road."

Brett completely agreed with her.

"That's our job," Yolan said.

"You couldn't exorcise it?" Brett asked.

"Not this time. Ghosts can have a real mind of their own, just like people."

"What do we do now?" Vernon asked CJ.

"We'll have the car inspected, and then someone can take it to wherever it belongs, once someone picks up the tab for Brett's damages," CJ said.

"Ready to go home?" Brett saw that Ellie was shivering, and he didn't want her out in the cold any longer if they could go.

She was staring at the car again though. "He died in a blizzard? In the car?"

"Yeah," Yolan said. "Shorty had a wife and son he left behind. The son kept the car locked up in a garage but let reporters see it for news stories over the years. He never would do anything with it. Just left it like it was with a crumpled front bumper, bloodied broken windshield that Shorty's head impacted with when the car hit the tree, and the tons of bullet holes all over the car. A real mess. A lot of newspaper accounts about the guy and his car were written periodically over the years.

"When Shorty's son died, he willed the car to his grandson. He wanted to showcase the car the way it looked before his grandfather wrecked it and pretend his grandfather had never been a bank robber. The grandson inherited the car and refurbished it. He swears the car has a mind of its own. He called us to see if we could do anything about it. We were interested to see if it was truly haunted. It was different than other ghost stories we've done, and we're always trying to find unusual stories for the show."

"The previous owner was a bank robber? A violent criminal? But your first priority is to do a TV show on it. Instead of your first priority being people's safety." Ellie narrowed her eyes.

"How did we know it was really haunted? That's the

deal with what we do. People say things are haunted all the time. We have to investigate them to prove they are or aren't. Ghosts don't always appear for us even if they do exist. We had mechanics look it over, and they assured us it was safe. At least from a physical standpoint. We'd taken it out several times and nothing happened. So we were certain we had to check it out when it was snowing, just like the grandson said we had to. We didn't know the ghost would take over the car like that and sideswipe another vehicle."

"Had that happened when the grandson was driving it?" Brett asked.

"No. Though he said sometimes he'd see his grandfather's face in the rearview mirror. He looked similar to the grandson's father at that age. The grandson looks similar to the grandfather too. Anyway, the ghost didn't do anything that would endanger the grandson except give him a near heart attack."

"In a case like that, it sounds to me like the car should be buried with its owner. It belongs to him. Once it's buried, that will be the end of that, and he'll be at peace," Ellie said.

"So who is haunting *you*, Ellie?" Vernon sounded pissed. "I hear you need a ghost exorcised yourself. Should you tear down the inn and bury the rubble to get rid of your ghosts?"

"It's obviously not the same thing." Ellie tilted her head to the side in a scornful way. "Shorty most likely died in a violent way in the car. He was probably attached to that car. And trying to separate the two could be impossible. What if the owner dies in a car crash that Shorty causes? Wouldn't you feel responsible?"

"You might be right," Yolan said. Vernon looked furious with him for agreeing with Ellie. "The Plymouth was his getaway vehicle. In the business he was involved in, nothing would have been more important to him."

"Getaway car for a bunch of violent criminals?" Ellie asked.

"He was one of the bank robbers, but the Feds got tipped off somehow and the others never made it out of the bank alive. He was the only one who escaped and tore off in the car. The feds and local police were chasing him, and the snow was coming down heavily. Snow and ice covered the roads already. He hit another couple of cars, but they were big and heavy like his and didn't suffer much damage. His car was riddled with bullets before he lost control, slid off the road, and hit a tree.

"They thought maybe he'd been shot. Despite the barrage of bullets, he never suffered one gunshot wound. After plowing into the tree, he lay gasping for breath, and the feds asked him why he did it. Why had he robbed the banks? He said the bank had foreclosed on his family's farm. His father committed suicide. His mother died of a broken heart two weeks later. And Shorty wanted revenge," Vernon said.

"Okay, so he got his revenge. Sometimes spirits like that won't give up no matter what," Ellie said. "No matter how capable you think you are at showing them the way out." She directed her last comment to Yolan.

He inclined his head a little in acknowledgment.

Vernon's phone rang. "Yeah? Okay, we'll meet you there." He ended the call and said to Yolan, "Come on. Let's go. We need to meet with the lawyer at the jailhouse."

"Who's going to drive the car?" Yolan jerked his thumb in the direction of the vintage car.

"Stanton. Unless you want to. No way am I driving it."

"Not me," Yolan said. "He's in charge. He can handle it or have it towed."

"He'll have to pay to have it towed. If all of this can be believed, no one's driving that car in the snow from the ski resort," CJ said.

"He'll love to hear that," Vernon said.

Yolan and Vernon climbed into their van and drove off toward town.

"What do you think, Ellie?" CJ asked.

Brett pulled her in close to warm her up.

"It's haunted. I wouldn't even want to ride in it."

"Could you exorcise it?" CJ asked.

"Maybe, but I really wouldn't want to try. Not if you have to drive it to get him to make his presence known. The car was used in criminal activities. The owner was a criminal. I told you what I'd do with it."

"I can imagine what the owner of the car now would say to that." Brett rubbed Ellie's arm to warm her further. "Are you ready to go now?"

"Yeah."

They said good-bye to CJ and left.

"I was surprised to hear Yolan couldn't exorcise Shorty." Brett turned the car heat on high for Ellie.

She settled back in her car seat. "That's the thing. Making a claim like that is setting yourself up for failure in this business. We have to have an open mind and learn what we can about the entity. In no way do I automatically believe I can always take care of the spirit. Sometimes I can. Sometimes not."

"If we can't get Matilda to leave, we'll have to move the piano, won't we? Maybe back to my house?"

"Or to our house, if you'd rather move it there. It's closer. But she may disturb us just as much. She hasn't bothered you in the past. She might not if the piano is returned to your house. How do you feel about it?"

"Whatever you want to do is fine by me. I know we can't have her disturbing your guests. You said Chrissy was angry about Matilda being there. How do you know that's what it's all about?"

"She told me. Well, us. My sisters and me."

"She spoke to you?"

"Yeah. Some ghosts will. Others won't or can't. We never know for sure."

"What I don't understand is why the change? I never heard Aunt Matilda play before."

"Maybe she's angry you moved the piano out of her family's home. Or because of the two of us were kissing. Well, it's like she popped in to chaperone us and that was it. Now she's here and can't or won't leave."

"Do you think moving the piano back to my home will appease her?"

"Truthfully? I'm not sure. There was a case at a castle I read about concerning a woman who had a minor title and was destitute. A laird took her in and gave her lodging, clothes, and food free of charge. She was his ward. When she became pregnant by someone on his work staff, he flew into a rage and killed her. The castle has been haunted ever since. Visitors to the castle—now a museum—periodically see a young woman in the clothes of the earlier century in the library. Visitors and staff have been telling stories forever about the woman and the laird.

"So the castle's preservation society finally had the floor taken up to see if they could find any evidence that the woman had been buried there. Lo and behold, the woman's remains and those of her unborn child were discovered. They buried the remains in a cemetery plot at the castle. She had such a fit about it that they returned her to the library and buried her where she had been before. So sometimes what you think will be a textbook way to give a person peace doesn't work at all."

"I would never have thought it. Stories I've seen about ghosts always show that finding the remains of someone who has been murdered and giving them a proper burial works. You must read up on a lot of cases."

"Some. When we're trying to deal with one, mostly in the business of renovating Victorian inns, we'll see if anyone has encountered what we have and how they dealt with it. Sometimes we find a solution that works for us that way. Sometimes we don't. That's why we always say what works for one won't necessarily work for another."

"So did the woman at the castle settle down there?"

"She did. Some say they still see her, but she seems to be at peace where she is."

"I hope my great-aunt died of natural causes and not because of anyone neglecting her or a drowning, accidental or otherwise. If it isn't about how she died, what else could be causing Matilda to manifest herself?"

"Us?"

"She doesn't think we should be together?" Brett was ready to move the piano to some other household if that was the case. But he didn't want Matilda disturbing anyone else either. His great-aunt wasn't going to dictate who he should see though.

"I believe she enjoyed helping to teach me lessons. So I don't think that's it. Maybe because you and I are practicing together, it's made her want to play again. Playing the piano brought her real joy." Ellie was silent for a moment, while Brett tried to think of anything he could recall of Matilda when Ellie asked, "How did she meet her husband?"

"He came to her for piano lessons. That was the story, anyway."

"A grown man went to her for lessons? That's kind of unusual, isn't…" Ellie smiled at Brett. "I mean, you always wanted to take lessons. I wouldn't think an older bachelor would suddenly take an interest in it."

"I think that was the family joke. Great-Aunt Matilda was busy teaching piano lessons to pay the bills. She didn't have time for frivolity."

"Courting wolves?" Ellie asked.

"Right. So when he saw her, he fell hard for her. She wouldn't take the time from her busy schedule to date him. She always said she didn't need anything else. He wanted to prove to her that she did. So to convince her he could love her for who she was, he took lessons from her."

"Was he good at it? Did they play duets together?"

"No. He tried really hard, or she wouldn't have been won over. And she loved him for it. Just as she loved all her students who gave it half a try."

"And she mated him?"

"Yes, with the condition that she be able to teach and play to her heart's content whenever she wanted to. She made him the happiest wolf ever."

"I really love your great-aunt. I wish I could have met her when she was alive."

"I'm sure she would have loved you."

"But no kissing until we were…" Ellie blushed. "Unless we were mated wolves."

Brett laughed and pulled into the inn parking lot. "We got away with it last night."

"We did." She smiled, but then frowned. "You said she was seeing someone. In a boat. Not her husband?"

"She was widowed by then. I'm asking around today about who the other man was. I've asked if anyone had seen them boating on the river before her death. Unfortunately, many of the people who grew up with her or knew her the best are dead. The doc even. My grandmother. Her two girlfriends she was out with the day that my great-aunt died. Both were widowed. Remer's grandfather. Probably the other man who she'd been seeing."

"I keep thinking about what she left behind in the boat—and his glove. Would they have been drunk? Would the doc have noticed alcohol on her breath?"

"He probably would have, but he didn't mention that in his findings. Maybe the water washed the scent away? Or maybe she never drank any wine. Maybe it was all the guy's idea to drink, and she wasn't interested."

"But the bottle was empty. Not just partially gone?"

"Yeah."

"Let's say a man brought her home after she'd drowned. Her clothes would have been soaked. That would have been suspicious. If he changed her out of them and into a nightgown, he would have had to dispose of them, right?"

"Agreed. He couldn't leave them lying around. He couldn't hang them out to dry. Grandmom would have noticed." Then Brett frowned. "I do remember one thing. My grandmother was fretting over locating a dress that was Aunt Matilda's favorite. It was her nicest, and Grandmom wanted to have her buried in it."

"Let me guess—you think she was wearing her favorite dress when she went out with the stranger on the boat."

"Yeah, I do. And unless anyone saw him with her dress, and whatever else she was wearing that day, I don't know how we would hope to learn the truth."

"How can I help to research this?"

"You have guests checking in today, right?"

"Yes. We've hired some staff to do the check-ins and other work. That way we can go to the ball. Laurel is going to relieve them for a time so they can attend too."

"Sounds like a good plan. You have your hands full. I'll keep asking around, seeing if I can learn anything that might give us more of a clue."

"All right. But if you need help, let me know."

"I will." They got out of the car and Brett pulled Ellie into his arms and kissed her. "Do you think Matilda's okay with us kissing?"

Ellie glanced back at the inn and Brett saw the lace curtains in the attic room move. "I don't know about your great-aunt, but Chrissy seems to approve."

He laughed, kissed Ellie on the mouth and gave her one more heartfelt hug. He had planned to ask her at the ball if she would mate him, so he wanted to stick to the plan and make this as memorable as could be. But right now, he wanted to just plain ask. "I'll see you at seven."

Chapter 14

ELLIE FELT LIKE DANCING ON AIR AFTER RUNNING with Brett as wolves. The way he hugged and kissed her, the reluctance he exhibited in leaving her... She really thought he might ask her to mate him right then and there. He was organized about everything—his research, his writing—and she didn't think spontaneous was his style. She was thinking of asking him, but she thought he wanted to do it his way and make it extra special at the ball. She didn't want to ruin it for him. If she had this all wrong and he didn't ask her? She was going to sock him.

After leaving Ellie off at her house, Brett was finishing an article at work when he got a call from Yolan Wernicke. Brett hadn't been expecting to hear from the Wernicke brothers. Especially not from anyone other than Stanton. So when Yolan called, Brett wondered if it was a ploy to learn more about the ghost Brett wanted to exorcise. Though they clearly had their hands full with the haunted car. "Stanton was bragging that you wanted a job done in secret. He said he asked five thousand dollars for the job since it wouldn't be televised. He said you wouldn't tell him if the ghost is at our cousins' inn, but he highly suspects it is since you're seeing Ellie, and your brother is mated to Laurel."

"He wants too much for the job. And it wouldn't work anyway." Brett wouldn't verify where the job was.

"If it's for our cousins, I'll offer my assistance for free. I'm the only one of my brothers who actually has any abilities. Stanton just runs the show. He would have sneaked me in to do the real work in any event. To make up for how we treated my cousins, I'd like to make amends. So if they need a ghost exorcist at the inn, I'll do it."

"It has to do with my great-aunt." Brett was sure that the Wernicke brothers wouldn't know about her haunting the inn.

"Okay, well, like I said, if it's for my cousins, it's free. For anyone else—"

"Can you really exorcise a ghost?"

"Yeah. I've taken care of dozens. We have testimonials on our website. They're real. I can give you a list of names and numbers to call to verify that the claims are genuine."

"Thanks, I'll…think about it." Brett was afraid that if the sisters learned of it, his wolf would be cooked. Working with Yolan was a last resort. He really felt his great-aunt was his problem to resolve since he had given the piano to the ladies and caused all the trouble to begin with.

Brett looked up other ways to commune with ghosts. Ouija boards. Séances. He didn't figure he could get away with using an Ouija board without someone catching him at it. Besides, he'd have to include someone who knew what he was doing. Same thing with séances. He'd be better off trying to speak with Matilda on his own. The question was, when would he have enough time to talk to her alone?

He called CJ and told him about Yolan offering to help get rid of the ghost and that he wouldn't charge anything for the job if it was to help out their cousins.

"You trust him? As soon as he knows the ghost is at the inn, do you think he'll keep it secret from the women? Or Stanton? Hell, what am I even saying? No, you did enough with the sage, and they were okay with it. Believe me, they wouldn't be amused if you tried to sneak the Wernicke brothers in. Or even one of them who professes to have the ability to take care of ghosts."

"I would think you would want to help them out. What if Matilda scares off all their guests? Then what? You'll be kicking yourself that you didn't try to help any way that you could."

"All right. Then either you tell Ellie what Yolan proposed, or I'll tell Laurel and let them decide. It's your choice."

Brett considered it for a moment. "I'll tell Ellie." He was the one who had talked to Stanton and then Yolan. He had to be the one to tell Ellie about this.

They ended the call, and Brett punched in Ellie's number. "It's my fault that Matilda is haunting your inn. I want to do something to help."

"No, it isn't, Brett. These things happen."

"Okay, if you say so. I hope you aren't annoyed with me, but I still really feel my great-aunt's presence is my fault. If I hadn't given you the piano, none of this would have been an issue."

"If I hadn't kissed you, it might not have been."

He sighed. "That wasn't an option."

She chuckled. "So what have you done now?"

"I spoke to Stanton about exorcising a ghost."

She didn't respond.

"Ellie?"

Still no response. Then he realized the phone line was dead.

Hoping it wasn't just because she was pissed off at him, he called her back. She didn't answer the phone this time. "Great." He had two options: call CJ and let him tell Laurel what he was trying to do, or go over to see Ellie in person.

This was his matter to handle, and he had to make it right with Ellie.

He left work and headed over to the inn, though he wasn't sure if she was there or at the house.

When he arrived, he saw her car was gone, but Laurel's and Meghan's were at the house. He knocked on the door to the house and waited. No one answered. He hurried down the path to the inn, knocked on the back door, opened it, and called out. "Laurel? Meghan?" He heard someone in the lobby and someone in the basement, and headed for the lobby first.

Expecting to see one of the sisters, he was shocked to the core when he saw his great-aunt sitting at the piano, staring at him as if *she* had seen a ghost.

Chapter 15

ELLIE COULDN'T BELIEVE BRETT HAD TALKED TO Stanton about their ghost when he knew they didn't want to have the ghost busters in their inn trying to profit from them.

She drove her sisters to Silva's Victorian Tea Shop to celebrate that the inn was now ready for guests—if they could help the ghosts find their way to their new home. She'd had to move her date with Radcliff to lunch tomorrow.

Before they got out of her car, Laurel asked, "Okay, so Brett made a mistake, but what exactly did he say about talking to Stanton?"

Ellie was fuming. "That he called him about our ghost. That's enough, isn't it? When he knows how we feel about our cousins with regard to the inn and revealing anything paranormal about it? I don't know when Brett talked to him, but I can just see Stanton over here bugging us about helping us out and trying to figure an angle where he can make some money or get more publicity, or something, at our expense."

"I agree. Why would Brett do something like that?" Meghan asked. "He knows how we feel, and he really cares about you. So he had to have a good reason, don't you think? Did you even give him a chance to talk about it? To tell you what he was thinking?"

Ellie shook her head. "I was so mad that I just ended the call."

"Call him back and hear him out. We need to know what Stanton is going to do next," Laurel said. "I think it would be a good idea to learn exactly what was said."

Ellie let out her breath. She knew Laurel was right. "All right. Go inside and get us a table. I'll call Brett and talk to him, learn all the details, and see what he has to say for himself."

Laurel squeezed her shoulder. "Good idea. We'll see you in a minute."

Ellie pulled out her phone but waited until her sisters left the car. Then she selected Brett's contact number and called him as she watched Laurel and Meghan enter the tea shop. Brett didn't answer, and she ended up getting his voice mail. She didn't want to leave a message for him like this. She really wanted to talk to him now that she'd cooled down a bit. She figured he was off on an assignment and couldn't talk to anyone else right this minute.

Waiting to record her message, at the sound of the beep, she said, "Brett, what exactly did you tell Stanton?" Then she hung up and stared at the tea shop, seeing her sisters taking seats beside one of the windows. She was certain Brett would want to talk to her when he could.

She let out her breath again and left the car to join her sisters. Talk about having to make a real effort to enjoy what was supposed to be a celebration!

"Any luck?" Laurel asked as Ellie sat down with them.

"No answer. I'm sure he has work to do and can't answer the phone now. He always shuts it off for interviews."

Her sisters were still waiting for her to tell them more.

"I left a message."

"A nice one?" Meghan asked, one brow arched.

"A to-the-point one."

Laurel laughed. "Well, he did try to call you back, so I'm certain he would have answered if he could have and will call as soon as he can."

Meghan ordered a grilled cheese sandwich. "He will. Be nice to him. I like him lots better than Fred, the guy you had planned on mating before."

Ellie did too. She still wasn't happy about him going behind their backs on this though.

Brett felt frozen in place. His cell phone rang, but he didn't dare touch it. He was afraid one little move and his very lifelike great-aunt Matilda would vanish into thin air. He still couldn't believe it was her.

He opened his very dry mouth to speak but then closed it, not sure what to say. He heard noises in the basement, but he didn't want to call out to the sisters and have his great-aunt disappear on him. He was a reporter. Think like a reporter!

Only she wasn't a news story. She was his beloved great-aunt. Well, the ghost of his beloved great-aunt.

"We miss you and your piano playing, Aunt Matilda." Even though she was his great-aunt, she never wanted to be called *great*. It made her feel too old. "We hope you like the framed sentiments." He motioned to the wall where the plaque was hanging. "I liked that photo best of you, sitting at the piano where you loved to be."

She just watched him, didn't move, didn't say anything. He kept expecting her to speak, but then she wasn't really…real. How could she speak?

"I really care for Ellie. She was upset when you disapproved of our kissing."

His great-aunt tilted her head down, giving him a disapproving look.

He couldn't help but smile a little at her. "She told me you helped her with her first lesson. She's been afraid she couldn't ever complete anything, and you gave her the willingness to give it a try." Brett shifted his gaze to the piano. "I love playing the piano. And we hope to do a duet at the inn sometime during Victorian Days. So thanks for helping her." Then he thought he should get down to business and see if there was a way to learn from Matilda what had happened. "I... don't know how to put this without just coming out and saying it. And I don't know if you would know what happened to you exactly either. But everyone thinks you died of pneumonia from a cold. Maybe took a bath and it chilled you further."

She frowned.

"Were you out in a boat instead? Did you drown?"

She ran her hand over the top of the piano and stared morosely at it.

He didn't know what to say next. How could he tell his great-aunt he wanted her to leave so she didn't disturb the guests arriving soon? He was afraid he would hurt her feelings. He never wanted to do that. There were really only two options that he could see, because he didn't believe it was in her power to avoid playing the piano, not as much as she loved it. So he had to help her find her way to the other side somehow, or maybe he could offer to take the piano back home. He hated doing it when it looked so nice in the inn lobby, and he thought more people would enjoy seeing it and maybe playing it there than if he kept it at home. Besides, how could he ask the sisters to give it back when he had just given it to them?

"Do you want me to take the piano back home to my place? I'll talk to the sisters, and I'm sure if they felt you'd be happier about it being there, they wouldn't mind." Would she play at his house? All hours of the night? And he would hear it? If he had Ellie over for a barbecue, would Matilda be standing there watching them, not happy he was taking advantage of Ellie? Or that Ellie was being too forward?

"You were dating a man, weren't you?" At least as evidenced by what had been left in the rowboat. His grandmother was afraid of the water and would never go near it. "We need to know who he was. Did he have anything to do with your death?"

She looked up at him and didn't say anything. Though he imagined he would have a stroke if she started to talk to him.

"What do you want me to—"

The back door to the inn opened, and Brett swung around as Ellie called out, "Brett? Are you in here?"

"I'm here."

"What are you doing in there?"

"I came to see you." He looked back at Matilda, ready to tell her that they'd work it out somehow, and if she'd died as a case of foul play, they'd discover the truth, but she'd vanished. He stared at the bench seat, not believing it.

"We were at Silva's tea shop until none of us could remember locking the door. I ran home to lock it and saw your car out front. What are you doing here?" she asked again.

"You wouldn't answer your phone. I came to talk to you in person, to explain everything." Then he smiled and joined her, taking her in his arms, but she was stiff and still annoyed with him. He wasn't releasing her for anything. "I spoke to Matilda."

She snorted. "How far did that get you?"

"Wait, if none of you were here, who's down in the basement banging around? You wait here. I'll check it out." He headed down the stairs, and she waited at the top with her cell phone in hand.

"Be careful," she said, concern in her voice.

He turned on the light switch and checked all the rooms, the bathrooms, to find no sign of anyone. He twisted the knob on the back door, but it was locked. "I guess it was just Chrissy." He headed back up the stairs, not believing all of this. Why had his great-aunt appeared before him now? Why was Chrissy making such a racket to get his attention when before he never knew she existed?

Ellie's jaw was slack.

Brett closed the basement door and took Ellie's hand and led her into the common area.

"You heard Chrissy?"

"I saw my great-aunt. And yeah, I heard Chrissy." He took a seat with Ellie on one of the love seats.

"You talked to her? Matilda?"

"I did. She didn't say anything."

"Did you ask her how she died? If it was some way other than what the coroner's report stated?"

"Yes, but she only frowned. I thanked her for teaching

you your first lesson, and I asked if she wanted me to move the piano back to my place."

"What did she say?"

"Nothing. She didn't say anything."

Ellie made a disagreeable sound. "Ghosts don't always just talk like we do. They do other things to help us understand what we need to know."

"All right. Well, she didn't do anything either. Just vanished when you came in the door."

"Where was she?"

"Seated at the piano."

"Okay, tell me what you told Stanton."

"Nothing. I just said I had a…" Brett paused. "Maybe we should talk about this somewhere else."

"Okay." Ellie and Brett started to lock up the inn when she got a call. "Yeah, the door was unlocked, and we had a visitor."

Brett wrapped his arm around her shoulders and walked her to the house.

"Brett. And guess what? He heard Chrissy banging around in the basement, who knows why, and he saw Matilda. Talked to her even." Ellie glanced up at Brett. "No, she didn't talk to him, and as far as he knows, she didn't tell him anything." She paused, listened, shook her head. "We haven't gotten that far. I'll pick you up later. CJ will? Okay, fine. No, thanks, I'll make some lunch here. Talk to you later."

When they reached the house, she asked, "What do you want for lunch?"

"Anything is fine with me."

"Are grilled cheese sandwiches all right?"

"Yeah, sounds good."

"Okay, tell me your story." She cut up cheese to add to the sandwiches, buttered the bread, then placed the sandwiches on a griddle pan.

"I didn't tell Stanton the ghost was at the inn. I asked him if he could exorcise one. He said he could. For five thousand dollars."

Ellie slid the spatula under one of the sandwiches and flipped it to grill the other side. "Wow. I'm in the wrong business."

"I don't know if he ever gets that price. He wanted to share the exorcism on his show, but I said no."

"You didn't tell him the ghost was at our inn?"

"No. I just wanted to know if he really could exorcise a ghost."

"And you were willing to pay that much money to do so?"

"No. That's why I used the sage."

She smiled as she served up the sandwiches. "Okay, but I don't believe he would have given up so easily."

"Yolan called today, saying he wanted to make it up to you and your sisters and would exorcise the ghost for free."

"So Stanton *does* know the ghost is at the inn," she said as she set the plates on the table.

"I didn't tell him it was. I said it was my ghost to exorcise."

Ellie studied him. "You really think it's your fault."

"Yeah, it is. I'm the one who gave you the piano. And then kissed you next to it. It's like it awakened her. I don't know. Anyway, I know you're troubled that she's going to cause problems for you with your guests. I feel I'm responsible."

Ellie got them glasses of ice water and a jar of pickles. "So what did you tell Yolan?"

"That it was my ghost. And he said he wouldn't do the job for free if it wasn't at the inn."

"So he's fishing for information for Stanton."

Brett took a bite of the sandwich. He hadn't planned on having lunch with Ellie, thinking she was having lunch with Radcliff, but if she could get over being mad at him, this was great. "Could be, but he sounded sincere that he wanted to help and make amends. He told me something interesting too. He said only he can really exorcise ghosts. That Stanton is in charge of the show, but Yolan is the only one of the three brothers who has the ability."

"So Stanton was going to send him in to do the job?"

"He said he was coming alone, but Yolan said Stanton would have sneaked him in because Stanton couldn't have done the job himself."

"Huh. That's interesting. I wonder why he told you that."

"Maybe he really does want to get on your good side." Brett finished the sandwich. "The sandwich was great."

"Thanks."

"Listen, I didn't tell Stanton the ghost was here, but Yolan said since CJ is mated to Laurel and I'm dating you, Stanton believes it has to be haunting the inn. So if he bothers you about it, that's the story."

"Do you really want to take the piano back?"

"No. It looks great in the lobby. It needs to be where it can entertain people."

She smiled a little. "You're afraid your great-aunt

will return home with you and play music at your place in the middle of the night."

He chuckled. "The thought did cross my mind."

"So what do you want to do?"

"I want to help guide her to the light."

"Sometimes spirits stay because they have unfinished business here. A message they need to get across."

"Like she died because someone killed her or neglected her."

"Or some other message. I asked her if she didn't believe she died of pneumonia. A sheet of music flew off the piano stand. That's how they communicate. Not by talking. At least not that I've heard—most of the time. Meghan is more auditory. She hears things that Laurel and I don't hear. I see things sometimes that the others don't see. Laurel senses things, and her skin crawls. The hairs on her arms and nape stand up. She's like a wolf that senses something's presence even if she can't hear or see or feel it.

"For some reason, Matilda is reaching out to me. We tried a séance, but only Chrissy showed up. She wants Matilda out of her home. That may be why she was banging around in the basement. I think Matilda is reaching out to you now because you aren't doubting her existence. At least that's what I think. Maybe it's because we're learning to play her piano, like we're her last students."

"You said they communicate in different ways. So if she tossed a song sheet off the music stand, what was the message?"

Ellie shrugged. "That she was trying to say something about her death was wrong? Or that she was angry that she died. That's all I can figure."

Brett took her hands and squeezed. "Are we okay?"

"Stanton will probably be a problem."

"Matilda, and maybe Chrissy too, are going to be a bigger problem when your guests arrive. How much do you want to bet?" Then he cleared his throat. "So what happened about lunch with Radcliff?"

"Lunch with him tomorrow. I'm surprised you didn't know about the change in plan since you seemed to know about all my other dates."

He smiled, then lost the smile. "I suppose you're having dinner with his brother tonight."

"Yes, and you don't need to chaperone us. Really."

He pulled her from her chair, knowing he had to get back to work, but he had to ask her one question. "Are you still dreaming about me at night?"

She gave him a wicked smile, which he took as a powerful *yes!* Right before he kissed her.

Chapter 16

BRETT HAD PICKED UP TONS OF OLD FAMILY PHOTOS from CJ's house to go through before he went to the tavern for dinner that night. The one he had for the memorial had been perfect, picturing Matilda at the piano with her grandnephews standing around it. But now he was looking for one that might show the dress she loved so much. Not that they'd ever find it. Yet, he was still curious. What if he could show her the photo and ask her if that was the dress she wore the night before she died?

He was sifting through the photos at his desk at home, looking for the ones when she was older, but one photo caught his eye. An old car that wasn't vintage but new in the photo. And his mother when she was younger, holding hands with a man standing in front of it. She was smiling, he was smirking, and Brett swore that was the car that Stanton was driving the night he'd hit him.

The 1930s gray Plymouth. Though in the picture, he couldn't tell the color. He flipped the photo over, and on the back, written in his mother's handwriting, was *Bill Smith and Me*.

He couldn't believe it. A human boyfriend before she met his dad and married him? Did she know he was a bank robber?

He called CJ. "You won't believe what I found." He continued to sort through the photos, looking for one of his great-aunt, and found one where she was with her sister and a couple of guys—all decked out. It was dated six months before she died. Was this the dress? He recognized one of the men. Theodore. But not the other. "I found a photo of Mom with Bill Smith. Shorty Bill Smith and his car. She looks like she was about eighteen in the photo."

"The bank robber?"

"Yeah, and the car that Stanton was driving. I also found a photo of Matilda with her sister and two men six months before she died. Theodore and someone else. Maybe we can make a copy of it and send it around the pack to see if anyone knows who he was."

"Okay, we can do that. Are you going to the tavern tonight?"

"Yeah. Are you?"

"No. Laurel wants me to spend tonight home with her."

Brett chuckled. "Okay. Well, looks like about that time. Got to go. Talk to you later."

"You'll have to show me the photo of Mom and the thug. I can't believe it."

"Me either. I wonder if Dad knew about it."

"I'll have to dig up news reports of who the arresting—well, would-have-been arresting—officers were. If Shorty hadn't died."

"Okay, let me know what you learn."

"Will do." After they ended the call, Brett headed over to the tavern, parked, and went inside.

"I thought you were crazy for suggesting that Ellie date other guys," Sam told Brett as he arrived early for dinner, took a seat, and got a beer.

"You changed your mind?"

Sam shrugged. "The place is packed every time she

arrives to have a meal with another guy." He handed Brett a mug of beer. "Yesterday when she canceled on Radcliff for lunch, I swear the whole pack knew about it, and it was the deadest it has ever been in here."

"Well, enjoy it while it lasts, because after she dines with Radcliff and his brother, she's not dating anyone else."

"Are you sure about that?"

Brett eyed Sam, wondering if he'd gotten wind of something. "Yeah." He took a swig of his beer. "She hasn't gotten any more calls from bachelor males." Not that he knew of.

Sam dried another beer mug and set it behind the counter.

"Well, do you know something I don't?" Brett asked him.

"I don't want to be the bearer of bad tidings, but I heard through the rumor mill that Sarandon asked her to go out with him in the morning."

"She doesn't eat big breakfasts, as far as I know."

Sam leaned over the counter. "That's all I know. If you want to know more, you'll have to ask Sarandon."

No way was Brett going to ask his brother what was going on. Knowing him, Sarandon was going to lecture Ellie, not date her. Where would they be going in the morning? Silva made cinnamon rolls to go, but her tea shop was only open for lunch. Unless Sarandon had made special arrangements with her.

Brett wasn't going to try to track them down, as much as the reporter in him wanted to—and the wolf in him too. He heard the door jingle and glanced back at it. Silva was chatting happily with Ellie as they walked into

the tavern. He wanted to sweep Ellie right out the door
and have dinner with her—and forget that her date was
closing the door right behind her.

—⁓—

Poor wolf, Ellie thought as she saw Brett, beer mug in
hand, take a seat where Darien and Lelandi usually sat
when they came here. The place was packed except for
a table reserved for her and her date. None of the other
Silvers showed up, which made it even harder to see Brett
sitting there all alone, staring into his mug of frothy beer.

"Want to ask him to join us?" Kemp asked. "It's
almost painful to watch him suffering so."

Ellie laughed. She loved the guys she had dated. They
were all so decent, though she suspected they would
have been a lot more forward if she wasn't really dating
Brett. She loved Brett most of all. "No, he wanted this.
Besides, I've told all of you it's only for fun."

"Unless someone else made your heart skip for joy,
right? I mean, that's why we all were begging you to
go out with us. Not because we wanted to teach Brett a
lesson, but mainly because we all hoped we would have
a chance to be that one and only for you."

"Of course. And I warned Brett that could happen."

"I bet he wasn't happy with that notion."

"Besides that I was dating wolves from the pack?"

Kemp laughed. "Serves him right. If I had been
dating you, I would never have suggested it." He drank
his beer and set the glass aside. "So, I hear Sarandon
asked you out."

"You know, we were never with a pack, and I really
have a hard time believing how fast word gets around."

"Your secret is safe with me."

She shook her head. "If you know, I'm sure everyone knows."

Kemp looked over at Brett. "Including him."

She had no idea what Sarandon had in mind, though she suspected he was going to give her a long talk about dating Brett, or what he was really like, or something. At least, she hoped that was all this was about. She hadn't planned to go out with anyone else, just lunch with Radcliff tomorrow. So she'd begrudgingly agreed to go with Sarandon in the morning, after he said he'd bring some fresh cinnamon rolls from Silva's shop, hot coffee, and green tea.

This time when she ended her dinner and thanked her date for a lovely time, she headed home and knew she wouldn't see Brett tonight…except maybe in her dreams.

But after she finally retired to bed and heard the wolf howl again at the inn, she headed to Meghan's room and knocked. "Hey, Meghan! Did you hear the wolf howl?"

After a couple of minutes, Meghan opened her door, wearing a long-sleeved flannel shirt, her eyes squinting. "What?" She was still half asleep, and Ellie suspected she hadn't heard a wolf howl.

She let out her breath and told her sister what she'd heard.

"No. And I don't want to hear a wolf howling. Put some earplugs in. Night." Meghan closed her bedroom door and returned to bed.

It was true that Meghan could sleep through about anything when she was tired enough, but Ellie wished someone else would hear the wolf. Preferably Brett so that he could identify if the wolf was his aunt. Of course after Ellie went to the inn to check it out, she saw nothing of a wolf or Matilda in her human form. Ellie retired to bed finally, wondering if she even had any earplugs… just in case.

The next morning, CJ called Brett as he was trying to concentrate on writing an article about Shorty Bill Smith and putting a local spin on it.. "Hey, did you hear Sarandon's taking Ellie somewhere this morning?"

"Yeah, I did."

"Well, I wouldn't worry about it. He's not interested in her. He only is concerned about you."

"Yeah, I'm not worried about it. Unless he upsets her."

"I'm sure he'll be careful."

Sarandon had better be, but Brett couldn't quit thinking about what they were doing, and he was trying to keep occupied until he knew. "I have something else I need to discuss with you. I spoke to Ellie about Yolan's exorcism offer. She said no, but we were talking more about what could be the reason for Aunt Matilda's death. Do you know who I can speak with that might know who she was seeing?"

"Maybe Bertha Hastings. She's been a friend of the family forever, and she's older than our mother but younger than our great-aunt."

"Okay, I'll check with her. I'll make some calls. Let you know what I discover." And that's what Brett spent the rest of the morning doing. Calling all of the older pack members about who had seen Matilda in the days before and after she had died.

"Her son, your uncle Ned, had been there," Bertha Hastings said as he sat down with her at her kitchen table. The place was always decorated with flowers no matter the time of year. Bertha's bed-and-breakfast was cheerful like Bertha was, her white hair coiled in a bun, the fragrance of roses scenting the air.

Uncle Ned had died in a boating accident, so no help there.

"Your grandmother was there, of course," Bertha said. "They really were close, you know."

"Remer, the piano teacher, said my grandmother was jealous that Matilda could play the piano so well."

"Nonsense. She was really proud of her sister's accomplishment. She bragged about her sister's success all the time. Sure, she wished she were as talented as Matilda, but she never said anything that made it sound as though she was envious of her. Matilda was jealous that Caroline had a boyfriend though."

"Grandmom did?"

"Yeah. Theodore Cochran, Remer's grandfather, in fact. He had a real courtship going on with your grandmother. But she wouldn't agree to mate him and stayed with her sister instead. Some wolves never want to take another mate. Both your great-aunt and grandmother were that way."

"So Matilda wasn't seeing Theodore." Brett pulled out the picture of his grandmother and great-aunt with the two men.

"Oh my," Bertha said, smiling at the photo. "That's such a nice photo of them. Okay, that's Benjamin Wheeler and Theodore."

"Tell me about Benjamin."

Bertha shrugged. "He was a builder. Built a lot of the early homes in the area. My bed-and-breakfast even, though at the time it was just a home. He did have a hobby though. He loved to play the piano, and he and your great-aunt would play duets together. This was after her mate died. Come to think of it, I remember hearing Theodore at her house the one day. I was a kid, came over for piano lessons, and he was upset with her. He was angry that Benjamin was over there all the time, worried that Benjamin really wanted to see Caroline, since she was living there too."

"Was he upset with Grandmom for not mating him?"

"He was. He tried courting another widowed wolf to make Caroline jealous, I believe. She just called him an old goat. Then she changed her mind and said he was just being a dog. So it didn't work on her. He quit seeing the other woman and kept hanging around Caroline after that, I guess figuring that he enjoyed her company more even if she wouldn't mate him."

Brett smiled, imagining his grandmother telling Theodore that.

"I think after Matilda died, he thought your grandmother would mate him, but she said she was too set in her ways. He died five years later. Six months later, she also died."

"All of natural causes?"

"Of course. Why would you ask that? Oh, don't tell me. Matilda is haunting the piano."

"How did you come to that conclusion?"

"It's the only thing I could think of that would make you question their deaths. You recently moved the piano to the inn. The sisters are sensitive to ghosts. I just added up the facts."

"Well, we're trying to take care of it and not let on that it's happening."

"She's playing the piano?"

"Sometimes. They're afraid she'll play when the guests are trying to sleep at night."

"Well, if you need my help, let me know. I'd be happy to talk to her."

He frowned. "You can see ghosts too?"

"No. I can still talk to her and see if anything I say helps. Oh my, you don't think Theodore had anything to do with Matilda's death, do you? I mean, maybe he thought if she were gone, Caroline would mate with him."

"Sounds like a motive. But how to prove it if it really happened that way." He studied the photo. "Grandmom wanted to have Matilda buried in her favorite dress, but she couldn't locate it for the funeral. Was this the dress she was thinking about?"

"It certainly could be. She only wore it for special occasions. You can't tell from the picture, but the dress is forest green. She loved that color."

It had nothing to do with Matilda, but wondering if Bertha would know anything about the other photo, he pulled it out and showed her.

"Oh, oh, I'm surprised your father didn't get rid of that photo."

"Granddad had it for some reason. He passed it down to us."

"Well, that's Shorty Bill Smith. The bank robber who hit our local bank. He had gotten sweet on your mother around the time your dad met her. Your dad led the posse that took off after Shorty and killed him. Or the man actually killed himself, from what eyewitnesses said."

"How did Mom take the news?"

"She was shocked. She never knew Shorty was a bank robber. She always told your dad he had saved her from ruin. Exaggerated, of course. Shorty was human, and she wouldn't have ever married him and changed him."

"I bet Dad wouldn't have liked that. About my great-aunt, everyone was there to see Matilda for the funeral, right?"

"Everyone but Theodore. He'd come down with a bad cold and wasn't feeling well. 'Course, Caroline went to take him her homemade chicken soup and wanted to check on him after her sister had died from a cold that wasn't all that bad. On top of that, the poor man had fallen and bruised the side of his head something terrible. But then they had a falling-out, I think over the fact that she wouldn't marry him even after her sister died, and I don't think they spoke to each other again."

"A bruise from falling?"

"He said he'd spilled some water on the floor, slipped on it, and hit his head on the table going down."

"Did she believe him?"

"I guess. She was worried about him."

"Thanks, Bertha." If not that, was it as Ellie had said? Matilda was angry she had died when she did, and it had nothing to do with anything else? But what if Theodore had gone out with Matilda in the boat the night before she died?

<center>~~~</center>

"Omigod, Sarandon, this is beautiful." Ellie did a pirouette under the green metal roof of Matilda's burned-down home. Three picnic tables were situated on the cement slab, with a grill on a separate slab and even outdoor lighting for night use. The fireplace had been refurbished, and a marble memorial plaque was attached to one of the pillars. Nearby she saw a wrought iron arbor that she hadn't noticed before. It was freshly painted white, and there were a few rose canes climbing over the arbor. Then Ellie saw the gazebo. It was beautiful.

"Jake had old photos of her tending her roses around the gazebo, so we could replicate it just like it had been during its glory years. As you can see, we built stone planters around the roses so when they begin to grow, everyone can enjoy them."

Sarandon folded his arms across his chest and smiled. "You suggested it to Brett, he mentioned it to the rest of us, and Eric told me to make it happen. I wanted you to see it first since it was your idea and we wanted to know if you thought we needed to make any changes."

Tears in her eyes, she smiled at him and turned to see the view. "It's glorious. Just perfect. I couldn't suggest anything different. When will we commemorate it?"

"We'll have a ceremony soon." He frowned at her. "Your lunch date is the last one you're having with any of the other guys, right?"

"Yeah, except for our breakfast date. That's it."

"Well, breakfast with me doesn't count."

"Sure it does. Maybe not in a boyfriend-girlfriend way, but we are on a date, Sarandon Silver." She took his hand and led him to the table where he'd set the bag of cinnamon rolls and the tray of coffee and tea.

They sat next to each other so they could watch the river flow by, a cinnamon roll in one hand, a hot

beverage in the other, and just listened to the birds singing in the trees as the sparrows woke to find a meal. The
sky was turning pink and orange and blue, the breeze
stirring the leaves and pine needles. She wished Brett
were here with her enjoying the beauty of the woods and
the river, having breakfast with her, seeing the sun rise.
What a way to start a day.

───※───

Brett didn't have any plan to stay away from the tavern
while Ellie had her last date. He wanted her to know
he was the follow-up date for tonight and every other
occasion. Though the truth of the matter was, he was
barely holding it together and couldn't wait for these
dates to be over. He still didn't know what her date with
Sarandon had been about.

"Hey, Ellie," Brett said, smiling down at her and nod-
ding his head to Kemp. "Want to come to my place for
dinner tonight? And then we can go to the inn to practice
our lessons."

She gave him a small smile back as if she knew he
was laying claim to her in the tavern in front of everyone there.

"All right. And a run after that to your favorite
childhood getaway."

Feeling overjoyed they were on again, and no one else
was going to slip in, Brett smiled. "Yeah, I'd love that."

She motioned to the box of chocolates. "I need to run
if I'm going to keep eating all this chocolate."

"I suppose I can't join you for a run tonight, can I?"
Kemp asked.

"No," Brett said firmly.

Kemp laughed. "I didn't think so, but I thought I'd ask. Just in case. We haven't ordered yet. Did you want to join us?"

Brett grinned at him, slapped him on the back, and sat down, mostly ignoring Ellie's look of surprise. She had to know that he was serious about her, and sitting back and waiting for her to get through all these dates with other wolves was killing him.

Ellie thought the world of Kemp for inviting Brett to dine with them. She was surprised he'd offered, as if he knew it to be a foregone conclusion—she and Brett were a couple. And she was a little surprised Brett would accept, but she thought he must have been desperate to end all this business with her dating other wolves.

They had a lovely time visiting. When they were done and it was time to call it a night and get on with piano lessons and a run, Brett paid for their meals. Kemp argued with him, but Brett insisted since he'd kind of taken over the date.

Kemp had laughed and thanked him and thanked Ellie for a lovely time. Kemp gave Ellie a quick kiss on the cheek and said good night before Brett could react to that. He helped her on with her jacket and pulled her in for a real kiss, which had the patrons in the tavern whistling, clapping, and cheering.

Ellie laughed, and Brett looked like the happiest wolf in the world.

When they arrived at the inn for piano practice, the first thing they noticed was the song sheet for "Mary Had a Little Lamb" resting on the floor.

"I tell you she's trying to share something with us." Ellie pulled out the one for "Louie, Louie Wannabe" and placed it on the music stand.

As soon as she did, the sheet lifted and fluttered to the floor. Brett and Ellie stared at the song sheet as if it were going to move again.

"She doesn't like that song? I love it," Brett said.

Ellie chuckled. "No, she wouldn't have it with the rest of her music sheets if she didn't like it and didn't think it was a good song to teach to her pupils. I'm sure she's trying to tell us something."

Brett opened the bench seat and began pulling out the separate music sheets, and he started setting them up one at a time. Every time he put up a new sheet of music, it was tossed to the floor. Carefully, Ellie gathered them up as if they were treasured possessions.

When he set the sheet music for "Sweet Caroline" on the stand, the name caught his attention. His grandmother's name. He and Ellie waited to see what happened next. He hadn't even reached for the next single sheet of music, just knowing this could be a clue.

"Your grandmother..." Ellie said, practically whispering the words.

Brett just stared at the song sheet, still waiting for something to happen, for Matilda to highlight her sister's name in lights or do something more significant to indicate they were on the right track.

"Okay, so she's trying to tell us something about your grandmother," Ellie said, drawing closer to the song sheet and reading it. "It's a love story between a boyfriend and Caroline."

"Remer's grandfather, Theodore. He wanted to mate her, but she wanted to stay with her sister instead."

"Was he unhappy about it?"

"Yeah. Tried to make her jealous by dating another woman."

Ellie's eyes widened. "And then?"

"My grandmom called him an old goat. And then a dog."

"Oh, wow," Ellie said, smiling. "Being a dog is worse than anything."

"Yeah, because they run around and don't mate for life. So when she didn't fall for it, chase after him, or try to make up to him, he came back to her." He explained all that Bertha Hastings had told him about Matilda, Theodore's bruised head from a fall on a wet floor, his fighting with Matilda over Benjamin being in the same house with Caroline, and the falling-out that he and Caroline had after Matilda's death.

Brett and Ellie read over the song sheet.

"I don't know. It's just a love song between a man and woman named Caroline," Ellie said. "I don't see any significance to the words."

Brett put up the rest of the song sheets, one by one, but nothing happened with any of them. Matilda had given them a clue, and if they couldn't figure it out, she was done trying.

Ellie put "Louie, Louie Wannabe" back on the stand and began practicing. "I'm surprised she didn't mind this kind of music."

"She loved all music, kept up with the ages, and

wanted to make sure that everyone, young and old, enjoyed it when she played. She said it kept her youthful too."

"She sounds really sweet."

"She was. Both she and Grandmom were funny together. Grandmom was my dad's mother. Aunt Matilda married a man who died young but gave her one son, Ned. He died in a boating accident. It flipped over, he was struck in the head, and he drowned. That was after she'd died."

"I'm so sorry," Ellie said.

"Uncle Ned was fun to be around. He took us kids boating all the time. We really missed him."

"No foul play, right?"

Brett smiled at her and shook his head. She stood up so he could practice playing. He played the same song she had and then went back to playing "Mary Had a Little Lamb." Afterward, they played the duet again.

"We're not perfect and probably won't be by the time the guests are here, but I think we'll be passable." She smiled up at him. "Are you going to dress up?"

"Yeah, I wouldn't miss it for the world." He let out his breath. "What are we going to do about my great-aunt?"

"Talk to her. I don't know what else to do. My sisters and I tried a séance, and that just riled Chrissy up. Your great-aunt only seems to want to express herself to the two of us, for whatever reason."

"Because we're courting each other," he ventured.

She smiled at him again.

He took that as an affirmative and decided to carry it a little further. "And we're in love."

Her smile broadened, and then she laughed.

He smiled back. "Well, don't tell me it's not true."

"Are you ready to run?" Ellie had such an impish smile on her face that he wondered what she was up to.

As soon as they drove out to the woods, stripped, shifted, and ran to his favorite spot, he couldn't believe what he saw. His great-aunt's burned-down home was now a beautiful memorial. He read the sentiments etched on the marble plaque while Ellie's soft wolf body pressed against his as if she was reading the memorial too, but he knew then that she and Sarandon had been here earlier today. He smelled their scents, cinnamon rolls, coffee, and tea. He howled with joy.

And she howled with him. Off in the distance, a couple more howls rent the air—Jake's and his mate's.

If Ellie liked the idea, he thought this would be the perfect place to have their wedding. If she wanted one. Wolves didn't always have them. Mating was for life, which meant no marriage certificate was needed to make it binding.

He thought the world of Sarandon for having added all the wonderful touches to the site. And he assumed his brothers would want to commemorate it with a pack gathering. What better way to do so than to have a wedding here? And soon.

On the drive back home, he told her how beautiful it was.

"I didn't know anything about it. Sarandon brought me out there this morning to show me. I believe he wanted me to show you."

"I was afraid he was going to scold you for dating the other guys. It was killing me not to know where the two of you had gone."

"I think it was a peace offering on his part, maybe from all your brothers, even your cousins, for hassling my dates."

"They hassled them?"

She raised her brows at him.

"You mean they were there to watch you eat with the other guys? What did you expect?" He smiled.

"I hadn't expected all of them to be there for that first date." Ellie leaned against the car window and peered out at the sky.

"That's what happens in a pack. One show of unity, and that's all that was needed."

She turned to look at Brett. "You were there for every date after that!"

"Well, sure. Just in case your date hadn't gotten the word."

She laughed and leaned back against the seat. "I couldn't believe you barged in on my lunch date with Kemp."

"He had a choice. He didn't have to offer. He just knew he didn't stand a chance."

"Next time you suggest to me that I should date others—"

"There will *never* be a next time, believe me."

Chapter 17

THE NEXT DAY, SILVER TOWN WAS ABUZZ WITH excitement. Dressed in Victorian attire, ladies, gents, and children were visiting the various establishments, celebrating the annual event.

Ellie couldn't believe she'd awakened so late and no one had gotten her up to help at the inn. She hurried to dress in her corset and petticoats, but had a horrible time trying to fasten her gown. As she started to walk over to the inn, she saw Chrissy peering out the lace curtains in the attic room. *Great.*

Ellie entered the inn where Laurel was setting out fresh flowers for the guests' arrivals, but she could smell that a couple of new wolves, a male and female, had been in the inn lobby.

"One couple already arrived," Laurel said. "Check-in isn't until noon, but since we don't have guests to clean up after, I figure it's fine."

"Sounds good to me. I'm sure they're excited to get ready for the ball. Did you say anything about you-know-what?" Ellie glanced at the silent piano.

"No." Laurel tilted her head at the way Ellie was holding her gown up. "Here, let me help. Meghan said you were having trouble sleeping, so we let you sleep in a bit. You know, because what if someone asks you to mate? Then you'll never get any sleep." Laurel winked.

"Thanks, Laurel. You and Meghan are the best. But if he doesn't ask…" Ellie sighed. "I just saw Chrissy in the attic room. At least she seems to have settled down a bit. Maybe she's adjusting to Matilda being here." As soon as the words were out of her mouth, Chrissy floated by.

"No, she is *not*," Chrissy said in a whispery kind of way.

"Wait. Why is Matilda here? Did she say?" Ellie asked, but Chrissy had vanished in the direction of the basement door.

Ellie hurried for the stairs, but then paused and asked Laurel, "Were the guests who checked in upstairs or in the basement?"

"Basement. Blue room."

"Great." Ellie hurried down the stairs to the basement and wondered if they should have left the lavender room vacant. Would Chrissy like company or be upset by it? Too late to do anything about it. All the rooms were booked now.

Ellie opened the door to the lavender room, entered it, and shut the door. Chrissy didn't appear before her, but the room was cold, as if she were there.

"Chrissy, I know you are here. Do you know why Matilda is staying here at the inn? Or why she's so attached to the piano?"

Suddenly, Ellie's lips felt like she'd pressed ice cubes against them. "Kiss? Love? We know it had to do with moving the piano here. But why is she here? Why are you still here, Chrissy?"

"Home," Chrissy whispered in a ghostly way.

They had all assumed that. Just like the Scottish lass who had been murdered and buried beneath the floor.

Chrissy had been born here and had never lived anywhere else. This truly was her home.

"She…" Chrissy paused.

"She what, Chrissy?"

"She wants…"

Ellie felt like she was standing on the edge of a cliff, waiting to hear what Matilda wanted. They wanted to help her find peace.

"…me to play."

"The piano?" Ellie couldn't believe it. Matilda wanted to teach Chrissy to play so she'd know the joy of playing too? Then Ellie realized what a disaster that could be. It would be bad enough if Matilda played the piano when the guests were sleeping.

Wringing her hands, Chrissy appeared and nodded, looking as though she was completely out of her comfort zone.

"Chrissy, if you play, will Matilda leave?"

Chrissy bit her lip, nodded, and vanished.

"If you learned to play well?" Ellie asked, assuming Chrissy was already somewhere else. She didn't think Matilda would agree to leave if Chrissy played a few notes and that was it. Maybe Chrissy was in the attic room. Ellie normally didn't chase a spirit from room to room. She gave them their space, figuring it was futile anyway. But she really did need answers.

Ellie dashed up the stairs to the hallway and headed for the stairs to the upper floors. She caught Laurel's eye.

"Trouble?" Laurel asked.

"If you define *trouble* as a reluctant Chrissy forced to take piano lessons from Matilda so she will go away—Matilda, that is—and the two of them choose any time of the day or night to practice, I'd say that is an affirmative."

"Oh, just great."

"Now what?" Meghan was wearing a red gown with a low-cut bodice and a corset that was lifting her boobs even more than usual. She looked as though she was ready to snare a wolf mate.

"Tell her. I'm going to try to get more answers." Ellie raced up the next flight of stairs, but then walked up the ones to the attic room and gently opened the door. In there, the air was chilly. "Chrissy? Just how well do you have to play before Matilda feels she's succeeded in teaching you?"

Ellie's phone rang, and she pulled it out of her pocket. "Yeah, Laurel?"

"Attic room guest, Rose McKinley, is on her way up. I just wanted to warn you."

Rose's brother, Ryan, and his mate were the pack leaders in Green Valley, and his wife, Carol, had future visions. So Ellie thought Rose might be all right with the idea that a ghost sometimes visited the attic room.

"Okay, I'm leaving." Darn it. Ellie wanted to ask if her sister could delay Rose for a few more minutes, but then the room warmed and Ellie figured it didn't matter anyway.

She greeted Rose on the stairs. "Here for Victorian Days?"

"Yeah, I could hardly wait. I'm glad you opened the inn early so I could get dressed and check out all the places." Rose owned a garden shop in Green Valley, and the sisters ordered all their fresh flowers and plants from there.

"Enjoy your stay. If you have any trouble, just let any of us know." Ellie prayed that none of the guests had problems of the ghostly kind or any others.

Laurel and Meghan were smiling at Ellie when she returned to the lobby. "What?" she asked.

"Well, are you going to pop the question to Brett at the ball?" Laurel asked.

The piano began playing a tune, and the three sisters stared at it. Then both Ellie and Laurel looked at Meghan to find out what the music was. "The Zombies, 'Tell Her No.' I think it says 'no' more than sixty times. So you have your answer from Great-Aunt Matilda."

The ladies laughed, but Ellie thought Matilda would be happy if she and Brett mated.

"Well, maybe he'll ask you at the ball," Meghan said. "You know, you've been so cautious with him that he might be waiting for you to let him know in no uncertain terms that you want him."

More guests arrived, and the song ended.

Ellie sighed, hoping that they wouldn't have a mass exodus of guests during the first week they were open again. And if Brett was afraid to ask her to mate, she would be asking him, with or without Great-Aunt Matilda's approval.

What made Victorian Days even more special this year was that the MacTire sisters were participating, and Brett was getting ready to ask Ellie to mate him.

That morning, he headed over to the inn to play a duet with Ellie on the piano for the special program they were putting on. They'd actually practiced two duets, in case anyone wanted to hear another.

Ellie greeted him in a burgundy gown with wide puffed sleeves, the skirt full and flowing. She was also wearing petticoats—he could see the top floral one because of the open-front gown—a corset, and a chemise beneath the gown. Even though most day dresses for the period were higher necked, for this event, most of the women were wearing gowns that had very low necklines and were worn off the shoulders, gowns that were supposed to be for evening affairs.

He gathered Ellie in his arms and crushed her against him, kissing her while everyone assembled there waited for them to play the duet. In fact, the inn was overflowing with pack members, some on the stairs watching, others gathered around the piano. He seriously had considered asking Ellie to mate him right here and now, but he was afraid Matilda would ruin it if she didn't like him doing so in front of the crowd.

Even if Matilda didn't care for the idea, the rest of the pack was all smiles.

"You're beautiful," he whispered in Ellie's ear as he led her to the piano bench.

"You are too," she said, smiling up at him before taking her seat.

She'd been so worried she'd make mistakes, but he had laughed it off, saying if anyone did, he probably would, and no one would be the wiser anyway, except for Remer and Mervin and Matilda. Brett didn't see any sign of his great-aunt though.

He joined Ellie, and they played the first duet beautifully, no mistakes at all. When everyone wanted to hear more, they played another. Because they hadn't practiced a whole lot of different songs, they stuck to all the simple ones they knew for beginners: "Mary Had a Little Lamb," "Louie, Louie," and several Christmas songs.

They made a few mistakes as they continued to play, but everyone cheered them on as if they were famous pianists, and Brett loved that he and Ellie could do this together.

Then they gave up the piano to Remer, whom they'd invited to play for a few hours today. He had his business cards on hand for any interested prospective students. Mervin played after that, while Ellie gave Meghan a break by helping to check in guests.

"So when are you going to mate Ellie?" CJ asked Brett in private in the common room while everyone else was milling around in the lobby. "Laurel wants to know."

Brett laughed. "She doesn't think I'm too bad a choice now for her sister?"

"Not after you began to see Matilda. I still can't believe you started to."

"She liked me best of all her grandnephews."

"Ha. You were such a suck-up. Doing odd chores for her whenever we visited her."

"As if all of you didn't." It was true. Without a mother, and with a father like theirs, Brett had cherished the hugs he got from their great-aunt.

"So when are you asking Ellie?"

"Soon." Brett had waffled so many times about how he wanted to do this—at the pack's first ball, right on the dance floor, at dinner or out, or at home over dinner. He'd even wished he could have when they were at his great-aunt's memorial spot, but they'd been wearing their wolf coats. He'd finally decided that asking her at the dance would be the most memorable.

"It has to be a special occasion."

Brett was amused that his brother was trying to guess when he was asking the big question.

"The ball tonight?" CJ's eyes lit up with specula-tion. "That's it, isn't it? You'll be dashing in your Victorian suit, and she'll be wearing a ball gown. Yep, if I could have done so with Laurel, that would have been my choice."

Brett had wanted to propose a mating to Ellie at the Victorian Days opening ball for that very reason. They would be all dressed up, it was the first time the ball had taken place, and he really couldn't wait a moment longer. "Okay, yes, but I want it to be a secret."

"Your secret is safe with me."

"No telling Laurel."

"I won't, but she may already suspect what's going to happen, like I did."

"I don't want any fanfare. I'll do it with Ellie, and we'll announce it to the pack later."

"A big announcement in the paper?"

Brett smiled. "It'll be in the paper, but after I propose and she accepts."

"Is there any doubt?"

"Unless the she-wolf agrees, there's always a chance of rejection."

Chapter 18

BRETT HAD LOOKED SO DAPPER IN HIS GENTLEMAN'S Victorian ensemble when he joined her at the inn that morning that Ellie had wanted to haul him off to her house and ravish him. He'd finally had to leave the inn and put in an appearance at the paper. Even though the newspaper hadn't been in existence that long, its office had been made to look like an old-timey one, and they even had an old printing press on display for Victorian Days. Brett had to operate it for a while for show-and-tell and hand out free samples of the paper, highlighting the articles he'd written on past Victorian Days, all the events scheduled for this year, and a page-and-a-half article on the Victorian Inn because it was their first year to be open for the celebration.

Since it was such a big deal today, Brett wished he could have announced his mating—well, upcoming nuptials to Ellie—but he would in tomorrow's paper.

Ellie was delighted when Silva dropped off finger sandwiches for everyone milling around the inn and listening to the music. People were going in and out and seeing how the other businesses were celebrating the occasion. But she was serving her special pies only at her tea shop. She had about thirty tables for guests, another ten out back in the courtyard when the weather was warmer, but today she was filled to capacity. Her business had tripled since she'd opened as the word spread about her great pies, soups, and sandwiches.

She'd hired four of the local wolves to serve meals for the Victorian Days festivities. Two were men dressed in Victorian striped trousers, button shoes, pin-striped vests, bowler hats, white shirts, and red bow ties. They were bachelor males and getting as much of a kick out of working there as the women who were flocking to see them there. They had other jobs, so this gig was just a couple of hours for them, and the tips were high.

Sam hadn't liked it very much. He'd come over to interview the wolves himself to make sure they knew that Silva was off-limits—as if anyone would be dumb enough not to know that.

———

That evening, Meghan had dropped Ellie off at the building the pack used for inclement-weather gatherings— and now for the ball—because Brett was running late.

Now Ellie watched as Brett searched the crowd, trying to catch sight of her. He was wearing a black wool frock coat, a charcoal-gray John Bull top hat, and charcoal-and-light-gray-striped trousers. His cherry-red jacquard vest with black embroidery was really elegant. A white Victorian men's dress shirt with a high standing collar set it all off. He was also wearing one of those black silk puff ties that Ellie loved, a diamond tie tack that sparkled a little in the overhead lights, a silver pocket watch, and black leather lace-up boots. She whistled at him, and he turned to see her and laughed.

Though she hadn't known what he was going to

wear, they were a perfect match since she was wearing a red ball gown trimmed in black lace.

The building was decorated with fresh flowers, and a table for grazing had been set up along one wall. Then someone began playing a waltz, and both Brett and Ellie turned quickly to look at the piano. Even though the music wasn't coming from Matilda's baby grand, it had given them a start. Mervin was playing.

"Can I have this dance?" Brett asked Ellie.

She pulled out her Victorian dance card and opened it. "Well, it looks like the first dance is free."

He considered the book and smiled. "I imagine in years past, it *was* full."

She slipped the dance card back into her velvet purse and smiled. "You're just lucky you chased all my other suitors away."

He pulled her into his arms and began to dance with her across the room. "That's good, because I wasn't in the mood for sharing."

"You are such a wolf."

"When it comes to you? Absolutely."

At first, not too many wolves were dancing, but then couples began to join them and Brett pulled Ellie tighter. She loved feeling him close like this, all dressed up as if they were from an earlier time. He began to kiss her and continued to dance with her across the wooden floor in a lovers' embrace.

———※———

Brett had wanted to ask Ellie to mate with him all day, and he hated that he hadn't been able to pick her up at the house in time to bring her to the ball. Rose had been running late with the flower delivery to his house because she'd set up the flowers at the ballroom too. And then she'd helped him to set up the flowers he had bought for Ellie the way they both thought would make the best impression.

Now on the dance floor, Brett couldn't hold back a minute longer. He kissed Ellie's ear and whispered into it, "Will you agree to be my mate, Ellie MacTire?"

As soon as she beamed up at him, he knew it was a yes, and his whole outlook brightened. He couldn't believe how much he'd been sweating this out. He should have known she'd say yes.

That *was* a yes, wasn't it?

CJ and Laurel danced near them, and Brett was certain his brother knew he'd asked, but had she accepted? All CJ did was raise his brows at Brett in silent question. Brett just smiled back, and Ellie rested her head against Brett's chest. They danced nice and slow, and he loved the way she held him close—as if they were already mated wolves, in love, and meant only for each other.

"Will you be my mate, Ellie?" he asked again, needing to hear her say yes, to be clear about it, to hear her say she wanted him like he wanted her.

She smiled up at him. "My sisters told me you'd propose to me at the ball. I wasn't sure." She wrapped her arms around his neck. "What made you finally ask?"

"I've wanted to for a long time. I wasn't sure you were ready, and I didn't want to hear you say no because I'd asked too soon." He let out his breath and kissed her forehead. "And I didn't want my great-aunt to come between us."

"I think she'll be pleased."

"That's a yes?" Brett figured he sounded so hopeful and thrilled at the same time that it made her smile again.

She nodded. "I couldn't love a wolf more than I do you, Brett. In the year I've known you, you've always been eager to please and fun and, well, almost perfect."

"Almost?"

"Until you suggested I date other guys, asked Stanton to exorcise our ghosts, and—"

"I didn't ask him to exorcise your ghosts. Just mine. And I didn't really ask him to do so. As to dating the other guys, I…" Brett paused. "Hell, why didn't I think of that? What were you wearing the next night after you wore the moose T-shirt? Wait, let me tell you. Tiger-striped pajamas."

She gaped at him. "We had dream sex."

"Yeah, hell yeah. That guy who had the nerve to ditch you? And all the other guys you dated? No way could any of them have been your mate."

She smiled. "I guess we should have discussed what I was wearing more. I thought one of my sisters mentioned something about me and my moose T-shirt, since Laurel got it for me when we lived in Minnesota and I loved the moose up there. I believed that somehow you'd heard of it, then made a lucky guess or dreamed of me wearing it." She placed her hand on his cheek. "Will you be mine?"

He laughed. "Yes, without hesitation and with all my heart. I've loved you since the first time you kicked me out of the inn when it was under construction and I was in the way."

She laughed. "Should we have asked your great-aunt

first?" She looked up at him with such a serious expression that he just smiled down at her.

"No. This is between you and me." He glanced around at the pack members at the ball. "And well, the pack, since everyone seems to have stopped dancing and is watching us to see what's going on. I'm sure they all figured I might ask you to mate with me tonight."

She laughed, turned beautifully red, and tightened her arms around him.

CJ howled. Laurel joined in. Then the rest of the pack members howled.

Wolf matings and wolf cubs were two of the most celebrated occasions in a wolf pack. Ellie just laughed and howled too. Brett's brothers and cousins added jauntily to the chorus, but Brett howled the loudest. It was a good thing the great hall was way out in the woods on the pack leaders' property.

⌁⌁⌁

Brett and Ellie slipped off early from the dance to make the mating a done deal. Everyone congratulated them as they left, so their departure wasn't exactly discreet. They were eager to turn their fantasies into something real.

Her car was parked in Brett's driveway and Ellie was so surprised. She laughed, thrilled her sisters had done that for her.

She realized Meghan would now be alone in the house. That might make her decide to look harder for a mate, if Peter wasn't the one for her.

Brett pulled into the garage and parked, then hurried to sweep Ellie out of the car, big gown and all. "Lots of petticoats?"

"Like in the old days."

"Corset?"

"Absolutely. Not a loose woman, you know."

He smiled. "A chemise?"

"For modesty."

"Bloomers or pantaloons?"

"Never as a wolf."

He grinned and rushed her into the house. She was trying to see all she could of it before he carried her into the bedroom. Most of the wolves who mated didn't get a new house to suit the two of them. Usually, one of the partners sold off their home, and the couple moved into the other. Since Meghan lived in the house behind the inn, and they'd always keep it, Ellie figured Brett's home would be hers too.

Brett flipped on a light switch, but before he had, she'd smelled the roses. Not the ones from her other suitors, but dozens in vases of fresh roses all over the room, sitting on the dark oak dresser, the end tables, and a tall bookshelf. The bedroom looked like a floral wonderland.

What if she hadn't said yes?

She smiled at Brett, loving him. "You are a romantic at heart." Or was he trying to prove that he could outdo her other suitors in the romance department? He didn't need to prove anything to her.

She wondered if he'd bought a ton of chocolate for her. She hoped not, or she'd have to surreptitiously give it away. She'd never be able to run it all off.

He set her down on the floor and she observed how clean everything was. The bed was neatly made, and a couple of Jake's pictures of a river and woods hung on the walls. Was Brett a perfectionist? Or had he made a special effort to clean up before he brought her here? That might have had something to do with him not taking her to the ball tonight.

She realized she still had a lot to learn about him. Just as he had a lot to learn about her.

She wrapped her arms around him and gave him a slow, lingering kiss as he held her tight and kissed her back. She figured she had a lifetime to learn all there was about him, but for now, this was all she wanted. Kissing, loving, mating.

He growled as he tried to unfasten her dress. "I think I made a mistake."

She reached up to unfasten his jacket. "How's that?"

"Way too many clothes." Then his brows arched.

She laughed, knowing just what he had in mind. For the first-time mating, they didn't need to remove *all* their clothes.

Then later, they could get naked and take it at a slower pace.

Brett yanked off his jacket and unbuttoned his vest, tearing it off and tossing it on a chest at the foot of his bed.

She couldn't remove her gown without his help. Instead, she sat on the bed and began untying one of her laced-up boots. He was hurrying to take his shoes off, and then his trousers and socks.

Kneeling before her, he helped her remove her other boot and slipped his hands up her stocking-covered leg until he reached her garter and unfastened it, sliding the stocking down in a gentle, sexy caress. After pulling it off, he did the same with the other stocking, his hands gliding over her skin as he slid the stocking down her leg.

"Hmm," she said, their hearts beating faster, their pheromones calling to each other in a primal wolf way.

"I've wanted you like this from the beginning," he murmured, his voice husky with desire. He ran his hands in a smooth caress up her legs, pushing them apart. Then he rose to yank off his boxer briefs. Still wearing his long shirt and puff tie, he moved in next to her and kissed the swell of her breasts in the low-cut gown.

Her skin tingled and heated with the whisper of his warm breath caressing it, his warm velvety tongue licking the upper swell of a breast before he kissed her mouth. It was a slow kiss that stirred memories of every real kiss he'd given her, of every fantasized kiss he'd bestowed upon her. Even so, this was different. This was the prelude to the consummation that would make them mates for life.

Suddenly, the frantic pace slowed and they enjoyed the moment—the kissing, touching, tasting, and breathing in each other's sweet and tangy woodland scents. As wolves, all of their senses were heightened, making the experience even more real and pleasurable.

She slipped her hand under his shirt and caressed his taut back muscles, while he nuzzled her cheek and then kissed her neck. She thought that if they were going to slow the pace, maybe he could help her out of her gown. But as soon as she tried to unbutton his shirt, he pushed up her gown, petticoats, and chemise and began to stroke her between her legs.

She arched—his strokes insistent, her body pliable—needing his touch. She wondered if he had been going

slower because he was trying to regain control over his
rampant need for her. She felt instantly empowered by
the notion and gave in to the ecstasy.

His breathing was unsteady, hers just as ragged.

The joining, the mating… How could they have
doubted their connection, despite their dreams, despite
their physical compatibility?

She felt caught up in the dream, and yet it was more
vibrant, more colorful. His crisp white shirt and tanned
skin, his dark hair and nearly black eyes—they were
real. In her dreams, she realized, she hadn't enjoyed the
smell of him or the sound of his thumping heart or his
heavy breathing. She hadn't felt the true warmth of his
touch, the way his tongue stroked hers and his mouth
teased and pressed against hers. Or the way his fingers
stroked her until she felt the climax shudder through her.
He inserted a finger inside her and smiled.

"I love you," he said, kissing her lips again and cen-
tering himself before easing into her and claiming her
for his mate.

"I love you right back, dream mate of mine."

———

Brett felt he was dreaming, that he'd captured his wolf
like he had every night for weeks, and yet it wasn't a
dream. He tried to hold back, to enjoy every moment,
but with Ellie still dressed in her beautiful gown, looking radiant and sexy, he couldn't prolong the inevitable
any further.

He nibbled on her ear as she ran her hands through
his hair, her touch a gentle caress, and he wondered if
she was seeing him in a new way like he was seeing her.

He was hers, just as she was his. No longer were they courting wolves, but mated.

He felt the end coming and held on, keeping still, trying to delay it, but she was stroking his ass, and he couldn't last.

He thrust again and again and spilled his seed deep inside her, smiling to think he might be the next wolf with pups on the way. He hadn't really given any thought to it before this.

For a moment, he stayed inside her, resting against her, but then he kissed her. Before they fell asleep, he needed to help her out of her clothes. He didn't want all that fabric between them—not when they cuddled, and certainly not the next time they made love tonight.

"It was even better than our dream sex, more real. Not that it didn't seem so real before." She stood while he unfastened her gown.

"I realized I'd never smelled our pheromones when we were dream mating." Brett still had come, despite not having that added stimulation.

"Agreed." She stepped out of her gown, and he began to untie her corset, kissing more of her breasts the more he revealed. She was getting all hot and ready for him again. "It was more vivid, and yet the other seemed just as real, in a dreamy sort of way, when it was happening."

She eyed his long shirt and then removed his tie, careful to secure the diamond tie pin to it so it wouldn't get lost in all the clothes. Then she began to unbutton his shirt, wanting to see all of him naked.

He started to pull off her petticoats—three of them,

which gave the gown fullness and kept her warm outside in the chillier air. The top petticoat had been on display beneath the open-fronted gown.

"We have to move your clothes over here. I had thought about asking Laurel about moving some of your things, but I wanted to keep my proposal a secret."

"It's still Victorian Days for four more days, so I'll still be wearing Victorian gowns." She opened his shirt and found his cock was beginning to stir.

"Maybe you can wear fewer petticoats?"

She laughed. "We'll make dates, and I'll be sure to start undressing a half hour beforehand."

He smiled and kissed her, his hard body pressed against hers, completely naked while she was still wearing her chemise. He ran his hands over her breasts in the semi-transparent gown.

"This, I can handle. Though I don't mind all the rest if I'm not in a hurry. For now, the chemise has to go." He pulled it gently over her head and laid it with their other clothes on the maple chest.

They snuggled in bed, the blankets covering them, and Ellie kissed his naked chest. "If I dream of having sex with you again in the middle of the night—"

"It will be the real thing." Brett kissed her cheek. "I wonder if, when Darien and Jake are apart from their mates for any length of time, they still have dream sex. Then again, I have no intention of testing that theory any time soon."

She smiled and closed her eyes, knowing she was right where she needed to be.

They were dozing when Ellie's phone rang in the middle of the night, and she glanced at the caller ID. *Meghan*. She wouldn't be calling Ellie at this late hour when she was newly mated to Brett unless there was real trouble.

Chapter 19

"YOU HAVE TO COME HELP ME DO SOMETHING. Anything. The piano is going crazy. Can Brett and his brothers get ahold of the movers or something and move it?" Meghan said frantically to Ellie over the phone. "Not only that, but then the howling began. You were right. One of the ghosts is howling. And running around the hotel as a wolf. I had three calls from human guests asking me to get ahold of the police or animal control."

"I'm getting dressed. I'll tell Brett. We'll be right over." Ellie pulled her chemise over her head. "Are you at the inn right now?"

"Yes. We passed out earplugs and told the human guests that animal control would take care of the wolf right away, but earplugs aren't working for the wolves. Nor are the questions about why a baby grand piano is playing like it's a player piano when that's not possible. Or why a wolf is running around the lobby. I've tried to get ahold of Laurel, but she and CJ must have turned off their cell phones."

"So who is howling?"

"Matilda. Can't be Chrissy because the one playing the piano is doing a horrible job of it."

"We'll be right over." Ellie looked at the corset. No way was she going to get laced up in that and put on all the petticoats.

Brett was already dressed in jeans and socks and calling

his brothers. He paused to dig in a drawer, pulled out a pair of light-gray sweats, and handed them to Ellie. She smiled at him and yanked off her chemise, then slipped on the pants and pulled the sweatshirt over her head.

"Okay. Hurry before we lose our guests," Meghan said.

"Will do. I'm staying on the line. Just hold on." Ellie kept her sister on the phone to give her moral support but asked Brett, "Where do we move the piano to?" She started lacing up one of her boots. She'd have to move her clothes to Brett's or at least grab an overnight bag for a few days.

Brett had finished dressing and laced up her other boot, then they headed for the garage.

"Your house. We can move it through the french patio doors. Otherwise, we need to get the professional movers to take it anywhere else. I can call them, but they're not wolves and I doubt they move pianos in the middle of the night. Not to mention it could spook them if she started playing while they're moving it. I could see them dropping it and running if Matilda decided she didn't like that we're moving it from the inn."

"Agreed."

Brett called his brother Sarandon and cousins Tom, Jake, and Darien. They all lived in the area. Eric lived four hours away, so Brett didn't call him.

"We're on our way," Darien said. "Congratulations to you and Ellie again. See you over there."

"Thanks, Darien." Turning to Ellie, Brett said, "I'll take my car and drop by CJ and Laurel's house. I know she'll want to be there to help calm the guests, if she needs to."

"Okay," Ellie said to Brett, then she told Meghan on the phone, "I'm on my way. Be over in a few minutes. Brett's running by CJ and Laurel's place to alert them about what's going on."

"All right. But hurry." Meghan sounded completely frazzled.

"We'll take care of it. We should have already moved the piano." Ellie gave Brett a kiss, then got into her car and drove off. He was right behind her.

"Yeah, we should have." Meghan paused. "Omigod. The Wernicke brothers just arrived."

"What?" Ellie was careful on the snowy roads, but she sped up a bit.

"Who told them?" Meghan asked, irritated.

Brett better not have, or he was in hot water.

"Got to deal with this. Bye." Meghan ended the call before Ellie had a chance to respond.

As soon as Ellie arrived at the inn, she saw Chrissy peering out the attic window. *Great*. Ellie hoped she wasn't bothering Rose, who was staying in that room. Then Ellie wondered if Matilda had been giving Chrissy lessons. When Meghan had said the piano was going crazy, Ellie thought that Matilda was trying to teach Chrissy how to play, and she was either having a difficult time mastering the right keys or she was angry and doing whatever she could to annoy Matilda.

No music was playing. And no wolves were howling. Ellie didn't trust that it wouldn't start back up if they left the piano where it was. Or that Matilda wouldn't start running around as a wolf again.

"Who was playing?" Ellie asked as Meghan rushed outside to greet her. "I saw Chrissy in the attic window."

"Both of them at first. At least I think so. One was playing perfect notes, and the other was making lots of mistakes. So I figured Matilda was trying to teach Chrissy, and it wasn't working out very well. Then the howling began. Maybe because Chrissy kept playing to annoy Matilda. Maybe because it was hurting her ears. And of course, our guests had to see if a real wolf was in the lobby. And of course, they saw it. Or at least a couple of people did. Not everyone. You know how it goes."

"And the Wernickes?"

"Yeah, they're in there. Offering to help fix things."

Brett got out of his vehicle. "CJ and Laurel are getting dressed and will be over in a minute."

Sarandon parked, and Jake soon joined them. Ellie saw Darien's car approaching.

When he joined them, Darien asked, "Where are we moving the piano?"

"To the house," Ellie said. "Sorry, Meghan, but if you want to stay with us tonight, you can."

"I'll be fine. I don't think Chrissy will leave the inn. I can sleep through Matilda's beautiful piano music."

Laurel and CJ arrived after that.

All the Silver men went inside to move the piano, while Meghan stayed outside with Laurel to explain what had happened, including that the Wernicke brothers were there.

When the Silver men began to move the piano, Ellie grabbed Stanton's arm and hauled him aside. Speaking for his ears only as his brothers assisted with doors and the piano, she asked, "What are you doing here?"

"I heard Brett and you agreed to become mated

wolves. I wanted to congratulate you and pay Brett for the damages to the car. I thought you both would be over here."

"Right. In the middle of the night? I can't believe you can't come up with a better story than that."

"The inn's open now. I figured someone would be over here."

"You wouldn't be here just to check out Chrissy, would you?"

"That wasn't Chrissy playing," Stanton said.

"How would you know?"

"She worked as a maid for years. Most likely she wouldn't have had the money to pay for lessons or the time to indulge in practicing." Stanton motioned to the framed memorial on the wall. "If I had to guess, I'd say Matilda was playing the piano. Yolan said he'd help you with the ghost for free. We all will."

Ellie wondered if Darien had read Stanton the riot act at the jailhouse over the hit-and-run incident, ghost or no ghost, and then decided to allow Stanton to help. Pack members' safety was Darien and Lelandi's main concern. Darien could have banned Stanton and his brothers from the Silver pack's territory since none of them had reported the accident.

"At the house then." Ellie knew she should ask Laurel's permission, but if the Wernicke brothers could help resolve this, then at this point, they had to try.

"Okay. Good. Tonight?"

"Be my guest. If you can do it, maybe Matilda will find some peace and Chrissy will be relieved she's gone. But no TV show production."

"Right."

She and Stanton hurried after the men. Stanton actually helped to carry the piano, and Peter dropped by and helped Meghan move the piano bench to the house.

"What was she playing?" Ellie asked Meghan.

"Bach's 'Love Song.' Beautiful piece. Do you think she's trying to tell *us* something?" Meghan smiled at Ellie.

Ellie sure hoped Matilda would be all right with the mating. Not that the ghost could do a whole lot about it. She wondered if Matilda knew Ellie and Brett were mated now. She frowned. Would Matilda stay with the piano or with Chrissy at the inn? What a mess. She turned to Laurel, who was directing where the piano would go. "Stanton offered to help us exorcise the ghost. I said he could. It's free of charge."

"I thought Yolan was the only one who could do that," Laurel said privately to Ellie.

"Not sure now. I'm just worried that this is going to backfire. Chrissy says she didn't want Matilda there, but what if she misses her?" Ellie ran her hand over the top of the piano, wondering if moving it here would help or cause more trouble. And what about Chrissy? Ellie hadn't wanted to upset her.

"I hadn't thought of that," Laurel said.

After moving the piano to the MacTire sisters' home, Yolan tried to communicate with Brett's great-aunt. "Matilda, do you want to return to Brett's home?"

Everyone gathered around and watched the piano for any indication Matilda was there and intended to respond. Nothing happened.

Brett didn't believe Yolan would have any success at it. He truly believed that if anyone could, he would be the one to convince her. Besides his grandmother, whom he was really close to, Brett had been the closest to his great-aunt, though he'd been a kid when she died.

"Is there someone else in the room that you'd like to speak through?" Yolan asked.

That would be creepy, and Brett hoped Matilda wouldn't decide to jump into his body and start talking. He'd seen a few stories on TV where that had happened, either with or without a séance. He glanced at Ellie who was watching him. Had that ever happened to her?

"Anyone at all? Brett, maybe?" Yolan glanced in Brett's direction.

Brett stiffened. He couldn't help it. The idea just didn't appeal. It was two in the morning, and he wanted to return to bed with his new mate. Though he also wanted to help the sisters resolve the ghost issue, help his great-aunt find her way to her new home, and give Chrissy some peace. He hoped Meghan's sleep wouldn't be disturbed all night either.

Everyone looked so serious, waiting for any indication that Matilda was present. What if she had stayed back at the inn with Chrissy?

"Aunt Matilda," Brett said, not wanting to prolong this any further, "I wanted to tell you that Ellie and I are mated wolves, if you didn't know already. We'll talk in the morning."

"Thank you for helping me with my piano lessons, Matilda." Ellie slipped her arm around Brett's waist. "I have to say this is the first time I've ever stuck with anything, and I'm thoroughly enjoying playing the piano with Brett."

"Hey, let's clear out," Darien said in the pack-leader voice that said he was in charge.

Yolan looked disappointed that he hadn't had any success. Everyone began to leave, all except for Darien, who motioned that he needed to speak with Brett and Ellie.

Meghan was waiting for everyone to leave so she could return to bed, but Darien said to her, "I want you to come and stay with Lelandi and me for the night."

Even though Ellie had made the offer for Meghan to stay with her and Brett, and Laurel would have offered if she'd had the chance, Darien's was not an offer. His was a pack-leader order. Brett knew Darien well enough to suspect what was coming next.

"Just pack a bag and you can ride with me, unless you want to take your own car," Darien said.

"I'll drive my own car so I can return tomorrow without inconveniencing you." Meghan went up the stairs to her bedroom.

"Okay, I want you and Ellie to stay here tonight. Alone," Darien said.

Brett had suspected as much. How were they going to get in some good loving if Matilda was staying where they were? But Darien knew how close Brett had been to Great-Aunt Matilda.

"You're the only one of us who plays the piano now. You've mated Ellie, and Matilda was working with her at the piano. So I think if anyone has a chance of reaching her, it's going to be the two of you. Good luck."

Darien shook Brett's hand and gave Ellie a hug. Then he and Meghan left, and Ellie and Brett were alone.

"Well, what do you want to do?" Ellie asked.

Go to bed with his mate and make love to her—naked this time. "Okay, she talked to us with the song sheets the one time."

"She played music to answer one of our questions, but Meghan's the one who's so good at knowing what the songs are. I might not know them."

"Let's bring out the song sheets." Brett started to set up one at a time. "Okay, why are you here, Matilda? Do you feel you have unfinished business?" He kept placing one sheet of music up after another, and each time, a puff of air sent the sheets flying just like before.

When he put "I Will Survive" by Gloria Gaynor on the stand, it stayed put, as if Matilda was trying to tell them that was the clue.

"I will survive," Ellie said. "So is she saying she won't leave? That whatever made her die won't stop her from staying with her beloved piano?"

"Aunt Matilda, you went out in the rowboat with Theodore. Correct?" Brett thought they might finally get somewhere with this.

The piano started to play "She Loves You" by the Beatles.

"'She Loves You,'" Ellie said, "and it says *yeah, yeah, yeah* a number of times."

Brett felt chills race up his spine. "Did you fall overboard?"

The Beatles' song played again.

"Yes," Ellie whispered the word. She swallowed hard and reached over and squeezed Brett's hand.

He wrapped his arm around her waist and held her close, hating that Matilda had drowned and no one had known it. He suspected foul play, or why wouldn't Theodore have told everyone what had happened?

"Did you and Theodore have a fight?" Brett rubbed Ellie's back.

The Beatles song played.

"Over Grandmom not marrying him?"

She played the Zombies' "Tell Her No."

"I don't understand," Brett said. "Do you mean Caroline wasn't there? She should have been there? With Theodore instead of with you, Aunt Matilda?"

The Beatles' song played again. "Yes!" Ellie said. "Why would he have asked her out on the boat when he was seeing your grandmother?"

"To make up to Matilda? Maybe he hadn't been very nice to her because he wanted to marry Caroline, and he didn't like that she was staying with Matilda instead. So he asked her out to make peace with her."

Yeah, yeah, yeah…

"Okay, the part about the Zombies' song "Tell Her No"… Did that mean Matilda thought Caroline shouldn't marry him?" Brett asked.

Matilda pounded out the Beatles' song again.

"Okay, her answer is yes. Because the boating accident wasn't an accident?"

The Zombies' song played again.

"No," Ellie said. "It *wasn't* an accident. Do you think Remer might know anything about it? About what had happened between his grandfather and Matilda?"

"I don't know. Do we wake Remer now and ask?" Brett asked.

"I'd say so," Ellie said. "For Matilda's sake, I think we should, despite the hour. Remer may not know anything about it, and I hate upsetting him, but we need to resolve this if we can."

Agreeing, Brett called Remer and put him on speaker. "I'm sorry to be calling in the middle of the night, but we have a situation that needs to be rectified. Apparently, my great-aunt Matilda went boating with your grandfather and…"

"You had to call me at this hour to tell me this?" Remer definitely wasn't a night owl.

"We have a bit of a situation. Matilda wants this resolved and—"

"She's dead."

"Right. Since we moved the piano to the MacTire sisters' inn, Matilda has been playing it from time to time. We moved it to the MacTire sisters' home in back of the inn to give the inn guests some peace tonight."

"A…spirit," Remer said skeptically.

Brett saw Ellie looking at him, her expression saying she was used to skepticism concerning her ability to witness ghostly happenings. Once Brett had seen what he had, he'd forgotten that a lot of people wouldn't believe.

"Okay, I know that could be hard to swallow if you don't believe in ghosts. I wasn't a believer either until Matilda made her presence known."

"I don't understand. As far as I know, my grandfather was interested in mating your grandmother. She wouldn't. They had a falling-out and never spoke to each other again," Remer said, sounding tired and annoyed.

"She—Matilda, that is—said she drowned while boating with your grandfather." Brett didn't tell him she had said Theodore drowned her, but if Remer knew the history, he would know that wasn't the story anyone had shared at the time.

"Okay, so you're saying…?"

"She said it wasn't an accident."

"A ghost said this."

"Yeah. If we can prove this was the case, hopefully, she can rest in peace." And so could they. "We wouldn't need to tell the world, if you'd prefer. But just learn the truth."

"You need to have evidence that something happened, other than the word of a ghost."

"Yeah. After Aunt Matilda was found dead in bed, her gown on backward, her hair still damp, Grandmom couldn't find her sister's favorite dress to bury her in. Not only that, but both Grandmom's towel and Matilda's had been used that night."

Remer let out his breath in a disgruntled manner. "I thought you'd discovered something that could have connected my grandfather with her death. Like he'd lost a glove in her bed or something."

"Glove?" Brett asked, surprised. He was about to get to the part about the rowboat and what they'd found in it. Why would Remer have mentioned that particular article of clothing? Why not anything else? Like maybe a cuff link? Brett quickly described what pack members had found in the rowboat after Matilda died.

Remer became deathly quiet.

Brett was sure he knew something about the missing glove. Brett gave Ellie a light squeeze. She gave him a harder one back.

"I'm not agreeing that anything you've said has merit. But if you want to come over at a decent hour in the morning, I'll show you what I have. My grandfather's steamer trunk is in the attic. I looked in it once and saw what I thought were my grandmother's things that he'd preserved and one of his gloves. I thought it was odd he only had one glove in the chest, but I didn't give it any thought after that. You're welcome to look in the morning. I'd prefer that you don't mention it in the newspaper, if you learn that there was foul play. I'll understand if you have to share with your families, which include our pack leaders."

"Understand," Brett said, glad they might finally have some resolution.

"Night," both Ellie and Brett said.

Would Matilda accept those conditions?

"Matilda, is that all right with you?" Ellie asked after they ended the call.

Matilda didn't respond.

"She's either thinking this all over, or she's gone to bed like *we* need to," Brett said, taking Ellie's hand and leading her to the stairs.

"Do you think she's happy for us? That we're mated?" Ellie asked as they climbed the stairs.

The Beatles song began to play, and Ellie smiled. "I'd say that was a yes."

"But her response means she is still here." Brett closed the door to Ellie's bedroom. He hadn't thought they'd be here tonight—or any night, really.

"Do you think she'll be bothered or will bother us if we make love?" Ellie slid her hands up Brett's shirt.

"We're mated wolves, and if she's going to hang around, she'll have to get used to it. She seems to stay by the piano, so at least she won't be watching us."

Ellie groaned. "What do we do now with the piano?"

"We'll ask her where she'd prefer us to take it." Brett began kissing his mate, wanting to make love to her naked this time, only in *her* bedroom. "I'm all awake now. What about you?"

"I'm ready for some more wolf loving." She began to pull off his sweatshirt, and he did the same thing with hers, baring her beautiful breasts to him.

He definitely preferred her wearing sweats to the gown for some quick loving. He was glad Ellie wasn't too tired, but hoped his great-aunt wouldn't be upset by it and try to interfere.

This time, he trailed kisses down Ellie's chest, licking and suckling a nipple. She let out a soft moan. Arching her back, she pressed her abdomen against his stiffening cock, making it jerk, and he wanted inside her all over again. He slid his hands down the sweatpants she was wearing and started to stroke her with one hand, the other holding on to her as she melted against the bed. As soon as her head hit the pillow, he heard a crinkling sound beneath it and Ellie's face turned red.

He waited for a moment for her to do something about what was under her pillow, but she just smiled.

"Did you want to move it first?"

She let out her breath in exasperation, then grabbed a manila envelope from under her pillow, shoved it in her bedside table drawer, and slammed it shut.

He sat beside her and took her hand in his, gently caressing it and waiting for her to say something, anything.

"Oh, all right." She jerked the drawer open and shoved the envelope into his hands.

Red Hot Rush was stamped in red letters on the envelope, which was addressed to Ellie from her aunt. When he looked inside, he saw the artwork and smiled, slipped the envelope back in the drawer, and shut it.

Then he began kissing her all over again, loving her for being Ellie.

The sex was amazing, but only because she was amazing and this was meant to be.

He began stroking her again and kissing her eager mouth, soaking up the smell and feel of her, tangling his tongue with hers, wringing her out until she shouted, "Omigod, yes!"

He smiled and worked on her boots, then yanked off his. She was tugging off the sweatpants while he unfastened his belt and dropped his jeans to the floor.

Then he joined her in the bed, kissing her as she slid her hands over his back, caressing and pumping him up before he slid his cock inside her and began to thrust.

Soft piano music began to play in the background. Brett smiled, and they began kissing again, and he continued to thrust. Nothing was stopping him from loving his mate.

When he came with the final plunge, he breathed out her name, "Ellie, my mate, my love."

"You are fantastic," Ellie whispered against his lips. "And I love you with all my heart."

They collapsed in each other's embrace, ready to sleep the rest of the night away.

But Brett had to ask about the photos first. "I thought you said you didn't want them. The photos, I mean."

"I didn't. My aunt sent them to me anyway."

Brett kissed the top of Ellie's head. "And you tucked them under your pillow. Why?"

"Meghan saw me with the package, and I didn't want her to see what was in it."

"Ahh. Then if you want me to, I can get rid of them for you."

"Ha! The last time you got rid of them, do you see where they ended up?"

He laughed. "Underneath your pillow."

Early the next morning, Brett and Ellie woke to soft piano music. Ellie cuddled against Brett, his hand gently stroking her back. "Nice easy music to listen to while waking up."

He let out his breath. "What if she doesn't want to leave? Even if we learn the truth this morning? What if she stays with the piano wherever we put it?"

"Well, we could take it back to your house."

"Our house."

"Right. Then it wouldn't disturb anyone."

"I keep wondering why she revealed herself now and not earlier."

Ellie kissed Brett's cheek and got out of bed. "You kissed me, and I was about to kiss you back. I was leaning against the piano, and we must have earned her Victorian ire. That's all I can figure. Once she was out, she couldn't leave."

"What if it doesn't have to do with us?"

"What do you mean?"

"What if it has to do with the place? The inn?"

"She's been playing here too."

"Right. So she was 'awakened' and now is here to stay unless we can help her to move on. What if there was something about my place that made her feel at home?"

"And she quit playing. The movers are going to think

we're crazy if we keep having the piano moved back and forth."

Brett smiled, then frowned. "As long as she doesn't play while they're trying to move it."

Chapter 20

THE NEXT MORNING, BRETT AND ELLIE ARRIVED AT Remer's house. Ellie really felt bad that his grandfather might have been involved in anything to do with Matilda's death.

Remer greeted them at the door and motioned them in. "I should have had you come over last night. I'm sure you must have needed some kind of resolution one way or another. I had a friend come over and help me move the steamer trunk from the attic to the living room. I don't remember my grandmother at all. She died before I was born. From what Matilda had said, my grandmother had been friends with both her and Caroline. It wasn't until after Caroline's husband died that Theodore started to court her."

Ellie took hold of Brett's hand as they looked at the old camelback wooden steamer trunk, with its leather straps and brass fittings still in excellent condition.

Remer opened it for them, and they looked inside. They found a lady's parasol, a faded forest-green dress, gloves, stockings, shoes, a few other articles of women's clothing, and one man's glove.

"Does that help solve the mystery?" Remer asked.

Brett handed him the picture of his aunt and grandmother with Theodore and Benjamin. "It appears to be the same dress she was wearing and the same parasol she had six months before her death. Though you can't tell from the photo, Bertha Hastings said the dress was forest green."

"I'm sorry. Dad said he'd been worried about his dad when he'd had a terrible fall around the same time that your aunt died. Granddad said he'd slipped on spilled water and hit his head. Dad thought he should move in with him, but Granddad said he was fine. Granddad didn't go to Matilda's funeral, and shortly afterward, he and Caroline broke up. We thought it was over her refusal to mate him. He'd told my father she'd marry him now that Matilda was gone. Dad thought he shouldn't get his hopes up. I'm...sorry."

"You didn't have anything to do with it. It still might have been that she stood and fell out of the boat. Your grandfather worried how it would look to my grand-mother. So he covered up the whole affair. He did want to marry her after all," Brett said.

"Could be. But would Matilda come back to say she hadn't died accidentally if it was an accident?"

"Yes," Ellie said. "If she wanted her family to know how she died, whether it was accidentally or not. She didn't want her sister marrying him because he hadn't told anyone the truth."

Remer nodded. "I don't know what else to say except I'm sorry. Feel free to take her things with you. And...I hope you're still agreeable to lessons?" Remer looked desolate about it.

"Oh, absolutely," Ellie quickly said.

"Agreed. Thank you," Brett said.

Ellie thanked him too, and then they left. "What are you going to do with her things?"

"What about displaying them with her memorial in

the inn lobby? Make a glassed-in case and include the picture of her and her sister all dressed up."

"With Theodore and Benjamin? Do you think she'll object to Theodore being in the picture?"

"Maybe, but we could give it a shot. Or I can have the photo of her and her sister blown up and remove Theodore from the photo."

"Okay, sounds good."

With the movers scheduled to arrive at the house later that afternoon, Brett and Ellie returned there, made love, showered together, dressed, and headed downstairs for a late breakfast. She hoped this would resolve the piano-playing issue. If it didn't, she wasn't sure what else to try.

"Did you want us to move the piano back to Brett's home?" Ellie asked Matilda, hoping she'd get an answer.

"Our home," Brett reminded Ellie, and she loved that it was now her home too.

Matilda didn't respond.

"I don't normally eat big breakfasts, but I'm famished. What about you?" Ellie asked. "It must have been all of our workouts."

He chuckled. "Breakfast will help give us energy for more."

"Are you off from the paper today?" She made omelets filled with cheese, bell peppers, and ham while Brett made coffee and tea and set the table.

"Yeah. No way would they make me work today."

"Good. I haven't talked to my sisters about not going to work at the inn today, but I suspect they already understand I'd rather be with you for the day." Ellie glanced at the piano. "Matilda might be feeling a bit

unsure, not knowing where the piano should be now."
Ellie served the omelets.

Brett made some toast for them. "Why would she be
upset about us taking it to the inn?"

"Maybe she just couldn't communicate with you.
Then she realized we could see Chrissy. I'm not sure.
However, she liked helping to teach me to play. Maybe
that made her feel alive again. This had been her calling.
She failed at teaching Chrissy, but she'd failed with stu-
dents before, so she knows that's a hazard of teaching."

"All right. I just hope she's happy with the piano
being back at the house."

They had just finished breakfast when Brett got a
call. "Hey, CJ? Okay, putting it on speaker."

"I just got a call from Stanton that he and his brothers
are stranded a couple of miles out of town headed in
your direction. The classic Plymouth made them get out
of the car, and then it drove off into the woods on that
rarely used road to Lover's Leap."

"Are the brothers all right?" Ellie hurried to put away
the food.

"Stanton says he has a broken leg. I'm headed over
there, but I thought you might want to meet us out there.
The other brothers only have scrapes and bruises."

"We're on our way." Brett quickly told him what
they learned about their great-aunt.

"Hell," CJ said.

"Yeah, I know. Be there soon." Brett ended the call,
helped Ellie with the food, grabbed their jackets, and
they headed out to the car.

Ellie was dressed in jeans and a sweater and boots.
Brett was dressed similarly. She was glad they'd

both had a chance to pick up a change of clothes that wasn't Victorian.

"I can't believe Stanton and his brothers were still driving that car. They should have buried it like I said," Ellie told Brett.

"The show must go on."

"It's a good thing the car didn't kill them."

No matter how much Brett tried to believe the car was possessed, he had a really hard time envisioning it. "You don't think it's just a publicity stunt for their show? Just to dramatize things a bit? Then they got a little out of hand and Stanton was really injured?"

Ellie processed that for a few minutes. "Knowing Stanton, anything is possible, I suppose."

"You really think the only way to end this is to bury the car?"

"If you can't exorcise ghosts—and the brothers have already tried to do it with some of the conventional means—I'd say so. The only other way to deal with it might be if Shorty's grandson attempted to communicate with him. There's no guarantee that will make any difference. What if the car was buried and it still honked its horn from the grave? No telling, really."

"Unless Shorty is buried somewhere in a private grave, I don't see that we can bury it with him or near him," Brett said.

"No. I want to see where it ended up. Maybe we can put the ghost to rest so Stanton can't try to exploit it any further for his TV program."

"Okay, well, you let me know how I can help."

She smiled at him. "Thanks, Brett, for going along with all this."

"We're mated, Ellie," he said. "That means we're in this together. We're partners in everything, including this ghost-buster business."

"I love you."

"I love you right back, honey."

They saw Stanton sitting in the melting snow off the road, CJ's taillights glowing red as he pulled over to park up ahead.

Brett pulled behind CJ's car and parked. He and Ellie got out to hear the brothers' story.

Vernon and Yolan had splinted Stanton's leg using a couple of tree branches and Vernon's shirt torn into strips.

"The ambulance is on its way," CJ said. "So what happened exactly?"

"Shorty told us to get out of the damn car, or he was going to kill the lot of us," Vernon said.

"You heard him?" Brett asked. "All of you?"

"Well, no," Vernon said, both he and Stanton turning their attention on Yolan.

"He spoke through you," Ellie said to Yolan.

"That's what Stanton and Vernon told me. I blacked out and don't remember anything. Not until Vernon shoved me out of the car and I hit the pavement."

"Sorry, but at least Shorty slowed down for a few minutes so we could get out. Shorty inhabited Stanton's body and used him to do what he wanted. Stanton didn't have control, but he was in denial that Shorty had taken over his physical being," Vernon said.

"So you pushed Yolan out of the car and…?" Ellie prompted.

"I told Stanton to jump while he had the chance. I

jumped out after Yolan, who was just coming to. The car sped up, and Stanton was still at the wheel. I ran after the car and grabbed the driver's door handle, yanked the door open, and seized Stanton's arm. I expected him to fight me because he wasn't leaving the car. Then I realized Shorty was controlling him. I jerked Stanton out of the car before it roared off, then took that side road. At that point, Stanton fell, landing harder than we had on the paved road, and broke his leg."

"Are you all right?" Ellie asked Yolan, who nodded.

"Hell, I'm the one who was injured," Stanton said, annoyed.

"Do you want to come with us?" Ellie asked Yolan. "We're going after the car."

"Yeah, unless you want me to drive it. If that's the case, I'll pass." Yolan gave her a half smile.

"No. You're going to help me get rid of Shorty or the car."

"That works for me."

"Hey, we need to return the car to its owner in good shape," Stanton said.

The ambulance's siren told them it was on its way, and Ellie, Brett, and Yolan climbed into Brett's car.

"Vernon?" Brett offered.

"I'll go with Stanton," Vernon said. "He'll be hell to live with if one of us doesn't go with him to the clinic."

Stanton grunted.

"Don't get yourselves killed over this," CJ warned. "We've got enough damned ghosts running around."

"We'll be careful." Brett had no idea how they were going to manage that. He drove his car to Lover's Lane and saw the fresh tracks in the snow. "It's a one-lane road, so if he decides to come back while we're trying to catch up to him, we could have a collision."

"Will he be able to pick up speed out here? The road is rough, and it curves so much." Ellie was staring straight ahead, Yolan in the back peering between them.

"His car is bigger and heavier, but everything you mentioned will help to slow him down." Brett glanced in the rearview mirror. "Yolan, you need to sit back and put on your seat belt."

"Can't see anything from back here."

"You'll fly headfirst into my windshield if he hits us with any force."

Yolan snapped his buckle in place.

"So you said the side road goes to Lover's Leap. Does it loop around, or would the car *have* to come back this way?" Ellie asked.

"It dead-ends at a cliff. To my knowledge, no one has ever leaped off there, but it is a scenic spot where trysts occur occasionally, I've heard."

"Not you though, right, Brett?" Ellie was smiling when she asked.

He laughed. "Not me."

"Why in the world would the car go this way and not continue on down the main road?" Ellie asked.

Yolan cleared his throat. "This is where Shorty turned to lose the feds and the local sheriff's men, but they saw his tracks in the snow, continued to follow him, and then shot at his car. He hit the tree and died."

"I remember hearing that story. At the time, I didn't know about the bank-robber part of it or the shooting. Just that someone had hit a tree and died out here. It was that tree right there." Brett slowed down so everyone could get a look at the pine tree.

Some of the bark was gone, there was a big dent in one side, and the tree was leaning over a bit, despite how tall it was.

Brett drove past the tree.

Ellie's heart was beating faster like his was. "So the road has a turnaround up ahead?"

"Yeah, and a parking spot. It's always been a narrow road, but the trees have encroached even more."

They heard a distant crash, and Ellie looked at Brett. He wondered if the car had driven off the cliff. But then they heard the engine revving up and the horn sounding *ahh-woo-gah*, and Brett knew the Plymouth was headed back their way.

"It's coming." Brett started to back up, but the curves were making it difficult as he looked backward and twisted and turned the wheel, navigating down the narrow road. The Plymouth's engine roared as it approached. They'd never make it back to the main road and out of the Plymouth's path in time.

"Brett!" Ellie braced for impact.

"God, we're all going to die!" Yolan shouted.

Brett wanted to sock him for being such a damn alarmist. Brett's car nearly slid into a tree on an icy patch. "Keep your cool, man."

"I had to say it," Yolan said, and this time his voice was unsteady, but he sounded like he'd been trying to make a joke. "They always have an ass screaming that in a movie."

"Brett!" Ellie grabbed his arm.

He turned to see the menacing car with the big steel

grill and heavy-duty bumper only feet away. A man wearing a suit, tie, and white hat with a black band around it stared back at him. He looked to be mid-twenties, his face clean-shaven and his expression hard.

Everyone braced for the car to strike. It hit—and yet nothing happened. It was as if the Plymouth had driven straight through them and vanished behind them.

In shock, all three of them sat there staring out the back window.

Was the car still parked at Lover's Leap?

"The bang we heard earlier." Ellie sighed with relief. "Do you think he drove the car off the cliff?"

"Maybe." Shaken, Brett drove back toward the cliff, having a devil of a time fathoming that a ghost could have taken the car, destroyed it, and created a ghost car. Ellie had had years to process this stuff. He was such a newbie that it all seemed so unreal. Disquieting.

Her heart was racing like his was, so it must have been just as genuine for her, and she was just as upset about it as he was.

When they arrived at the parking area, they saw the car sitting at the edge of the cliff, the engine running. It looked tangible. Was it?

Brett wasn't sure what to do. Should he block it in, move out of its path, or park next to it? At least if he parked next to it, the car couldn't hit his.

He left space between them and parked. The car's engine was still revving. "What do you want to do?"

"I think it's already done. I think that's the ghost car, though it looks so real." Ellie got out of the car, and Brett and Yolan hurried after her.

Suddenly, the car tore off over the cliff and fell to

its demise on the rocks below. No resounding crash occurred this time. They all moved to the edge and stared down at the crumpled car on the jagged rocks, the river rushing by. On the bank stood a man wearing the same 1930s suit, white hat, and shoes as the car's earlier driver. He glanced up at the cliffs, tipped his hat to them, turned, and walked across the river. He didn't wade in it, instead floating on top of it, and then his body faded to mist and he was gone.

Brett wrapped his arm around Ellie. She was shivering, either from the cold or the shock of it.

"Hell, the owner isn't going to believe we had nothing to do with this." Yolan folded his arms and blew out his breath in the frosty air.

Ellie cast him an annoyed look. "You had everything to do with it."

"How do you figure?" He gave her a growly look right back.

"You drove the vehicle in winter." She looked back down at the car. "I think he's found his resting spot."

"He got away." Brett didn't think he'd ever make it as a ghost psychologist, but that's what he assumed had happened. The ghost had to make his escape from the Feds and other police officials, and then he could go on his way.

"Yeah. The feds can't chase him anymore. And"— Ellie glanced at Yolan—"no one else will ever drive his car again."

Yolan snorted. "Stanton is going to be pissed."

"Better pissed than dead." Brett moved Ellie back to his car. "Ready to go home?"

"And do what?" Ellie asked.

He knew she meant about the piano.

"I'll call the movers and have them take it back to our house."

Yolan climbed into the car. "Maybe we should toss it down there with the car."

Ellie rolled her eyes at him.

"Hey, what if they hit it off?" Yolan actually looked serious.

"My great-aunt and a bank robber?" Brett could just imagine her scolding the guy for taking up a life of crime. He backed up, turned around, and headed toward the main road.

"So what do you want me to do?" Yolan asked.

"Go with CJ to the hospital. We have other business to take care of," Brett said.

"I can help. I'd much rather help you try to deal with your great-aunt's situation than see Stanton at the hospital."

"We've got this." Ellie relaxed a little in the seat.

Brett sure hoped so because he truly wanted his great-aunt to be happy, but he didn't want her to disturb them if she chose to play the piano at inopportune times.

He called CJ and asked if he was still there.

"Yeah, just determining what happened here by the tire tracks in the snow. What happened with you?"

"We're returning. Can you give Yolan a lift to the hospital?"

"Sure. What about the car?"

"At the bottom of the cliff."

"Okay. I heard a really distant bang but then heard your engine, so I knew you were still driving and figured you were okay."

"Yeah, we're okay, but Lover's Lane visitors might have a ghostly experience if they come this way."

"The car's really at the bottom of the cliff?"

"Yeah. No more ghost story for Stanton." Brett made it to the main road, drove to the site where CJ was parked, and let Yolan out.

CJ leaned against Brett's car door as he rolled down the window. "I'll go check it out."

"Can we leave it there?" Ellie asked.

"This land is pack territory. If the Plymouth's owner wants to pay to haul it out of there, he can. It would probably cost too much to be bothered with. He can just get the insurance money and go from there. Otherwise, I'm sure Darien will agree to leave it there as a wildlife refuge."

"Just be careful when you drive that way. If the ghost car comes at you, threatening to smash you, it seems real." Brett didn't want his brother having a heart attack over a ghost car.

"Or it might be gone now completely," Ellie said.

"Okay, gotcha. Come on, Yolan. We'll take a drive on Lover's Lane, take a look over Lover's Leap, and then I'll get you back to town." CJ waved at Brett, then they took off.

"At least that resolved the issue of anyone driving the car and causing an accident," Ellie said.

"As long as he doesn't scare somebody to death on Lover's Lane. I can see word spreading and everyone heading that way to see the car at the bottom of the cliff and attempting to witness the ghost car." Brett couldn't quit thinking of what had happened to them. "Why did the car come back toward us after it crashed? I would have thought that if Shorty had found peace, the car wouldn't have been driving on Lover's Lane again."

"He died when he crashed his car into the tree, yet the need to get away must have been so great that he was tied to that car until he could make his escape from those who would incarcerate him. By sending the physical car over the cliff, he made sure no one else could have it. He must have realized that he couldn't have escaped the men going that way. That he had to head back the way he'd come, return to the main road, and disappear. That's when we saw the ghost car drive through us."

"Then we saw him with the car at the bottom of the cliffs," Brett said.

"Right. He was ready to leave his physical car behind. He tipped his hat in greeting, thanking us for releasing him."

"We didn't."

"Shorty was a man who was used to being in charge. He wasn't going to go quietly. He had to prove to himself that he could do it. Don't you think?"

"Could be. What if we had buried the car near his body like you had first suggested?"

"It might not have worked. It's really hard to second-guess what a person is thinking, whether alive or in spirit. I think this was where he needed to be to actually be free."

Brett was glad, as long as they didn't have any more trouble with Shorty's ghost.

When they arrived at the MacTire sisters' house, no one was there. Brett suspected Laurel and Meghan were at the inn.

He kissed Ellie. "I'll help you pack some of your

clothes and take them to our new home. And I'll move things around at the house again so the piano can be dropped off."

"Okay, sounds like a good idea." They packed her clothes in a couple of suitcases, and she called Meghan to ask if she could use hers too.

Brett hauled the bags downstairs and out to the car, so glad he and Ellie were now mated. He still couldn't believe he had seen a ghost car drive straight through him. It was so real that he'd expected to hear the crash and he'd been so worried that Ellie might be hurt.

"Movers will be here in just a bit. I'll be back after I get this done," he said.

"Maybe you should just stay there and be ready for us."

"You might be right. I'll unpack your bags and then move the furniture and wait. And I'll see if anyone can have a memorial display box made, pronto, to store Matilda's dress and parasol." He gave Ellie one long, lingering kiss and hug and hoped they wouldn't have any further trouble with Matilda.

Chapter 21

"WELL?" LAUREL ASKED AS SHE AND MEGHAN dropped by the house after Brett left, as if they'd been watching out the inn windows and hadn't wanted to intrude, which Ellie was glad for. She'd found some boxes and had packed a few personal things she also wanted to take to the house.

"She played music while we made love, either to accompany it as background music, or so she wouldn't hear us," Ellie said.

Laurel laughed. Meghan looked shocked.

Ellie taped up the box. "She played for us this morning too. A nice, soft wake-up tune."

"So she's still here," Meghan said, exasperated.

"Yeah." Ellie told them about Matilda's clothes in Theodore's steamer trunk. Her sisters were shocked like she knew they would be. "We're having the piano moved back to Brett's house. That way you'll have peace. I'm not sure about us. Still, she never did anything while the piano was there before, so maybe that location will make the difference."

"What about the wedding?" Meghan asked.

"We haven't talked about it yet." Ellie wasn't even sure if Brett would want to have one.

"Well, decide already! I need to know what to wear," Meghan said, eager to participate in a wedding.

"Victorian gowns." Ellie didn't hesitate.

"Should we have the wedding at the inn, then?" Meghan asked.

Laurel laughed.

"I mean *your* wedding." Meghan smiled at Ellie.

"I don't even know if he'll want a wedding. It's not something we have to do."

"Yes, he will." Laurel spoke with authority.

Ellie and Meghan laughed. Ellie knew if Brett was waffling about that, Laurel would tell CJ and he would set him straight.

"CJ called me about the bank-robber ghost." Laurel grabbed a cup of jasmine tea.

"Did he and Yolan see any sign of the ghost car or Shorty when they drove down Lover's Lane?"

"No. CJ said he was expecting it because Yolan kept telling him it wouldn't be real, as if Yolan was trying to reassure himself that it wouldn't be." Laurel stirred honey in her cup of tea.

"Yolan was really scared when he saw it run into us. Thankfully, it wasn't the physical car." Ellie fixed herself a cup of mint tea.

They heard the movers park their truck, and Ellie tensed. "I hope that Matilda doesn't play the piano while the men are moving it."

Laurel greeted the movers, and one of the men said, "Haunted, eh?"

The women all looked at him as if *he'd* turned into a ghost.

He smiled, showing off a missing tooth. "We get one of these once in a blue moon. Sometimes folks move them, thinking they'll get rid of the ghost in their home. Sometimes it works, sometimes it doesn't. Sometimes the new owner sends it right back, saying the piano doesn't work. Guess we'll have to start having a disclosure clause on pianos." He began placing a pad on the piano. "Was this the property of a person who died a violent death?"

"She…might have," Ellie said, not really wanting to give any details about it.

The mover raised a dark brow as he covered the piano with another furniture pad. "She, eh? So I guess a disclaimer clause wouldn't work in all cases. Hey, did you know that you have to disclose if someone died in a house now if you're trying to sell it? People will believe in anything these days."

"So you don't believe in ghosts?" Ellie thought from the way he talked that he did.

"Nah. Bunch of hogwash. If someone believes in it enough, I suppose they can imagine just about anything. And here we are, getting paid to move the piano back where we got it in the first place." He paused and looked at Ellie. "So, is the owner upset about you returning it? I hate having to deal with any issues with the previous owner. We just move pianos from one place to another. Don't want no drama at all."

"No. He called to have you move it back. We're married, so no problem with moving it." Ellie smiled.

"Congratulations. And good. Some guy nearly drove us off the road yesterday. Just don't need any more issues this week. He swore the old car was haunted. See what I mean? People will say anything. Luckily, he gave me a hundred dollars for my trouble even though I didn't have any damage. He was desperate to give me the money though. Never seen anything like it. Didn't smell liquor on his breath, or nothing."

"Vintage Plymouth?"

"Yeah." The mover raised a brow. "Don't tell me you seen the car?"

"Yeah."

"It's not the dead people you got to worry about." The mover helped the other men lift the piano. "It's the living that are scary."

Ellie couldn't agree more.

―⁂―

Ellie called Brett, telling him that the movers were on their way with the piano. Her sisters were staying at the inn. "We need to talk about the wedding." She figured it was a foregone conclusion. Not *if*, but *when*.

"I've been thinking about it," Brett said.

And he sounded enthusiastic. She loved that he'd been thinking about it when she hadn't given it a thought.

"What if we have it at my great-aunt's old home? Where the picnic benches are. We could move the benches and have the wedding with the pack gathered around in the woods. A winter wedding," Brett asked.

"Victorian clothes. That sounds great to me." It was still Victorian Days after all.

"Okay, that works for me. Uh, will you be wearing tons of petticoats and the corset and all?"

"Yep. You're just going to have to learn how to undress me faster. No scissors involved. What if we move the piano out there to play the wedding songs?" she asked.

"The movers will think we're crazy, and I'm not sure about the weather as far as the piano goes."

"What if the piano is played for a joyous occasion

one last time where her home used to be? And that makes her happy?" Ellie hoped he would agree then. What if it did?

"We'll do it. Whatever it takes. When do you want to do it?"

"When the weather is clear. We'll have to plan it around that. I'll check the ten-day forecast, and you can tell the movers you'll need them to move it twice more. Once to the memorial site, and back again to our home."

"I'm sure they'll be happy to get the money. We should have just left it at your house."

"Then Meghan might not be able to get any sleep. And it's already on its way there."

"Okay, it's a deal."

"Who will play the songs at the wedding?" she asked.

"Remer or Mervin. Both were her students. I'm sure if she's still hanging around the piano when we have it moved out there, she'll be pleased."

"Okay, I'll be there in a little bit."

When Ellie arrived at the house, the movers had already left. Brett pulled her into his arms and gave her a warm embrace. "We still need to move the rest of your things, but whatever you want changed at the house, please go ahead and do it."

She looked at the collection of rocks sitting on a couple of shelves in the living room and smiled. "I see all your magic rocks. They're beautiful."

He lifted a topaz crystal. "This is the one that Eric found for me. He found a yellow diamond for CJ."

"Wow."

"We didn't know it was a diamond at the time. I thought my clear crystal was prettier."

"It's beautiful." She ran her fingers over an amethyst stone and turquoise. "They're all beautiful."

"Which do you like the best?"

She shook her head, unable to decide.

He took her into his arms again and kissed her forehead. "So what gown are you going to wear for the wedding? Daring red? Pretty blue?"

"Winter white. A faux fur muff, a white wool cape trimmed in faux fur. I think it'll be pretty."

"You'll be beautiful. What about the bridesmaids? The groomsmen?"

"What was your great-aunt's favorite color?"

"She wore a lot of green. Forest green. I remember because I said something about it to her. She told me she loved the forests and her gardens, and wearing green made her feel at home in them."

Ellie nodded. "I'll check with the shop that sells and rents Victorian clothing and costumes for other events to see if they have what we need, or we can change the color scheme. I was wondering if you made any other changes concerning the piano that would have made a difference in it coming to life."

"I had it refinished. And I had the bench recovered. I also had to have it repaired so that it would work properly. Remer played it and made sure it was perfect."

"Remer. Did you hear or see anything unusual after you made the changes when the piano was still at your house?"

"No. I didn't see her when I kissed you either. Remember? I thought I was going too fast for you."

She wrapped her arms around his neck. "Not fast enough, it seems."

They had to make wedding plans. She had to unpack her bags. But nothing seemed as important as hauling her mate back to bed.

The wedding was held two days later, in short order, mostly because Matilda played nearly nonstop. Just anything and everything. They didn't know if she was happy they were mated and joyfully playing, or annoyed they'd brought her back here, or what. She'd even howled once in the living room after they'd cried out in pleasure in the bedroom! They had to do something about it. And fast!

One of the local carpenters had built a beautiful cabinet for their living room where they had hung Matilda's gown and parasol near the piano, with the memorial right next to it. And on top of that, they had set their first hand-carved wolves. They'd already had a ton of requests for them, but the first were in loving memory of Great-Aunt Matilda. They had cropped a print of the old photo so that only she, Benjamin, and her sister were in the shot. Even so, Matilda hadn't seemed to want to leave.

Ellie and Brett had begun working on a brown, rust, and beige macramé hanging to go on their living room wall and were having a ball working on the craft together. With someone to work with, Ellie had no trouble sticking to lessons and instructions. But the most fun project they'd been working on lately was clay pottery. Though after watching *Ghost* with Demi Moore and Patrick Swayze and being caught up in the sexy moment where he was sitting with her between his legs, shirtless, the pottery wheel spinning, his hands sliding over hers as she was trying to mold her vase… Well, Ellie and Brett hadn't quite finished their piece yet either.

Today she was getting ready for the wedding, and she couldn't wait.

"Omigod, Ellie, did you see the paper?" Meghan opened the newspaper and showed it to her while Laurel finished adding pearls to Ellie's hair. "A full-page photo of the two of you dancing at the ball, your lips locked in a sizzling kiss, declaring your love." Meghan handed her the paper.

Ellie couldn't believe it. She smiled. Brett didn't do anything small.

"Come on, ladies," Laurel urged. She and Meghan helped Ellie climb in the car, handing her the train to hold in her lap.

"We don't want to be late for the wedding. But, boy, CJ couldn't believe that announcement. Their cousin Jake took the photograph. CJ said it was a way to ensure that everyone in the pack knew you two were a couple," Laurel said.

Meghan laughed. "As if anyone could be clueless about that."

"You are so beautiful," Laurel said to Ellie as she drove them to the memorial site.

"So are the both of you." They were wearing forest-green velvet gowns and wool cloaks of the same color.

It was a sunny day, thankfully. The snow had mostly melted, but it was still chilly. Perfect for a Victorian wedding. Ellie had learned that no one had ever had a wedding during Victorian Days before, so that made this year's extra special.

When they arrived at the site, Ellie smiled to see the whole pack gathered, almost everyone in Victorian dress, except a handful who showed up in their wolf coats to honor that part of their heritage. The gazebo and pillars were covered in roses. It was the most gorgeous sight she'd ever seen. Jake was busy taking pictures of her, while Brett's oldest brother walked her toward the gazebo to give her away to the groom, the handsome wolf waiting to marry her.

Remer was playing the piano nearby, smiling.

She joined Brett, and they said their vows and kissed. Ellie had been so wrapped up in the ceremony that she hadn't even given Matilda a thought until she saw her standing near the gazebo tending the roses. She smiled at Ellie and Brett, whose attention had been on Ellie until he realized something had diverted her and he'd looked in the direction she was staring.

Wearing her favorite dress and matching the bridal party, her parasol hooked over her arm, Matilda nodded, then walked off, but before she faded into the woods, she morphed into the wolf and vanished.

"She is home," Ellie whispered to Brett.

"She is."

They couldn't be sure until the movers returned the piano to their home one last time. As soon as they arrived home to wait for the piano delivery, they noticed that in the spot on the floor where the piano normally sat, a big, white faux-fur bear rug had taken its place, the card on it signed: With all our love, Laurel, Meghan, and Aunt Charity.

Ellie laughed. And she swore Brett almost looked embarrassed, his ears tinging a little red. She loved it. It would be perfect in their bedroom. But then he seemed to recover and smiled. "I know just who will be *my* model lying on that fur rug."

Then her face warmed with embarrassment. "Only for you."

That night, as Brett and Ellie made love, the piano was silent, and Ellie knew Matilda was truly home.

Just like she was with Brett here, making her fantasy dreams come true.

"You are so beautiful," Brett said, "better than any dream."

"Ditto, wolf of mine. This was where we were meant to be."

Read on for a sneak peek of

SEAL WOLF
UNDERCOVER

**Coming soon from Terry Spear and
Sourcebooks Casablanca**

Prologue

Six months ago
San Diego, California

FORMER SEAL AND CURRENT PI VAUGHN GREYSTOKE leaned back on his barstool in the Kitty Cat Club in San Diego, smelling cats everywhere. He wasn't sure what to make of the packed place. His twin brother, Brock, slapped him on the back. "Drink up. You're way behind."

Douglas Wendish, a friend from their wolf pack in Colorado, was dancing again with his date. Vaughn's date was more for show, and Brock looked a bit too tipsy to do anything more than sit and stare into space. Around them in the jungle-themed club, rock walls covered in moss, genuine potted palms and ferns, and vines criss-crossing the ceiling created the illusion they really were in the Amazon rain forest. Women in skimpy leopard-skin bikinis and men in leopard-skin loin clothes were grinding on elevated platforms. The chirping of crickets, the calls from the macaws, and the sound of water rushing over rocks played in the background, while the music offered a riveting South American jungle beat.

Lots of gyrating females were twisting around on the floor, but only one really caught Vaughn's eye. She was a dark-haired beauty wearing a tight, black skirt split up the side that showed off shapely legs, a pair of sparkly sandals that exposed red-hot toenails, and a low-cut blouse of leopard print that revealed a nice swell of breasts. Unfortunately, she seemed to be taken already.

Vaughn watched her dance with the redheaded guy— sensuously, but not like they needed a room. The way she moved her body made Vaughn feel like *he* needed a room. *With her*. Observing her, he was swept up in the jungle heat, the warm bodies, the cold beer, the infectious laughter, and her hot moves. Then the redhead she was with leaned down and kissed her. She wrapped her arms around his waist, tilted her chin up, and kissed him back. In that instant, Vaughn wanted more than anything to be on the receiving and *giving* end.

"Hot," Brock said. "Wonder if she smells like she's got a ton of cats at home too."

Fine with him. As long as he had her.

"Have another beer," Brock said. "That might cool you off."

The only way Vaughn would cool off was by taking an ice-cold shower.

A woman—who smelled overwhelmingly of cats— asked him to dance, and so he did, if only to get his mind off the brunette.

"I'm Kira. You must be new here," the blond purred next to his cheek, her body pressing closer to him than he really wanted.

"Name's Vaughn. Does it show that I'm new here?"

"Colorado license plates," she said.

He smiled. Here he thought she had heard an accent, though he didn't believe he really had one. "So you live around here?" he asked out of politeness.

"Yeah, nearby. You pulled up when we did. I always notice out-of-state license plates."

She sounded like a private investigator or a cop. "Own a lot of cats?"

She smiled in a wicked way. "Love them." She didn't say that she owned any, though. "What about you? Own a lot of dogs?"

He smiled back. Wouldn't she be surprised if she knew he was all wolf? "Dogs are man's best friend."

"So I've been told. Are you going to be around for a few days? Return to the club?"

"Not sure. Do you hang out here all the time?"

"Every chance I can get." Kira glanced at his table. She must have been wondering about his date. "She looks bored."

"She doesn't care to dance."

Vaughn danced with a few more cat women who didn't seem to mind that he smelled like a dog. Afterward, he took his seat at his table. Douglas returned with his date, but Vaughn had already forgotten her name.

No wait, Wendy. If Douglas mated her, she'd be Wendy Wendish.

Douglas pulled out his camera and began taking pictures. *Again.*

"Hey, see someone I know. Be back in a minute." Douglas took off and started talking to some guy, probably about boating, as much as he loved to boat. Vaughn, Brock, and Douglas were all going out on the water tomorrow. One of these times, Vaughn was going to convince Douglas to take a plunge and show him how much fun swimming as a human could be.

Vaughn watched the brunette laughing at something the redhead said at their table. She turned her head in

Vaughn's direction, as if she realized someone was watching her. He hadn't meant to be staring at her, but everything about her appealed, and he just couldn't take his eyes off her.

He smiled. She smiled. In that instant, he felt they'd made a connection, as lame as that was. When she left the club tonight, she was going home with the muscular guy who had his arm wrapped around her like he was afraid he'd lose her. From what Vaughn could tell, she hadn't once shown any interest in anyone else but her date. Oh sure, when she was seated at her table and sipping her drink, she watched other dancers, but she wasn't focusing on any one person. Not like he was focusing on her.

Her gaze caught his again, and he couldn't help but smile. Not that her checking him out meant anything. But he sure could fantasize.

—◦◦◦—

Formerly an army intelligence officer and now a PI, Jillian Matthews had agreed to go out with her brother Miles's friend as a favor, but man, did the guy have octopus arms. Oh sure, he was fun, but he was way more interested than she was. The guy several tables over? Now *he* got her attention. If she didn't know any better, she'd say he was all wolf, though some human males showed the same wolfish interest in a woman, even if she was with someone else. She'd never consider dumping a guy on a date when he was being nice, especially when it was to pay her brother back for his help in solving one of her cases. But she'd made it clear it was only one date, reserving the right to change her mind.

Everything about the club was a blast—the music, drinks, dancers, and atmosphere—yet it was the man at the other table who truly stole her attention. He had dark hair, chiseled features, tanned biceps. He was muscular, but not muscle-bound, and had a darkly intriguing smile that made her melt.

"Would you like to come back here tomorrow night?" Miles asked.

She smiled at her brother. She'd love to, if that other guy was going to be here.

"Sure," she said, secretly wishing she could meet tall, dark, and intriguing. Maybe he would ask her to dance, or she'd ask him. The guy's date looked bored, and Jillian hadn't seen him dance until other women began asking him. As soon as the blond did, it was like a signal to other single women that he was available. If Jillian had been on her own, she would have asked him to dance too. She'd help him move that gorgeous body right up close and personal. Her own date wasn't interested in dancing with anyone else, so she curbed the inclination. She could envision hanging on to the guy too, if he still piqued her interest and didn't allow any other woman to take a turn with him.

"Hey, you ready to go?" Miles asked, breaking into her fantasy. "If I'm going to help you on that next case, I need some sleep."

Miles's date was a human woman, and Jillian knew her brother too well. Sleep wasn't what he had in mind at all.

"Yeah, agreed."

"I can take you back to your hotel," Jillian's date said to her, as if he were looking for some mattress action too.

"Oh, thanks so much, but no, that's fine. Miles is right. We have to get up before the crack of dawn."

She and Miles rose from the table, Jillian's date not making a move to leave. "See you tomorrow night then," he said.

Not if she could help it. She gathered her sweater and bag, and though she didn't want to seem too obvious, she glanced back at the dark stranger. He inclined his head a little to her, and her whole body flushed with heat.

He was so hot. Yeah, he was the one she wanted tomorrow night, whether he had a date with him or not.

Suddenly, a scream caught Jillian's attention. One of the corner chains holding a dancer's platform had broken loose, and the dancer on it screamed again. Thank God the dancer had reacted quickly enough to grab one of the remaining chains holding it up before she fell. Dangling twenty feet above the patrons, she clung precariously to the end of the chain, looking up as if she was thinking of trying to climb it. Before Jillian could do anything, the wolfish guy she had been admiring had climbed the ladder to the platform. He leaped to one of the chains still holding the platform and shimmied across the top to reach the chain the dancer was holding on to.

The music was still in heavy jungle beat mode, most patrons unaware of the potential tragedy unfolding before them. Jillian rushed to tell a server to get help and to turn off the music so the guy rescuing the woman could concentrate.

"Hell, that's part of the show," the server said, smiling at her. "You're not from around here, are you?"

"The guy trying to rescue her is part of it too?"

The server glanced up at him. "No. Once in a blue

moon we get some hero type that has to show off how macho he is. He must not be from around here either."

"He could injure himself! Kill himself even!"

"Safety nets spring up and will catch them if they fall. We've only had one case where we've had to use them, and everyone, including the would-be hero, loved it."

Then the man managed to climb down the chain to the woman and had her crawl up his body. As agile as she was, she probably could have made it up the chain by herself if the heroic guy hadn't tried to rescue her. The dancer wrapped her legs around his waist and her arms around his neck as he made the treacherous climb.

Even so, Jillian was practically holding her breath. The visitor wasn't part of the show, and any misstep on his part and the two of them could fall. Maybe he knew this was part of the show. Maybe the waiter didn't realize it.

The music was still playing, but a lot more of the patrons had stopped to watch, probably because only *once in a blue moon* someone came to the dancer's rescue.

At the top edge of the platform, the guy made his way across the wooden edge until he reached the next corner chain. He paused there for the longest time. The music was still playing, the only lights the ones high-lighting the dancers on their platforms. The other dancers no longer moved, riveted by their fellow dancer and the heroic guy. If he jumped to the ladder and missed, that would be the end of the show, and the dancer and the Good Samaritan would fall. What if the net didn't appear in time?

Jillian wanted to do something, anything to help him. All she could do was watch lamely and pray he was successful.

He leaped for the ladder and her heart stopped. One of his hands grabbed the ladder, the other swinging to grab hold also. Then he climbed down, the woman still clinging to him.

Jillian wanted to give him a hug, thank him for being a hero, wishing she had a guy like that in her life. When he reached the floor, the woman he'd saved gave him a big kiss, several other women crowding around him to give him hugs and kisses, and her brother said, "Show's over. Let's go."

As it turned out, Miles had a job the next day, and he left bright and early. Jillian got another PI case and headed back to Tacoma. The hot guy would just be one of those dreams she had when she needed some fantasy in her life. But really, who wouldn't admire such able-bodied heroism?

Chapter 1

Present day
Oregon

"MILES, CALL ME WHEN YOU GET THIS MESSAGE. I'M working with a group of jaguar shifters on a case and don't know when I'll get back to our cabin. I'll be working for the jaguars' boss, Martin Sullivan, on the case. Call me."

Jillian Matthews parked in front of the log cabin where her brother had intended to visit with his friend Doug. Douglas Wendish was a wolf like them, but she'd never met him. She thought her brother might already be there. But he would have answered the phone, wouldn't he? Maybe they were running as wolves. She couldn't help but be anxious about Miles—he'd been shot only a week ago running as a wolf in these same woods.

As soon as she got out of her car in the cold, misty Oregon forest, she knew something was wrong. Smoke curled from the stone chimney, as if welcoming a visitor inside to warm up, but chairs on the front porch were overturned, the smell of fresh blood wafted in the air, and the door was wide open.

Her heart beating triple time, she pulled out her Glock and called Leidolf, the local red pack leader who owned the cabins, to ask for backup and possibly his EMTs for medical support.

"Wait for backup," Leidolf said in a commanding pack leader way.

"Going in. Call you when I know more." He wasn't her pack leader, and someone inside could be injured or dying.

She pocketed her phone and readied her Glock. Listening for any sounds, she approached the deck and heard someone moaning inside. She took a deep breath and smelled other scents.

Humans. Wolves. A cat.

She climbed onto the deck, making it creak, but she kept moving forward cautiously in case someone inside might still be a threat. Other than the low moan, she couldn't make out any other sounds.

Barely breathing, she quietly stole into the cabin. When she saw a boot behind the couch, her heart thundered and she rushed around the furniture. A blond-haired man was sprawled on his back, his hand gripping his throat, blood trickling through his fingers.

"Hold on!" She bolted for the kitchen nearby, grabbed a bunch of paper towels, and raced back to him. Holding the towels against his throat, she asked, "Douglas?"

The injured man stared at her, his blue eyes half lidded, and he gave a little nod.

"You're going to be fine." She set her gun on the floor next to her so she could reach it if she needed to, then quickly called Leidolf back while holding the towels against Douglas's wound. "Douglas Wendish needs an ambulance ASAP. He's lost a lot of blood." Leidolf would have the records on who rented his pack's cabins and would know he was a wolf.

"Everyone's on their way. ETA—ten minutes. Cause of wound?"

Jillian considered the bite wounds on Douglas's arms and his neck. "Someone bit him on the throat and arms. Looks like he was trying to defend himself."

Jillian took in a deep breath, trying to smell any sign her brother had been there, worried he could be a victim too. But he hadn't been here. So where in the world was he? "Do you know who bit you?" Jillian asked Douglas.

He shook his head weakly.

She heard the ambulance and breathed a tentative sigh of relief. Douglas was in bad shape, but at least with the paramedics here, he might have a chance. This couldn't be a coincidence. They'd already had a case of a jaguar shifter being shot at Leidolf's ranch, the shooting of her brother, and now this. Leidolf had asked her to help the jaguars in the United Shifters Force to figure it all out.

As soon as Leidolf's officers arrived and the paramedics took care of Douglas, she drove back to her cabin, anxious to see if Miles had taken a wolf run and returned there. At least she could leave Miles a note to warn him what had happened in case he didn't check his phone right away, if he still wasn't there. She prayed he wasn't in trouble again.

When Douglas had called Vaughn Greystoke, worried about not being able to reach his friend Miles, Vaughn told him he'd meet with him and look into it. Vaughn had been on a missing persons case in southern Oregon that he'd resolved and wasn't too far from Douglas's location. And Douglas was one of his pack mates from Colorado, and a close friend, so he knew Vaughn was nearby.

Douglas texted back forty-five minutes later: My friend got ahold of me. No need to worry about it. Case of miscommunication. Thanks!

Vaughn was almost to the cabin, so he figured he'd just drop in, say hi, and return home to Colorado. When he tried to get ahold of Douglas to tell him that, there was no response.

Vaughn didn't want to jump to any conclusions, but he couldn't help it. That was some of the trouble with being a wolf, SEAL, and PI. After asking for Vaughn's help, Douglas wouldn't have ignored Vaughn's call. Perhaps he had gone running as a wolf with his friend. Vaughn would have called the local pack leader, Leidolf, to have some of his men check on Douglas, but Vaughn was so close to the cabin's location, he would probably get there before Leidolf could send anyone.

When Vaughn arrived at the cabin, no vehicles were parked there, and two chairs and a small table had been knocked over on the deck. A light rain was falling and a gentle breeze was blowing.

He got out of his Land Rover, gun readied, and moved quickly to the porch. He smelled Douglas's blood right away, several wolves—some of them Leidolf's men's scents—and a cat's scent. His heart pounding, he rushed into the cabin, navigated around the sofa, and came face-to-face with a big, male gray wolf, his nose touching the blood on the floor before he whipped his head around.

Vaughn was startled, and the wolf looked just as shocked to see him. Before he could prepare for the wolf's reaction, the wolf leaped at Vaughn. Huge paws slammed against Vaughn's shoulders. Without being able to brace himself in time, he fell backward and hit the floor hard, losing his Glock under the damn sofa.

He grabbed the knife in his boot, but the gray wolf didn't attack him; instead, it shot out the door.

"Damn it to hell." Vaughn shoved his hand under the sofa for the gun, pulling it from the accumulated dust bunnies. He shook it off and raced out of the cabin just in time to see the direction the wolf had run.

Vaughn holstered his gun, immediately called Leidolf, and began to strip.

"This is Vaughn Greystoke. I'm at Douglas Wendish's cabin near your ranch and—"

"We've got him in surgery. Jillian Matthews found him and called me. He's in a drug-induced coma."

"Hell."

"We're taking care of him."

"A wolf was here. I'm going after him. Get me a nearby cabin so I can investigate this, will you?"

Leidolf told him which cabin he'd give him, the same one he'd stayed at last year when he'd taken a vacation there. Leidolf would have his men park Vaughn's vehicle there. Vaughn gave him the code to unlock the car door. "Going after him."

Then Vaughn threw his clothes, cell, and gun in the car, locked it, and shifted. He tore after the wolf, hoping he'd reach him quickly. He intended to get some answers from him pronto. Vaughn prayed Douglas would pull through after the vicious attack he must have suffered.

Loping through the Oregon forest as a wolf, Vaughn was hot on the trail of the other. For the moment, he and the other wolf were running through the evergreen forests near the Columbia River Gorge, the sound of yet another waterfall rushing over the top of a cliff nearby. A light, icy rain continued to fall, the guard hairs of his outer coat repelling the droplets.

For about an hour, he chased the wolf through the underbrush of the misty forest, the birds diving for cover in the Douglas firs and western hemlocks as soon as they saw him coming. He wondered where the wolf was going. The wolf had been looping around as if trying to reach a location, but then moving in another direction, most likely fearing Vaughn would catch up to him.

Then somewhere in the deep forest ahead, the wolf suddenly howled. Calling for help? Out there?

That meant he'd stopped long enough to howl. Vaughn raced forward to close the gap, trying to reach him before he ran off again. Or before reinforcements arrived.

Why else would the wolf howl? Other members of his pack must be out there. Maybe he thought he could scare Vaughn off, making him *think* a wolf shifter pack was out there and would back him up any minute. Vaughn had used that ploy himself a time or two. He wasn't giving up on his prey no matter what. He had to learn the truth. Had the wolf standing next to the bloody mess on the cabin floor been the same wolf who had torn into Douglas? If the blood on the wolf's muzzle was any indication, and the way he had run off, Vaughn would have to say he certainly could be.

Yet how had a she-wolf, Jillian Matthews, found Douglas, called Leidolf for help, and not been injured by this same wolf?

The chance this wolf would have left Douglas for dead, run off, then returned after Leidolf's people had come for Douglas would be pretty slim. Unless the wolf had nearly killed Douglas in anger, then got his rage under control and came back to get rid of any evidence. Maybe he realized he hadn't made sure Douglas was dead and went back to see. What if Jillian had witnessed the attack, and that's how she knew a wolf had severely injured Douglas and needed Leidolf's help?

Leidolf hadn't said Jillian had seen the attack though. Not that Vaughn had given him a chance to respond much. Except for a quick mention that Leidolf would give him the cabin closest to Douglas's on the north side while he investigated the attempted murder, Vaughn hadn't had time to do anything else but agree. He was certain Leidolf had as many questions for him as Vaughn had for Jillian. Like how had Vaughn happened to be at the cabin so soon after the incident when he lived in Colorado.

And Vaughn wanted to know who Jillian was. Douglas's girlfriend? He didn't remember Douglas dating anyone by that name.

Right now, Vaughn was so busy tracking the wolf's scent that when something hit a tree near him, and then a shot rang out, it took him a second to realize someone was shooting at him. He growled low, irritated anyone would be hunting out there. He continued his pursuit, another round slamming into a tree near his chest. No damn hunter was going to stop Vaughn in his mission. He had to take down the wolf and learn if he was the one who had nearly killed Douglas. Vaughn dodged around a hemlock, hoping the hunter would think he'd taken off in another direction. But Vaughn couldn't detour from his path for long or lose the wolf. As soon as he was in the clear again, a third round clipped the shrubs in front of him. *Damn it!* He would soon be out of the shooter's range. Just a little bit farther. Then he felt the kick of the fourth round impact with his right shoulder and the sound of the round firing right afterward.

Trying to dodge behind a tree to get out of the hunter's sights, Vaughn stumbled over fallen branches. He didn't have time to look for the shooter. The hunter fired another shot and the round whizzed past Vaughn's head, sinking into the trunk of a massive maple tree with a thud. *Hell.* No matter how much he wanted to continue on the wolf's trail, he couldn't. Not with the shooter actively hunting him down.

Right before Vaughn sidetracked to the river a few feet below a rocky cliff, he saw something golden moving so fast in the undergrowth, he could barely believe his eyes.

A big cat? Jaguar? Shifter? What in the world was going on? He'd never seen a jaguar shifter before.

Vaughn jumped into the river, the cold water enveloping him as he went under. He surfaced and let it carry him away, the whole time mentally cursing the shooter.

What of the cat he'd witnessed running through the woods? He hadn't imagined seeing a jaguar. He wasn't delirious. Yet seeing one of them in an Oregon forest was like finding a unicorn. Had one gotten free from the Oregon Zoo? Or a big cat reserve? Then again, his pack leaders had said jaguar shifters lived among them. Taking the wolf down had to be priority, yet he wished he'd been able to chase after the big cat too and learn what it was doing there.

Hell, maybe the jaguar, and not a wolf, was responsible for Douglas's wound.

Jillian couldn't believe that a *lupus garou* could be trying to kill her brother. The wolf chasing Miles had to be a shifter. She knew he wasn't running with Miles for fun. Not with the way her brother had howled, calling to her for help. If the other wolf had been in trouble too, he would have howled along with her brother. No, he'd been hell-bent on Miles's trail. Worse, she worried he could be the wolf who had nearly killed Douglas.

She ran through the woods to track where the wounded wolf had gone once he'd finally veered from her brother's path. Wild wolves had been sighted in Oregon, so at first she'd thought it might have claimed the territory and was chasing Miles out of the area, or worse, wanting to kill him. When she couldn't scare him off with the first three rounds she'd fired, she was certain he was a shifter. She found drops of blood collected on vegetation, the light rain already diluting it, and followed them to the river, where the trail ended.

In the misty rain, she glanced in the direction the river was flowing and thought she saw a wolf's head bobbing up and down in the water. She couldn't be certain, considering the conditions: the water was dark, the object was far away, and the day was overcast.

She continued to watch until whatever it was disappeared beyond a bend. Her heart pounding, she ran in the direction of her cabin, hoping her brother was there and could tell her what was going on. If she didn't need to hang on to her rifle and cell phone, she would have shifted and run as a wolf. Much faster that way.

She was glad the wolf was no longer chasing her

brother, but she did hate that she'd had to shoot him. With their shifter ability to heal faster than humans, though, she knew he would be fine in no time.

As soon as the cabin came into view, she hurried to the front door, unlocked it, and called out to her brother. He didn't respond. She stalked to the back bedroom, but he wasn't there. Why wouldn't he have come here? Unless he was afraid of bringing the big, bad wolf to their doorstep.

For now, she had other business to take care of. She left a message for her brother, telling him to call her at once, that she was working with some jaguar shifters. And that Douglas was in dire straits after someone attacked him. She would be staying at the red wolf pack's ranch part of the time. She considered trying to track down her brother as a wolf, but with the other wolf wounded and leaving the area, she figured Miles would be okay for now.

Teaming up with jaguars was something totally new for her. Never in a million years would she have believed she'd be working with a combined force of jaguar shifters and a wolf—and with another, if they could solicit his help. On the way over to her cabin, Leidolf had informed her about a hardcore Navy SEAL, turned PI, who was in the area and was also investigating the attack on Douglas. From what she'd read in his profile, he was a loner in his investigative work—and single, though she just happened to notice that information by chance. A photo Leidolf had sent to the team showed he was one hot-looking specimen of a wolf. And he looked a hell of a lot like the guy she'd seen at the Kitty Cat Club in San Diego. The Good Samaritan. That meant he had been a wolf all along. She should have known.

She quickly packed a bag and left to join the shifters at the cabin nearby to meet up with the SEAL wolf, hoping she'd hear from her brother soon. She also put in a call to Leidolf for an update on Douglas's condition.

———

Vaughn bobbed up and down in the icy water, thankful his wolf's double coat protected him from the chilling cold. He had to take care of his wound first, hoping it wasn't too bad; he would heal quickly enough. He was certain the gray wolf couldn't have suddenly armed himself with a rifle, so he was still running as a wolf, and that meant Vaughn could try to find his scent again.

What if he had an accomplice? Maybe that's why he howled. To get help from a wolf shifter friend or pack member who would shoot Vaughn instead of coming to his aid as a wolf. The shooter wouldn't have been some random hunter then. A marksman lying in wait while Vaughn tried to take down the wolf seemed too damned convenient to be mere coincidence.

Because of the numbing effect of the cold water and the shock from the impact of the round on his shoulder, he wasn't feeling any pain. *Thankfully.* He'd make it to shore close to where his cabin was and slip into the place, take care of this bloody mess, rest a while, eat, and take off again.

Lupus garous healed faster than humans, but they didn't heal instantaneously. He couldn't wear a bandage on his shoulder as a wolf either. He would need to rest his shoulder for a time before he could shift again. Chasing the wolf as a human, Vaughn would never be able to catch up. Not until the wolf settled somewhere.

Vaughn recognized the trees and shrubs near the water's edge, and the telltale marker he'd run past before that marked where his cabin was situated, just north of Douglas's—three stacked boulders, the result of an avalanche centuries ago. He fought the swift flow of the currents so he could scramble onto the rocky shore. He could tell his strength was already dwindling.

He needed to get an update from Leidolf on Douglas's condition and let his pack leaders know about it too.

He was trying to keep on his feet, stumbling over rocks and branches, stumbling when there were none. He was a little north of his cabin, not too much farther to go. He was sticking to the woods and avoiding the river view in front of the cabin, just in case. The next couple of cabins were about half a mile away, including the one where Vaughn had found Douglas's blood. Vaughn was nearly in view of his cabin when he heard a woman's voice as she spoke to someone else.

"We'll just wait for him. You're so impatient, Everett."

"We should have tracked him down."

Staying low and prowling closer, to his surprise and irritation, Vaughn saw two men and a woman standing on his front deck, drinking bottled water.

What the hell? He didn't need this aggravation. Why did they want to see him? He didn't know them from Adam.

The woman was a brunette, hair tied back in a pony-tail, and her eyes were dark brown. A man with shaggier dark hair and green eyes looked like he was with the woman. From the man's protective stance, Vaughn was certain they were together. Another man was occupying his own space on the other side of the deck, watching the river, his short-cropped hair black and his eyes blue, a square jaw that looked like it could take a fist. His eyes narrowed, his expression was ominous.

All of them were dressed in jeans, rain jackets, and hiking boots. The men looked hardcore, like they could dish out some real punishment. The three were in great shape; regular hikers in the woods, Vaughn guessed. Something about their postures and appearances suggested they were former military or police. They just had that official look about them. Leidolf's people? Nah. He didn't recognize any of them.

All of them could be wearing shoulder-holstered weapons. He couldn't tell from the lay of their jackets.

Furious with them for intruding, he remained hidden in the woods, standing perfectly still. What the hell were they doing here?

He couldn't just walk up to them as a wolf. A wounded wolf. They'd shoot him for sure if they were armed. He couldn't sneak around to the back and get into his cabin that way, as Leidolf's cabin rental manager had to have locked all the windows.

Then again, his bags were still in his vehicle parked nearby, courtesy of Leidolf.

If Vaughn could have sneaked inside somehow, he could have grabbed a towel and pretended to have taken a shower—except hiding the gunshot wound still would have been problematic. If he shifted and headed for the cabin naked as could be, he would be sporting a bullet hole in his shoulder, bleeding all over the place, with no way to explain how he got shot.

Screw 'em. He didn't have time for this.

He had to stop the bleeding, and he assumed they weren't leaving. If anyone asked, he'd tell them some damn hunter shot him accidentally. Why was he running around naked in the woods as chilly as it was? He was conducting survival training. He was sure they wouldn't believe him, but he didn't owe them an explanation anyway. He just hoped none of them called the police to report the gunshot wound. He'd heal faster than normal, and because of it, he couldn't see a human doctor.

The pain was just beginning to hit, and he growled low with annoyance.

All three people glanced in his direction, as if they'd heard his low wolf's growl. Which would have been impossible. Unless he hadn't growled as low as he thought he had, as angry as he was. *Or* unless they were wolves. What if they were members of the pack the wolf he'd been chasing belonged to? Because of the way the breeze was blowing away from all of them, he couldn't smell them any more than they could smell him. What if one of these people had shot him? *Terrific*.

Not having much of a choice, he shifted and headed out of the woods in the raw, the chilly air bracing. With a narrow-eyed look that meant he would shift again and take them all on, he said, "What the hell are you doing trespassing on private property?"

Acknowledgments

Thanks so much to Donna Fournier for all the time she takes to brainstorm with me before, during, and after the process of writing the book. And to Dottie Jones, Sarah Fisher, and Donna Fournier, who were invaluable in catching my mistakes. I couldn't do it without you. Thanks to Deb Werksman, Amelia Narigon, and the cover artists who made the book shine.

About the Author

Bestselling and award-winning author Terry Spear has written over sixty paranormal romance novels and four medieval Highland historical romances. Her first were-wolf romance, *Heart of the Wolf*, was named a 2008 *Publishers Weekly*'s Best Book of the Year, and her subsequent titles have garnered high praise and hit the *USA Today* bestseller list. A retired officer of the U.S. Army Reserves, Terry lives in Spring, Texas, where she is working on her next werewolf romance, continuing with her Highland medieval romances, and having fun with her young adult novels. When she's not writing, she's pho-tographing everything that catches her eye, making teddy bears, and playing with her Havanese puppies. For more information, please visit www.terryspear.com, or follow her on Twitter @TerrySpear. She is also on Facebook at www.facebook.com/terry.spear. And on Wordpress at Terry Spear's Shifters: http://terryspear.wordpress.com.

WOLF HUNT

SWAT: Special Wolf Alpha Team delivers sizzling
paranormal romantic suspense

Wolf shifter Remy Boudreaux is glad to be back in New
Orleans, prowling the French Quarter with his pals from
the Dallas SWAT team. NOLA's as sultry and tantalizing as
he remembers. And so is Triana Bellamy, a beautiful Creole
forensic scientist who's also back in town. Soon they are
drawn together into danger—and with a hurricane bearing
down from the Gulf, all hell is about to break loose...

"SWAT is hot, hot, HOT!"

**—Kerrelyn Sparks, *New York Times* bestselling
author for *In the Company of Wolves***

For more Paige Tyler, visit:
www.sourcebooks.com